Cover design by Michele Maakestad

Back cover photo by Robert Davis

Published by All Writes Reserved Publishing, LLC

ISBN-13: 978-1540583307

DEDICATION

To all my loved ones who have passed on but would have enjoyed seeing this book come to fruition: my parents and two brothers. Also for my gentle cousin who inspired the Tevan character.

TABLE OF CONTENTS

ACKNOWLEDGMENTS

Many people have helped me get this story published. Thanks to Tony Brimeyer, Linda Fritts, Barbara Malmberg and Marty Novak for their expertise and invaluable assistance.

Special thanks to all my family. It was their "gentle" nudging that got me back to working on the project, which became two novels — Seers of Verde: The Legend Fulfilled and its sequel, Return of the Earthers. Some of them served as inspiration for the characters: Stazia, Verinya, Amaura, Flyn, Gerro, Lyllen, Grig (Seers), Nyrthka (Seers), Xander (Seers), Athal, Maelys, Varie and, of course, Tevan (see Dedication page).

Much appreciation to Dennis W. Green, Rob Cline and S.V. Brown for their kind words.

Works of M.L. Williams

Seers of Verde: The Legend Fulfilled, Book 1

Return of the Earthers: Seers of Verde, Book 2

The Fixer: Death of the Demon Machine anthology: https://
mlwilliamsbooks.com/2016/08/16/anthology-of-death-of-a-demon-
machine/

Coming

Memoir anthology (2017, title TBA)

The Fence (late 2017 or early 2018)

Book 1 — Seers of Verde: The Legend Fulfilled story . . .

The planet XR-309 looked like a shining emerald when it was discovered by Earth bioformers. Thick green moss covered the mountains and valleys. The simple plant life was proof the new world could sustain life and be perfect for colonization.

A little more than a century after its discovery, a spaceship transporting 2,000 colonists set off to settle the planet, christened Verde Grande — Grand Green One — in old Earth Spanish. The ship's arrival was greeted by tragedy after an attack by vicious Tanlian space marauders.

The last landing party split off from the main group and flew over a treacherous mountain range in a desperate attempt to draw the marauders away from the defenseless people already on the ground. Colonists on both sides of the mountains were able to fight off the vicious Tanlians, but victory came with a heavy price — all their technology was lost, and the spaceship that delivered them was destroyed.

A second Tanlian attack was repelled with the help of Taryl Bryann, a young seer. Believing their people were killed or captured, the planet's colonization sponsor abandoned the world.

In the ensuing years two very different cultures evolved on the planet. A powerful group of Seers, descendants of Taryl Bryann, use their mind-control abilities to watch over and protect their people in the great Verdan Valley from intermittent flyovers by the Tanlians. The peaceful existence of the Verdan people, however, is achieved at the expense of the "others," the Nuvens across the mountain range.

For two centuries the Seers have diverted the Tanlians' attention to this hunter society which has thrived despite repelling repeated attacks by the marauders. The Seers also have kept the two cultures apart in a misguided effort to protect the Verdans.

Much to the Seers' dismay a group of young Nuvens, led by a mysterious young woman who is immune to their influence, manages to cross the previously impassable mountain.

Efforts to stop the Nuvens from contacting the Verdan populace meet with tragic consequences when a confrontation turns deadly.

Unable to stop the inevitable encroachment of thousands of Nuvens flowing into the Verdan Valley, the Seers sponsor a secret group of warriors — the Sankari — to kill and terrorize the interloping "pagans" in the hope of driving them back across the mountain.

Faced with yet another threat to a peaceful existence, the Nuvens rise to the challenge and fend off attack after attack. Growing weary after a generation of fighting, Nuvens in the Verdan Valley seek help from their ancestral home — the Valley of the Heroes.

Elite Nuven warriors — Defenders — are recruited to help fend off the Sankari. A stalemate soon develops between the Sankari and the Defenders.

The Seers and the Sankari grow desperate after seeing the Nuvens spreading out and building their temples across the Verdan Valley.

They escalate the hostilities by enflaming the Verdan population with false accusations of crimes by the Defenders. The temples are marched on by Verdan forces, but the Nuvens again hold strong and repel the attackers.

In an effort to lull the Nuvens into relaxing their defenses, the Seers orchestrate a false truce. The Sankari leader has a plan to attack through the air, something that has not been accomplished before. Only ten young Nuven warriors stand in the way of his goal — to eliminate the Defenders once and for all.

. . . And now Return of the Earthers

Seers of Verde Book 2

RANSACK

1

The village children squealed with delight at the wondrous sight of hundreds of gliders swooping out of the sky and landing in the nearby wheat field. Even the adults in the remote mountain village stared at what looked like a flock of huge black birds gently drifting into their midst. It was not unusual to see a lone glider or sometimes two or three but never hundreds.

However, one old Nuven was upset by the arrival of the intruders. Ancia Fawzer shouted as she marched toward the Verdans who were trampling the village's field. Amused and curious, all the inhabitants of the village fell in behind the determined little woman.

"Stop, stop. Have you no respect?" she yelled at a Verdan who stood with his arms folded while flashing a satisfied smirk. "This is our wheat, we need this to get through the winter," Ancia snapped. "Oh my ancestors, half the field is down!"

The Verdan shrugged as he surveyed the scene. "My apologies, but my men and I needed an open area to land."

Ancia was not to be placated. "We expect to be compensated for this damage Verdan," she growled, pointing a crooked finger at the stranger. "Who are you and why are there so many of you?"

"We are merely hunters," the Verdan chuckled as he watched the Nuven villagers crowd around the angry old woman. "It looks like the entire village has come to greet us," he replied, gesturing toward the curious onlookers.

1

Ancia turned and glanced around at the crowd behind her. Indeed, all forty-seven of her fellow villagers were gathered around. "Humph, we don't see many strangers here, and we like it that way," she said. "Hunters you say? What are you hunting and why are there so many of you?"

The stranger smiled at Ancia. Behind the old woman, he saw his men slowly close ranks around the unsuspecting Nuvens. He stepped forward. "Our prey is the most dangerous in the Verdan Valley, and we intend to exterminate it once and for all."

Ancia shook her head. "If you are after mountain cats, there are too many of you. They will be scared away."

The Verdan winked at the old woman. "No, we hunt something even more dangerous — Defenders." Before she could react, he jabbed a knife into her chest and pulled it out quickly. Ancia gasped, took a step back then fell in a heap. The villagers had no time to react as dozens of javelins hurtled into their midst. The attack happened so fast, only a few people managed to scream in fear. Men, women and children quickly collapsed from the onslaught of the deadly missiles.

One of the other fliers approached the first Verdan. "Any further orders General?"

Manor Stillinger inspected the pile of bodies with a grim satisfaction. "Yes lieutenant, make sure all those vermin are dead then check the village for anyone that might be left. After that, block all access to this village. Cut down trees, create landslides, whatever is necessary. We don't need any unwanted guests to give us away."

The General was temporarily distracted by a whimpering child, but its cry was abruptly cut off. The lieutenant stared wide-eyed at the dead Nuvens. "Do your duty son," Manor said matter-of-factly. "Once we kill the Defenders, the other Nuvens will either leave or convert to worshipping Mother Verde. Then we will be done with this unseemly business."

For the most part, the Seers' attempts to win over the Nuvens at Temple Darya, especially the Defenders, had failed. The women were watched too closely to become reliable spies. Verinya had not dared to reveal her love affair with Aron Nels to the others even though this was what High Seer Rufina had hoped would happen. The young Seer had not seduced the Defender. Instead, the two had fallen in love and swore each other to secrecy.

Only Defender Egan Pozos suspected, but he had pledged his loyalty to his circle brother and Verinya.

During first meal, Lanella told her companions their work was done at Temple Darya. The High Council was calling home all the Seers it had dispatched to the Nuven temples. Their "help" would no longer be required, Lanella explained. She had made transportation arrangements. They were to leave soon after the meal.

Verinya tried to smile at the news, but her stomach twisted in knots. Lanella was surprised at Verinya's tepid reaction to her news. "Are you feeling well? You look flushed."

Verinya fought to control her emotions. The thought of leaving without contacting Aron filled her with despair. "I am well Lanella. I am just tired, tired of this place," she said softly.

Lanella smiled. "I understand. I cannot wait to return to my quarters at the fortress and take a lovely, private bath." The four other Seers agreed with exuberance. It was a common practice for Nuvens to bathe in large public pools of chilly water. Many Verdans were accustomed to the luxury of hot water in private receptacles.

Verinya had no chance to slip away from the other Seers or even to scribble a note to Aron as they prepared for their trip home. With only an hour to get ready, the women scrambled to gather their possessions.

A familiar shout stopped Verinya as the Seers were stepping into the carriage the Defender elders had loaned them. "Vera, where you go?" Tevan's face was contorted with worry as he ran toward her.

The Seer hugged him and gave him a gentle kiss on the cheek. "I am going home with the other Seers," she said slowly. "I will miss going to market with you my friend."

Tevan shook his head with disbelief. "I don't like. Aron go. Vera go. Tevan sad, I want to see Mama and Papa." Verinya blinked away the tears as she faced her friend. She did not know Aron had left the temple earlier. Now there would be no farewell between them.

Tevan smiled, almost as if he understood her swirling emotions. "Don't worry Vera, Aron say he come back and take me home. I will wait. Then we go home. I will ride a horse all way home."

She nodded. "Take care of Aron for me," Verinya whispered in his ear. He laughed and slapped her on the shoulder in his usual good-natured gesture. Verinya positioned herself by a window so she could see Tevan waving to her as the carriage rolled away from the temple.

"You had the right idea to use that simpleton to reach his cousin," Lanella clucked as she leaned over to watch Tevan waving goodbye. "Too bad it didn't work. Perhaps if you had more time."

Verinya fought to contain the grief that swelled within her. "Yes, it was a good idea," she said as the carriage turned slightly on the road, blocking her view of Tevan.

2

Natono Gallu trudged wearily along one of Temple Darya's parapets. The Defender trainee could hardly keep his eyes open. He and most of the young Nuven men were exhausted after three days of celebrating the retreat of the Verdan army. It was still dark, but the first rays of dawn were threatening to peek over the mountains.

The young man stopped to look up at Luz Primo but stared, puzzling at the curious sight. The full moon blinked on and off as if passing clouds occasionally hid it from view. However, the night sky had been clear. The stars and both of Verde's moons shone brightly. He strained to see the source of strange whooshing noises overhead, when a whistle made him whirl around.

Natono did not have time to react when a Verdan glider swooped down, knocking him from his perch. The only sound was a thud when his body hit the ground, killing him instantly. Verdan fliers successfully repeated their attacks on all the temple watchers.

No alarm was sounded as several hundred Verdan warriors silently drifted over the walls and landed inside. Once on the ground, Sankari veterans crept up and overwhelmed the guards at the gate. The giant doors which had stood so steadfast under the catapult attack were now easily swung open to allow more of the enemy into the temple. Sankari and their fellow Verdan warriors scurried through the hallways looking for Defender barracks.

The first alarm finally rang out when a door to a room filled with a sleeping Defender circle was kicked in. Half of the Nuvens in the room were slaughtered before they could protect

5

themselves, but one of them managed to reach the bell in the window. The bell had only chimed three times before its ringer was cut down by the invading Sankari. However, the alarm had done its job.

Almost instantaneously, Defenders throughout the temple swarmed out of their rooms like angry bees protecting a hive. Many of the Nuvens charged headlong into overwhelming numbers of Verdans who were waiting for them. Now bells rang throughout the temple to warn the Defenders, but the invading Verdans were everywhere. Knowing their surprise attack had at last been discovered, the attackers grabbed torches and set fire to anything that would burn.

The battle was fought throughout the temple: in the halls, dining areas and finally out into the outside square. More Verdans, who had been waiting for a signal from the fliers, now poured through the open gates to reinforce the invaders.

Nuven archers raced to the parapets, but were unable to shoot with any accuracy. Defender and Verdan combatants were everywhere. It was impossible to shoot at an identifiable target in the half light of early dawn. The Nuven archers were forced from their perches after becoming targets of enemy bowmen.

One veteran Defender circle made a heroic effort to reach the temple's gates. With a frantic determination and disregard for their safety, the circle savagely cut through the mass of Verdans who blocked their way. But the Nuven warriors eventually succumbed to the crushing surge of their attackers. The last Defender from this circle was less than 10 meters from the gate when he collapsed from more than a dozen wounds inflicted by Verdan javelins and knives.

————————

Egan Pozos took a quick break from cutting through the thick brush of downed trees as Circle Sankarikiller tried to reach a Nuven village that had been out of contact for days. He scrambled up a boulder to try to peer over the trees that blocked their way.

Unable to see anything, Egan looked down the mountain toward Temple Darya. Even from this distance, something looked wrong. A massive smoke cloud arose from the direction of the temple, which was almost a day's ride away.

The Defender yelled for Witt Peyser to take a look. The Steward grumbled as he clumsily pulled himself up the rock beside Egan. It only took one sickening glance for Witt to interpret the tragic scene. He swore loudly as he bounded down. "The temple is on fire! It looks like it's under attack."

As one, Circle Sankarikiller and Witt raced down the mountain to where they had left their horses tied. It seemed like it took them forever to make the descent. However, they covered the distance in less than half the time it had taken to climb it. At full sprint, the Defenders leaped on their horses and galloped at top speed toward Temple Darya.

Curious about what all the noise was about, one of the youngsters in the Defender trainee barracks peeked out the door, stared momentarily in disbelief then slammed it shut. "Verdans are in the temple, they're down the hall!" he screamed as he grabbed a crossbeam to secure the door. The boy had barely called out the warning when the door shuddered from a crash on the other side.

Farren Hamish instinctively yelled orders, "Grab your bows and form two lines. Wait to shoot until they've broken in, first line then second line." One young man ran over to him, his eyes wide with fright. "Tevan, stay behind me," Farren ordered. Before the trainee could say more, the door exploded into pieces followed by a swarming group of Verdans. "Fire!" Farren yelled. The initial Verdan charge halted as the trainees' arrows dropped them in their tracks. The attack continued as the second covey of arrows flew into their midst dropping many of the invaders.

The trainees only managed to launch their arrows a third time when the Verdans reached their ranks. One of the attackers thrust a javelin at Farren. The youngster deftly avoided it, drew his knife and plunged it into his enemy's sternum.

Farren had just pulled his knife out of the fallen Verdan when the hilt of a javelin smashed into his face, knocking him to the floor. With one eye filled with blood, he tried to focus with his good eye and winced with resignation when he saw the attacker raise the javelin for a fatal strike.

A shadow passed over Farren and then a sickening sound of bone being crushed reverberated in the room. The Verdan attacker collapsed in a heap, a look of surprise glowing in his dying eyes.

"No!" Tevan shouted, brandishing his favorite walking stick as he stood over his wounded friend. The solid, gnarled walnut piece, carved for Tevan by his favorite carpenter and reinforced with iron at the head and tip by a blacksmith, dripped with the fallen Verdan's blood. Farren reached up and tried to pull Tevan back, but the man child looked down, calmly shook his head and clasped his hand.

"I will take care of you, Farren," Tevan said with a maturity he had never exhibited before. The attack had triggered something that had lain dormant for most of his life but now spilled out as the Nuven warrior — a Defender — he was bred to be. For the first time in his life, Tevan saw the world as an adult. His mind was clear.

Shouting a war call and remembering the tactics he had seen the brothers of Circle Sankarikiller practice during their combat exercises, Tevan waded into the battle swinging his walking stick with blinding speed. Verdan after Verdan fell to his furious blows. Moving with the expertise of a veteran Defender, the furious young Nuven dodged and parried his attackers' attempts to bring him down with their javelins. Skulls were smashed, jaws broken, arms and legs shattered and ribs crushed by Tevan's blows. The screams of pain from his victims only strengthened his resolve and unnerved the Verdans. He did not stop to kill a wounded foe but kept wading into the swarm of attackers swinging his deadly weapon.

Tevan had nearly forced the group of Verdans out of the door when a new batch of Sankari rushed him en masse, urged on by a furious Manor Stillinger, who had raced to the scene of the skirmish. This time, the young Nuven could not fend off all javelins that were thrusting savagely at his body. Groaning with pain, Tevan grabbed the throat of the nearest Verdan and squeezed with his remaining strength. Both men were dead before they hit the floor.

———————

A splash of water in his face finally roused Farren. The Defender trainee coughed as he regained consciousness. The room was filled with bodies, Verdan and Nuven. Many of the enemy were calling out in pain and were being attended by med techs. His right eye was swollen shut from the blow and his head pounded painfully. Farren tried to move but found his arms and legs were securely tied. He sat on the floor with his back up against a wall.

"Good, you're awake," a deep voice growled from beside him. "My men seem to think you are the leader of these younglings. You pups and this Defender put up a fight, killed too many of my men," a gruff-looking Sankari said as he pointed at Tevan's body, which lay at Farren's feet.

Despite attempts to be brave, tears streamed down Farren's face when he saw Tevan and then spotted the bodies of his fellow trainees lined up nearby on the floor. The youngster looked up at his questioner and then gazed into the faces of the men standing with him.

Instead of finding the Verdans laughing and gloating over their victory, they stood staring at him with grim expressions. Most were covered with blood, and many sported bandages. Even though the Verdans had achieved their long-sought-after victory over the Defenders, it had come at a heavy price.

The Nuvens had fought furiously, killing hundreds of the Verdan attackers. Many Sankari had fallen that day. Barely thirty had survived the bloody battle. During the fighting, it became a familiar sight for a Defender to frantically slash his way through a wave of untrained Verdan fighters to reach and ultimately kill a Sankari. Only the sheer numbers of opponents finally overwhelmed the Defenders.

Manor Stillinger knelt next to Farren. "Even though you killed Verdans this day, I understand you were only trying to protect yourselves. I have a proposition. If you beg my forgiveness and disavow any loyalty to the Defenders, we will free you. I imagine your mother and father will be anxious to see you." Manor leaned back and flashed a generous smile. "If you refuse, you will suffer the same fate as your elders — death. Well youngling, do you have anything to say to me?"

Farren leaned his head back and nodded. "Well, finally, a young Nuven with good sense," Manor crowed, gesturing to his men. "What is it you have to tell me?"

Farren whispered something unintelligible. "Speak up youngling, what is it?" Manor said leaning in close. Saying a silent prayer to his ancestors, the last Defender trainee spewed a mouthful of blood squarely onto his tormentor's face and smirked at his small victory. The general yowled in surprise and sputtered angrily. After wiping himself off, Manor took great pleasure in killing the young Nuven.

Not long afterward, a breathless lieutenant rushed over to Manor. Muttering at the mess the youngling had made of his face and uniform, the general glowered at his junior officer. "What do you have to report? Make it quick, we have wounded to gather and bodies to collect."

The ashen-faced officer looked sick as he saluted. "Sir, we have disturbing reports from the other nine Nuven temples. There have been counterattacks. Our forces have suffered heavy losses."

Manor stared in disbelief then grabbed the lieutenant by the collar and shook him. "Counter attacks? From whom? Common Nuven folk?" The young officer trembled in fear at being manhandled by the most feared man in Verdan society that he wet himself. Manor swore at the pathetic sight and tossed the lieutenant up against a wall. "Damn you, give me your report!"

One of the general's aides stepped between the two men. "Sir don't kill him before he gives us the news. He's only a courier." Manor nodded and took a step backwards with his arms folded tightly. His eyes still glowed with rage.

"Sir, the other temples have been overrun and our forces have been driven out by, by . . ." the young officer stammered then choked. He looked like he was going to vomit. Seeing his commander's face turning bright crimson, the aide grasped the courier's shoulders. "Out with it man or the general is likely to hang you from your heels," he said as soothingly as he could manage.

Taking a deep breath, the lieutenant blurted out his shocking message. "Hundreds of Nuven women have attacked. They have killed every Sankari and driven out the common Verdan fighters who were left in the temples. The women are making their way to Temple Darya. They may be here by nightfall."

Manor's expression changed from rage to shock in a blink of an eye. "Women killing our men?" he blurted in disbelief. "We've never had reports of women warriors."

The young officer nodded and cleared his throat. "Sir, the women are carrying many weapons — bows and arrows, javelins, knives and clubs. They call themselves the Daughters of Defenders."

The aide, an older Verdan wearing the insignia of a colonel, quickly turned and saluted Manor. "General, with your permission, I recommend we withdraw to safety. Many of our fighters are wounded and exhausted. We cannot withstand an attack."

He paused briefly to read a status report handed to him by a junior officer, "Sir, an old Nuven woman is mourning a pile of bodies. She is crying about the deaths of Circle Sankarikiller."

Manor allowed himself to let out a sigh of relief. "We have achieved our objective, the Defenders are dead. We will reconnoiter later."

On their way out of Temple Darya, Manor Stillinger and his party passed a tall woman with a long gray braid weeping loudly over the bodies of ten young men. She sat cross-legged in their midst and swayed back and forth in her grief. The general reined his horse to a stop.

"Circle Sankarikiller?" he asked. His aide nodded and smiled. Manor snorted, not masking his derision. "They look so young. Good thing we did not allow those pups to grow up." Manor swung around and ordered his forces to continue their exit in double time. He did not want his victory turned into a humiliating defeat.

The mourner continued her loud wailing until the Verdans were out of earshot then stopped abruptly. "My only regret is my Daughters of Defenders did not arrive in time to wreak vengeance on those murderers," she snarled at the retreating enemy. A young woman rushed over to help Nyrthka, the last surviving child of the hero Raaf Vonn, to her feet. The elder suddenly felt old and frail. Her brothers were dead, and she had just witnessed the greatest tragedy to have befallen the Nuven people.

"See to it these archers are welcomed by their ancestors in a hero's pyre. They have served us well in life and again in death. Do it quickly. Those monsters may come back with reinforcements," Nyrthka said, gesturing toward the retreating Verdans. The first female Defender turned to her younger companion. She held out her arm for support as the two women slowly walked away from the temple.

Nyrthka turned one last time to sadly gaze upon the ruins of the temple which had borne her aunt's name — Darya, the quiet one who had led the Nuvens to the Verdan Valley. "I will pray to my last breath that Circle Sankarikiller is safe," she said. "They are the only ones left to take vengeance."

3

Circle Sankarikiller rode their horses hard for better than two hours when they first came upon the fleeing Nuvens. The Defenders listened grimly as a sobbing old merchant explained how the Verdan invaders had flown over the temple's walls and caught its Defenders by surprise.

Witt just shook his head at the shocking news. He could not believe the impenetrable Temple Darya had been breached. "How many Verdans were in the attack force?" he asked the old man.

The merchant shrugged. "At least hundreds. It was hard to tell with all the fighting and shouting. Verdans were everywhere, especially when they opened the gates."

The young Defenders had never seen their steward look this ill. A ruddy-faced woman clucked sympathetically while she patted Witt's head. "There's nothing you can do for those at Temple Darya now. You and these young ones would have been killed, too, if you would have been there. Maybe the ancestors were looking after this circle. We've seen survivors from the other temples, but all the Defenders have been killed."

Witt looked at her, too stunned to say anything. "What? The other temples, they've all been attacked?" he stammered. By now, a large crowd had gathered around Circle Sankarikiller. Several other Nuvens echoed what the woman had told Witt.

"I was getting ready to open my vegetable stand at Temple Arafa early this morning when the Verdans swooped down upon us," said a tall man with thin, mussed straw-colored hair. "My woman and I barely made it out alive before they burned everything, just like at Temple Darya. Luckily we had horses nearby and escaped before the Verdans killed everyone."

13

Witt struggled to his feet and stared at the young Defenders. They were too stunned by the news to say anything. The idea that all the other Defenders in the Verdan Valley were dead was almost impossible for them to accept.

"Oh, no, Tevan!" Aron Nels cried out as the reality finally struck him. The Defender ran over to the old merchant. "Did the young ones escape the temple, too? My kinsman Tevan was with them. Did you see them?"

The old man shook his head. "I know Tevan, all the merchants do, but I did not see him or the other boys. There was too much fighting, people were running everywhere." Without saying another word, Aron bolted from the group, leaped on his horse and furiously spurred it into a gallop.

"Stop him, he'll be killed!" Witt shouted at the other Defenders who also were racing toward their horses. The Steward sprinted to his horse, knowing he had to stop his Defenders before they martyred themselves in a foolish attack on an enemy with overwhelming numbers. For once Aron was not riding the fastest horse. Within a few minutes, his Defender brothers had caught up with him. However, no one tried to stop him. They all raced together in determined silence toward Temple Darya.

Witt managed to join the circle after furiously goading his horse to catch up. The riders only slowed to search groups of escapees in a frantic attempt to find Tevan or demand news about him and the other young ones. However, none of the fleeing Nuvens had any hopeful reports.

It was almost sundown when Circle Sankarikiller crested a ridge not far from the temple. All-too-familiar crashing sounds brought them to a halt. Even the frantic Aron was forced to stop. The circle was horrified to see Temple Darya's walls crumbling under a steady rain of boulders from four catapults. This time the machines were much closer than they had been during the earlier assault, so the stones were striking with much more force than the Verdans' first attempt.

Smoke still billowed from the temple as the Verdan boulders thundered into the walls. A gaping hole where the gates had been grew wider and wider with every strike of the missiles. Whole sections of the walls had been smashed away.

With a curse, Aron tried to ride toward the temple, but he was pulled off his mount by nine pairs of hands. He furiously tried to fight off his circle brothers, but they clung to him with stubborn determination. All knew certain death awaited him if he managed to make it to the temple.

Witt intently watched the catapults for a few moments then gestured for the Defenders to listen to his orders. Even Aron had calmed down slightly, but two circle brothers stood nearby just in case he decided to escape again. "We may not be able to save anyone in the temple, but we can stop those catapults. The Sankari would not be anywhere nearby once those rocks started flying."

Egan surveyed the situation and nodded vigorously. "Those catapults are only manned by six or eight people," he said. "I'd bet they are not expecting to be attacked."

Still wearing his worried frown, even Aron agreed to the plan. Just as the Defenders expected, the catapult crews were caught completely by surprise. Circle Sankarikiller swept upon the first machine without being noticed. Its crew died in their tracks, killed by the deadly aim of the Defender archers. The circle successfully slaughtered all four catapult crews without any resistance.

One of the Verdans manning the last catapult tried to escape, but the hapless man was run down by Aron. The angry Defender spent longer than necessary to kill the man, stabbing him repeatedly with his knives. He only quit when his victim's blood covered his face and dripped into his eyes.

The young Defenders were overwhelmed by the carnage that greeted them when they finally entered Temple Darya. Bodies were strewn everywhere — Verdan and Nuven. Their horses balked and refused to move.

The smell of blood and death spooked the animals. Even Witt Peyser, the battle-tested steward, was shocked and sickened by the sight. Several of the young Defenders gagged and had to turn away.

"Why haven't the Verdans taken care of their own dead?" Egan Pozos asked after he regained his composure.

Witt surveyed the scene. "They will probably send a clean-up detail with wagons to pick up their bodies and take them back for burial." Aron slowly made his way through the bodies, looking carefully for any recognizable features. He doubted Tevan and the other youths would be among the slain fighters, but there was no way of knowing where the battle had taken them.

As the circle moved toward the center of the temple, a miraculous sight greeted them. Three elderly Nuvens solemnly stood at the entrance of one of the barracks. One of the elders called for the circle to halt and requested a private audience with Witt. The Steward stepped into the room and returned shortly, grief etched in his face.

Shaking with dread, Aron approached Witt followed by his circle brothers. "Is it Tevan?" he asked in a hoarse, barely audible voice.

Witt nodded and put his arm around the Defender. "Tevan and the other trainees were killed," he said, trying to choke back tears. "Please don't look Aron, it is not the way to remember him."

The young Defender was not to be deterred. "Tevan is my kinsman. I am responsible for him being here. It is my right to see him." The elders and Witt reluctantly moved aside but signaled for the other members of the circle to follow him. Aron's stomach churned violently when he saw the blood-soaked bodies lying on the floor of their barracks.

In a daze, the Defender walked toward a familiar figure. A primeval scream of rage and sorrow poured out as Aron fell to the floor embracing his dead cousin. Tears streamed down the faces of the circle brothers as they helplessly watched Aron stroke Tevan's blond hair. The other Defenders walked gingerly among the other dead youths, patting some of them gently.

Witt attended to Farren. He noted the multiple knife wounds. "You must have made your killer angry. May your ancestors welcome you with open arms, brave Farren. Your courage was equal to any Defender's," he said kissing the trainee's forehead.

A sobbing Aron started to scoop Tevan up in an attempt to carry his body away but was stopped by Witt and the three elders. "We can't touch them yet," Witt explained to the grief-stricken Defender. "The elders overheard Verdans planning to come back to collect their dead. We have to leave the boys here or the Verdans will know there are Defenders left alive."

Aron shook his head and continued to try struggling to his feet with Tevan's body. "No! He is my kinsman," he shouted. "It is my duty to take him home." Egan and the other circle brothers gently tried to stop Aron, but he fought their efforts, growing more frantic as they tried to pull him away.

He appeared to be entering into the first stages of the rage, that uncontrollable fighting trance Defenders could will themselves into when their lives were threatened.

Witt grimaced at what he had to do. As the circle struggled with Aron, who was growing more frantic by the moment, Witt pulled out a large knife and struck the young Defender on the back of his head with the hilt. Aron shuddered from the blow then collapsed into his circle brothers' arms. Witt examined the young man and assured himself he had only knocked him out.

"Quick, take him. We need to leave the temple, Verdans are on their way. They must not be able to tell we were here," he ordered. The other members of Circle Sankarikiller eyed their steward with suspicion but did as they were commanded. Seeing their misgivings, Witt explained his actions.

"It appears you may be the last Defenders left alive. We have to make sure the Verdans believe you are dead until it is safe for you to reveal yourselves." The circle brothers eyed each other sadly, and one by one said, "aye."

4

Fires still smoldered in the ruins of Temple Darya when hundreds of concerned Nuvens arrived at dawn to search for survivors. At first they crept in slowly, frightened that Sankari fighters still lingered, waiting to kill any Defender sympathizers. After a few brave souls scouted the ruins and gave all-clear signals, the Nuvens rushed in to help anyone they could find.

Not long afterwards, Nuven scouts reported the Verdan attackers had retreated to the safety of Verde City. They were not returning to retrieve their dead.

Disguised as a med-aide, Witt helped find members of Circle Sankarikiller, disguised as wounded archers, scattered just beyond a crumbled wall. All of the young men had suffered many superficial injuries and were groggy from slight head wounds. He pointed to a collapsed structure. "Obviously, the archers had fallen when it toppled."

This made sense to the sympathetic rescuers who quickly helped treat their wounds and carried them to safety. Surprisingly, dozens of wounded Nuvens were found. Most were badly wounded archers who were discovered in the ruins. Several died in the arms of the rescuers. None of the temple's veteran Defenders survived. Although the Nuven warriors had fought bravely and killed dozens of the enemy, the Sankari and their allies had overwhelmed them.

Many of the Defender's bodies had been mutilated. Some were missing ears, and others were grotesquely disfigured. With great respect, the Nuven rescuers gathered the bodies and carried them to where the proper funeral rites could be conducted. Dozens of funeral pyres burned brightly that night as the heroes of Temple Darya were mourned.

Witt slipped away in the early morning after paying his respects at the funeral pyres. He had never experienced such a feeling of helplessness as he now abandoned his Defender circle to uncertain fates.

With the help of the three surviving elders, he had put the Nuven warriors in the "waking sleep." Even the highly agitated Aron Nels, who almost had gone into the rage when he found his murdered kinsman, finally succumbed to the trance. Witt's charges now were being cared for by sympathetic Nuvens. Their wounds were being treated, and they were being fed.

Some of the disguised archers were regaining consciousness. It was time for the circle's Steward to leave before his Defenders saw him. Witt did not want to take the chance his presence might stir memories he had so painstakingly worked to bury until the time was right for the awakening.

Witt had known the young Defenders all their lives. From infancy through childhood, Witt had observed them. When they reached their early teenage years, he had stepped in to train them as an elite circle. Another bond tugged at him. It was much more than his attachment as mentor, but he had sworn an oath to never speak of his connection to these young warriors.

Now, before his Defenders even had the chance to prove their worth and maybe help turn the tide against the Sankari, the circle had to be broken up and protected for their own safety. The young men now would scatter and fashion very different lives from what they had been trained and bred for — to infiltrate Sankari ranks and kill this enemy which had terrorized and slaughtered so many Nuvens. Witt had no idea if they would flourish or languish in aimless lives. He had no recourse but to follow the survivors of the battle to the Nuven Valley.

The elders knew the Sankari would not rest until they were assured all known Defenders — elders, warriors and even young trainees — were dead.

The only sanctuary left for the handful of survivors was the valley from where their forefathers had come from just a few generations ago. For more than 200 harvests their ancestors had searched in futility for the Verdan Valley. Now the proudest sons of these brave people were returning in defeat.

Witt was not afraid to make the difficult trek, but a terrible loneliness ached in him as he trudged along the pass where he hopefully would find safety among distant kinsmen if they would accept him — again. This was not the first time he had visited the ancestral valley. More than twenty harvests ago, Defender elders had sent him there on a recruitment journey. His mission was to bring back kinsmen of Nuven Defenders who could help turn the tide against the Sankari.

Witt was successful, but the younglings he had brought back with him to Verde Valley were the Defenders he was now abandoning. His mind was so filled with defeat, sadness and frustration that he did not notice the silent watchers who followed him as he trudged his way through the gap. A few times a shadow, which seemed out of place, would catch his attention momentarily, but Witt either ignored it or did not care to investigate.

On the fourth day of his journey, Witt awoke with a strange feeling he was not alone. This time, he listened to his instincts. Witt lay on his bedroll for a few minutes, listening carefully to every sound around him. He opened his eyes just wide enough to see through slits but noticed nothing. Witt slowly inched his hand to his knife belt, which lay beside him.

Just as his fingers reached one of the hilts, someone from behind ordered him to stop. "You are growing slow and lazy in your old age, Witt of Clan Peyser. Twenty harvests ago, you would have had your knife at my throat before I could defend myself."

Witt tensed for a moment but smiled at the familiar voice. Rising slowly, he saw ten imposing bearded men standing with folded arms. All were smirking at the good-natured insult. "It is true, I have grown slow," Witt said. "It is good to see you kinsmen. My heart is heavy with many troubling events. I'm afraid I do not return in triumph."

One man approached Witt, placing a hand on his shoulder in a respectful greeting of the Nuven Defenders. "The other travelers from Verde Valley have told us of the sad news," said Jep, the leader of Clan Peyser. "The young ones, are they safe?"

Witt nodded. "Many loyal Nuvens are caring for them. The young ones are in no danger as long as they do not awaken to their old memories. It will be many harvests until they are ready to avenge their brothers."

Jep eyed Witt closely. "It has been many days since you have smiled, kinsman. The young ones will survive if they are worthy and the ancestors will it. You are welcome here until they awaken."

Witt reached out to grasp Jep's shoulder. "You are correct kinsman, the first time I have smiled in days was at the sound of your voice."

Jep laughed. "I know another who should bring you an even bigger smile. Gwena Hanzell knows you are returning, she is eager to see you again."

Witt stared at Jep, surprised at hearing the name of the woman who he had loved the first time he visited the Nuven Valley. "She speaks of me?" Witt asked hopefully. He had often thought of the dark-haired woman after he had returned to Verde Valley. She had lovingly accepted him without condition and even supported him when he was bound to carry out his mission.

Jep slapped Witt on the back. "Gwena never bonded with another after you left. She has been waiting for your return. She and a *few* others are anxious to hear of the fate of your Defenders."

Witt winced at the mention of "a few others," which incited raucous laughter among his clan members. He flashed them a rude gesture but smiled as he turned to grab his sparse camping gear. The Steward was now eager to see what life had in store for him until he was needed in Verde Valley many harvests from now.

5

Word of the victory over the Nuven Defenders quickly spread through Verde Valley. At first, people from the cities and villages rushed out to welcome their heroes, but most celebrations were muted by the wagonloads of bodies to be buried or the wounded who needed care.

Sounds of laughter and cheers turned into wails of grief as relatives identified their fallen loved ones. The victory had come at a terrible price. Almost every Verdan family had lost family or friends.

Much to the surprise of most Verdans, the Defenders had not given up once their temples had been breached by the surprise attack from the gliders. Nuven warriors in all ten temples fought violently to their deaths, often killing dozens of the poorly trained Verdan troops and targeting Sankari whenever possible.

Surviving troops were not in a celebratory mood. Even those lucky enough to not have been wounded tromped home, exhausted from the battles. Many sported haggard looks, haunted by what they had seen and the friends they had lost in the fighting.

High Seer Rufina rushed over to greet Manor Stillinger when he and the surviving Sankari marched to Fortress Bryann to deliver news of the victory the day after the Nuven temples had fallen. Her welcome was subdued, however, as she reviewed the surviving Verdan fighters. Barely more than 50 Sankari stood at attention in front of her, and half of them appeared to be wounded.

"I am thrilled at your news General, but where are all your Sankari? Do they dare slight the Seers who have protected them all these harvests?" Some of the men looked down in embarrassment and sorrow at her remark.

Manor shook his head. "No Sankari has shirked his duty of appearing before you, High Seer. These brave men are the survivors of the Defender wars."

Rufina gasped in shock at the reality of his words. "But, Manor, there were hundreds of Sankari. This is all that's left? These few men?"

The normally arrogant officer nodded. "Yes, High Seer. The Defenders fought like cornered mountain cats. One lone Defender at Temple Darya killed more than a dozen of my Sankari and other troops before our forces finally overwhelmed him. We also have lost hundreds of Verdan support troops."

Manor looked grimly at Rufina, then bowed stiffly. "However, High Seer, we have accomplished our objective. The Defenders have been exterminated and their temples have been destroyed. The Nuven population is now at your mercy. They have no one to turn to now except the followers of Mother Verde."

Rufina expected to feel euphoria at the news she had been waiting years to hear — the destruction of those pagan temples and the demise of the Defenders, the champions of the Nuven religion. However, the loss of so many Verdans to achieve this goal was sobering.

The High Seer forced herself to smile bravely as she personally thanked the surviving Sankari. Moved by their dedication, Rufina was about to order a week of celebrations to honor all victorious Verdans when one of her aides, a young Seer, stopped her. "I beg your forgiveness, High Seer, but many Verdans are mourning their dead."

Another Seer stepped forward, her face was flushed with anger. "Cara, how dare you speak to the High Seer in such a manner," Lanella scolded.

Rufina held up a hand to stop the argument. "As much as our brave warriors deserve to be honored, the celebrations can wait until our people are finished grieving." The High Seer paused. "We also will give the Nuvens time to conduct their funeral rites then we will reach out and welcome them to worship Mother Verde. This is a time for healing."

Cara shrugged. "We have to find the Nuvens to tell them of our honorable intentions first."

Rufina looked surprised. "What do you mean, find them?"

Cara shook her head. "I am told every Nuven in our cities and villages fled when the temples were attacked. They have abandoned their villages and escaped into the mountains."

Rufina smiled. "I'm sure they fled out of fear. The Nuvens will be back once they learn we mean them no harm as long as they pledge loyalty to Mother Verde."

Two weeks later, however, no Nuven had returned to Verdan cities and villages. A few adventurous Verdans, who had done business with Nuvens before the temples were attacked, set off to search for their former partners. Upon their return home, the Verdans reported many Nuvens had found safety high in the mountains in secluded, highly fortified villages. They refused to trade with the Verdans and threatened any glider who dared to fly too close.

The Verdan merchants also bore troubling news. During their retreat to the mountains, the Nuvens had ensured their enemies would not gain from the terrible victory they had perpetrated on their people. They burned their grain fields, cut down their orchards and herded their livestock along with them.

The Nuvens' absence began to weigh heavily on the Verdan population. Fresh produce, meats and grains were becoming rare commodities. In the three generations since first setting foot in the great valley, the Nuvens had taken over the role of food producers. They willingly hunted game, cared for domestic livestock, grew the crops and produce, which the Verdans came to depend upon.

After another lunar had passed, riots started to break out in Verdan marketplaces as people fought for a chance to barter with the few vendors who had managed to procure food.

Several groups of foolish Verdans attempted to carry out raids against the Nuvens in their well-fortified strongholds, but few returned alive. No serious war campaign was organized because the Verdans had lost their desire to spill more blood.

Even the Seers were not immune to the shortages. Rufina grew more irritable by the day. She missed her favorite fresh fruit dishes. Bread and other baked goods also were becoming scarce. Finally, at the insistence of Verdan leaders, Rufina reluctantly approved a plan to send negotiators to bargain with the Nuvens.

Amson Kunder warily regarded the Verdans seated before him and the other elders. The normally jovial man was chosen to be the Nuven spokesman because he was level-headed and slow to anger. The irony of the moment was not lost on Amson. Two lunars ago, his people had fled in terror from the Verdan cities after hearing their temples had been destroyed and beloved Defenders slaughtered.

Now a group of Verdans were seated in front of him, begging to negotiate for food and other goods the Nuvens had offered at market for many harvests. The balding man with bushy hair put a hand over his face. His body started shaking slightly then the convulsions grew more pronounced.

Alarmed, several Nuven elders rushed to Amson's side only to be startled by an eruption of laughter. He waved them off while the Nuven and Verdan negotiators stared at him. Across the table, Cara shook her head and chuckled loudly.

"This is quite incredible don't you think?" Amson blurted out between guffaws. "You destroy our temples, kill our favorite sons over an incident that some say was now a huge misunderstanding. Now you tell us all is forgiven and you wish for us to supply you with food and other goods."

Cara met Amson's eyes and both burst into hysterical laughter much to the discomfort of their fellows. The Seer regained her composure first. "This tragedy on both sides could have been avoided. Whoever wanted this war has realized the terrible cost on both sides. We Verdans have learned a terrible lesson and lost our taste for bloodshed."

Amson studied the Seer carefully. He would have risen from the table and taken the other Nuven elders with him if she hadn't exhibited her feelings. "Why should we trust any Verdan? The people defending our temples thought a truce was in place when the fliers attacked. How do we know you do not want to regain our trust so you can wipe out the remaining Nuvens? Your request to convert us is an insult. We will not abandon the worship of our ancestors."

Cara sat quietly for a moment. She knew the next few minutes would make the difference between success and failure. "I cannot speak for every Verdan, but I assure you most of us want peace. Trade between our two peoples will be the best way to start healing wounds. We both offer vital goods and services that will benefit Nuven and Verdan."

Amson nodded in agreement. He liked this Seer. She seemed to speak with honesty and sincerity. "My fellow elders need to discuss your offer. I'm sure we will have conditions to propose the next time we meet. Come back in a week. We will have an answer." Cara stood, bowed respectfully and left with her fellow negotiators.

One week later, she and the other Verdan representatives met again with the Nuvens. Amson welcomed her warmly, ignoring the others. He carefully unrolled a scroll. "Before I read these conditions, I want you to know almost half our people want nothing to do with you Verdans. If you refuse any one of these conditions, this is the last time we will speak."

Amson picked up the scroll, glanced around the room and began to read.

"Number one: All attacks on Nuvens will cease immediately. Any unprovoked attack will be considered an act of war, and we will cut off all trade." Seer Cara nodded in agreement.

"Number two: You will let us worship in peace and to that end, you will allow us to restore Temple Darya without fear of reprisal. We will not rebuild the other temples. They will become shrines to honor our fallen heroes."

The other Verdan negotiators started to object but were cut off by a wave from Cara. "We will approve this only with the condition our Mother Verde priestesses be allowed to speak to your fellow Nuvens."

Amson raised his bushy eyebrows as he peered over the scroll. He looked up and down at his fellow Nuven negotiators. Only one objected, shaking her head vigorously. Another shrugged, and the others looked slightly amused at this attempt at conversion. "Approved," he said, scratching a note on the scoll.

"Number three: We will resume trade of goods, but all Verdans will honor our first asking price for this harvest. There will be no bargaining. We will offer fair prices."

"Perfectly acceptable," Cara said.

Amson cleared his throat and continued. "Number four: We will kill any Sankari we catch in our villages or spying on us without fear of reprisal."

"Number five: We reserve the right to fire upon any glider who flies near our villages." Cara sighed but nodded her approval.

"Number six: We wish to retain all rights as Verdan citizens as dictated by law."

"Number seven: A copy of this signed peace accord will be displayed for all to see in every Verdan city and village."

Amson and the other Nuven elders rose. He presented the scroll to Cara. "This scroll is to be returned to us in a week signed by the High Seer and the twelve recognized leaders of Verde. If it is not returned, we will not talk again."

Without another word, the Nuvens rose and abruptly left the room. Six days later, Cara made the return trip. She was escorted by a solemn-looking young Seer who had served at Temple Darya.

Cara smiled as she handed the signed scroll to Amson. "The Verdan leaders were quick to sign your document. The High

Seer took longer, but she misses her peaches." The second Seer asked in quavering voice if anyone survived at Temple Darya, especially the innocent known as Tevan.

Amson nodded. "Only a few badly injured archers were left alive my dear. Ah, so you were Tevan's friend. I'm afraid he perished with a group of younglings." Verinya let out a sob. She was not ashamed of showing her grief. No one suspected she also mourned for one of the young Defenders.

Moved by her show of emotion, Amson reached over and clasped her hands. "I am told this Tevan died fighting the murderers," he said then paused. His face flushed with embarrassment. "I apologize for my frankness."

Verinya stared in shock at the news. "Tevan could not have fought anyone. He was gentle. He had the mind of a child."

Amson shrugged. "We do not know why he changed. Some of the wounded Verdans were talking about a wild Defender who killed many of their number with an unusual weapon — a walking stick.

"Perhaps he learned something from his kinsman Aron Nels."Verinya buried her head in her hands. More tears streamed down and dripped off her chin. Amson turned to his fellow Verdans at the table. "If this Seer can mourn for one of our people then perhaps there is hope for a peace."

6

"Push, girl, push, Ah, that's it. I can see the head now. Take a breath and push," Cara gently coached the mother-to-be. Sweat streamed down Verinya's face as she gave another push, then moaned in pain. But her efforts were rewarded this time. The older Seer skillfully cradled the baby's head and shoulders as it emerged.

"It's a boy, very healthy," Cara said, smiling, as the infant let out a wail, filling his lungs with air for the first time. She quickly cut the baby's umbilical cord and tied it off. Verinya laid back, exhausted but sat back up quickly as another powerful contraction coursed through her body.

"The second baby is coming right behind the first one," Cara said calmly. "Get ready to . . ."

Verinya didn't need to be told what to do, she obeyed her body's demand. The young Seer strained, took a quick breath, grunted, then gasped from the exertion. After three more sequences of contractions and pushes, Cara reached down and helped guide the twin into the world.

"What a beautiful girl," she said carefully holding up the newborn so Verinya could see. "And look, red hair, what a surprise," the older Seer laughed.

Not to be outdone by her brother, the baby girl let out a lusty cry to tell the world she had arrived. Verinya smiled weakly then sank back on the birthing table. A gray-haired Seer cooed and cleaned up the new mother while two other Seers gently washed and examined the twins.

Cara checked on the newborns then attended to Verinya. "You did well," she said, stroking Verinya's damp hair. "They are small, but that is normal for twins. They look healthy."

Verinya sat up with some help from the gray-haired woman. "Please, I want to see my babies." After an approving nod from Cara, the twins were handed to their beaming mother. She cradled them tenderly for a few minutes then handed them back to their caretakers and relaxed back to the table. Cara stayed with Verinya through the final stages of the birthing process and made sure the young mother was going to be fine.

"Watch her carefully, but let her rest. There will be time for questions later," she said loud enough for all in the room to hear, especially a serious-looking woman, who watched from afar. After washing, Cara approached the visitor. "Verinya has presented us with two fine youngsters," she told Rufina, who stood frowning, her arms folded tightly against her chest.

The High Seer raised her eyebrows slightly. "Has she confessed who the father is?" Rufina asked.

Cara shook her head. "No. All she has said was the father died at Temple Darya. She refuses to name him."

The High Seer shrugged with indifference. "Perhaps we should expel her and those bastards from the fortress. I will not tolerate any Seer who refuses to cooperate with us."

Cara smiled and pointed toward the babies. "Now that would be a shame. The little girl already shows the strong sign of a Seer with her dark red hair. And the male also has red hair and a loud voice. I think he will make a fine Tarylan guard when he grows up."

Rufina's expression softened. "We need more Seers. Too few girls are being born with the gift. Even though the Defender wars are over, we need more sons of our Seers to serve as Tarylan guards."

The High Seer paused for a moment. "We shall keep the babies, but if Verinya does not cooperate, she will be expelled." With that edict, Rufina swirled around and departed. She did not see Cara shaking her head in disbelief.

Verinya stood patiently before the High Council. She was terrified at what the council was threatening her with, even though she did not visibly show it. Gathering her courage, she tried to plead her case again with the elder Seers. "With all due respect to your request to name the father of my twins, I cannot. Their father was a formidable fighter who died at Temple Darya. News of these babies will bring his family great distress."

Rufina was growing irritated with Verinya. In the High Seer's opinion, the Council had been too patient with the young mother. It had been one lunar since she had given birth. The babies were robust and growing. However, Verinya had refused every command to name the father. Other Seers had tried to embarrass and even anger her into a confession by accusing her of not knowing who had fathered her babies. Instead of being upset, Verinya just smiled at the innuendoes. This infuriated her interrogators even more.

"You have told the Council all this before," Rufina snapped. "We are not concerned with distressing the father's family but want to know which Verdan lineage the children come from."

Verinya shook her head. "I cannot. I pledged to protect his identity. Forgive me, but I stand by my promise." The young Seer did not dissuade the council from their line of questioning. She wanted her elders to believe she was protecting a highly placed Verdan family — the truth would be more damning.

Verinya was frightened what the Council might do to her twins if it knew the truth — the babies were fathered by a hated Nuven Defender, especially one of the unreadables the Seers had been so concerned about. She was worried the elders would order the babies killed for fear of continuing the Defender bloodline. Kind Cara was the only Council elder who supported her. The older Seer had grown fond of Verinya while helping her through childbirth and continued to look in on her and the infants.

Rufina rose and looked up and down the Council table then addressed Verinya. "This is our final request Verinya. Tell us who fathered your children."

Verinya also looked up and down the table. Cara was the only elder who did not frown at her, but she looked worried.

"Forgive me, I will not," she said softly. The young Seer was prepared to be assigned the dirtiest chores in the fortress probably for the rest of her life.

Rufina snorted in disgust. "The High Council cannot tolerate your refusal to comply with our request. Tomorrow, after first meal, you will be expelled from the fortress. You only will be allowed to return if you come to your senses."

Verinya stared in shock at the verdict. "My babies, what about my babies?" she asked, wildly looking from one elder to another.

Rufina smiled. "You will not have to worry about your children. They will be cared for and remain with us in the fortress."

Cara did not worry about showing her displeasure with the decision as she rushed over to comfort Verinya. The young Seer was bent over, sobbing with grief at the thought of being driven away from her children. "Shame on you, all of you," the normally affable Seer scolded her fellow elders. "This is entirely unnecessary."

Rufina started to reply, but stopped after seeing Cara's angry glare. Even the High Seer dared not reprimand Cara, who was loved by all.

"Our decision is final," Rufina said quietly as she and the other elders left the room while Verinya's sobs echoed through the chambers.

———

A few hours after the Seer elders had delivered their terrible edict, Verinya stroked her daughter's hair while the baby girl nursed. The young mother shivered from the thought of being torn from her children. The infant stirred a bit but continued to suckle peacefully. It was her turn to nurse from Verinya.

The babies alternated feedings with their mother. The twins were growing fast and required more milk than Verinya could provide. A wet nurse fed the other twin when its sibling was with Verinya.

"Oh Arynna, how could the elders be so cruel to force me away from you and Gerro," the young Seer whispered to her daughter. As was her right under Seer tradition, Verinya named her babies. She christened them Arynna and Gerro. Not even Rufina could refuse the young mother this right. No one suspected the girl's name was derived from her father, Aron Nels of Circle Sankarikiller. The name, Gerro, meant "warrior" in one of the Old Earth languages. He also was named in honor of his Defender father.

Arynna fell asleep when she finished feeding. The little girl always slept contentedly when her stomach was full. Her brother was very different. He squirmed and kicked. If something distracted or upset him, the boy would screech his displeasure. Whoever was caring for him would have to patiently pace back and forth, patting him gently in an attempt to calm him. Sometimes it took several minutes to settle the little boy down.

"I could take you anywhere, and you would not even stir, would you?" the new mother said to her daughter. A disturbing idea formed in her mind as she gazed lovingly at Arynna. The thought of being forcibly separated from her babies so distressed Verinya that she was willing to undertake a desperate plan.

The Seer knew there was nothing she could do to change her elders' minds. Verinya could, however, control when she left and what or who she could take with her. Moving with determination, the Seer gathered all the belongings she and Arynna would need for a journey. Verinya choked back tears as she thought of Gerro. Escaping with her daughter would be another blow to the elders. The other Seers already were doting over the little girl. They hoped she would grow up and join their ranks. The only others who helped with Gerro were the wet nurse and Cara. Caring for one baby on a journey into the unknown would be difficult enough. She knew bringing her son would be an impossible task.

Verinya did not delude herself that she could escape the fortress while carrying two babies and their necessary belongings. The placid Arynna barely made a peep when she was carried, but the restless Gerro might give away the escape plan if he decided he was unhappy.

As darkness set in, Verinya lowered her bundle of supplies, which she had tied to an escape rope, out her window which was only three levels off the ground. Taking a deep breath to steady herself, the Seer fastened the sleeping Arynna to a carrying harness on her chest. The young mother took one last loving look at her sleeping son and stifled a sob as she kissed his cheek.

After making sure no one was watching, Verinya donned a bulky cloak and sauntered out of the fortress as if she was going for a peaceful evening walk. No one paid attention to her as she left the fortress. Arynna never made a peep. Verinya was afraid her wildly beating heart would wake the baby but the infant slept soundly as her mother made her desperate escape.

As soon as Verinya was out of sight of the guards, she doubled back, found the bundle she had lowered from her window and hurried away from the fortress. The young Seer knew there was no turning back. The elders were going to expel her from their midst and tear her away from her babies. At least she was leaving under her terms and taking a precious cargo with her. Verinya had spent so much time worrying and planning her departure, she had given little thought to her destination.

Again, her throat tightened with fright. She did not know where she could hide if the Seers wanted to pursue her to reclaim Arynna. Once she reached Verde City, Verinya walked quickly, turning down many side streets in an attempt to lose herself among the multitudes. After keeping up the frantic pace for almost three hours, she made it to the outskirts of the city.

Without realizing it, Verinya found herself in the Nuven section of the city. The houses were simpler than their Verdan counterparts, but the Nuven district again bustled with craftsmen, merchants, shopkeepers and innkeepers who had returned after the peace agreement was signed. Exhausted, she stumbled into a quiet-looking inn to rest and feed Arynna who was now stirring a bit. The baby fussed as she tried to nurse from her nervous mother. Verinya had not eaten or drank since she made her escape. Arynna was not getting very much milk for her efforts.

A woman with a kind face and twinkle in her eye brought Verinya some cool water and bread without being asked. "You look troubled my dear. Can I help?" the woman said with a distinct Nuven accent. "I am Luta Petran, the owner of this humble establishment. If you need a place for the night, you are welcome here. The rooms are simple but clean."

Verinya gladly accepted the offer and ordered a hearty hot meal. The Seer knew she would need her strength and rest if she were to continue her journey. Luta asked if she could hold the baby. Verinya studied the woman for a moment then gladly agreed, eager to relax and eat in peace for a few moments.

"Ah, what lovely red hair this darling has. She favors you very much." Luta turned to the baby and cooed, "Perhaps you will grow up to be a beautiful Seer like your mother."

Verinya almost choked at Luta's words. She looked desperately at the older woman. "How do you know?" Verinya was frightened the older woman would report her to her elders.

"Your hair, your eyes, your clothes told me you were a Seer. Your daughter resembles you too well. Only Seer characteristics are that strong."

"We don't see many Seers in the Nuven section, especially frantic young mothers with newborns. The Seers usually protect their own, so when one such as yourself passes through, she must be in trouble. Don't worry dear, whatever secret you are guarding is safe with me. With respect to yourself, I do not owe the Seers any allegiance nor do I fear them."

Verinya stared in wonder at Luta. She had only been in the inn for a few minutes and already the older woman almost knew her story. Knowing Luta could turn her over to the elders if she wished, Verinya decided to trust her. The innkeeper reminded her of another woman who had helped her — Cara.

"Forgive me but for reasons I cannot reveal, I had to escape the fortress with my baby. The elders were going to expel me and keep my babies."

Luta looked surprised. "Babies? You left one behind?"

Verinya slowly nodded then burst into tears. This was the first time she had grieved for abandoning her son.

"Oh you poor dear," Luta said, kneeling to hug the sobbing woman. "Whatever made you leave must have been terribly important." Trying to choke back her tears, Verinya told Luta the babies were fathered by a prominent Nuven. She feared for her children's safety if the Seers found out.

"A Nuven father, eh?" Luta said, her eyes lighting up with pride. "I can see why those witches would not like that. Our bloodlines rarely have been mingled." Luta comforted Verinya for a few minutes. "My dear, there is only one place you can go where the Seers have no influence and where you and your daughter will be welcomed."

Verinya cocked her head in puzzlement. "Do you mean the Valley of the Heroes?" she asked incredulously.

Luta nodded. "You honor us with the proper name. Most Verdans would have said Valley of the Hunters. Only there can you raise your daughter in safety. If you wish, my mate and his brother will gladly take you there after you rest here for the night." Verniya rocked Arynna for a few moments, then consented. At least her daughter would grow up away from the Seers' influence.

7

The little boy chortled with delight as he was tossed into the air. The young father grinned as he caught his son then spun him around by his arms. When he was finally plopped down, the three-year-old collapsed to the ground giggling happily.

"My turn Papa, my turn," squealed his older sister, tugging on her father's sleeve. Grabbing the five-year-old girl, the father gave her a similar ride — tossing her into the air and spinning her in a dizzying circle. She laughed with delight when she careened back and forth then fell over after he put her down."Ride, Papa, again please, please," the little boy begged after he finally regained his balance.

The fun was cut short, however, by their concerned mother. "Aron Nels, stop it. You will make those children sick," Stazia scolded. The children yelled for one more ride, but his mate had made up her mind.

Trying to hide his amusement, Aron playfully scolded the youngsters. "Don't argue with your mother. Flyn, you got sick last time."

The boy pouted. "I won't get sick this time Papa, I promise, please. I like to fly."

Not to be outdone, his sister tried her luck one more time. "I never get sick Papa, I love spinning." Aron knelt down. "Now Amaura, you heard your mother. Besides I have another surprise for you and Flyn." The word "surprise" made the two children forget about the ride. They begged to hear more.

Stazia looked at her mate curiously as she patiently fed one-year-old Lyllen. She was a bit concerned because they had not talked about any surprises for the two oldest children.

"Romal asked me for help in the orchard," Aron told his mate. "I haven't been there since I was injured in the battle. It's been seven harvests. He has had no help since his sons have set off on their own."

Stazia looked puzzled. "I understand, but what does that have to do with Amaura and Flyn?

Aron smiled. "I could take them to the orchard. Mother and father can't help pick fruit any longer, but they would love to care for the children."

Not understanding what her parents were talking about, Amaura butted in. "What is the surprise, Papa?" she demanded, looking very serious with her hands on her hips.

Her father laughed. "Would you like to visit Gram Norene and Gramp Ural?"

Amaura looked disappointed. "Yes I would, but is that the surprise?"

Aron winked at Stazia. "Oh, I almost forgot. Would you like to see where the honey fruit comes from?"

"Honey fruit!" the two children screamed in unison. Flyn had gone off to play but came running when he heard his father mention the sweet, mouth-watering treat. "Take us to see the honey fruit please Papa. Please, please," he shouted as he clung to Aron's leg, swinging back and forth.

Stazia looked dubious. "You want to take both of them? I know Norene and Ural will take good care of them, but the trip is long for two little ones."

Aron gave his mate a big hug. "Don't worry, I will take my time traveling there, and Romal will return with me. He and I will make sure the children are safe." Looking at her mate, Stazia could tell this trip was important to him. He often had told her about the great fun he had exploring the grove when he was a child.

The family's most difficult task over all the years was keeping the orchard hidden from outsiders. They guarded the secret of the honey fruit with a religious fervor. The delectable treat was in great demand by anyone who had tasted it. The fruit sold out immediately whenever Aron's family offered it at market. Sales of the fruit had sustained his family for years.

Aron had never mentioned returning to the orchard since he and Stazia had bonded. The two met a few weeks after he had been found badly injured from the battle at Temple Darya. Stazia was helping her sister, a med-aide, care for the wounded. The two young women had volunteered with a Verdan group that offered to help care for anyone wounded in the battle — Nuven or Verdan.

Aron's physical wounds healed but an apparent blow to the head had apparently erased most of his memory of the battle and his duty at the temple. The young Nuven was enchanted with the dark-haired, green-eyed young woman with the quick wit. He teased her until she finally paid attention to his advances. One harvest later, the two bonded in Verdan tradition, much to her family's delight.

The bonding of a Nuven to a Verdan was rare. Strife usually arose between families when they argued over which religion the new couple and their children would follow.

Aron refused to convert to worshiping Mother Verde, but he did not insist on following the precepts of the Nuven ancestor worship. After recovering from the battle, his desire to observe any religion had slackened. He was just happy to be alive.

Stazia raised her hands in resignation. "Go help your brother but be careful with our little ones. Amaura and Flyn might be a handful for your parents."

Aron kissed his mate on the forehead and chuckled. "We are just visiting the orchard. What harm can come of harvesting honey fruit?"

REVENGE

1

It had been a long twenty harvests for Witt Peyser. He had spent the majority of the time in the Valley of the Heroes, biding his time when he would be needed to assist his charges. After returning unnoticed to the Verdan Valley two harvests ago, the Defender steward had carefully crafted and spread the legend of a circle of Nuven heroes who someday would surface to challenge and hopefully kill the hated Sankari.

Witt traveled from village to village, usually stopping at marketplaces to tell his tale to the vendors and tavern keepers, who were always eager for good gossip or to hear a good story. They would be eager to spread those stories, keeping the legend alive. The old man would cackle as if he had heard the story for the first time from a sage at the previous village he had traveled through.

His story always started the same. "You can't believe what I just heard at a little village I was passing through." This always drew his listeners in, eager for something interesting they could pass on. Witt would pause, shaking his head of white hair in wonder as if he didn't believe the fable. "They heard there were still Defenders alive. Can you believe that? Defenders!" He would either pause for a slow drink or pretend to lose his thought. After being prodded, Witt gladly continued his story.

"They," he never said who, "say the Defenders are waiting until the time is right and then will take revenge on the

Sankari." At the mention of the enemy Verdan warriors Witt would spit in disgust if appropriate. His listeners often would guffaw or sympathetically shake their heads. But they would want to hear more.

"I heard a young circle of Defenders escaped before Temple Darya fell. They've been in hiding, just biding their time." At this, the listeners would demand proof of the story. "They say an old Nuven helped a circle of young ones escape. The old man swore this on his deathbed to an innkeeper in one of those mountain villages. Went to his ancestors swearing this was the truth."

Witt would pause. "Imagine that! Defenders still alive. I hope I live to see that." Then he would bid his listeners a good-natured farewell and would shuffle away before the story could be debated. It hadn't taken long before Witt would hear the story retold to him in new villages. He gladly reinforced the tale. "Why, I just heard the same thing in another village. There must be some truth to it." He would shake his head in apparent amazement at hearing this incredible tale from a stranger.

The Nuvens were primed and ready when the first Defender announced himself two harvests ago. The hero energized his people's hopes by killing five of the Sankari before dying from his wounds. It was well known if one Defender was still alive, perhaps there were more, even a full circle of ten. The Nuven population eagerly waited for more Defenders to come forward to fulfill their destiny.

Witt could not have foreseen the first Defender's awakening. He had planned to guide them, help them to remember and prepare to seek revenge on the Sankari as each came forward, but their awakening had been unpredictable. As designed, the young Defender circle had dispersed after being put in the living sleep. They drifted back to their families and forged new lives. The Defenders were supposed to "awaken" after twenty harvests with the help of their steward — Witt.

However, when the 20th anniversary of the fall of Temple Darya neared, the High Council of Seers announced plans to hold a huge celebration in honor of the Sankari's heroic triumph. Witt shuddered at the news, then swore he would travel as far as he could from any place celebrating this ignominious event. He later rued the day when he made that decision.

The scope of the celebration was stunning. Almost every Verdan village hung posters advertising the weeklong festivities, which would culminate in a huge parade featuring the Sankari. A play was commissioned by the Seers to be performed every night in the capital city's giant arena. It was to be a re-enactment of the battle where the Defenders were defeated once and for all.

For decades, the Verdan populace had been told the Defenders were a threat to their culture and religion. Lies were spread that the Nuven warriors were terrorizing the countryside, burning villages and slaughtering innocents. Witt was so furious when he heard those falsehoods, he often had to leave before he gave himself away. Nothing could be further from the truth, but few were alive to testify to it. The Sankari had always been the aggressors. Their attacks started shortly after the Nuvens had refused the Seers' "request" to stop building temples shortly after they started moving into Verde Valley. The speed at which the temples were being built worried the Seers. Many Verdans were attracted to the Nuven religion of ancestor worship. It was a fresh idea after generations of the stranglehold the Seers had exerted.

Fearing they were losing control to these pagan interlopers, as they saw the Nuvens, the desperate Seers recruited and trained the Sankari, a secret warrior class. The Defenders suspected the Seer-Sankari collusion but nothing could be proven. Now with this new play, the fall of the last Nuven temple was going to be repeated over and over. People would toast to the heroic deeds of the Sankari. Songs and stories would echo through the performing halls, spilling out into the marketplaces, schools, even into the cradles of cynicism — the taverns. Witt was sickened by the very thought of it all.

Tanzer Unota had lived through the Battle of Temple Darya. He blamed his memory loss due to wounds he suffered as an archer. The Nuven always harbored an unexplained gut-wrenching hate toward the Sankari but managed to keep it to himself. Now an accomplished craftsman, Tanzer was startled to receive an official invitation to attend the first re-enactment of the battle.

At first he adamantly refused but finally gave in to the entreaties by his mate and four children. His family was thrilled at the chance to mingle with the elite of Verdan society. They had never witnessed such a spectacle. With great trepidation, Tanzer attended the play with his family. As the re-enactment unfolded showing courageous Sankari vanquishing the barbarous Defenders, a sickening feeling swirled in his stomach and swept through his body. He tried to control his trembling. Cold sweat rolled down his body soaking his clothes. Closing his eyes tightly, he tried to calm himself by taking deep breaths.

When Tanzer opened his eyes, his brain exploded with those long-suppressed memories. He remembered seeing the aftermath of the Battle of Temple Darya, but he was witnessing the events in a waking flashback.

A serene calm spread through Tanzer as he stared off into space reliving his life as a young Defender. The unlocked door that had harbored his secret had swung open in his brain. Tanzer remembered everything and knew what he had to do. The next day he bid his family farewell telling them he had to travel to one of the distant valleys to meet a potential client. One week later, the first Defender to come forward in 20 harvests challenged and killed a Sankari in the capital city's huge marketplace.

A large crowd gathered to watch the duel. Many assumed this was all part of the anniversary celebration — an impromptu performance. It became apparent the conflict was real when the Sankari's blood gushed over the ground after his neck was neatly sliced open by the Defender's knife. Filled with adrenalin after the fight, which was over quickly, the Defender used the dead man's blood to write a challenge to all other Sankari.

When finished, Tanzer faced the crowd as if he were an actor acknowledging a standing ovation, "We have returned to take revenge on the murderous Sankari. The truth of Temple Darya shall be told." Leaping onto a nearby horse, he bolted away through the crowded market before the Tarylan guards arrived at the scene. Buoyed by the promised return of one of their heroes, thousands of Nuvens gathered to dance the night away around huge bonfires. Frightened Verdans refused to venture from their homes.

Jolted by the news of a Sankari's death at the hands of a Nuven warrior who should have been long dead, the Seers immediately canceled the remaining celebrations. The Defender's challenge was accepted, creating the first public duel in almost one hundred harvests. He killed five more Sankari in the arena before he finally fell. The victorious Sankari was unable to relish his victory, since he died from the wounds shortly afterward.

To his credit, Tanzer, the first Defender to awaken, gave a heroic account of himself. He managed to kill four more Sankari before succumbing to his wounds. News of his death triggered the awakening of a second Defender. And on it went. The chain of events was unleashed, out of Witt's control. Often, by the time he heard another Defender had come forward, the warrior had either been killed or was preparing for a duel. With the Defenders' lives dwindling, Witt hurried to find the remaining members before they too awakened.

2

Aron Nels hid in the branches of the giant fruit tree fighting to quiet his heavy breathing after the frantic chase. The attack had come so quickly, he barely had time to flee. He stood straight up in the crook of two heavy limbs, his back flattened snug to the tree trunk. The heavy canopy of leaves and flowers hid him — for now.

After finally regaining control of his breathing, Aron cleared his mind. As sweat slowly trickled down his face, he concentrated on all the sounds and sights in his area. A light breeze slightly swished the leaves around him. Bees and other insects flitted and buzzed among the flowers. A bird broke into a song in a nearby tree. All was as it should be.

What seemed forever but actually was only several minutes later, a twig snapped nearby. The bird cut short its song and flew away. Something moved through the underbrush near his tree. It stopped often, then continued slowly, examining everything in its wake as if it was looking for something.

Aron knew what the hunter sought — him. This was the attacker who had ambushed him near the river. Somehow the assailant had tracked him to his hiding spot. He begrudgingly admired the hunter. Not many could have followed his frantic escape as he sprinted in a zigzagging pattern through the trees.

The orchard keeper had done his best to elude the pursuer. He leaped over fallen logs and scuttled through heavy brush until he found a familiar, ancient tree where the branches could support his weight. However, now he could hear the searcher pace from tree to tree, looking for his prey. At each tree, the hunter clumsily scaled the lower branches. Finding nothing, he would drop back to the ground with a thud.

Aron followed the other's progress. The pursuer finally reached his tree. The branches shook as the other man scrambled up. Moving slowly and quietly, Aron positioned himself directly above the other. Assuming he would have only one chance to strike, Aron poised in a ready-to-attack position.

The other man stepped out on a lower branch in an attempt to better scan the upper branches. This was his chance. Aron let his missile fly with tremendous force. Sensing movement from above, the pursuer moved with cat-like speed. But the large fruit still hit him, exploding after striking his shoulder, knocking him to the ground. With a blood-curdling scream, Aron leaped from the tree to subdue his victim but found nothing when he landed on the ground. Out of the corner of his eye, a blurred shape shot toward his head, hitting him squarely in the face.

It was Aron's turn to be knocked down. Before he could sit up, a foot pressed down on his chest, pinning him. Aron could do nothing. He had been defeated. The two men stared at one another momentarily. Aron's captor removed his foot and sat beside him smiling broadly, proud of his achievement.

"You'll have to do better than a piece of fruit to knock me down, father," Flyn Nels chuckled as he watched Aron sit up and clean the pulp off his face.

The elder Nels finally managed a smile. "How did you find me so quickly? You don't know the woods that well."

Flyn said nothing but let out a loud sniff and pointed to his father. "You were working very hard to escape. You left a heavy trail of scent. I recognized your odor," he said shrugging.

Aron raised his eyebrows. "Scent?"

Flyn nodded matter of factly. "On the ground, in the brush, even on some of the trees where you must have stopped briefly. Why are you looking at me so strangely? You have told me you can smell rain coming when it's hours away. I have seen you find a herd of grazers by smelling them from downwind."

Trying to look stern, Aron grumbled, "You still sound like an old woman when you climb, son. You will never ambush prey if they hear you."

Flyn grinned. "That's why I hunt the ravines and grasslands. I can see and smell the prey, plan my attack. Speed and a good aim with the bow will bring down most animals."

Rising together, both men sauntered back to the stream where Flyn initially "ambushed" his father by hurling a rotten windfall that exploded all over his back. "Just in time, son. You can help me carry some of these fruit baskets back to the cabin," Aron said.

Flyn grunted as he picked up one of the heavy baskets. "You will get your revenge on me yet."

"Can you stay for second meal?" Aron asked as they trekked toward the cabin with their loads of fruit. "Romal will be happy to see you."

An older man walked out of the orchard, carrying more fruit. "Why should I be happy to see this cub?" Romal growled. "He never comes around to help any more now that he finally learned how to use a bow."

Flyn sauntered up to Romal. "Good to see you, too, uncle," he said, slapping the older man on the back.

"Well, as long as you're here, we might as well feed you," Romal said, his eyes twinkling, revealing his good humor.

Flyn licked his lips. "Sounds good after the trip here, but it will have to be quick." The two other men looked at him questioningly. Flyn looked away for a second then faced Aron.

"This is what I came to tell you. The Tarylans have captured another Defender. A death duel will be held tomorrow, two hours after first light. I'm sorry, Father, I wanted you to hear it from me instead of some gossip who would have gotten the details wrong. Uh, there's one other thing," he paused, looking embarrassed. "My hunter circle wants me to go with them to watch the duel. I've never seen a Defender before."

Aron's face paled at the news. Saying nothing, he snatched up his basket of fruit and stomped angrily toward the cabin. Romal glared at Flyn. "You know your father fought with the Defenders at Temple Darya, where he was wounded and lost his memory. He thinks one of them saved his life, dragged him to safety."

Flyn looked down at the ground, scratching a line with his boot toe. "I know how he feels Uncle, but it's a chance to see a real Defender. Perhaps this duel will be different. Maybe the Defender will defeat more Sankari than the last one did. That would make Father happy."

Romal shrugged as he picked up his basket. "Yes, but they always kill the Defenders, don't they? How many of them have been killed so far?"

Flyn looked at his uncle. "This is the eighth one."

Romal looked surprised. "Eight already? That probably means only two are left. Those damn Sankari won't be happy until all the Defenders are dead." He just shook his head and followed his brother to the cabin.

Nothing was said during the meal. Aron concentrated on his food, angrily stabbing the pieces of meat as he ate. Finishing, he pushed his plate away. Aron folded his hands together, his elbows propped on the table. "Why do you want to go?" he asked in a low voice, not trying to mask his feelings.

Flyn met his father's gaze. "I want to see one of those famous warriors you have told me about since I was a crawler."

Aron's eyes narrowed. "Which side will you sit on?" Romal stopped eating but said nothing. He looked at his nephew questioningly.

Flyn looked up and smiled. "Nuven," he said proudly. Don't worry father, I will cheer for the Defender." Aron rose slowly from the table looking very tired. He said nothing, but the sorrow in his eyes told his son how he felt. Flyn rose to follow his father outside but stopped to squeeze his uncle's shoulder.

"Next time, stay longer, pup," Romal growled good-naturedly. "We could use the help. Our backs aren't as young as they once were."

"I promise, Uncle."

Aron did not look up when his son approached. He was busy rearranging fruit in small baskets, which would make for easier delivery to their customers. Without warning, Aron tossed two large golden apples to Flyn, who easily snatched them with both hands.

"Which one is the honey fruit?" Aron asked, testing his son.

Flyn felt both apples then carefully sniffed each one. "This one," he said, holding the apple in his left hand triumphantly aloft as if it were a prize. A deep bite of the fruit confirmed his declaration.

Rising, Aron reached out taking Flyn's face in his hands. Two sets of blue-green eyes stared into each other. "Your Nuven blood is strong son, always remember that."

Father and son embraced, giving each other hearty pats on the back. "Don't worry, Father, I'm sure the Defender will give a good account of himself in the arena." Aron allowed himself to smile. "May he send many Sankari to their ancestors." With a wave and a smile, Flyn turned and jogged steadily through the orchard.

Romal joined his brother on the porch to watch as Flyn disappeared into trees. "You don't have to worry about that one. He's grown into a fine man. Why, he's already a better hunter than you."

Aron snorted, giving Romal a strong brotherly shove. "There's more fruit to harvest or do you need a nap old man?" Aron said grinning.

"See if you can keep up for once," Romal answered as he grabbed two large empty baskets and headed for the orchard.

3

The bravado of the Defender was infuriating. High Seer Tanella glared at the hated Nuven warrior who gestured mockingly toward the group of Sankari seated above one of the arena's gates. The Defender had quickly killed two of the Verdan heroes. He refused to take his allotted rest period between duels and was calling for another challenger.

The Nuven crowd rose up in throaty admiration after his first two triumphs. The Defender was stirring up those unruly hunters even more by his antics. The crowd yelled for the next Sankari to dare challenge their champion of the moment. These Defender-Sankari duels had dragged on for too long for Tanella's liking. Twenty-three Sankari had been killed since the first Defender had come forward more than two harvests ago.

No two of their enemy had been alike in their methods. The first Defender had announced his presence by killing a Sankari in a marketplace and wrote his famous challenge to the remaining Sankari on a wall with the dead man's blood.

Other Defenders did not make their presence so public. Some hunted down unsuspecting Sankari, murdering them wherever they could find the opportunity — in their homes, on isolated streets, even in public places. The Defenders who refused to reveal themselves became the subject of extensive manhunts. They were finally hunted down by the Tarylan guards and killed after elaborate traps were set using Sankari "volunteers" as bait. Even then many men died trying to subdue these Nuven warriors.

A roar from the crowd told Tanella another Sankari had entered the arena to meet the latest Defender to announce himself. The High Seer watched with great interest as Manor Stillinger strode out to meet the Nuven.

Like the others before him, this Defender called out to his opponent. "I offer you life if you admit to the slaughter of innocent Nuvens and the massacre of the Defenders. Do you yield?"

Manor growled in response and drew his weapon. This was a sharp contrast from the previous Sankari, who answered each Defender with derisive yells and insults.

The combatants circled each other warily. The two men parried, thrust and dodged, trying to break through the other's defenses. Neither one could gain an advantage. The audience on both sides of the arena roared its approval with every jab and counter thrust. The duel continued like this for many minutes.

As the deadly contest dragged on, the Defender became more reckless. He took more chances, carrying the attack, trying desperately to penetrate Manor's defenses. Every time the Defender was repelled, he backed up breathing hard. After the latest unsuccessful maneuver, Manor attacked savagely but withdrew quickly. Unnerved, the Defender countered with a wild attack. The Sankari met him head on. Knife clashed with knife. The two combatants were chest to chest. It was now a test of strength like two bulls in a shoving match.

Manor was able to bring his arms down, shoving the other man backwards. The Defender charged again, but the Sankari turned and delivered a blow with his shoulder, knocking down his attacker. Before the Nuven could get to his feet, Manor jumped on top, plunging a knife into his chest.

In a violent reaction, the Defender rolled Manor over, stabbing him in the side. As he raised another knife to plunge into the wounded Verdan, the Defender trembled and collapsed, dead. Manor managed to push the body off him and struggled to rise. Tanella smiled with relief as the Verdan side of the arena erupted in a victorious roar. The Nuven crowd sat down with a disappointed groan. Many wept as they prepared to leave.

"That's the eighth Defender who has surfaced," the High Seer said to the captain of the Tarylan guards. "If their circle is intact, we must assume two more are left," she said while watching Manor being attended to by med-aides. Tanella paused for a moment as more movement in the arena caught her eye. She frowned as a Nuven honor guard picked up the Defender's body and carried it out of the arena.

"We shall keep up our patrols and offer protection to the surviving Sankari," Gerro, the Tarylan captain, assured her.

Tanella shot him an angry glance. "Surviving? You make it sound like our warriors are lucky to be alive."

He shrugged. "Perhaps they are. I have never seen more skillful warriors. They fight like someone of my years, not mid age." She would have chastised the captain even more, but he had been the only Verdan to have fought and had a hand in killing two Defenders.

Gerro had more respect for Defenders after his encounters with them. One of the first Defenders to reveal himself had attacked and killed a Sankari in a marketplace. Gerro had happened on the attack during a patrol. The Tarylan managed to kill the Nuven after a bloody hand-to-hand fight.

In the second incident, Gerro and his squad discovered the Defender forcing his way into the home of a Sankari. The captain was still amazed at how fast the Defender had moved. The Nuven had seemed to feel where the attacks were coming from, turning and twisting to avoid the six guards' knives and slashing out to counter any blows. Not unlike the Defender who had just fallen in the arena, the Nuven had lunged at two of Gerro's men, cutting their necks wide open before he collapsed, succumbing to their weapons.

The Tarylan captain had been wounded in both encounters. His shoulder was still slightly stiff from a stab wound he sustained in the marketplace skirmish. A long, jagged scar ran across his chest to serve as a reminder of the second Defender.

Gerro had grown up hearing the tales of the brave Sankari warriors, but his opinion changed after meeting many of them.

The Sankari were not held accountable to laws. They expected other Verdans to cater to their needs. Food, possessions, even property had to be given to them if they demanded it.

A med-aide bowed before Tanella. "High Seer, we have stabilized him. He should recover fully."

Tanella praised the aide's efforts then dismissed her with a wave. "We must find those two remaining Defenders," she hissed. "There are twenty-five Sankari left who survived the Defender wars. We must protect our heroes."

Gerro bowed. "Yes, High Seer, we shall remain vigilant." The Tarylan captain dared not question Tanella's opinion of the Sankari.

———————

Flyn Nels sat with his head down, still mesmerized by the familiarity of the Defender's tactics. Fascinated by the deadly drama, Flyn had found himself flinching and twitching as if he were the one fighting. The outcome was disappointing. An overwhelming sadness engulfed Flyn, surprising him with its intensity. He wiped away the sudden rush of tears. His friends said nothing when they saw his reaction. They had known each other since they were children and had survived many hunts together.

The circle of young men had bonded during those hunts, when they depended on one another to carry out their duties. One wrong move could have been fatal to them all. Flyn was always the point man, the leader who directed their movements and carried out the plan when stalking the grazers. Many times it was his arrows or javelins that brought down the huge beasts as they stampeded in terror.

Flyn rose in respect as the Defender's body was carried out of the arena. "A hunt," he said to his circle. "I need to go on a hunt to get this out of my mind."

———————

Almost all the Nuvens had left the arena after sadly watching yet another Defender fall at the hands of the Sankari. This was the first Defender-Sankari duel Egan Pozos had witnessed. For some unexplainable reason, he had been unable to take his eyes off the Defender.

The flashes of strange memories started when the Defender had announced his name before the first duel — Gillo Baze. With each of Gillo's parries and thrusts, painful memories of other skirmishes surfaced in Egan's brain. How could this be possible? His memories of being an archer during the battle of Temple Darya became cloudy. This did not dim the exhilaration Egan felt when the first two Sankari fell to Gillo's knives. Now, as he watched the Defender's body being taken from the field, Egan doubled over in grief. Why? He was sure he didn't know this Defender.

Egan was told by med-aides he had been injured when a wall collapsed after the Sankari overran the temple. Something about that memory now seemed wrong. Egan did not recall being in hand-to-hand combat, until now. The Defender's death was causing a chain-reaction of memories to flash through his brain. Egan sat alone rubbing his temples, watching a dramatic play unfold before his eyes. It was like witnessing a performance of one of Verde's traveling theater troupes, only this was in his mind.

Laughter from across the stadium interrupted Egan's troubled thoughts. The surviving Sankari were standing, jovially pounding each other on the back for their good fortune to still be alive. Egan glared at the Verdan heroes. Hatred flooded into him so savagely it made him shake. Watching the Sankari as a hunter would study its prey, it become clear to Egan what he must do.

As he was leaving the arena, Egan passed an old man standing by himself, looking forlorn at what had just occurred.

"It's tragic, we've lost another brave Defender," the old man said shaking his head.

Egan stopped for a moment. "Perhaps he won't have died in vain, Uncle," he said, using the Nuven term of respect. The elder nodded and smiled at the fierce determination in Egan's blue-green eyes.

The Nuven started to leave but turned back, giving the elder a questioning look. The old man looked like one of the many people he had seen in his waking dream.

Witt's face lit up. "I've been waiting too many harvests to say this. I feared I would never get the chance. Welcome back, Defender."

Egan started to protest. "You honor me, but you are mistaken, Uncle. I served with Defenders at Temple Darya."

Witt reached out and clasped Egan's shoulder. "You were told you were an archer, Egan Pozos. You were injured and lost your memory." The old man took a step backwards and clapped his hands in a strange cadence then shouted: "Awaken, Defender!"

Egan blinked as if a mask had just been removed from his face. Stepping closer, he studied Witt carefully. Recognition finally shone in his eyes. "Steward, is that you?" he muttered in disbelief.

Witt chuckled. "Twenty-some harvests have brought a few changes to both of us, Defender." Egan swept Witt up in a bear hug, laughing with glee. He put his steward down only after the old man started to gasp for air. The Defender tenderly patted Witt's white hair. Egan thought he would be alone in his stand against the Sankari. At least now he had the support of the man who had transformed ten unruly boys into a promising Defender circle.

His last memory was of a much younger-looking Witt speaking softly, slowly and reassuringly. The Steward was attempting to calm Egan down after his circle was ordered to retreat when Temple Darya fell. Afterwards, he had wakened while being cared for by his family. He didn't remember how he had gotten wounded, especially that nasty bump on his head. "A cloud has lifted in my mind, Steward. I remember being with Circle Sankarikiller as if it were yesterday."

Witt patted him on the shoulder. "I know, but it's been twenty harvests. There are still too many Sankari left."

"How many Defenders have awakened besides me and . . ." Egan frowned looking back at the arena.

Witt shook his head and sighed. "Eight have awakened before you and now they have been embraced by their ancestors. He then named Egan's fallen circle brothers.

Egan's eyes widened at the realization. "Only Aron and I survive and so many Sankari are left," he said frowning. "Aron! Have you found Aron?"

Witt shook his head and motioned for Egan to follow. "If we are lucky, we will find him. He and his family disappeared into the mountains after Temple Darya fell. Come, we have a lot of work to do."

4

Standing at the edge of the 2,000-foot precipice, Flyn Nels took a deep breath as he felt a hot air thermal on his face. Flashing an encouraging smile to his circle, the young man backed up a few steps and then launched himself over the edge with a defiant yell. That first few meters of plummeting was always exhilarating just before a gust of wind caught his glider and swooped him aloft. He circled slowly until he caught another thermal, leaned into it and soared through the air.

Familiar shouts told Flyn the others had launched themselves behind him. Soon his friends pulled alongside him and the flock of colorful gliders soared through the valley, following one of Verde Grande's many uncharted rivers.

Below them, two of their circle brothers steered a boat through the water. The slower vessel would be needed for hauling back two lunars' worth of skins and other treasures after their hunt. Upon reaching a valley they wanted to explore and hunt, the fliers would post colored flags so the boat could find them.

Deeply troubled after witnessing the Defender's death in the arena, Flyn wanted to get far away. Only a hunt would help take his mind off that tragic event.

While flying, it was easy to forget how difficult it was to learn to glide. Young Verdans started under the watchful eyes of their parents. Families would hike up the foothills to find a spot that provided a respectable running start for the young flier and also a meadow of tall grass to cushion any unsuccessful attempts.

Being of Nuven blood, Aron was not interested in flying so he was reluctant to encourage Flyn. Flying was a peculiar Verdan talent that most Nuvens were reluctant to learn. Two centuries of defending themselves from the Tanlian space raiders had taught them death came from the sky. The attacks on the temples also cemented many Nuvens' distrust of flying.

During a visit to his mother's family, the young Flyn begged his grandfather to teach him to fly. A skilled flier as a youth, his grandfather finally agreed. On his first try, Flyn warily launched himself off a bluff, stiffened his body and promptly crashed into some bushes. Only his face was scratched. No bones were broken.

"You can't be scared," his grandfather said matter-of-factly while brushing him off and examining the glider for damage. "The wind is your friend. Jump hard into it, trust your glider to catch it." After catching his breath, Flyn tried it again. He darted off the bluff at full run, launching himself into the wind. The glider dipped slightly, Flyn instinctively shifted his weight and then soared over the meadow.

He grinned proudly when he heard his normally stoic grandfather let out a victorious whoop. A few attempts later, Flyn learned how to bank right and left. He no longer landed in a heap but set down gracefully — a flier was born. Aron was not pleased when his son excitedly told him of his adventure. He couldn't scold the boy after hearing the pure joy as Flyn proudly described his accomplishment.

It didn't completely take his mind off recent events, but it helped. Now Flyn and his fellow hunters were searching for game in one of the myriad canyons that had spread out from the main valley like the threads of a spider web. They hoped to find an uncharted area, one that had not been settled. In these small valleys, hunters often found predators that challenged their skills. The rare furs were sought after by Verdan merchants who paid very well for them.

The hunting party glided for most of the day, taking short breaks to rest and take nourishment. At sunset, they found a suitable clearing to rest for the night. Flyn and his circle repeated this cycle for two more days until they reached uncharted territory. They no longer swept over villages nestled in the sides of the mountain. No fishermen sailed over the river looking for a catch.

Not long after second meal, a split in the side of the mountain caught Flyn's eye. Signaling his intention to the others, he banked into the small canyon. A small tributary barely seeped through a fissure. *The boat will barely make it*, Flyn thought as he carefully guided himself through the narrow opening, followed by the others. The wings of the gliders almost brushed the sides of the canyon as the fliers cautiously made their way through.

"If this gets any narrower we won't be able to turn around," Hund Telfer yelled as a wall of rock jutted out directly in their path. Flyn leaned his glider close to the wall then eased his way around, following its rounded contour. Moments later, he emerged in a large valley covered with pines.

Wildlife was everywhere. Birds sprang from the trees squawking with alarm as the hunters floated overhead. Grazers barely noticed the fliers as they fed or drank from the river, which coursed through the valley. With a shout of joy, Flyn banked right and left looking for an open ledge or clearing partway up the side of the mountain to set down. Finally spotting a large ragged rock outcropping, he landed with a well-practiced soft plop. After a quick survey of the surroundings, he determined the location was safe and signaled the others to follow.

———

The hunting circle reveled in the amount of game they found in the narrow valley. Grazers were plentiful and fat, proving there was a good supply of food. Of course where one found game, it was natural that predators also inhabited the area. Flyn and his circle were not disappointed.

That first night, the air echoed with the screeches of night birds, howls of wolves and eerie screams of the giant mountain cats. Once during the night, a growl erupted from nearby bushes, but the beast did not bother the hunters who kept a healthy fire blazing while they slept.

"We were looked over last night," Yal Chim said the next morning when he found a large set of feline tracks not 30 meters from where the hunters had slept.

Flyn nodded. "We must be trespassing in the cat's territory. Good, we found our first target. Gather the circle for a predator hunt."

Yal knelt to examine the tracks. He poked a finger in the indentation and then spread his hand out over the surface. Checking behind him carefully, the tracking expert located the back paw prints. "These are the biggest cat footprints I have ever seen," Yal said softly as he did some mental calculations. "This animal may weigh more than 250 pounds."

Flyn's eyes flashed with amazement. "We had best be back to camp before dusk. I don't want that thing ambushing anyone after dark."

Yal nodded. "It's bigger than we are. I doubt if it's scared of us. I hope it's never tasted humans."

5

The early morning sun had barely cleared Mount Barrasca when activity in Verde City's marketplace begun to buzz around the vendors. Shoppers eager to be first to claim fresh, abundant produce, darted from kiosk to kiosk searching for the best deals.

Aron trudged through an already half-crowded marketplace to reach his stand. He was in no hurry to open for business. *It will be hectic soon enough and the produce will be quickly sold out. It never fails,* he thought.

No one noticed Aron, who wore an old hooded pullover to protect himself from the chilly air as he unlocked his station. The top door of the kiosk swung up to act as a canopy. Half of the bottom door folded into a counter. Once inside, Aron busied himself arranging the small baskets of fruit so they could be quickly plucked once the rush came.

A haggard-looking woman stuck her head over the counter to snoop while Aron was still moving the baskets. "What are you selling today keeper?" Without waiting for him to answer, she spotted the filled baskets. "Ah, just more fruit. Well, hand one over, let me give it a look, want to make sure it's fresh," she ordered.

Looking up with a half smile, Aron shook his head. "You touch, you buy. This is the freshest fruit in the valley, you have my word."

The old woman stared at him with disbelief. "Every vendor lets us check out their wares. Why, that's, that's Verde City tradition," she sputtered, clearly annoyed.

Aron shrugged. "I'm not from the city. Not my tradition, grandmother. I always sell my fruit and quickly I might add."

The old woman cackled with surprise. "A Nuven, I should have guessed with that beard of yours. You must not come down out of your hills very often. I'll forgive you for not treating me better. This time."

Dark red hair with some white streaks tumbled out when the hag removed her shawl which she had wrapped around her head and shoulders. Standing with a triumphant smile, she held out her hand again.

Aron smiled politely and crossed his arms, not budging. He had an inkling about this old woman, but she had no right to order him to comply. She had grown accustomed to having her way and was shocked when he did not comply. Dropping her hand in dismay, the woman shook her finger threateningly. "You will make no sales today, keeper. Your fruit will spoil. That will teach you some respect."

Aron further infuriated her by laughing. "Stand back grandmother, I don't want you to get trampled." Before she could protest again, he yelled to a young boy sauntering by, then tossed him a golden fruit. The youngster examined his gift, then tore a huge bite out of it. A stunned then delighted look crossed his face.

"Honey fruit!" the youngster shrieked with delight. "The honey fruit man is here. He gave me a free one!" Before the old woman could spit, Aron's kiosk was crowded with customers loudly begging for his produce.

"Now remember, there is one honey fruit in every basket. One basket per customer," he warned the people eagerly awaiting their turn.

No one accused him of shortchanging them of that precious fruit. For three generations, Aron's family had sold fruit throughout the valley. They had earned a reputation for honesty. Villagers and city dwellers alike always flocked to buy the delicacy which only the Nels family provided.

Every so often, Aron would stop to toss a free slice of honey fruit to a child, which drew cheers from the crowd. He was too busy grabbing baskets and taking coins in return to notice the old woman angrily stomp off. In less than an hour, Aron had sold more than a hundred baskets. He sat down exhausted — his arms ached, sweat soaked his clothing. A satisfied smile creased his lips while he gulped a much needed drink of cool water and closed his eyes.

Aron understood why Romal disliked this part of the business. Dealing with shouting customers made his brother nervous and irritable. The older Nels couldn't wait to return to the solitude of the orchard. Romal would gladly harvest from dawn to dusk, but he refused to put up with the noisy marketplaces.

"I understand you have sold all your fruit, keeper. That is disappointing. I was looking forward to trying the famous honey fruit," an intoxicating female voice purred, interrupting his reverie. Aron nodded wearily. Blinking, he was startled by the beauty of the young woman who peered with dark brown eyes into his kiosk, smiling politely. She looked familiar. Long bright red hair cascaded down her back.

With a start, he remembered the old woman who had demanded to inspect his fruit. Embarrassed, Aron started to offer an apology. "Oh, was the old red-haired woman your mother? I'm sorry, but I don't allow anyone to touch the fruit before it's sold."

The young woman looked surprised, then chuckled. "Really, you don't *allow* it?" she asked. "No, that was not my mother, but she is close to me." The young woman stared at Aron for a moment, then glanced away with a startled look. "When will you return with more of your special fruit?"

Aron thought for a moment. "Harvest is just beginning and there are many villages to visit. I could try to return in a lunar, perhaps."

She smiled. "I would appreciate that. I look forward to seeing you again."

One of the nearby vendors, who had been selling vegetables, sauntered over to Aron's stand after the young woman departed. "So, you're the honey fruit seller. Heard of you, but never set eyes on you before. That was quite a show," he chuckled, leaning over the counter.

Aron shrugged. "Oh, it's always like that. The crowds snatch up the produce because of the honey fruit."

The other vendor snorted, "Fsssh, I've seen crowds before. I meant the old woman. I've never heard anyone deny them before. She sure was angry, stomped off she did."

Aron looked puzzled. "Them? I only told the old woman she couldn't touch the fruit, not the young one."

The visitor squinted suspiciously at Aron. Looking cautiously over his shoulder, he carefully leaned over the counter. "Nuven, that was a Seer you just insulted. You never seen a Seer before?" he whispered. "They come to the market sometimes to mingle, sometimes to buy our goods. They think they're being clever, getting all disguised like that, but you can always tell."

The realization startled Aron. Of course, the red hair, piercing brown eyes and arrogant attitude. He should have known. "No, I've never seen a Seer before. He paused. There was something unsettlingly familiar about that hair and those eyes. A memory scratched at his brain, trying to surface. But it remained foggy, just out of reach.

"I always sell my fruit and leave immediately. I've done nothing wrong." Aron shrugged, trying to convince the other merchant as much as himself.

Taking another look behind him, the other man offered Aron some advice. "If I was you, Nuven, I'd leave right quick. The Seers always get their way. Don't know what will happen when one of them gets told no."

Aron rose quickly and started to clean the kiosk when a thought stopped him. "I told the young one I would be back in a lunar."

The other vendor shook his head at Aron's quandary. "You upset one and made a promise to the young one. You're in a spot, Nuven. My advice is don't make two Seers angry. That won't be good. No, not good at all."

Reaching out, he gave Aron a fatherly pat on the shoulder. "You got to come back then but be careful my friend, the Seers can be a dangerous lot."

Aron shrugged. "I've done nothing wrong. I will apologize to the old one if I must. Maybe offer her a honey fruit."

The vegetable seller cackled. "Better have a whole basket of them honey fruits, Nuven. Good luck to you."

The other women tried to conceal their amusement while the old woman ranted about being insulted in the marketplace. "By a Nuven, no less. In the marketplace!" she finished angrily, thumping her hand on the dais, accentuating every word. By now she was breathing heavily, her cheeks flushed, red hot.

Sitting around the semicircular table, the listeners patiently waited for the hag to take a seat. "Thank you, Fionula, that was an interesting account," High Seer Tanella said, glancing up as another woman took her place at the dais. "Katine, I understand you followed up Fionula's complaint."

The young woman bowed. "Yes High Seer, I spoke with the vendor after the incident. He apologized. I don't think the Nuven understood he had offended the honored Seer."

Fionula stood up. "The Nuven didn't apologize to me."

Katine nodded. "Yes, that's true, Fionula. But you were not there later. You were lodging your complaint."

Tanella drummed her fingers against the fine marble surface of the table. "Fionula, obviously you had the misfortune of haggling with an ignorant Nuven. I don't think it is warranted to ask the Tarylan guards to drag a fruit vendor in front of us for an interrogation."

The old woman sat down with a loud thump, mumbling her disappointment. "High Seer, there was something different about this Nuven," Katine said almost as an afterthought.

Tanella impatiently gestured for her to continue. "Yes, yes, what is it?"

"This has never happened to me before," Katine continued, sounding embarrassed. "I, I could not read him. I saw nothing with my sight. However, I sensed no threat."

The mood of Tanella and the other Seers changed in a heartbeat. "You were blocked by the Nuven?" the High Seer asked sternly. Katine nodded, looking down, startled by the intense looks from the other Seers.

"What color were his eyes?" the High Seer asked.

Katine looked surprised, then thought for a moment. "His eyes? Ah, blue, yes they were blue."

Fionula stood up again, waving her hands. "They weren't blue, for Mother Verde's sake! They were as green as the moss on Barrasca."

Tanella sprang up out of her chair so quickly, it startled all in the room. "Where is the Nuven now?" she snapped.

A trembling Katine shook her head. "I don't know, High Seer. He said was traveling to sell his fruit in other villages."

Tanella threw up her hands in disgust. "He could be anywhere by now. We may never find him."

Katine cleared her throat and cast a nervous glance at her elders. "I may know where he will be in a lunar, High Seer." Tanella glared at the speaker and gestured for her to continue. "He said he would try to return to our marketplace," Katine offered, hoping this would placate the other women.

Tanella whispered with the other Seers at the table, then turned to the young Seer. "For your sake, I hope this Nuven comes back. Go sit with one of our artists. I want a very detailed drawing of this fruit seller. If he comes back, I want the Tarylan guards looking for him."

Aron scurried out of the marketplace. He wanted to escape the city as fast as possible without causing any further scenes. However, Aron noticed a hush followed him as he made his way through the marketplace. Vendors and their customers paused to curiously follow his progress. It had not taken long for word to spread that a hapless Nuven fruit seller had accidentally insulted a Seer. This had never happened before.

Many Verdans and some Nuvens mingled amongst them were curious about this bold vendor. Everyone had known him as the famous honey fruit dealer. Now there was even more fodder for the gossips. It didn't take long for the gamblers to spread through the market taking odds on Aron's fate. The best odds had the Tarylan guards carting him off to Fortress Bryann, never to be seen again.

All this was unbeknownst to Aron. Returning to the peace and quiet of the orchard never sounded so appealing.

6

Parwiz Shlabaw slammed down his mug of ale, cocked his head back and let loose with a giant belch. This brought a roar of approval and raucous laughter from his fellow revelers. The large man had a slightly round belly and short thinning red hair. His friends and family were helping him celebrate his 55th birthday at his favorite neighborhood tavern.

Looking pleased, Parwiz slowly rose and announced his next intention, to relieve himself to make more room for ale. He endured a chorus of good-natured insults as he shuffled toward the door to find the outdoor toilet. Two young Tarylan guards rose to escort him, but the old Sankari waved them off. "Sit lads. I don't think you have to worry about any Defenders tonight. Even those devils have to sleep."

The Tarylans looked uneasy, not knowing what to do. However, they relaxed when Parwiz slapped them both on the back and ordered a round of the tavern's finest for them. The two men were tired after their long shift. They did not argue with the offer to relax and enjoy themselves with a fine drink.

Ever since the first Defender had come forward and killed several Sankari, the Seers had ordered their Tarylan guards to protect the surviving Verdan "heroes." This had proven to be difficult, stretching out the Tarylan ranks as they watched over the Sankari night and day.

In a happy stupor, Parwiz shuffled toward the toilet. The party had gone well. He couldn't remember the last time he had downed so much brew, sang so much and laughed so loud. When reaching his destination, he let out a soft curse after seeing both doors were locked. Shifting his weight impatiently from foot to foot, Parwiz finally pounded on both doors after waiting for what seemed to him to be an interminably long time.

With a creak of rusty hinges, one of the doors slowly opened as a slight, small man walked out. "It's about time neighbor, thought I was going to explode," Parwiz grumbled, bumping the other man out of his way as he reached for the door. The old Sankari never saw the other man quickly move toward him with a drawn knife.

Parwiz only managed a surprised grunt when the knife plunged into the middle of his back. He collapsed from the blow and pain. Struggling to rise, a great weight pinned him to the ground. A hand snatched the hair on the back of his head, bending it back.

"You've grown fat and stupid, Sankari," a deep voice hissed in Parwiz's ear. "We have treated you Sankari as warriors, worthy of honorable deaths, but now you will die like the grazers you have become." Before Parwiz could utter a word, a knife quickly slashed across his throat. He died quickly as his life's blood gushed out in a steady stream.

"He's been gone a while," one of the young Tarylans said putting down his mug, looking out the door. "Do you suppose he passed out?"

His partner shrugged. "If he did, I'm glad it's not our responsibility to carry him home."

The first guard nodded in agreement as he rose to go look for the old Sankari. He had not been gone more than a few seconds when his scream startled everyone in the tavern. Grabbing torches, the crowd from the inn rushed to where Parwiz lay face down in a large pool of blood. In the confusion, no one saw the message which had been scrawled on the tavern's wall in the darkness.

The next day, Gerro frowned when he read the words which had been written with Parwiz's blood: "More of these fat grazers will die."

The captain of the Tarylan guards shook his head. "This Defender is different," he said to one of his nearby lieutenants.

"There was no confrontation, the kill was done quickly, efficiently. Apparently this one is not interested in a public duel. He may be much harder to find."

An exhausted messenger hurried over to the Tarylans. The man slumped over wheezing loudly as he handed Gerro the piece of paper. "Damn," the captain exclaimed loudly, then angrily threw the paper to the ground.

"What is it, sir?" the lieutenant asked, surprised by his leader's display of emotion.

Gerro shook his head in amazement. He snatched the message to reread the details. "Apparently this Defender killed another Sankari during the night, got him coming out of a pleasure house. Only one wound, too, a knife directly in the heart. Again, there was no struggle."

The lieutenant stared wide-eyed at the news. "He's hunting them like animals," the young officer murmured.

Gerro glanced at the message again before he walked away. "Slaughtering them like grazers, more like it."

———

The two men ate first meal in quiet. Neither looked nor spoke to the other. They listened to the hubbub in the street. Everyone was talking about the shocking news — two Sankari had been killed that night. An unknown Defender was suspected of savagely cutting them down, then escaping before anyone saw him.

Egan Pozos brought a spoonful of porridge to his lips then put it down slowly. He watched the passersby with a keen interest. It was easy to eavesdrop on their conversations. "It was almost too easy, steward. The Sankari did not have a chance. There was no honor in killing them," Egan whispered, absent-mindedly stirring his bowl.

Witt Peyser studied his charge between bites of his meal. Leaning over the small round table on the outdoor patio, he spoke softly, but his eyes burned with intensity. "Did the Sankari worry about honor when they attacked and slaughtered our people at Temple Darya and the other temples?" he asked, snapping his spoon angrily on the table.

Egan nodded, resting his chin on folded hands that were propped up on the table. A chill ran through his body while the memory of the night's events tumbled through his brain. The Sankari in the pleasure house had died quickly. Egan followed him to the house and ambushed his target when the other man departed from his amorous adventure.

Killing the Sankari outside the tavern went differently. Egan waited in the shadows for several hours before Parwiz came stumbling out. He scurried ahead to the toilet before the drunk could get there. The Defender jammed one door shut, then waited inside the other stall, knowing Parwiz would become impatient.

Egan saw the Sankari's face but instead of hesitating, he instinctively attacked, driving his knife deep into Parwiz's back then slashed the man's neck with a deadly stroke. With adrenaline still coursing through his body and inspired by the first member of his circle to awaken, the Defender scrawled his bloody message on the tavern's wall.

Egan finished his porridge but stared off into space, deep in thought. "Steward, there is something else. Killing those men was so easy. My mind turned off and something else took over. I barely felt remorse. In fact, just the opposite," he said staring hard at his companion.

Witt nodded but didn't look up from his food. "Your circle was bred specifically to kill Sankari," he said, carefully measuring his words. "We needed young men who, if needed, could infiltrate and kill the enemy without remorse. They were pressing their attacks on our temples. We wanted warriors who could slow them down, maybe force them into a truce. You were born with those instincts. The other teachers and I helped you hone them. However, Temple Darya was destroyed before we could send you among their ranks."

Egan frowned while he mulled over what Witt had just told him. He conceded it made sense. The steward's story explained why he felt a strange satisfaction after killing the two Sankari. Some of his long-lost memories were now making sense.

After a long pause while reflecting on his past, Egan addressed the task before him. "It will be much more difficult to kill the others. They will be guarded very closely now. Perhaps I should not have written that message."

Witt smiled. "We can be patient as long as we wish. We have waited more than 20 harvests for our revenge. Besides, it makes me rather pleased to know many of the Sankari will spend sleepless nights wondering if an unseen knife will end their life." The two men sat at the table, enjoying the warm morning sunshine and listening to the worried passersby.

7

Romal shook his head at Aron's story, but a twinkle in his eye gave away his amusement at his brother's predicament. "So you insulted a Seer. Now that's a first. Wish I'd been there to see that. That can't help business," he snorted with laughter.

Aron sat back in his chair, glowering at Romal. He should have known better than to expect sympathy from his older sibling. Romal's misgivings about selling their produce in Verde City had proven right. For years he had argued they should be content just to do business with neighboring villages.

"You have to go back now," he urged Aron. "We don't want those Seers interfering with our business. What'd that other vendor tell you?" Romal asked, but didn't wait for an answer. "Give them a whole basket of honey fruits, huh? That just might work. Let that old witch pinch them all she wants, then let her eat her fill. However, if you do that, it will come out of your shares at the end of the season."

Aron nodded. "I would not mind if that's the worst that would happen after all this. The Verdans seem frightened of the Seers."

Romal grew serious as he thought about the consequences. "Be careful around those women. I've heard stories. Can't believe most of them though. I do know they control that strange religion the Verdans practice."

Aron grimaced, wishing he had other options. At this moment he envied his son, Flyn, who probably was enjoying another carefree hunting adventure. *I would even try to fly one of those damn gliders if I didn't have to go back to Verde City,*

Aron thought as he headed for the orchard to pick that basket of the delectable fruit.

Flyn and his circle were stunned by the vicious attack of the big cats. The hunting circle had followed the large tracks for the most part of a day, ending up in a small clearing of giant oaks. However, the tracks stopped suddenly.

The hunters retraced their steps and examined the surrounding area carefully — nothing. With the sun setting quickly, they found a large hollowed out spot in the side of the mountain and settled down for the night. As before, they kept a large fire blazing mainly to deter any predators, especially the big cats they were trailing. If the animals had dared approach their first campsite, there was a good chance they would investigate again. Halfway through the night, the fire had died down to about half its size when the attack started. Hearing nothing so far, their sentry had dozed off. Ear-splitting roars from only a few meters away startled the hunters awake. Two pairs of green eyes glowed in the night as the cats circled the camp.

Seeing the hunters move, the huge felines rushed close to the fire, snarling and angrily pawing the air. Flyn reached for a weapon but could find nothing in the half light. He touched a large log during his frantic search. Cocking his arm to throw it at the beasts, another thought shot into his mind.

With careful aim, he chucked the log into the fire. The shower of sparks drove the cats back momentarily. Following his lead, the other hunters grabbed the nearest sticks, hurling them into the fire.

The flames shot into the air, lighting the scene. The dark brown cats backed away quickly, turned and bounded away into the night before the hunters could grab a weapon. Flyn and the others looked at each other in shock. It was not unusual for a wounded animal to turn on a hunter or stay to protect its young, but they had never seen a predator attack without warning.

"I've never been the hunted before," Flyn said, casting a nervous glance around while his circle brothers nodded in agreement. "What say we leave these cats to themselves and go hunt grazers?" The hunters' unanimous decision to leave was accentuated by a feline scream from the nearby underbrush. The fire burned even brighter than ever for the remainder of the night.

At dawn, the hunters armed themselves and set out for their original campsite. They looked back frequently to guard against another surprise. Returning to their gliders, Flyn and the others flew across the river in search of prey that wouldn't turn on them. Someone in their party remembered cats didn't like water. They hoped that was so.

8

Egan Pozos had followed the Sankari turned merchant for two weeks. The man wandered through the marketplace in the mornings, buying raw supplies of hides, produce and hand-crafted goods. He then would resell the items at a handsome profit to shopkeepers who would turn the materials into finished goods.

It soon became evident to Egan, the Sankari kept to a strict routine. The Defender positioned himself in a different corner watching the man from the front, the back and either side. With each passing day, Egan grew more frustrated. He saw no clear opportunity to get to the Sankari without dozens of people watching and perhaps blocking any escape.

One day while watching the merchant haggle boisterously over a load of produce, the man suddenly swore and ducked as a bird swooped down, just missing his head, to grab a piece of fruit which had fallen to the ground. Instinctively, Egan retraced the bird's path to the rooftop, where it had been roosting. Later that day, he inspected the building where the bird had been roosting. Finding large vines covering the back, he easily scampered up to the roof. Peering carefully over the roofline, Egan was greeted with an open path to the produce stand.

The next day, just before sunrise, Egan crawled back onto the roof to avoid attracting attention. He was content to wait for hours, even days if necessary. The Defender wanted the perfect shot — no witnesses, either from the populace or the Tarylan escorts.

Egan had picked the perfect spot — the sun was rising behind him, a well-lit view stretched out before him. If anyone happened to glance in his direction, they only would see a shadowy figure against the bright sun. The vendors arrived at daybreak. Kiosks were opened and cleaned. Wares were laid out in anticipation of the haggling customers.

It was a perfect early autumn morning, the sun quickly warmed the chilly air. Before some of the vendors were even ready, eager buyers started to swarm the marketplace. Egan settled back, content to watch the activity below. A half hour had barely passed when the merchant made his appearance on the far side of the market.

He slowly worked his way through the rows of vendors, haggling over prices until he got his way. On the rare occasion of being denied a bargain, the Sankari would protest loudly and gesture menacingly as he stomped away.

Egan followed the merchant's every move. Finally, his target turned down the row of produce stands near where the Defender lay in wait. When the old Sankari bellied up to the stand just below Egan, the Defender glanced up and down the row. As usual, the Tarylan escorts had grown bored. They lagged behind, more than content to flirt with the pretty young women milling about.

The merchant picked up a freshly picked red apple to examine it closely. Before he could start haggling, the fruit jumped from his hand, rolled slowly down the counter and landed on the ground with a soft thud. It was several moments before the vendor, who had been busy with another customer, noticed the Sankari slumped over the counter, an arrow jutting through his neck. The screaming and confusion that followed the bloody discovery gave Egan plenty of time to slip away unnoticed.

One person in the market looked with interest at the chaos that exploded after the merchant's death. Some of the people ran screaming from the area, getting in the way of Tarylan guards who rushed in looking frantically for the killer. Vendors quickly closed their kiosks and hid inside. With a sly smile and low chuckle, the old man slowly made his way out of the frantic crowd.

Cara's thoughts raced as she hurried toward the emergency meeting of the High Council of Seers. She had never seen her fellow Seers in such a state of confusion and worry. The deaths of two Sankari had rattled the women who had seen themselves as protectors of Verdan society. Even during the war twenty harvests ago, when the Sankari clashed with the Defenders in an attempt to force the stubborn Nuvens into submitting to their beliefs, there had been a plan. The Seers were in control.

The latest killings of the two Sankari unnerved the Seers even more. What frightened them so was this enemy was proving to go undetected among their people. They did not know how many Defenders were hunting Sankari. Most guessed there could be no more than two of those Nuven warriors left, perhaps even one very crafty killer.

Only one other time had the Seers experienced such a phenomenon — with Circle Sankarikiller. Until two harvests ago, the Seers thought the Battle of Temple Darya had eliminated that problem. In previous generations, the women had protected Verde from Tanlian attacks with their special sight. The Seers had successfully thwarted and confused those outworld raiders. However, in doing so, they had exposed the Nuvens to the very same danger from which they had shielded the Verdans.

A realization made Cara stop with a shudder. They were now as helpless against this enemy as the Nuvens had been with the Tanlians. What really worried the Seers was the secret they all protected — their connection to the Sankari. If the truth was ever revealed, would the Defenders turn their vengeance to them?

Cara shook her head violently to rid her mind of that paranoid thought. She had been one of a handful of Seers who had objected to the training and eventually unleashing of the Sankari to attack and terrorize the Nuvens among them. She had been horrified and saddened by those tragic events of 20 harvests ago.

So many deaths, Verdan and Nuven, Cara thought grimly as she continued toward the meeting of the High Council. Before passing through the giant oak doors that opened into the council chambers, the Seer stopped to admire the door which had been ornately decorated. The other remained untouched.

Another Seer brushed near her and also stopped to look. "The craftsman, a Nuven, finished one, but then disappeared," the short, round woman said disapprovingly. "His family said he was called away to a job in another village. Imagine that, forgetting to fulfill his obligation to us. And I've been ordered to find the lout and make him finish the job." Turning with a swish of her robe, the older Seer continued on her way.

An unusual sight greeted Cara when she strolled into the council chambers. A man was sitting in the audience section. His back was toward her as she approached. Taking her place at the council table, Cara recognized Manor Stillinger. The normally abrasive Sankari leader looked pensive as he fidgeted uncomfortably in his seat.

A few moments later, after the last of the Seers had been seated, Tanella called Manor to the dais. Never before in Cara's memory had a man been called before the council. "General, I hope you appreciate the honor we bestow upon you today," Tanella said in her coldest, most formal tone. "Very few men have been invited to stand before us."

Manor offered a respectful bow. "Thank you, High Seer. The honor is mine to stand before this august body." Many Council members nodded, appreciating the compliment.

Tanella wasted no time. "General, it must be as clear to you as it is us. The Sankari are in grave danger from this Defender or Defenders who are killing your warriors without warning."

Manor nodded. "Yes, High Seer. Many of my men are, uh, concerned about the situation. The last two killings were tragic."

She grimaced. "Indeed General, that is why we called you here. You must get control of your men. We can't afford to have any more slain in drunken stupors or coming out of pleasure houses."

Manor looked down at the floor, his face reddened with embarrassment. The Sankari leader was not accustomed to being scolded in such a manner, but he dared not disrespect her.

"We have decided to take extraordinary measures," Tanella said, waving her arm around the table. Cara raised her eyebrows in surprise. She had not been a part of any Council decision.

The High Seer continued. "From now on, General, all your men will agree to be under constant surveillance by the Tarylan guards, no exceptions. Our guards will be posted in their homes. They will escort them wherever they go. We can't have our heroes slain by these murderers."

Before Manor could respond, a young woman hurried into the council chambers. A Seer at the end of the table took the messenger aside to hear the news. The Seer turned pale while she listened. Dismissing the young messenger, the older woman approached Tanella, whispering the news.

"We have lost another Sankari." The High Seer sat back, shaking her head in disbelief. "He was killed in the marketplace in daylight. An arrow through the neck. No one saw anything."

Looking up at Manor, Tanella slammed her hand on the table. "General, you have your orders! Let's see if we can get through the day without losing another Sankari."

After Manor had scurried away, the High Seer rose to address the Council. Her face glowed with anger. "I want Seers scattered everywhere the Sankari go. I want them in the marketplace, watching, talking to the vendors. Go into the taverns if you must. Visit the surrounding villages. Someone, somewhere has to know something about this murderer. In the name of Mother Verde there can't be more than two of those vermin left."

After dismissing the Council members with a broad sweeping motion, Tanella collapsed heavily in her chair. Rubbing her temples with her fingers, the High Seer almost fainted from the violent headache that now enveloped her.

9

When the alarm sounded, Gerro and his men bolted for the marketplace. They had trouble navigating through the crush of people frantically rushing away from the scene.

Gerro stood aside to let an elderly man pass. Something about the stranger seemed odd. The old man was peacefully taking his time while a mass of frightened people swarmed about him. "Be careful, uncle, or you could get trampled here," Gerro advised. "Do you need help?"

The elder started to wave off the captain but stopped with a surprised look. "Do I know you, Tarylan?" he asked.

Gerro shook his head. "No uncle, I don't recall meeting you. I was concerned for your safety among these frightened rabbits."

"Thank you for your concern, uh, Captain is it?" the old man asked, glancing at Gerro's insignias. "May I ask your name, sir?"

Bowing with respect, he responded. "Gerro, I am Captain of the Tarylan guards."

The elder's eyes lit up at the name. "You don't have to worry about me Captain. I have seen many people die. Too many I fear. One more doesn't frighten me."

Gerro nodded. "Yes, we've all seen our share of death."

The old man paused. "You remind me of a brave warrior I knew long ago. But he was a Defender. I mean no disrespect."

Gerro bowed. "I accept it as a compliment. The Defenders I have seen have been impressive warriors. I am curious. The Defenders seem to fight with so much fervor. Do you suppose there is any truth to their accusations against the Sankari?"

Witt looked away thoughtfully. He was surprised by this question from the renowned captain. It could be a trap, but Gerro seemed sincere. "Who is it to say it is not true? There was a terrible battle at Temple Darya. It seems something powerful is driving these Defenders."

Gerro nodded. There was something about this old man he admired. Perhaps he was an old warrior, a kindred spirit. "May I ask your name, uncle?"

Smiling, the elder returned the bow. "Witt Peyser. I'm just an old Nuven trying to enjoy my last few harvests."

He started to walk away but turned back to eye Gerro once more. "You're a credit to your blood, Captain, remember that. May the ancestors watch over you."

Gerro smiled as he watched the old man amble away. "And may you be at peace with Mother Verde, uncle." When Gerro reached the spot where the Sankari was killed, his Tarylan guards were scrambling over the area, frantically searching for the killer. The captain was certain their actions were futile. He was sure the Defender had quickly escaped. However, a cadre of Seers also swarmed the area, so his men went through the motions.

They rounded up every suspicious Nuven but all had solid alibis. Everyone provided multiple witnesses — Verdan and Nuven. Even the Seers could not find a viable suspect among them. All were surprised at the audacity of the killer, but some Nuvens refused to condemn who they thought to be another avenging Defender.

Gerro did not admonish these proud Nuvens. It was evident they believed their people had suffered a grievous wrong at the Battle of Temple Darya. The Tarylan Captain admired the Nuvens. For the most part, they were straightforward and honest. He would much rather deal with Nuven vendors. You could trust what they were selling to be what they claimed it was, unlike some of the Verdans who were experts at bait-and-switch tactics.

Gerro was curious how the Defender managed to kill the merchant without being seen. He patrolled the immediate area, examining corners, kiosks, anywhere that could harbor an unseen attacker. None of the places seemed likely. The captain walked over to the stall where the Sankari had been slain. He turned in a circle, studying all the vantage points.

A shadow temporarily passed overhead. Glancing up, Gerro watched a flock of birds swoop over the area, then land onto the roof directly overhead. They noisily squawked their displeasure at being chased from their daily meal of picking up scraps. Squinting into the sun, Gerro turned back to look at the kiosk. Twirling quickly back around, he shook his head, looking back at the birds. A few moments later, the captain stood on the roof, looking down at the scene. A few leaves from the vines were scattered around. He knew now where the Defender had hidden.

When he returned to the marketplace, an angry Seer awaited him. "The High Seer says the deaths of these last three Sankari are unacceptable captain," she snapped. "You must step up your efforts to kill this Defender."

Gerro shrugged. "Tell Tanella we are doing all we can. The only way to protect the Sankari is to keep them locked up, under guard. I'm sure they would not agree to that."

The Seer was not to be assuaged. "We want to talk to your guards who were with the Sankari when he was killed. Perhaps they could have prevented his death."

Gerro frowned and pointed to the roof. "The Defender hid up there and waited for a clear shot. There was nothing they could have done. It would have been difficult to see the bowman." The Seer shrugged, not bothering to look where Gerro pointed. She glowered at the merchant's two guards. Yanof Bosh and Milgar Paylon stood nervously nearby. Their guilt-ridden faces clearly showed how the two young men felt.

"Have those two report to Fortress Bryann immediately, Captain. We want to hear their version of the incident."

Gerro nodded. "We will be there shortly."

The Seer shook her head vigorously. "No, Captain, only those two. High Seer's orders." Before he could protest, the woman paced away. Gerro escorted Yanof and Milgar to the fortress. However, he was denied entrance to the hall where they were to be questioned. To his surprise, two Sankari manned the doors. The Captain loudly announced his intention to wait for his men and took a seat on a nearby bench. After more than an hour had passed, Gerro challenged the Sankari at the door but again they denied him access.

Growing angrier by the moment, the captain waited one more hour. Rising, he marched to the door, but the Sankari moved to intercept him. This time, Gerro was determined not to be denied. "Let me enter or there will be two less Sankari for the Defender to kill," he snarled, reaching for his knives.

At that moment, High Seer Tanella and General Manor Stillinger stepped out to face the angry captain. "I demand to see my men," Gerro said, not cowed by the presence of two of Verde's most respected figures.

Manor gestured dismissively. "Stand down, Captain, we have detained them. They are being held until we determine their punishment."

Gerro stepped forward, his hands on his weapons. "You are not my superior, Sankari. Stand aside." Manor took a step backward, surprised at Gerro's ferocity. The two other Sankari exchanged nervous glances. They all were familiar with the captain's fighting prowess. To date, he had been the only Verdan to survive a fight with a Defender, let alone kill two of them.

High Seer Tanella stepped between the two men. "Captain, we have determined your guards were negligent. You will be notified of our decision. Now, I order you to leave."

Gerro stared in disbelief at the woman. "I protest any action against my men." He then stomped away. At dawn the next day, Gerro appeared at the gate of Fortress Bryann again demanding to see Yanof and Milgar. He paced outside the gate for almost an hour before Manor appeared.

The Sankari flashed a grim smile. "Your wait is futile, Captain. Those two incompetent guards were executed at first sun. Perhaps now your men will take their responsibilities seriously." With a sneer, Manor wheeled around and strode away without another word. Gerro was stunned. His breath left him as if he had been punched in the stomach. Growing ill at the thought of the deaths of his two men, Gerro stumbled back to his lodging, his mind swirled in a dark fog.

10

A Seer slowly approached the two men who were enjoying second meal outside a small tavern not far from the marketplace. The men glanced up but continued eating. The short, rotund woman chuckled when she reached their table. "Ah, I found you Nuven. You thought you could get away from us."

Egan Pozos twitched slightly at the unwelcome intrusion. Instinctively, he slipped a hand to a knife inside his jacket. His eyes swept over the area looking for a company of Tarylan guards but saw nothing out of the ordinary. Incredulous at being discovered by a lone Seer, Egan's mind raced, plotting how he could quickly kill her without causing any commotion.

Witt Peyser rose and politely bowed to the Seer who was looking very pleased with herself. "May we be of assistance, Honorable One?"

She smiled, folding her arms over her chest, her gaze never leaving Egan. "Nuven, you were paid to finish your handiwork on the Council chamber doors at Fortress Bryann. I am here to hold you to your pledge. You are ordered to return with me to finish your work."

Egan relaxed his hand on the knife, returning her smile. He had forgotten about the carving job he had started at the fortress since he was awakened to his lost memories. "My apologies. I was called away on urgent family business Honorable One. I will return to the fortress as soon as I can."

The Seer smirked. "And slip away again? No Nuven, you will fetch your tools and accompany me to the fortress now."

She shook a plump finger in his face when he started to protest. "I'm sure some of the Tarylan guards will be happy to escort you to the fortress if you refuse to comply."

Witt broke the mood with a laugh. "Shame on you for forgetting to finish the job. You had the honor of working in the fortress of the honorable Seers. Many of our people would envy you this opportunity." Egan raised his eyebrows in a questioning look, not believing what he heard Witt say. "Go finish the work for the Seers," the older man said, pretending to admonish Egan. "Your other duties can wait. You cannot turn down an opportunity such as this."

The Seer clapped her hands. "At last I've found a Nuven with some common sense." For a moment, Egan thought about using his knife to dispatch this pest, but fought the urge. "I will return to the fortress with you after I finish my meal and fetch my tools," he said.

The Seer started to argue but was stopped by Witt. "While you wait, Honorable One, let me fetch you some fresh pastries drizzled with hot jam. The baker does a wonderful job here," he cooed.

Licking her lips, the Seer inhaled the aroma of fresh baked goods wafting from the nearby kitchen. "Agreed. It's been two hours since I've eaten." Witt took the woman gently by the arm and led her to a nearby table. Within moments of being seated, the Seer was greedily sampling all the specialties of the house: fruit-filled muffins, sugar-glazed pastries, several slices of pie and lightly toasted fresh bread.

"Ah, that should keep her occupied and in a good mood for at least an hour," Witt said returning to his seat.

Egan stole at glance at the Seer who was indulging herself loudly. The woman obviously would be in no hurry to leave her feast. "The fortress? Why should I return there to work for those women?" he whispered.

Witt sat back, taking a sip of freshly brewed tea. "I understand many of the Sankari are holed up at the fortress. We always suspected there was a connection between the Seers and

Sankari, what better place for a curious Nuven to keep his ears open? Some interesting opportunities might present themselves."

Egan kept eating but smiled at the plan.

Three hours later, Egan and the Seer were walking through the gates of Fortress Bryann. At Witt's suggestion, Egan dressed the part of an artisan. He wore a bright red tunic with long billowing sleeves. A stylish feathered beret was cocked to one side of his head. While walking through the fortress with an overly emphasized saunter, no one suspected he was carefully noting how many guards were posted at various positions.

The guards mostly were Tarylans, but occasionally he caught a glimpse of a middle-aged man traipsing past, wearing the tell-tale red scarf that identified him as a Sankari. When spotting one of his enemy, Egan struggled to quell the instinctive urge to strike out.

A Tarylan stopped them to do a routine search at the entrance to a stairway that led inside. The guard raised his eyebrows in surprise when he discovered Egan's carving knives and woodworking tools — small hammers, scrapers, brushes and other strangely pointed tools.

"Let us through," the Seer ordered grumpily, holding her aching sides. Nodding her head at Egan, "This one's here to finish work on the Council chamber doors. Just look at him, he's no threat."

Egan removed his hat and bowed with great flair to the guard. "At your service, kind sir. I am just a craftsman here to ply my trade." Straightening back up, he gave the Tarylan a wink and slightly pursed his lips. The guard rolled his eyes and stepped aside to let them pass. After climbing six flights of stairs, the Seer guided him to the empty council chambers. All she could manage to do was point at the unfinished door. The poor woman was huffing and puffing from the exertion of the stairs after gorging herself at the bakery.

"There, Nuven, finish what you started," she gasped, collapsing on the nearest bench. With a great groan, she rose to leave. "You will be quartered here until your work is done. You will be fed and allowed any supplies you wish. We will check your progress from time to time."

Egan plunked down his large tool bag. Frowning, he examined his earlier work on the first door. He now understood why it had bothered him to etch out the figures in the massive oak door. The Seers had commissioned him to carve a scene depicting the Sankari victory at the Battle of Temple Darya. They had rejected almost a dozen prospective sketches before approving the scene of victorious warriors chasing the barbarous Defenders from the temple. On the second door the Seers wanted a scene of Verdans going about daily life — the marketplace, children at play, people at work.

A young woman appeared and shyly introduced herself — Dira Lineu. She was to be his assistant. "Very good," Egan said as he rolled up his sleeves. "This is a messy business, bring some old blankets to spread out. It will make clean up go much easier." Dira started to leave but stopped to watch as he unpacked his tools. Her eyes grew big when she saw his collection of knives. Egan smiled. "Ah, I see you like my tools. You may be surprised at how some of these can be used."

11

The woman almost dropped the roasted lamb she was removing from the oven. "You insulted a Seer? How could you do such a thing?" Stazia looked incredulously at her grimacing mate.

Aron shrugged. "Never met one before. I thought she was just a nosey old hag."

Amaura giggled. "No father, just a nosey old Seer, that's much worse." Aron glared at his oldest daughter. She was not making it easier for him.

Lyllen, the youngest daughter, looked more concerned. "What are you going to do, Father? Did you apologize?"

Aron gazed out the window. He had feared his mate and daughters would react like this. He almost wished he was facing the Seers instead of his womenfolk. "I did apologize to the younger Seer," he said, pausing uncomfortably.

Stazia gazed at her mate, knowing he was holding something back. "So what did the younger Seer say?"

Aron cleared his throat knowing he would have to choose his words carefully to avoid causing them undue concern. "Actually, she seemed a bit amused. She said she looked forward to seeing me again in a lunar when I return to the Verde City marketplace."

Stazia shook her head in disbelief. "You're not going back, are you? The Seers are so unpredictable."

Amaura shook her head. "He has to go back Mother. The Seers know he is the honey fruit seller. It's better that he return when he said than having them come looking for him."

Lyllen agreed. "Yes, you need to go back father. But take Amaura and I with you. Perhaps we can help talk to the Seers."

Amaura raised her eyebrows at her sister's offer but quickly agreed to help. "Well, Father, you have said you needed help selling the honey fruits. Now you will finally have it." Aron and Stazia both started to protest but the determined looks on their almost-grown daughters' faces told them it would be useless.

Two weeks later, Aron and his daughters arrived in the marketplace at first sun to set up the kiosk. "That is strange, look at them," Amaura said, glancing at the other vendors who were not being shy about staring at Aron and his daughters as they went about their business.

Lyllen looked at her father. "Every vendor greeted you, Father. Is it always like this?"

Trying not to worry them, Aron forced a laugh. "Oh everyone knows the honey fruit man. I think the other vendors might be a little jealous. I almost always sell out in an hour. Mind you, it's a frantic hour."

Hands on her hips, Amaura glared back at the other vendors until they turned away, some looking embarrassed.

"Nuven, it's good to see you," the old vegetable vendor, who set up shop next door, greeted Aron. "You had been the talk of the marketplace until the killing. Most haven't said much about you, but I expect that will change."

Aron looked up with surprise, "Killing? Who died?"

The old vendor guffawed. "Nuven, you should leave your orchards more often. One of the Sankari was killed across the way. Arrow clean through his neck. Most suspect the Defender who killed the other two Sankari that one night," he said, taking time to spit into an old mug. "This has got many around here in an uproar. They don't know when the Defender will strike next."

Lyllen was wide-eyed at the news. "Is it always Sankari the Defender has killed?"

The old man smiled. "Don't worry young one, the Defenders only seem interested in the Sankari. Guess they're after revenge. Sure has got the other Sankari nervous. Most are being protected in the fortress. They don't come out too often."

Aron smiled. "I suppose not, especially if they are being hunted."

The old vendor spit again and nodded. "Good luck with sales today, Nuven. Try not to upset any more Seers."

As soon as Aron and his daughters had finished setting up, customers started inquiring as to what kind of produce they were selling. Smiling, Aron cut one of the honey fruits into four equal sections and handed them to children who were peering over the counter. It didn't take long for shouts of "honey fruit man" to ring throughout the marketplace.

Looking at his daughters, Aron pointed to a mid-sized basket in the corner filled with golden fruit, "That's not for sale — only if we get our special visitors. Brace yourselves, here comes the mob." As if on cue, a crowd quickly pressed around their kiosk with coins in their hands hoping to be one of the lucky ones to take home that delicious honey fruit.

Aron was proud of how quickly and efficiently Amaura and Lyllen worked. They laughed and joked with the customers while keeping sales moving briskly. He wished he had asked for their help earlier. Halfway through their sales, the crowd quieted to a hush. Aron was busy giving small slices of honey fruit to toddlers in the crowd, when Amaura called for him in a worried tone.

Looking up, Aron saw the reason for the interruption. The two Seers, whom he had spoken with the last time he sold fruit here, were standing at the counter. It wasn't the two women that drew his attention, however, but the six Tarylan guards standing behind them.

The younger Seer smiled. "It's good to see you again, merchant. I'm glad to see you are a man of your word." The older woman frowned. She held out her hand expectantly. Amaura and Lyllen glanced worriedly at their father.

"The Honored Seer wishes to examine our produce. Please give her one of the honey fruits," Aron said, bowing to the older woman. The hag snatched the fruit from Lyllen's hand. Taking a careful nibble from the golden fruit, her expression changed quickly to surprise.

"By Mother Verde, this is delicious," she chortled. "Nuven, you should have let me examine them last time. I would have taken the whole batch."

Aron bowed again. "My apologies for my behavior last time, Honorable One. However, this fruit is for sale. This is our livelihood. We cannot afford to give away a whole batch."

The old Seer snorted. "Such impudence. It is custom here to give us what we want." Aron was incredulous at the woman's apparent greed.

Seeing his expression, the younger Seer interceded. "Fear not, merchant, we never take everything from a merchant, just a sampling here and there, according to our needs. We understand perfectly selling this produce is your livelihood."

Aron sighed with relief and then was startled by a bump from behind. Amaura handed the basket of honey fruit to him and gestured toward the Seers. "Oh yes, as a token of my respect and to make up for my rudeness of the other day, I wish to give you a basket of our honey fruit," he said, carefully placing the basket on the counter in front of the two women.

This gesture drew impressed oohs and ahs from the crowd. No one among them had ever seen a whole basket of those sought-after treats. Even the old Seer was at a loss for words as she stared at the sweet-smelling basket. "You apparently have learned your lesson, Nuven, I accept your gift," she said. Then cracking a rare smile, she held up one of the fruits. "Don't worry merchant, I won't ask to examine your produce again as long as you save me a couple of these."

Aron smiled. "Agreed." Amaura and Lyllen relaxed a bit. Throughout the confrontation with the old woman, Aron hadn't noticed the younger Seer staring thoughtfully. To her companion's chagrin, she reached over and sampled one of the fruits. "It is delicious, beyond description," she cooed. "I have never tasted anything like this. What makes them so different?"

Amaura and Lyllen glanced nervously at their father, knowing he would refuse to tell the secret. Aron shrugged. "Ah, it is a difficult tree to grow and cultivate. It has taken my family many generations to grow them and even we are not always successful."

The younger Seer nodded thoughtfully. "It would please us greatly if you could show the gardeners at Fortress Bryann how to grow this delightful fruit."

Aron's mind raced at the ramifications of what the Seer asked of him. He knew the fruit would not grow and reach maturity if not planted in perfect conditions. Even if the young trees grew, there was so much more to producing the honey fruit, a secret his family had carefully guarded for generations.

"You have the first step in front of you," Aron said pointing to the basket of fruit, hoping he could stall for time. "Collect the seeds, dry them, plant them in your richest soil and hope for the best. It takes seven harvests for a young tree to fruit. Out of a hundred seeds, maybe a dozen saplings will grow to reach fruiting age with Mother Verde's help."

The young Seer raised her eyebrows in surprise when she heard Aron refer to the "Mother." Most Nuvens did not share the Verdan reverence for the planet but stubbornly clung to their strange ancestor worship. "You honor Mother Verde?" she asked.

Aron nodded. "I am bonded to a Verdan woman." Gesturing towards Lyllen and Amaura, he said, "My daughters and son were raised to praise the 'Mother' as well as their ancestors. We respect each other's beliefs."

The young Seer smiled. "As it should be — mutual respect. But back to the business at hand. I am positive our gardeners will want to hear the specifics of growing the honey fruit. When you are done here, you are invited to Fortress Bryann. You will be our guest, of course."

Aron knew this wasn't a good situation but could not think of a way out of it. The frightened looks on his daughters' faces didn't soothe his spirits. "I will be honored to speak with your gardeners, but I have told you all I am able to tell them. Let us finish up here and then I will go with you."

The young Seer nodded and looked behind her at the crowd still hoping to get a share of the fruit. "That is acceptable. Take your time, I will escort you to the fortress when you are ready."

One of the Tarylan guards stepped forward. "I will take charge of the Nuven," he offered.

Aron glowered at the Tarylan. "I gave you my word. I will not need to be put in their charge."

The Seer dismissed the guard. "I require no help. I am sure the merchant will come voluntarily." Looking at the older woman she said, "Help the Honored One back to the fortress. She will require assistance with the basket. I am sure the other Seers will be anxious to try this delectable fruit." The older woman started to protest but thought better of it. She had hoped to hoard the fruit for herself but now there were too many witnesses to get away with it.

The Seers and Tarylans stepped away to allow Aron and his daughters to finish their sales. Fearing for their father, Lyllen and Amaura wiped away tears while they waited on the last few customers.

One of the last buyers in line was an old man. He had been passing by when the commotion at the kiosk caught his attention. The elder smiled as he gestured for Aron's attention. "Don't worry about those women," he said, pointing to the Seers. "They always want more than they can have. I have a friend working at the fortress, a Nuven. Tell him hello for me if you see him."

Aron looked puzzled. The elder looked familiar, like a faded memory just out of reach. But he had no time to ponder now, there were more pressing things on his mind than placating this old man. The customer leaned over the counter. "My friend is Egan Pozos, the craftsman. Tell him Witt Peyser sends you with a greeting."

"Yes, yes, if I see him," Aron nodded absent-mindedly.

12

The gasps of delight flattered Egan Pozos. He had been carving away at the second door to the Seer Council chamber for less than a week, but the characters were starting to take shape nicely. Glancing over his shoulder, he winked at the small group of young women who were watching his every move very closely. They giggled at his attention.

Even though he had taken this job as a front to find out more about the Seer connection to the Sankari, Egan found himself getting lost in his work. He could spend hours detailing a child's face. The Nuven did notice something interesting. The longer he worked on the project, the more relaxed the Seers and Sankari became around him. They no longer hushed their conversations when walking past. Egan practically had become part of the furnishings.

He continued to wear flamboyant clothing and delighted in annoying the Tarylan guards with his pretended flirtations. Egan became known as the harmless craftsman. One of the young women stepped forward to offer Egan a drink. He had stopped to examine his workmanship. His sweat-soaked tunic clung to his body.

Frowning, Dira Lineu stepped in to intercede, but a glare from the other woman stopped her. Egan's assistant did not appreciate the attention some of the Seers were paying to him. She had only begun her Seer training, and the other woman outranked her. The Seer brushed very closely to Egan while handing him a mug of cool water. She smiled coyly when he touched her hands to accept the mug. He noted the woman's interest. The signs were obvious: slightly dilated pupils, the flicking tongue that unconsciously wetted her lips, the flaring nostrils.

Nuvens knew very little about the Seers. Stories abounded around these mysterious women. Bawdy tavern talk depicted the women as sexual beasts who would take any man they desire and bed him until he passed out from exhaustion. In the villages, old Nuven women insisted the Seers forced men to breed with them against their will just to procreate.

"Is it true what they say about you Nuven?" the Seer teased in a low whisper. "Some say you are immune to the charms of a woman, preferring other, ah, interests."

Egan shrugged, acting aloof. "It would be depend on the woman and what temptation she offered." Smiling with self-assuredness, the Seer turned to admire his work but made sure her breasts grazed his arm. He stepped into her slightly, making sure there was more contact than she had intended.

Egan gazed at the door as if in deep contemplation. "I am having trouble outlining one of the characters, a woman at the marketplace. I lack inspiration. I need her to be a beautiful example of Verdan womanhood."

A sly smile crept across the Seer's face. "Perhaps your inspiration will come to you in the night," she said, her pupils dilating even more.

"I would welcome such inspiration," he said, casting her a quick glance. The nights here have been lonely." Their eyes locked in an unspoken understanding. She took her leave and went on her way with the other women but not without casting a sly look back.

By the third hour after last meal, Egan's eyes were starting to get heavy. He had busied himself with bathing, cleaning up the two meager rooms he had been assigned and sketching the next day's carving work. Egan jolted awake when his head bobbed down suddenly, pressing his chin against his chest. Disappointed he apparently would receive no visitor this night, Egan shuffled around his quarters extinguishing the candles.

Just as the last flame died from a blast of his breath, an odd sound caught his attention — scratching. It took a moment for Egan to realize the sound was coming from the door. The darkened hallway made it difficult to see when he quietly opened the door. Egan could barely make out the silhouette of the veiled woman who glided into his almost pitch-black chambers.

Egan started to light one of the candles but was stopped. In a whisper, she told him she preferred the mystery of the darkness. "How can I carve your likeness if I can't see your beauty?" he asked. Without speaking, she took his hands in hers, running them up and down her face and body. Their kisses started out soft and tender but quickly gave way to passionate, hungry exploration. Both fumbled with each other's clothing in the darkness, but this only fueled their anticipation. Egan led her by the hand to his small bed, where they fell into a lusty full-bodied embrace. Their delirious lovemaking lasted several hours.

Much to Egan's delight, the Seer more than lived up to the tavern stories. And he did not disappoint her, proving to have the great stamina the Nuven men were rumored to possess. Just before Egan fell into a deep, fully satiated sleep, the woman rose, kissed him on the forehead and slipped out the door.

About two hours before sunrise, a soft but insistent rapping on his door woke him from a deep slumber. Naked and groggy, he stumbled across the room and peered out the peep hole.

Egan was startled to see the Seer who had flirted with him the day before. Her face was plainly visible, she wore no veil this time. Curious, Egan let the Seer in. As she glided into the room, her hands brushed against his chest. Sighing with delight, the woman rubbed her hands all over his body, reveling in the sensation.

Despite his exhaustion from the earlier lovemaking, Egan found himself excited at her advances. Reaching out, he pulled her close for a kiss. His hands eagerly explored her body.

Something was different. This woman kissed less passionately than before. She smelled different, even tasted different. Her body didn't feel the same to his touch — she was much more voluptuous. The Seer's breasts were larger and her bottom was much rounder.

Giggling, she half pushed him away. "There will be time for that later, Nuven. Don't you want to see what will inspire your carving?" Curious, but saying nothing, Egan lit the candles in his room and picked up his etching pad. The Seer slowly unfastened her cloak, letting it fall to the floor.

His artist hands had not betrayed him. Prancing before him in the nude, her body was nothing like he had envisioned it earlier in the night. The woman he had bedded was thin and petite. Her small round breasts easily fit into his hands and her hips were delightfully narrow. However, there was no denying the beauty of the Seer proudly displaying herself for him to admire and sketch which he did with great relish. After his fourth page of illustrating her in all positions, close up and at a distance, Egan declared himself inspired.

Laughing, the Seer pulled him from the chair and led him to the bed. Pushing him down, she slowly explored his body with her hands, lips and tongue. Barely letting him move, so unlike the almost violent throes of passion from earlier in the night, the Seer took her time. She gasped and savored the slow-building sensations. After both had been fully satisfied, the Seer quickly rose from the bed.

How odd, it was like being with two women, Egan thought as he sleepily watched the Seer get dressed. "I'm glad you waited for me," she said looking at him with a sly smile. "I was delayed last night due to an unexpected Council meeting." Delayed? Now Egan was more puzzled than ever. If she had not visited him earlier, then who had?

"I enjoyed being with you much more than the Nuven we questioned in the chambers earlier tonight," she said. Seeing his surprised reaction, the Seer explained. "A vendor from the marketplace was brought to the fortress. He is the famous honey fruit grower. Very strange though. He refused to tell our gardeners how to grow the fruit."

The Seer laughed at what occurred earlier. She looked at Egan, shaking her head. "You Nuvens are quite stubborn, aren't you. The other Seers, especially Tanella, grew quite frustrated with his refusal to cooperate. He kept claiming it was a family secret."

Egan raised himself up on his elbow. His face rested on a fist. This Nuven intrigued him. Not many would refuse a request from the Seers. "What happened to this vendor?" he asked then yawned trying to mask his interest.

The Seer shrugged as she turned for the door. "Nothing has been decided. But he has been, let's say, 'invited' to stay in the fortress until he decides to cooperate. Tanella does not like being told no."

Egan forced himself to chuckle. "You are detaining a vendor because he is refusing to tell you his secret to growing fruit? That seems like a severe punishment for such a harmless offense."

The Seer momentarily stared into space, "Yes, that is so, but there are other oddities about the man. With this mad Defender killing the Sankari, the Council is taking no chances with Nuvens who behave strangely."

Egan stretched lazily, but now his mind was racing. He had to find out more about this Nuven. "Perhaps I could talk some sense into the fellow," he volunteered. "This Nuven may not appreciate what an honor it is to cooperate with the Seers."

The Seer smiled. "An excellent idea. I will convey it to the Council. Now, you should get some rest, you look exhausted. I will be interested to see your inspired carving."

Egan rose to fetch himself some water. He was dehydrated from all the attention he had received. Out of the corner of his eye, he noticed the Seer admiring him. "By any chance, do you know the Nuven's name?" he asked. Perhaps he might be an acquaintance or I might be familiar with the family."

To his puzzlement, the Seer found his request to be amusing. "Familiar with the family," she laughed. "Aren't all you Nuvens of the same blood?" Egan fought to control a flash of anger at the old Verdan insult. He forced himself to shrug and smile at her cleverness. Still pleased with herself, the Seer stopped to think. "Oh, yes, I remember. His name is Aron Nels, if that's any help."

Glancing out his window at the rising sun, she bid him farewell. After carefully checking to make sure no witnesses were in the hallway, the Seer let herself out. Egan trembled with excitement at hearing the name — Aron Nels. His exhaustion had been replaced with rejuvenation. He paced back and forth, thinking of the opportunity this presented. Imagine what two Defenders could do when loosed on the Sankari.

But first he had to help awaken Aron's Defender memories. Somehow, he had to get his remaining circle brother to Witt Peyser. The old steward could help awaken this Defender as he had done with him. The problem was how could this be done?

13

Aron Nels had never felt more dejected than at this moment. The meeting with the Seers had been a catastrophe. After shutting up his kiosk in the marketplace and bidding his tearful daughters farewell, Aron voluntarily went along with the young Seer to Fortress Bryann. The Seers and their gardeners supposedly wanted to know more about the honey fruits.

Aron was not sure what awaited him. He assumed he would be questioned by three or four gardeners as to how to grow and cultivate the fruit that up until now only his family had provided. He was prepared to give general answers about planting conditions, water needs, fertilizing tips, pest control — such specifics only gardeners and orchardists cared about.

He was stunned to be led into a room of more than 30 Seers. About a dozen of them sat around a half-moon table. High Seer Tanella had wasted no time. She admonished him for insulting the old Seer at their first meeting. The gift of the basket of honey fruit was a nice start to repay his debt, she said, but then ordered him to cooperate fully with their gardeners to produce the hard-to-grow tree.

Remembering that moment, Aron put his head in his hands and rocked back and forth moaning softly. He wished he hadn't lost his temper, but it had happened. When the High Seer had issued her ultimatum, he had just stood there, refusing to move or say anything. He would not allow these strange women to steal his family's livelihood.

Aron had promised his father on his deathbed to keep the secret his family had guarded for so many generations. He tried to divert attention toward the skills of the Seer gardeners, who most assuredly could produce the fruit from seed. Much to his dismay a tall, older woman stood up to testify the Seer gardeners, indeed, had tried to grow the honey fruit from seeds, but had no luck. The saplings grew well enough for two or three years but eventually all withered away. The Seer gardeners wanted to see where the honey fruit was grown and study how his family was able to nurture it to a fruit-bearing tree.

During the questioning, Aron had the uneasy feeling he was being carefully scrutinized. Many of the Seers in the room stared at him with strange, blank expressions. Something about the stares made him uneasy. The hair on the back of his neck rose stiffly much the same as it would on a hunt when he sensed a nearby predator.

Then the questioning had taken an unforeseen turn. The High Seer demanded to know if he had known any Defenders. Deciding it would be difficult to lie to these strange women, Aron had answered honestly. Yes, he remembered meeting several of the Nuven warriors when he was an archer during the Battle of Temple Darya. Med-aides told him a Defender had dragged his wounded body to safety after the temple was overrun by the Sankari.

Aron finished his story, saying he did not see the Defender who saved him or any of the others after the Sankari victory. After he finished, an odd quiet fell across the room. All the Seers sat like statues, staring at him.

A friendly looking woman broke the silence. "I sense no coercion in this man," she declared to her fellow Seers. She looked at Aron sympathetically and implored him to cooperate with them. Aron shook his head and tried to explain his predicament one more time but was cut off by a visibly angry Tanella.

"We do not have to beg Nuvens or anyone else for that matter for anything. You will be our 'guest' until you decide to cooperate," she had shouted. Before Aron could respond, four Tarylan guards surrounded him and led him to the one-room cell where he now forlornly sat.

Egan Pozos started work on the giant door much later than normal. He yawned and sleepily greeted Dira Lineu. "It looks like you had a restless night, Egan," his assistant said smiling.

He nodded. "It was an interesting night. I've never had one quite like that." Staring at his uncompleted work on the door, Egan felt how insignificant this task was compared with his almost maddening urge to reach Aron. He picked up one of his fine carving tools and halfheartedly started working.

Seeing him working lethargically, Dira stepped close offering her assistance. Egan started to shoo her away, when a familiar seductive scent made him stop. He knew that scent. He had breathed it in deeply and savored the scent last night with the first passionate woman. Her hair and body exuded that lovely aroma. The memory of the scent was burned into his brain during their lovemaking.

Putting his tool down slowly, Egan turned and saw Dira smiling slyly. "Last night, it was . . . " but Dira put her finger on his lips, stopping him. She said nothing, but her smile answered his question. A rush of mixed feelings swarmed through Egan. She was so young, barely in her 20s, but what an incredible lover.

"Egan, if you are so sluggish after such a fitful night's sleep, perhaps the interruptions will have to be monitored carefully," Dira teased.

He looked at her much differently now. "I will welcome such an interruption any night," he smiled. Now filled with a refreshed vigor, Egan turned back to work on the door in earnest. He would just have to bide his time for the right opportunity to visit Aron.

The next day, Egan was returning to the fortress after shopping for supplies early that morning when he passed three women begging the guard to let them inside. The older woman was plainly Verdan, but the two young women exhibited Nuven features. Curious, he politely asked who they wished to see. The older woman clutched his hands when she heard his Nuven accent.

"I am Stazia. My husband is being held prisoner, he has done nothing to them," she told him. Her eyes crinkled with worry. "He is Aron Nels, the fruit vendor. Can you help him?"

Egan's eyes grew wide when he heard these women were Aron's mate and daughters. A closer look at the young women was obvious. He could see his old friend in their faces. "I have requested an audience with him. Possibly I can help convince him to cooperate with the Seers." He had to be cautious, not knowing who might be listening or watching.

Stazia shook her head with worry and confusion. "It is over those fruit trees. Why are the Seers so interested in them? Surely they will not harm him over that."

Egan tried to comfort her. "I suspect the Seers may be trying to set an example with your husband. They are not accustomed to being told 'no'. Also, this business with the Defender has upset them greatly. I am confident once they determine your husband has nothing to do with the Defender, they will let him go."

The women seemed heartened after hearing he was working to meet with Aron. Egan finally convinced them to leave after promising to do his best for Aron. This was an easy pledge to make because he already was determined to reach his old circle comrade somehow. Returning to the Council chamber door, Egan attacked his work with a frustrated energy. He dared not draw attention to his strong desire to see Aron. One Nuven insisting to see another of his people would fuel the Seers' suspicions even more.

Dira tried to get his attention, but Egan kept furiously scraping away at the door until an authoritative voice interrupted his labors. "My, my. Do you always put so much gusto into your work, Egan Pozos?"

Panting from his exertion, Egan turned around to see High Seer Tanella and Seer Cara curiously watching him. He bowed.

"No High Seer, I must have been caught up in the moment. My apologies for not noticing you earlier."

Tanella and Cara carefully examined the scene that was slowly coming to life out of wood. "Your work is coming along well, Egan," Cara said admiringly. Egan had always liked this Seer. She always made time to offer encouragement, even shared a joke or two. Cara was the opposite of the strict High Seer, whom he had never seen smile.

"Yes, it seems quite acceptable," Tanella said. Egan thanked her, knowing that was as close to a compliment she was ever going to give. The High Seer wasted no further time. "I am told you have requested to talk with the uncooperative Nuven Aron Nels."

Egan nodded. Trying to mask his excitement, he bent over and started to nonchalantly sharpen one of his knives. "Yes, High Seer. I think this Nuven is being very foolish. He probably grew up in one of the uncivilized outer valleys. I'm afraid those people are not taught the proper respect."

Egan was shocked to see Tanella looking amused. "Let me try to convince him to cooperate," Egan said, sensing he was winning Tanella's confidence. "He may be thoroughly intimidated by you and the other Seers. Nuvens naturally withdraw and are distrustful when they fear something. He may find it comforting to talk to me."

The High Seer gazed at the first door then at the second door that was being transformed into a masterpiece.

"Yes, you have our permission to talk with this Nuven. Perhaps during first meal tomorrow. Let him think about his situation for another night." Pausing for a moment, her mood turned serious again. "I will double your commission if you can get him to reveal any knowledge about this latest Defender."

Egan tried to contain his amusement. "Defender? Why would this fruit vendor know anything about him?" he asked.

Tanella and Cara exchanged nervous glances. "We find this Nuven to be a bit odd," the High Seer said. "We've only encountered a few like him before. Report to me after you've spoken with him."

Egan bowed again and turned to watch the two women walk away. His heart was beating so fast, he feared the Seers could hear it — all his prayers had just been answered. In his euphoria, he did not notice Dira staring curiously at him.

14

Dira could hardly catch her breath. Her whole body, which glowed with perspiration, ached from the frenetic lovemaking with Egan. He was lying on his side snoring heavily. In the candlelight, she could see the beads of sweat dripping slowly down his back.

This night had been wonderful but very different from their first encounter. The mystery was gone this time. Egan had picked her up as soon as she entered the room and carried her to his bed. He burned with exuberance and passion as if he were trying to quench a massive thirst. She had been caught up in the swell of emotion and spasms of ecstasy that swelled through her body.

Something very surprising had happened that night. During their lovemaking, Dira suddenly saw herself through Egan's eyes, his mind had opened up to her. It was her first Seer experience. This puzzled her. Up to now, none of the Seers had been able to see through him. This troubled them at first, but Egan had quickly gained their confidence through his craftsmanship and flirtatious antics. The Seers finally accepted the fact that he must be one of those strange Nuvens they could not reach.

With a snort, Egan rolled over, opened his eyes and sleepily smiled at her. Reaching up, he gently stroked her hair, then gave her a long, tender kiss. The emotion swelling in her heart almost took her breath away. The two embraced and fell into that deep, satisfied slumber only lovers share. Egan rose well before sunrise to bathe and prepare for what could be an eventful day. Dira playfully tried to lure him into more lovemaking but to her surprise he gently turned her down, claiming he was exhausted from the past night.

However, she could tell by his actions he was filled with an intense energy. This was the morning he was going to talk with the Nuven fruit grower who was being held captive in the fortress. "You seem preoccupied, Egan."

He solemnly studied her face, knowing he had to carefully choose his words. Even though Egan also had felt a strong passion for Dira, he was well aware she was training to be a Seer. Dira's loyalties most likely lie with those strange women. He knew he had to be careful around her. "I just want to make sure I win his trust. If the Nuven suspects I am there for any reason other than to help him, he will trust me no more than the Seers."

Much to her surprise, she watched him don traditional drab-colored Nuven garb, not the flamboyant colors he had favored up until now in the fortress. Dira sensed there was much more than he was telling her. She detected a new guardedness about him. "I hope it goes well. Just be yourself Egan, you have the gift of putting people at ease and gaining their trust," she said hoping to reassure him.

Egan smiled at her remark. He was not worried about gaining Aron's trust, but was concerned how to awaken the sleeping Defender in him. An even bigger challenge would be how to get him out of the fortress undetected. "I'm sure the meeting will go well. Yes, I can be very convincing," Egan said kissing her on the top of her head.

———

Aron was staring out the small window in the cell when the door swung open. Not looking up, he assumed it was the guard bringing him first meal — he could smell the food. Even though he was famished, he did not want to give the server the satisfaction of showing any appreciation.

"Put it on the table and leave me in peace," he snarled, not budging from his position. Hearing nothing, no tray being placed on the table or movement by the visitor, Aron whirled around to repeat his order but stopped short. Standing before him bearing a tray filled to the brim with pastries, meats and fruit was a smiling man who appeared to be a Nuven. Aron cocked his head, raising his eyebrows questioningly.

"Greetings, brother, I invite you to dine with me," the other man said in the Nuven dialect. Aron nodded and sat down, staring at his visitor. The aroma of the food was too tempting. He hungrily snatched a piece of meat and a pastry and began eating. The visitor joined him in the meal. In hunter tradition, they said nothing while they ate. After he had eaten his share, Aron looked up. "Thank you, brother."

The other man flashed a wide, easy grin. "It was my honor. I am Egan Pozos, a craftsman working in the fortress." That name sounded familiar. Where had he heard it? Aron cocked his head to one side trying to remember. So much had happened to him in the past several days that he had almost forgotten the encounter with the old man in the marketplace.

"Egan Pozos, I know that name. An elder sends you a greeting. What was his name? Ah, yes, Witt Peyser. That's who he said he was."

Egan laughed, shaking his head. "So you met Witt? Yes, he and I are close. You do not know him?"

Aron shook his head and leaned back in his chair. "I appreciate the meal Egan but why are you here? Why have the Seers let you see me?" Egan was disappointed. So far Aron showed no indication of recognizing him. Even Witt's name did not seem to stir anything in his circle brother. Why was he not showing signs of awakening to his past memories?

Egan decided to go slowly. It was important the awakening be done correctly or they both could be discovered and killed before accomplishing their duty. "I have gained some trust with the Seers," he whispered. He gave a shrug and glanced toward the door to alert Aron that someone might be listening.

"They think I can persuade you to tell them the secret of your fruit," Egan said. "Also, they are worried you might know something about the Defender who is terrorizing the Sankari."

Aron crossed his arms. "I will not betray my family. The secret of the fruit has been handed down by the ancestors. I have pledged never to reveal it. As for the Defender, I told them I do not know who it is."

Egan frowned. "I do not care about the fruit. I understand your pledge to your family, but we must get you out of here."

Aron scowled. "Why is it so important to you that I leave? I don't even know you," he said, wondering if this was another Seer trick to make him talk.

Sensing Aron's wariness, Egan looked him in the eye and detailed his meeting with Aron's wife and two daughters at the fortress gate that morning. He had met with them after hearing they visited the fortress every day since Aron's incarceration.

Egan described the women perfectly to prove he was telling the truth. "They are very worried about you. Is that not enough? Cannot this issue with the fruit be resolved? As for me, I can't explain how important it is. You will understand much more later. It is much greater than guarding the secret to the fruit. I swear it by my ancestors."

Aron solemnly regarded Egan. He sensed the other's sincerity. "I'm sorry, brother, but too much is at stake for my family. I don't understand what could be more important than that. Stazia is a strong woman with many family members to support her, and my children are grown."

Egan knew it was useless to argue. Rising to leave, he leaned over the table, "Trust me, brother, I will get you out of here somehow. If not by your cooperation with the Seers then perhaps there may be another way. Until we meet again."

The disappointment almost was more than Egan could bear. Aron had shown no sign of recognizing him. The Defender in Aron remained dormant. Egan was frustrated and felt a growing desperation. Aron should have recognized his name. Why hadn't he awakened? Assuming he was being watched, Egan knew he had to report to High Seer Tanella. Any deviation would be treated with great suspicion. He was in no mood to talk with that sullen woman but perhaps he could use his emotion to good use.

Not surprisingly, Egan was granted an immediate audience with the High Seer. "I have never met such a stubborn man," he told her, not masking his anger. "He refused to let me help him."

Tanella studied him for a moment and sighed. "Did you sense anything else about the Nuven? Did you ask him about the Defender?"

Egan shrugged with an exaggerated flair. "I truly believe he knows nothing about the Defender. It appears his only worry is about his *precious* fruit trees."

Tanella frowned. "Those fruit trees are enough to keep him here until he or other members of his family decide to cooperate. I will not be denied my request for that information. It will set a bad precedent if he does not cooperate with us."

Egan forced an agreeable smile. "Yes, Honorable One. With your permission, I will keep trying to persuade him. We had an amiable conversation until the fruit trees were discussed."

Sighing with frustration, Tanella nodded. "Agreed. I appreciate your help with your fellow Nuven. I'm sure you are anxious to return to your work."

Egan bowed and departed, relieved to be out of her presence. He sullenly went back to the door. Not even Dira's attempts to cheer him up were successful. Never had the wood chips flown so far from his furious carving knives. Egan worked on the door well into the night. He could meditate on his problems while he let his knives almost guide themselves through the wood. The intense woodcarver barely noticed when an exhausted Dira finally bade him good night.

15

At sunrise, Egan Pozos slipped out of the fortress. No one challenged his comings and goings since he now had the full blessings of the Seers. He made his way to the tavern to meet Witt Peyser for first meal. The old man gazed into space as Egan Pozos retold his meeting with Aron Nels. He did not seem surprised at their fellow Nuven's failure to awaken to his Defender memories.

Sighing, Witt shook his head as he remembered his last encounter with Aron, all those years ago after the battle of Temple Darya. "I feared this might happen with him. It took many hours to put Aron into the waking sleep. Much more so than you and the others."

Egan bowed his head, remembering the events of that sad day. "The memory of Tevan is the reason Aron has not awakened, isn't it?" Egan asked sadly.

Witt's eyes watered. "I may be the only one to help him awaken. It took a long time to put his mind at rest so I could place him in the sleep." Egan groaned at the predicament. Getting Aron out of the fortress might prove more difficult if he would not cooperate with an escape.

The steward spoke after a long, thoughtful pause. "The death of another Sankari would take the Seers' minds off Aron. Perhaps this would convince those women he has no connection to the Defender who is on the loose."

Egan stared thoughtfully into the distance. "Perhaps, but the Sankari are being kept under much better guard. Many have taken refuge in the fortress."

Witt smiled mischievously. "But not all of them. A few are still trying to go about their daily lives."

Egan's eyes lit up. "You have been studying a few I take it?"

Witt rose from the table, gesturing for Egan to follow. "You will be pleasantly surprised how easy it will be to reach some of them. I have even met and done business with a few of these fellows."

Egan's mood had improved greatly. At last, there was something he could do to help loosen Aron from the grip of the Seers. He also relished the thought of hunting Sankari again.

––––––––––

Zaim Hesson and the other men crowded around the bar, laughing uproariously at the joke one of their party just told. He shook his head with amusement and went to work serving the customers who filled his tavern. Much to the delight of his regulars, the large, bald Sankari had refused to hide in the fortress or, as he described it, "Run like frightened children to hide under the Seers' skirts."

After the Battle of Temple Darya, Zaim returned to work in the tavern his family had operated for generations. After his father's death a few harvests later, he had become the sole proprietor of the popular eating and drinking establishment. Zaim had become a local legend for refusing to change his routine after the Defenders starting attacking and killing his fellow Sankari. He delighted his customers by declaring, "If those Defender vermin want me, they can find me right here. I'm no coward."

Zaim was no fool, however. After the attacks on the Sankari had started, he hired two bodyguards to be nearby whenever he left his home. He felt even more invincible now that the Tarylans had posted four additional men to be with him.

"I would like to see one of those Defenders fight his way past these lads," Zaim bragged to two new visitors who seemed concerned about his safety. "I'll pay 200 golden to anyone who kills a Defender trying to reach me. Then I'll dry his carcass and hang it from the rafters. It'll be a fine addition to my prizes up there," he said, pointing up to where 10 pairs of dried ears hung from a low-hanging rafter.

The two customers laughed, raised a toast in his honor and excused themselves to find a table where they could talk in private. "I said you could get close enough to touch him," Witt said, as he and Egan found a secluded spot in the corner. He studied the surroundings and noted where the guards were posted. The tavern only had one door, which was guarded. Every spot in the tavern could be seen by the guards.

"This will be a difficult kill, although an enjoyable one," Egan said shooting a glance at Zaim who already was in the middle of one of his long-winded stories with another customer. That was one of the many bloody memories he wished would have stayed forgotten. Filled with bloodlust after their victory at Temple Darya, some of the Sankari cut the ears off dead Defenders for trophies. This was only one of the many insults perpetrated on the slain warriors and the temple.

"What does this Sankari value most?" Egan asked thoughtfully.

Witt swept his arm in a wide circle. "This place. The tavern has been in his family for generations. This is where he holds court."

Egan looked around with a different eye, taking stock of all the wood which was everywhere — the chairs, tables, bar, large support beams, rafters and, of course, the roof. He smiled as a plan formulated in his mind.

The Tarylans who were guarding Zaim in his home rushed to the door to see who was pounding on it in the middle of the night. A breathless, wide-eyed man stammered something about a fire at the tavern. Upon hearing this Zaim, under a full escort, rushed to the scene to the find the whole building engulfed in a giant ball of fire.

Flames shot high in the air, illuminating the night sky for hundred of meters. A giant explosion caused the roof to cave in. Hundreds of onlookers milled around in shock. Many tried to console the stricken owner. Zaim grew more and more frantic with anger and sorrow as he watched the destruction of the building his family had owned for countless harvests. He stomped back and forth shouting curses and wailing.

Gerro, captain of the Tarylan guards, had been notified when the fire alarm was first sounded. He ordered an extra squad of his men to patrol the area in an effort to protect the distraught Sankari. However, no one could calm Zaim down or reason with him. He stormed through the crowd shaking his fists and screaming in anguish. In a fit of rage, Zaim broke free from those trying to hold him back and ran to within a few meters of the flames. He stood there, a silhouette against the flames with his arms raised futilely to the sky.

No one heard a soft thud over the roar of the fire. A woman screamed when Zaim swayed back and forth, an arrow through his neck. The tavern owner finally collapsed when three more arrows struck his back in rapid succession. Seeing Zaim fall, Gerro twirled around to notice a lone figure run across a neighboring rooftop before disappearing over the opposite edge. With no time to call for reinforcements, the captain set out in a full sprint to chase the escaping killer.

Running through the alley between buildings, Gerro heard someone land on the ground. The archer had jumped to the street and started running. The captain was famous for being one of the fastest men in Verde, but even he could not gain on the stranger who darted among buildings and scrambled over fences.

Gerro turned a corner running at full speed when a deadly hiss made him jump instinctively to the side. An arrow sliced across his shoulder, causing a deep gash. Still on the chase, the captain ripped a piece of cloth from his sleeve and wrapped it around his throbbing shoulder. Gerro could tell he was bleeding profusely.

Stumbling a bit, he stopped to cautiously peek around another corner. But this time he was greeted by the sound of a horse galloping away. With a groan of pain and frustration, Gerro slumped against a building.

16

The first rays of morning were just beginning to lighten the sky when Egan stumbled to Fortress Bryann's gates. He banged on the large wooden doors with his fist and loudly demanded to be let in. One of the guards looked through a long narrow slit and grunted an acknowledgement. The door swung to admit Egan.

"Whew, you've had quite a night, Nuven. You smell like you fell into a barrel of ale," the guard said with a knowing smile. Egan proudly brandished a jug of ale. "Quite a night down there," Egan slurred as he shuffled unevenly past the guard. "Big fire destroyed a tavern. Another Sankari was killed; what a commotion." Squinting, Egan held up the jug. "Want a drink? I've had, urp, I've had enough I think."

The guard laughed. "No thanks, Nuven, better get yourself cleaned up and to bed. It won't be long before first meal." Egan lowered the jug, gave the guard a halfhearted wave and swayed into the fortress. He slowly made his way to his room making sure every guard within hearing distance saw him weave from side to side, bumping occasionally into walls.

When he reached his room, an upset Dira Lineu was waiting for him. She started to question why he spent the night outside the fortress but stopped when she smelled the ale on his breath and clothes. "Another Sankari was killed last night Egan. I was worried about you, but I see you've been drinking all night," Dira said, throwing her hands up in disgust.

Egan smiled sheepishly. He clumsily attempted to give her a hug, but she pushed him away. "Oh, don't be angry little one," he chuckled. "I went to visit a friend. We started telling stories and the ale kept coming. Then people in the street were shouting about a fire so we went to see what was going on."

Dira's eyes grew wide. "You were at the fire? Did you see the Sankari get killed?"

Egan took a deep breath and slumped against his door. "Saw huge flames coming out of the tavern," he mumbled. "Saw the Sankari yelling and carrying on. Then he fell like a tree that's been cut down. Dropped dead with an arrow in his neck and more in his back. Most suspect the Defender." Egan shrugged and started to fumble with his key, trying unsuccessfully to get it in the lock. With an exasperated sigh, Dira snatched it from his hand and helped him into his room.

"Get some sleep and wash yourself. You are disgusting," she snorted. "Well at least we know two Nuvens who couldn't have killed the Sankari — you and the fruit vendor."

Egan held up his jug in a toast. "Ah, here's to Aron Nels. I bet he would share a sip with me," Egan said, rising shakily looking at the door.

"Oh no you don't," Dira said forcefully and pushed him back to the bed. She grabbed the jug from him, stripped off his ale-soaked clothes, led him to the sink and washed him. Afterwards, she guided him to his bed. As he curled up, Egan sleepily held up his hand in an invitation to join him.

Dira laughed. "Maybe another time." She left when she was finally satisfied he would sleep away his drunken stupor. Egan waited a few moments to make sure Dira was not coming back, then sprang from the bed to quietly lock the door. *That was close*, he thought, letting out a huge exhale. Egan had almost gotten caught twice tonight — by the Tarylan who had chased him after he killed the fat Sankari and then by Dira, whom he had not expected to be waiting for him after he returned to the fortress.

Egan stared out the window. The night's adventure had been a success but now security around the Sankari would be even tighter. Killing more of them would prove to be an even greater challenge.

17

Nuvens throughout Verde Grande were struck with horror at the proclamation from the High Seer. Tarylan guards traversed the countryside, visiting every known village to deliver the ultimatum to the Defender who had been relentlessly killing the Sankari. High Seer Tanella gave the Defender one week to surrender to the Tarylan guards or the fruit vendor known as Aron Nels would be publicly executed.

Tanella had refused all entreaties on Aron's behalf from his family, Nuven elders and even Verdan officials. Hundreds of vendors in the marketplace petitioned for his release, but the High Seer refused to be swayed. Even a large contingent of Seers, led by Cara, implored the High Seer not to have Aron killed, but she angrily ordered them away.

Convinced by Manor Stillinger, Tanella decided the only way to capture the Defender was to start killing Nuvens. Aron would be the first example to show their resolve. After the proclamation, all contact to Aron was cut off. He was not told why. Egan Pozos became physically ill when he heard the news. The man who he had been trying to free was given a death sentence if Egan didn't give himself up.

The craftsman refused to come out of his room for an entire day. He ignored entreaties from Dira Lineu and even orders from other Seers to return to his work on the door. When he finally emerged, Egan spoke to no one. He took his meals by himself and returned to work in silence. The craftsmanship on the door took on a sad drudgery. He carelessly chipped away at the figures he had so lovingly created. Egan became more desperate as he worked. Normally, working on the door cleared his thoughts, but the dark storm in his mind grew in intensity.

Dira was worried about her sullen lover. She knew he was worried about Aron, but nothing she could say or do could placate him. He refused to let her visit at night. Even Cara, the Seer who liked to joke with Egan, tried unsuccessfully to break his mood. Egan only acknowledged her presence with a curt bow and a frown. Worried, she pulled Dira aside.

"Something has changed in him. His eyes are different," Cara said watching Egan methodically work on the door. "He was so full of humor before and now I feel a coldness."

Dira nodded. She tried to look away as tears filled her eyes, but Cara noticed. "Oh, my dear, I did not know you had such feelings about him," Cara said, taking the young woman's hands in sympathy. Dira started to mumble an apology, but Cara stopped her with a gentle smile. She looked sadly at the older Seer. "He has not been the same since the proclamation. Somehow, I think he feels responsible for the other Nuven."

Cara sighed. "I tried to talk Tanella out of taking such drastic measures, but I'm afraid Manor Stillinger has her ear. It was his idea." The Sankari leader was furious after hearing about the death of another of his men. He was determined to capture the Defender and did not care how many Nuvens had to die to accomplish this deadly goal.

"I'm afraid we do not understand the bond the Nuvens seem to have with each other. They had such a difficult existence for generations before they finally found their way to our valley," Cara sighed.

She was one of the few Seers who had grown up ashamed at what her predecessors had done to the Nuvens. The Seers had protected the Verdans with their gift of the sight, skillfully deflecting the Tanlians, those terrible space raiders, toward the Nuvens. To the Seers' amazement, the "lost ones" evolved with extraordinary survival skills. They managed to skillfully fight off most of the Tanlian attacks and even thrived. Cara admired the Nuvens. She agreed with the majority of the Verdan population who welcomed them as lost kinsmen. •

"Keep an eye on Egan," Cara said, patting Dira on the cheek. "He is a good man, but he may take it very hard if Aron Nels is executed. If that happens I fear we may lose our craftsman and our friend."

After Cara had departed, Egan slowly turned around to stare at Dira. She did not say anything but returned the stare with a loving look. "No, you Verdans will never understand the bond we Nuvens have for each other," he said somberly.

Dira gasped, "You could hear our conversation? But we were half a room away!"

Still expressionless, he cocked his head slightly.

"Oh no, did you hear everything?" she blushed with embarrassment.

Egan slowly approached her. Reaching out, he pulled her close, kissed her on the forehead and held her tightly. Finally pulling away, he gazed at Dira sadly. "If this gets me killed, so be it. I cannot allow Aron Nels to be executed. I have taken an oath to protect him."

Dira took his face in her hands. "I will not betray you, I swear. But what can you do to help him?"

Picking up his carving tools, Egan walked back to the door shaking his head in frustration, "I don't know. The whole situation seems impossible." That night Egan and Dira lay quietly together, savoring each other's presence.

The next day, Egan reluctantly returned to his labors on the door. The work went slowly. There was no inspiration or satisfaction in it now. He was at a loss as to how to help Aron. Escape seemed impossible. Guards were posted everywhere throughout the fortress, including one at Aron's door at all times. Dira stopped trying to cheer him up. She knew her lover was deeply depressed about Aron's apparent impending execution. No words were exchanged between the two while he worked.

Egan grew more frustrated with each stroke of his carving tools. Desperation slowly filled him. It was only two days now before the date of Aron's execution, and he was no closer to a solution. The consequences weighed heavily on him. Even if he gave himself up, Egan doubted the Seers would free Aron. Tanella would not forgive the fruit vendor for refusing to cooperate with her. Every instinct in his body fought against surrender. The surviving Sankari would be ecstatic and vengeful.

He did not doubt they would resort to torture. This would be partially done out of revenge but also it would be an attempt to extract any information about the Defenders, especially the surviving one, whom they desperately sought. Egan knew his Defender resolve was strong, but no one was immune to the effects of torture. Things could be done to the human body that would break anyone.

He worked throughout the day with his mind in a dark fog. Egan only stopped to eat a few bites of the food Dira brought. His stomach was so full of knots, he had no appetite. He kept methodically working, not even noticing it was now early evening.

From a distance he heard two men walking down the hallway, laughing and talking loudly. "Look what we have here!" exclaimed the taller of the pair. "A Nuven working on a tribute to us." Egan took no notice while he slowly etched out the characters in the second door.

"You keep working at that pace Nuven, and you will be an old man before you're through," sneered the shorter man. Again, Egan refused to acknowledge the visitors.

The tall one stepped over to the first door, smiling as he examined it. "Ah, it is good to see an accurate portrayal of our glorious victory over those heathen Defenders," he said admiringly. "Did you do this work? My compliments."

Stopping for a moment, Egan frowned slightly as he regarded the stranger. He nodded slightly then returned to work, his carving knife digging a little deeper and faster.

"Nuven, you were just paid a compliment. Answer my friend," the second man barked.

Dira stepped between Egan and the shorter man. "Please forgive him, his mind is elsewhere when he is working on his art."

The second man shoved Dira roughly aside. "I'm not interested in what your whore has to say Nuven. I am speaking to you. Do you know who we are? Show some respect." The taller man said nothing but looked amused at his friend's antics.

Egan slowly turned around. His eyes gleamed with hate. "I will answer you after you apologize to my assistant," he said quietly as he tried to control an instinct to strike out at the man.

The short Sankari snorted in disgust and slowly approached Egan. "Me? Apologize to the likes of her. Your assistant, eh? How does she assist you? To bed I imagine. Eh, lass?" The taller Sankari guffawed at his friend's cleverness.

Egan folded his arms. "You will get no respect here today, Sankari, be gone," he said in a warning tone. The antagonistic Sankari regarded Egan with a snarl, then took a swing at his head. Egan easily blocked the clumsy blow and instinctively jabbed his carving knife into the man's chest. The stunned Sankari fell in a heap to the floor.

The dead man's tall friend let out a yell and charged. Egan feinted to one side then deftly changed directions, tripping the attacker. The Sankari tumbled to the floor. As he clumsily tried to stand, Egan whirled, landing a skillful kick to the man's neck. The tall man grabbed his throat, stumbled backwards a few steps, then slumped over dead.

Dira held her hands over her face. She was too stunned to say anything. The whole attack had lasted less than a minute. Egan took a deep breath while he studied the bodies with a strange detachment. His sullen expression had vanished, replaced by a fierce look of purpose and determination.

"Now you know who I am," he said matter of factly. "I will not stop you if you alert the others, but I know now I have to free Aron or die trying."

A trembling Dira looked at Egan and then at the bodies of the Sankari. Taking a deep breath, she pointed toward the council chambers. "We can wrap them in the cleaning blankets and drag them in there," she said in a surprisingly steady voice. "No one will discover them for a while."

Saying nothing more, Egan and Dira quickly covered the bodies with the blankets they had spread to protect the floor and dragged the bodies into the darkened room. Only a small patch of blood from the first Sankari had oozed through the blanket. Dira fetched some nearby soap and water. While she was scrubbing the floor, Egan grabbed a hammer and large wood chisel and started to work furiously on the first door that depicted the Sankari victory at Temple Darya. Finally satisfied no trace of blood was left, Dira glanced up to see what Egan had been working on.

In huge Verdan script letters that covered the entire width of the door, he had chiseled out the word "MURDERDERS" over the scene where the victorious Sankari were marching away from the temple ruins. Egan bent over his tool box and grabbed a large assortment of knives. He stuck them in his craftsman's belt and pulled on one of his brightly colored shirts.

"It is time to free him," he said looking at her solemnly. Without another word, they headed for Aron's cell, extinguishing the lights in the hallway as they went.

18

Aron sat forlornly in his cell. It had been three days since anyone had spoken to him. No visitors had been allowed to see him, not even Egan Pozos. Worse, ever since that curious Nuven craftsman had spoken with him, Aron had been haunted with troubling nightmares.

He dreamed of fierce fighting, of being swarmed upon and dragged away by vaguely familiar young men. One of the captors in his dream looked like a young Egan. These visions caused him to jolt awake in the middle of the night, drenched in sweat. But the memories fled as soon as he opened his eyes.

The isolation had not troubled him that greatly. The guards saw to it he had enough food and water, but they no longer spoke to him. In fact, most refused to make eye contact. Aron was troubled when he thought of his family. He knew Stazia, his mate, and daughters would be sick with worry. However, there was no way for him to get word to them that he was well.

The guard's gruff voice outside his door startled Aron. Curious, he rose to look out the narrow eye slits in the door. He barely made out a young woman carrying like a food basket. Her companion was just out of his visual field, but now and then he caught a glimpse of a bright red shirt.

"This is highly irregular," the guard growled. "I was not told he would be allowed extra food. He was given third meal two hours ago."

A familiar voice chastised the guard. Aron smiled as he recognized it.

"We have permission of High Seer Tanella herself," a disgusted-sounding Egan snorted. "I will be happy to wait with you while my lovely companion fetches her. Although she may be a bit upset at being interrupted at this hour."

No one spoke for a moment, until the woman sighed and put down the basket. "I will go find the High Seer. I'm sure she will send word with another Tarylan guard. May I have your name? I'm sure Tanella will be very interested in who will not carry out her wishes."

The guard stood silent but shifted nervously on his feet. Dira turned and started to walk away. She had not taken more than three steps when the guard called her back. "I will allow it," he said resignedly. "No need to bother the High Seer. However, I will check that basket. Those orders are not subject to interpretation."

"Of course," Egan said cheerily, but Aron detected an edge in his voice. "Dira, kindly allow the guard to examine the basket. Now try not to handle all the pastries. They are quite fragile you know."

The guard mumbled his displeasure when Dira placed the basket at his feet. As he bent over to take a look, Aron saw a flash of red, then the guard's back filled his view, followed by a large crash against his door. Startled for a moment, Aron backed away, then he returned to the eye slit. Flashes of red and the Guard's drab green uniform spun in and out of view, followed by grunts of two men fighting.

The fracas did not last long. The guard stumbled to the door. His back filled the window, then it slid out of view. Egan's face now filled Aron's view. The craftsman had a nasty gash over his left eye, and his nose was bloodied. Stunned by what he had just seen, Aron stepped away from the door. He almost dared not to breathe. A key was inserted into the lock, and the door swung open. Egan and Dira quickly dragged the guard's body into the room, pulling it out of the way.

"What have you done?" Aron whispered in disbelief.

Egan flashed him a smile. Dira stepped back into the hallway to serve as a lookout. "I've come to free you, brother,"

Egan said. "We may not have much time to get you out of the fortress."

Aron stepped back, shaking his head vigorously. "The Seers will never allow me to leave now," he groaned, looking at the dead guard.

Egan put his hand on Aron's shoulder, looking him squarely in the eyes. "Brother, the Seers were going to have you executed if the Defender did not give himself up. You have become the bait. I swear it on my ancestors."

Aron shook his head in disbelief. "Kill me? What would that accomplish? Why would the Defender care about me?"

Egan nodded as he rummaged through the basket. "Oh, believe me, I care greatly," he said handing Aron a wad of brightly colored clothes topped off with a large plumed hat.

Aron stared at Egan. "You? You are the Defender? But you have been in the fortress working for the Seers."

Egan grinned. "What better way to hide than right under their noses? I would not have been able to rescue you if I had not been here."

Aron held up the clothes he had just been handed. "What are these for?"

Egan's expression and tone turned serious as he explained the situation. "Look at us. We are the same height, same build, even same hair color. The guards don't look twice at me as I come and go. You need to be me to get out of the fortress."

Aron tried to think of an alternative solution but could not. Everything had happened so quickly but for some reason he trusted Egan. As he stripped off his clothes and donned the brightly colored garb, Aron looked at Egan warily. "Why me? Why are you taking such a chance and putting yourself in even more danger?"

Egan sat down at the table, studying Aron with fondness. "You don't remember do you, Aron?" he asked sadly. "We are brothers of the same Defender circle. We were the only circle to survive the destruction of Temple Darya."

Now fully dressed, Aron stared in shock at Egan. "Defender, me? No! I was an archer, wounded at the temple. I am not a Defender. What you are saying is impossible. Do you have me confused with another?"

Egan shook his head. "No, you are a Defender, as I am. We were put into the waking sleep after the battle to protect us and to ensure we would come back to take revenge on the murderous Sankari."

Egan rose and called Dira into the room. "You and I are the last of the circle, Aron. Our other eight brothers and I have awakened and killed as many Sankari as we could. Now it is your turn." Egan turned and hugged Dira. "It is vital you escort him out of the fortress. He needs to find Witt Peyser. Only our steward can help him awaken to his Defender memories."

Egan looked at the dubious Aron. "I beg you to go with her, now! Do this for your family. Do this for Tevan who was killed during the battle."

Aron was stunned. How did Egan know about Tevan? He only had a cloudly memory of being wounded and finding his cousin's body among the dead.

Tears streamed down Dira's cheeks as she kissed Egan passionately, then held out her hand for Aron. She no longer questioned Egan's motives.

"If you are telling the truth brother, it seems I owe you my life," Aron said. "And you, what will happen . . .?"

Egan waved off the question. "Go. You have unfinished business with the Sankari." Aron nodded solemnly then embraced the man who freed him. The two regarded each other for a moment and exchanged a smile. Reaching for Dira's hand, the pair cautiously walked out the door.

Dira and Aron walked briskly down the hall until they came to one of the fortress' winding staircases. Before starting down, she studied her companion. Reaching up, she pulled the hat down so it partially covered Aron's face. "We can be in no hurry now, it will only draw attention to us," she said. "Try not to speak if possible."

Aron took a deep breath and offered his arm as if they were taking a lovely evening stroll. They sauntered down the stairs, came to another floor of the fortress and walked slowly past a guard who ignored them. Dira and Aron kept a steady pace down three more staircases.

During their heart-pounding journey, which seemed to be going at an agonizingly slow pace, several Seers greeted the pair with knowing smiles. Dira responded politely and Aron gave friendly waves. At last, they came to the front gate, which was still open but manned by a small troop of Tarylan guards. Slowing their pace, Dira and Aron headed for the opening.

Seeing the pair approach, one of the Tarylan guards called out. "Going to the city, Egan?" he asked good-naturedly. "I see you have a friend to help you back from the ale house this time." This drew laughter from the other guards.

Aron could feel Dira stiffen with fear. He patted her hand reassuringly. "Most assuredly my good man," he said softly then bowed.

Summoning up her faltering courage, Dira flashed the guards a smile and ran her fingers sensuously through her hair. Every guard admired the lovely young woman, ignoring Aron. "Don't worry, I will make sure this Nuven behaves himself," she said sweetly then winked. Aron gave them a friendly wave and continued walking. The guards roared with laughter and wished them a good time.

19

Egan waited nervously in one of the fortress's parapets. He had grabbed his bow and quiver and scrambled quickly to the highest point possible so he could watch when Aron and Dira had safely escaped. *Where were Aron and Dira? Certainly they had time plenty of time to reach the gates by now,* he thought.

Egan exhaled with relief when he saw two familiar figures walk out of the gates. Aron was easily distinguishable in his brightly colored shirt and large hat. Dira walked alongside, clutching his arm. Egan felt a pang of sadness as he watched the two fade into the darkness. This isn't the way he would have planned it, but he was not one to dwell on the unfairness of life.

With Dira and Aron now safely out of range of the Tarylan guards' bows, it was time to create a diversion to allow them to make it to safety. Egan stood up and nocked an arrow. Taking a step out of the small balcony, he fired at the guard in the nearest watchtower. The surprised man spun around after being struck and slumped over.

Shaking his head in disbelief that the man didn't call out or plummet to the ground, Egan crept out on the narrow ledge and made his way along the wall to the next balcony. He eased over the small rail to position himself for another shot. The guard in the opposite tower stood with his back toward Egan. The Tarylan was much farther away, presenting a more difficult target. If he only managed to wound the guard, the man could point Egan out, trapping him before he could escape to create more mayhem.

He would have to try for a kill shot. Egan's arrow struck the guard in the lower back. The Tarylan stumbled slightly then let out a piercing scream of pain before toppling out of his tower and hitting the ground with a sickening splat. As soon as he heard the guard cry out, Egan raced down the steps. The Defender could hear the alarm bells ringing throughout the fortress as he ran for his next attack point.

Gerro had been almost out of the fortress when he stopped to talk with his men at the front gate. The Tarylan captain had finished inspecting his men's barracks when he saw that strange Nuven craftsman and a young woman about thirty paces ahead of him. Something didn't seem right about the couple, which piqued Gerro's curiosity. He planned to keep his distance and follow them into the city. The guards at the gate were more than happy to retell the amusing confrontation they had had with the Nuven and the woman.

"You're sure it was Egan Pozos?" Gerro asked while he watched the couple saunter away. The sergeant of the guard chuckled. "Can't miss that one with those bright . . ." A scream from above stopped them cold. They all looked up to see a body crash to the ground.

Gerro rushed over to the dead man. A quick examination revealed the arrow. "Lock up the fortress, sound the alarms, we have an intruder!" he yelled forgetting all about the couple who quickened their pace as soon as they heard the alarms. "Get archers on the catwalks. We can't have anyone picking us off at will," Gerro ordered. "I want the entire fortress in lockup. No one is to move from their quarters without a Tarylan escort."

Manor Stillinger had just left the room of a particularly voluptuous Seer when the alarms sounded. Startled, he headed toward his room which was up another floor. Just as he reached the staircase, he grabbed a young Tarylan who was rushing to his post. The guard was about to pull away when he recognized the Sankari leader. He stepped in front of Manor to answer his question, but a strange tearing sound stopped him.

"What is going on?" Manor demanded, still hanging onto the other man. "Why have the alarms sounded?" The young man never answered. He gagged slightly and collapsed in

Manor's arms, an arrow protruded from his back. The weight of the guard caused Manor to stumble backwards. As he backed up against the wall, something buzzed by his face. It hit the opposite wall with a resounding crack and exploded into splinters — an arrow lay in pieces on the floor.

The old war veteran knew he was under attack. Holding up the dead guard as a shield, Manor clumsily backed down the hall to get out of range. Two more arrows struck the Tarylan as Manor dragged the body with him around the corner. Finally out of the archer's field of vision, the Sankari flung the dead guard to the floor and raced for shelter.

Egan cursed at himself. Four shots and he still didn't hit that damn Sankari. It was time to move again. He sprinted down the hall and ducked behind a huge tapestry. He emerged on a small corner balcony that overlooked one of the fortress's interior courtyards. The Defender stole a quick glance at the scene below. People were hurrying in a great panic.

One old woman with unkempt white streaks in her hair stood in the middle berating everyone to slow down. "It's that vermin Defender!" she shouted. "He only wants the Sankari. Don't panic, don't give him the satisfaction."

Egan took another look at her. He realized it must be the old hag Aron had told him about, the one who had caused him so much trouble in the marketplace. It was the woman who brought all that needless attention to Aron. Pausing for a moment, he listened to the foul-mouthed elderly Seer. Egan stood up to get a better view, then in a loud voice called out. "Honey fruit here!"

"Where?" the hag yelled, looking up at Egan. She had no time to call out a warning before an arrow buried itself between her eyes.

A stunned guard spotted Egan disappear behind the tapestry. Alerting his cohorts, a troop of Tarylans rushed up the stairs in pursuit of the fleeing Defender. Egan raced down one hallway and the next running for his life. He now was the hunted. Charging around a corner, he recognized the hallway where he had spent most of his time at the fortress, where the Seer

Council chambers were located as well as the doors he had crafted.

Egan bolted into the room and swung the doors almost closed so only a crack showed, just enough to shoot an arrow through. The Tarylan troop came charging down the hallway but stopped in a panic as arrows rained out at them. Two of the men fell before the others could back away to safety.

The hallway became eerily quiet while the stalemate ensued. Less than a quarter hour had passed when a voice called out: "Defender, I am Gerro, captain of the Tarylan guards. I request a truce to offer terms."

Egan smiled at the man's daring. "How do you know I won't drop you where you stand Tarylan?"

Gerro yelled back. "I don't. But most Nuvens I have known have been true to their word. I understand the Defenders were protectors of the Nuven way."

Egan laughed. "That's true, Captain. But I have no such faith in the Tarylans or the Sankari for that matter." To his surprise, a Tarylan appeared in the hallway, holding his arms straight out from his sides to show he bore no weapons.

"Defender, I am no Sankari. I keep my word," Gerro said as he slowly walked forward.

The great doors creaked open as Egan slipped through. He pointed his bow at the floor, an arrow nocked. Egan stared as a familiar face approached. Gerro stopped ten paces in front of him. "Why have you attacked Tarylans? I thought Sankari were your targets."

Egan shrugged. "You protect the Sankari. The sheep refuse to come out to play."

Gerro shook his head. "Certainly you know you would be killed in an attack on the fortress. No Sankari have been killed this night."

Egan gestured behind him. "You will find two more in there. I am satisfied with that. I have fulfilled my objective."

Gerro shook his head. "I don't understand, Defender." Egan silently held his ground. This Tarylan's resemblance to a young

Aron was startling. The Defender tried to blink away the memories of the two of them growing up together.

"Many have died here tonight," Gerro said. "It is my duty to stop it. I challenge you to a death duel."

Egan shook his head. "And if I kill you, then how many more Tarylans will challenge me or ambush me?"

Gerro bowed. "None. My word, Defender."

Egan studied the young man. The Tarylan was intense but he detected no hatred. The way he cocked his head when he spoke was so familiar. "I believe you Tarylan, but I have no such confidence in the Sankari or the Seers," Egan said. "No matter. Your challenge, my choice of weapons."

Gerro nodded. "Agreed; choose."

Egan held up his bow. "Thirty paces, arrow in quiver, bow at side. The ancestors will greet the loser."

The Tarylan bowed again and in a surprising move turned his back on Egan, showing he trusted his foe. A few moments later, Gerro returned with a bow in hand and quiver over his shoulder. "My lieutenant will count, if that is satisfactory," he said.

Egan braced himself. "To four, on the count."

Gerro relayed the message. A deep voice rang out. "Warriors, on the count, one, two, three, four."

A blur of hands snatched arrows from their quivers, nocked them and let them fly. One twang rang out first, then a breath later, another twang sounded. Neither man moved for several seconds until Egan took two stumbling steps backwards and collapsed, an arrow protruding from his chest. He slumped against and slid down the doors he had toiled on for so many days.

Gerro let out a deep breath. Egan's arrow had just missed his neck by an inch. The Tarylan captain somberly regarded the slain Nuven. He was bothered by something he saw in a blink as both men released their arrows. The Defender appeared to have winked at him. *No, that cannot be true. It must have been a shadow across the Nuven's face.* Gerro frowned at such a foolish thought.

Gerro called out the all-clear as he knelt near the dead Defender. He looked at the Nuven craftsman, then up at the door where he had carved out the word "MURDERERS." Victorious shouts from his men rang through the hallway.

Something Egan said puzzled him. The Defender said he had achieved his objective. What objective? The lieutenant who called out the count walked over to study the body. "With this one dead, do you suppose the Seers will execute the other Nuven?"

Gerro looked up. "Other Nuven? Oh, yes, the fruit vendor. Better go check on him. Who knows what the Seers will do."

20

Stazia and Aron's two daughters, Amaura and Lyllen, were sick with worry after they heard about his escape. Not long afterwards, the family was shocked to learn the mysterious Defender had apparently sacrificed himself to help free Aron. Barely an hour later, the Nels women were frightened by a loud clamor of voices outside their home. Peeking out one of the windows, Amaura gasped to see several hundred troops surrounding them.

"Mother Verde, they've come for us," Stazia moaned, hugging her daughters. A knock on the door startled them, but it was a soft, polite rap, not a demanding thump. Taking a deep breath, Stazia looked out the round window in the door then gasped with surprise. She quickly unbolted the locks and opened the door. An important-looking man adorned in a black uniform with gold trim stepped inside and bowed graciously.

"Forgive the intrusion. I am Rissom, steward of Clan Nels. I have been told my kinsman escaped the fortress. With your permission, we need to escort you to a safe place to protect you from any repercussions from the Tarylans."

Stazia grasped Rissom's hands in thanks. "Have you heard anything of Aron? We are so worried."

Rissom shook his head. "I'm sorry, I have no more information other than he is free and that the Seers are furious. Bowing again, the steward stepped outside and gestured toward his men. "We should leave quickly. You and your daughters need to make haste and come with us. My troops will stay here and guard your property. You need not fear the Tarylans. I have informed them all the Nuven clans will take it as an act of war if they attack this home or harm your family. However, that may not stop them if they are out for revenge."

The three women were whisked away to a secluded, well-guarded small fortress in the foothills of Mt. Barrasca. Along the way, more and more able-bodied Nuven men and women joined them to ensure their safety. All the Nuvens introduced themselves to Aron's family, then bowed with a closed fist over their hearts — a reverent gesture that pledged their lives.

One young woman, about Amaura's age, lingered for a moment near the Nels women. Her blue-green eyes filled with tears when she greeted them. "Thank you for your pledge my dear, but I sense you grieve for someone," Stazia said as she reached out and grasped the young woman's hands.

"I am Egatha Pozos, the oldest child of Egan Pozos. I, I . . ." Before she could finish, she broke into sobs. "My family did not know father was a Defender. He regained his memories so quickly he barely had time to say goodbye." The three Nels women surrounded Egatha in a warm embrace.

No one said a word after Gerro finished his report to the High Council. The Seers sat in stony silence, stunned by the events that had unfolded over the past few days. The color had melted from Tanella's face, turning a deathly pale. Her eyes gazed out at nothing. One of her hands trembled slightly.

Cara broke the silence as she read quietly from the report: "Nuven craftsman Egan Pozos revealed himself to be a Defender after killing numerous guards, Seer Fionula and two Sankari. The Defender was killed by Captain Gerro in a duel. Upon further investigation, it was discovered Nuven vendor Aron Nels had been freed by the Defender. The Tarylan guarding the Nuven's door had been killed and dragged into the cell."

She took a trembling breath. "The Nuven Aron Nels walked out of the fortress apparently with the help of Seer trainee Dira Lineu. Both remain at large."

Gerro listened with his arms folded. "That is correct, Seer Cara. Our efforts to find Aron Nels and Dira Lineu have been unsuccessful. The Nuven population, for the most part, has refused to cooperate with us. Unfortunately, many of the Verdans in the city also seem to be sympathetic toward the Nuvens."

Manor Stillinger had been staring out one of the giant windows in the council chamber. The Sankari general exploded in anger after hearing the report. "We had the Defender within our midst for weeks and no one suspected him. The other Nuven, whom we had under arrest, may be another Defender and now is missing, and with one of your Seers."

Cara frowned at Manor's outburst. "If I recall General, you interrogated Aron Nels and spoke with Egan Pozos," she said tersely. "Apparently both men slipped by your expert attention as well. In point of fact, Dira Lineu was a trainee, not a confirmed Seer." Flushed with anger, Manor looked at Tanella for help, but the High Seer sat with her head in her hands. He strode over to confront Cara for her insubordination but was blocked by an intense-looking Gerro.

"Stand down General," Gerro growled. "The Seer has spoken nothing but the truth. We all can take a share in the blame."

Manor was not to be placated. "I want all the guards who let that Nuven and the woman out of the fortress brought here at once," he demanded. "Order the Tarylan guards to kick down doors, burn Nuven homes if they have to. We must find them!"

Manor started to approach the High Council table when Gerro reached out, grabbed his collar and spun the Sankari leader around to face him. "You have no authority over the Tarylan guards. There will be no more interrogations or executions for failing to do their duty," Gerro snarled. "We will not destroy property or harm the population to do your bidding. You are a guest in the fortress, nothing else. Be careful that my Tarylans don't escort you and the other Sankari back to your homes where the Defender, if indeed one remains, will find you."

Manor started to protest but was stopped by an angry Cara. "This is a matter between the Sankari and the Defenders. You have brought much grief to our fortress. The High Council suggests you settle this vendetta as warriors if you are confronted by another Defender. You and the other Sankari may stay in the fortress as our guests. But mind you, our patience is wearing thin."

Gerro pointed to the chamber's new doors. "You may leave now, General." Speechless, Manor tried to regain what little dignity he could muster, turned and strode out. The huge oak doors, upon which Egan had labored for so long then vandalized, had been removed immediately at Tanella's orders. She wanted nothing to remind her of the tragic events that had taken place in the fortress.

Being attacked from within was a new experience for the Seers. For centuries they had used their gift of the "sight" to thwart aerial assaults by the Tanlians, those persistent space raiders. But now they had been infiltrated. No one had suspected. When the time was right, he attacked at will, leaving a blood trail throughout the fortress.

A Defender, the Nuven warrior they all sought, had lived and worked among them. Many Seers, including Tanella and Cara, had spoken to and eaten with Egan. Dozens of Tarylan guards enjoyed joking with him. One Seer, seated at the far right edge of the Council table, was bent over as if she had been hit in the stomach. Her hands covered her face in shame for making love to their enemy. She had been closer to him than almost anyone else, yet had not detected him as the Defender. Especially unnerving to the Seers was the killing of Fionula, one of their elders. No Seer had ever been killed by an enemy. The women's sense of invulnerability had been shattered.

Gerro sensed the Seers' unrest. He had never seen fear in their eyes before. They now looked like anyone else — Verdan or Nuven. "High Seer, do you want me to double the guards throughout the fortress?" he asked softly.

Tanella looked confused for a moment, then slowly nodded. "That would be most welcome, Captain," the exhausted-looking woman said in a hoarse whisper. "We are most unnerved by these recent events. The presence of your guards will be reassuring until the other Defender shows himself."

Gerro bowed. "We do not know if there is another Defender."

Rising with great effort, Tanella started to leave the room but stopped, looking back at Gerro. "Egan Pozos was willing to die to free the other Nuven. Do you think he would have made such a supreme sacrifice if Aron Nels wasn't a Defender? Something must be special about him, and we had him in our custody."

Tanella held up a hand as a thought occurred to her. "His family! His mate and two daughters were at our gates for days. Seize them and bring them here!"   •

The Tarylan captain held up his hands. "They have all disappeared, High Seer. We cannot find anyone who knew or was associated with Aron Nels or Egan Pozos."

The High Seer turned and stomped out of the room repeatedly mumbling, "How could we not see it? How could we not see it?"

21

Aron Nels stared warily at Witt Peyser. The old man seemed vaguely familiar, but he did not recall from where. The events of the past few days overwhelmed him.

After their escape from the fortress, Dira led Aron through a maze of streets and alleys in Verde City. She followed a map Egan had drawn for her. It seemed like the two of them had run for hours when she finally stopped at an old inn. One lone candle burned in the second-story window. On the first floor, three candles were placed in the left window and five candles lit up the right window.

After carefully studying the map and the inn, she cautiously approached the door. Dira knocked once, paused, knocked three more times, paused, then knocked five times. She had barely put her hand down, when the door swung open revealing an old man who welcomed them and quickly ushered them inside. Introducing himself as Witt Peyser, he let the exhausted escapees catch their breath and fetched them food and drink.

When they finished, he asked them no questions, demanded nothing of them. He led them to two comfortable rooms where they could rest for the remainder of the night. Aron had a fitful sleep. Disturbing dreams kept waking him. Visions of people he didn't remember and battles unknown to him kept flooding his thoughts. Dira hadn't fared much better. She cried herself to sleep, haunted by the sacrifice Egan had made on their behalf.

When the two finally settled down they slept well into mid-morning. The smell of fresh pastries and cooking porridge finally roused them from their heavy slumber. Witt greeted them and led them to a table filled with food. Again he said nothing, allowing them to eat in peace. The inn's doors were locked. No one else had been allowed to enter. Aron noticed the old man looked sad, as if he had lost someone close. His mind swirling with questions, Aron finally broke the silence. "You are a friend of Egan Pozos, the Defender?"

Witt smiled. "Yes, more than a friend. I've known him and his circle brothers all their lives."

Aron studied his plate, not knowing how to ask the next question. He was frightened of the answer. "The Defender made some outlandish claims," Aron said slowly. "He said I was a Defender, one of his circle brothers, but I have no memory of that."

Witt looked at him patiently. "Are you having strange dreams of fighting next to people you don't know, of being in places you don't remember?" he asked softly. Aron said nothing, but the troubled look on his face told Witt what he wanted to know. The old man measured his next words carefully.

"Egan was telling the truth. You and your circle brothers were put into a 'waking sleep' after the destruction of Temple Darya. Your circle was all that was left of the Defenders. We had to save you and the others. We put you in the 'waking sleep' so you could live undetected in Verdan society. Twenty harvests later, you were all to have awakened to take your revenge on the Sankari. We wanted the Sankari to have become fat and complacent, which they have."

Aron sat shaking his head in disbelief. "I, I don't remember any of that. I remember being wounded at Temple Darya. I was an archer."

Witt smiled. "Ah, you were much more than that. You and your brothers were the finest Defenders to be bred specifically for your mission. Your minds were impenetrable to the Seers. That is what frightened them so."

Aron sat in silence, scowling. "Egan said the same thing. He risked his life for me. He, too, believed I was a Defender."

Dira could not hold her tongue any longer. "Egan — what have you heard of him? Was he captured?" she asked.

Witt lowered his head in sorrow. "No my dear he was not captured. He would never allow that. I hear he terrified the fortress and killed many Tarylan guards, even a Seer before . . ." The steward stopped as emotion overwhelmed him. He rose to look out a window. Dira held her hands over her mouth, dreading to hear what she feared. Aron looked on in concern. "Egan died as a true Defender hero," the old man said hoarsely. "He was killed by Gerro, the Tarylan captain. I am told it was a fair duel."

Witt turned around, giving Aron an odd look. "This Gerro is an incredible warrior. He possesses skills far superior to any Tarylan or Sankari I have seen. He is credited now with killing three Defenders."

Dira wrapped her arms tightly around her chest, sobbing quietly. She suspected Egan had fallen to this fate but held out a desperate hope that he somehow found a way to escape. Aron bowed his head in sorrow. Egan had sacrificed himself to save him even though he did not remember the Defender. "I don't know what to think, who to believe. This is all so incredible."

Witt walked over, putting a hand on Aron's shoulder. "If you let me, I can help you remember," he said soothingly. "It will be difficult, even painful for you to awaken. More so than your circle brothers."

Aron looked up with a start. "Why?"

Witt shook his head as he remembered. "You went into the rage when you saw that Tevan had been killed. It took all of us to subdue you. You were wounded at Temple Darya, but it was from your circle brothers trying to stop you from attacking the Sankari. It took hours to calm you enough to put you into the waking sleep."

Shocked, Aron stood up. "You, you know about Tevan? I found his body amongst the dead after the battle?"

Witt put his arm around Aron's shoulders. Aron blinked back tears as he remembered taking the body back to Tevan's mother and father so they could give their son the proper funeral rites. It had been bittersweet for them — Aron had survived but their son, that sweet young man with the mind of a child, was dead.

His aunt's words still haunted him. After delivering Tevan, the young Aron collapsed from the rigors of the trip, still weak from the wounds he had suffered at Temple Darya. Thella, a kind but stoic woman, tried to comfort him. "If he was with you, he was happy. I'm sure you did all you could to protect him. We are grateful to you for bringing him home." Twenty harvests later, her words still stirred up sharp feelings of grief and guilt.

"If it is true, I want to remember," Aron said sternly, looking up at Witt.

The steward nodded. "Very good, but I will need help, and you need to prepare yourself. It will be very painful, much like a waking nightmare until you remember. You will have to relive those sad days."

Aron nodded slowly. "It is time to know the truth."

22

Aron's family waited for two agonizingly long days before a message from him was delivered by a mysterious old man just as night was falling. The elder Nuven shuffled up to one of the Nels guards, spoke with him briefly and was quickly ushered inside the house. Recognizing Aron's handwriting, Stazia sank into a chair and sobbed with relief as she devoured the note from her mate. Rising, she hugged the old man. "So you are this Witt Peyser he writes about. He says he is safe, but still in danger?"

Witt nodded. "Yes, my dear. It grieves him terribly that you cannot join him immediately. We fear the Tarylans will try to capture him again. If you go to him, it will be difficult to protect him or you. Many could be killed on both sides."

Stazia reread the note. "He asks for help from kinsmen and friends, but does not say why."

Witt leaned close to her. "Aron is about to undergo a painful awakening. He requires these men to help him through this. This will be a difficult time for all of them."

Stazia gripped Witt's arm, concern gripped her face. "Awakening? Tell me what is happening to Aron! Will this harm him?"

Witt tried to reassure her. "If I am successful at helping him remember some very painful events, he will be able to tell you himself. It will be a long process, and he may act much differently after he awakens."

The old steward let out a heavy sigh. "Defender Egan Pozos died so Aron could escape. Now it is up to me to help him remember who he truly is. After that, it will all be very clear what he will need to do."

Seeing Stazia's shocked and worried look, Witt arose and whispered in her ear. "Remember, no matter what happens, Aron loves you and your children."

––––––––––

The nine men listened with rapt attention while Witt Peyser explained why they had been called to help Aron Nels. The six Verdans and three Nuvens had known Aron for many harvests. The Steward told them what happened at Temple Darya and why Aron and his circle brothers were put into the waking sleep. Stazia's brothers and her sisters' mates looked at each in astonishment. The three Nuvans were soberly considering the facts.

"This is unbelievable! Aron, a Defender?" exclaimed Maje, the eldest of Stazia's brothers. "Did you suspect this?" he asked, looking at Aron's brothers — Romal, Erson and Wellin.

Romal stared at Witt. "That is why our family was sworn to secrecy when Aron was brought to us as an infant."

Erson nodded. "We were told it was a child of a kinsman who was in trouble with the Tarylans."

Witt smiled at the memory. "You and your brothers were delighted by the baby. You fought to hold him. Your parents were most gracious to accept him into your family."

Wellin was stunned. "It was you? You brought him to us?"

The old man nodded. "I've been with Aron and his circle brothers since they were born. They were all bred for a noble reason — to protect the temples and go undetected by the Seers. However, the Seers somehow learned of their presence and conspired somehow with the Sankari to destroy the temples before this Defender circle was ready."

The nine men sat in silence, absorbing what they had just heard. "Before you commit to this duty, be forewarned it will be a difficult task," Witt said, eyeing each man. "I may ask you to do things to Aron that will seem to be cruel but they will be necessary." Witt choked, pausing to regain his composure. "Aron may be injured in the awakening. He was in the rage when Temple Darya fell and may need to go back into that state to remember. It may be dangerous for you."

After a few moments, Romal rose slowly. "I've considered him a brother most of my life. I will not abandon him now." Erson and Wellin nodded in agreement.

Aron's friends — Malik Klinfer, Tuller Kranf and Kaj Striff — also stood. "Aron and I have saved each other countless times on hunts for many harvests. Whatever is asked of me, I stand by him," Malik said.

Tuller looked at the others. "Aron asked me for help. I will stay." Kaj nodded in agreement. The other men also stood and pledged their support.

"Aron has been our brother almost as long as I can remember," said Kaleff Remer, Stazia's youngest brother. "We will do what is asked of us. If he is a Defender, so be it."

The group whirled around in unison when someone coughed behind them. A gaunt-looking Aron greeted them with a nod, tears running down his face. With a whoop, Malik rushed over to his friend and embraced him. The others followed, surrounding Aron, pounding him joyfully on the back and shoulders.

Only Romal stood back a bit from the others. The other men ceased their celebration when they noticed the two brothers eyeing each other. A frowning Romal strode forward. "I told you not to go to the city. Maybe you will listen to your elder next time," he said sternly. However, he could not keep up the ruse, breaking into a wide grin and swatting Aron on the arm.

Aron finally allowed himself to smile. "It's good to see you, too, brother." Turning to the other men he said, "It's good to see all my brothers." Laughter echoed off the walls as the happy reunion continued through the night.

23

Aron Nels could hardly see Witt Peyser even though the older man was sitting only a few meters away. The room was almost pitch black. The only light came from a small flame in the fireplace on the opposite wall. Witt had been chanting and singing in a low, steady voice for almost a full hour.

Aron was having trouble focusing on the older man's face. He turned to peer into the darkness, searching for his new circle of brothers, but they all were sitting out of his field of vision. The only sound came from Witt who now was chanting the same mantra over and over in a low monotone.

Aron's head bobbed as if he were fighting sleep. The chanting seemed to grow slower. His mind relaxed, focusing on nothing else but the soothing words that drifted through his consciousness. Even though Aron's eyes were half open, they did not focus on anything in the room. At Witt's coaching, his breathing slowed. The chanting become slower and slower until it finally stopped.

Witt sat in silence, studying the half-conscious man in front of him. Aron looked so peaceful but now the difficult task was ahead — to awaken the Defender who had been sleeping for more than 20 harvests. The steward gestured for the fire to be stoked so he could see Aron's face clearly. Witt stood with his arms raised. He beseeched his and Aron's ancestors to guide them through these next difficult hours.

Witt moved to within centimeters of Aron and placed his hand on the younger man's head. "You are Aron Nels, tenth Defender brother of Circle Sankarikiller," he chanted slowly. "Defender, your brothers call upon you to awaken." At that signal, Aron's new circle loudly called out the names of his

deceased Defender brothers. Malik Klinfer was the last to call
out a name — Egan Pozos. Witt studied Aron's face carefully.
He caught the eye twitch when the Defenders' names were
called out.

The steward chanted again and again then signaled for the
chorus of names. This was repeated over and over. Every time
he beckoned the circle to call out the names louder than before.
Aron was now visibly reacting to the chanting. His face
contorted, head rolling back and forth and his eyes were
twitching rapidly. The chanting and shouting of names had gone
on for almost a half hour, when after Malik yelled out the name
of Egan Pozos, Aron sat up straight, eyes wide open and loudly
called his name — Aron Nels. The room went silent. Aron sat
perfectly still, staring into space.

Witt called out. "I am your steward, who are you warrior?"

"I am Aron Nels, tenth Defender brother of Circle
Sankarikiller, present sir," Aron shouted. Witt hunched over. He
was already exhausted and there was so much more work to do.
Several of the circle members rushed to his aid, helping him to
his feet and gave him water. It had been more than twenty
harvests since he had supervised an awakening, most were
completed in less than a half hour. This was going agonizingly
slowly.

"Prepare yourselves. If he awakens at the wrong time, he
may attack," Witt whispered to the circle. "Remember, he will
awaken as a Defender in his 20s who can move with great
quickness." Witt sat down a few meters away from Aron.
"Defender, what are your orders,?" he barked.

Aron replied. "To guard Temple Darya at all costs, sir."

"What will you do if the Sankari attack?" Witt prompted.

A fierce smile flashed on Aron's face. "Show no mercy. Kill
them sir."

Witt took a deep breath and looked at each of the other men
in the room. They were all somber and determined. "Defender, I
call on you to remember. Temple Darya has fallen to the
Sankari. All have been killed."

Aron cocked his head to one side, his face contorting slightly. "Sir, Circle Sankarikiller would not have allowed that. We would have died defending the temple."

Witt nodded to Malik, who was now stationed across the room. Aron's friend cupped his hand over his mouth and screamed in a high-pitched voice, "Aron, help me, Aron! Let me go! Aron, Aron."

The awakening Defender's face contorted, sweat starting to bead on his face. "T-Tevan. Is that you? What's wrong?" he mumbled.

Witt steeled himself for what could be the most painful part of the awakening. "Yes, it's Tevan. He needs your help. The Temple is under attack. Remember, Defender."

Again, Malik mimicked Tevan's plaintive call for help. Now in a state of torment, Aron sprung to his feet and whirled around looking frantically in all directions but was still unable to see anything. "Defender, remember, Temple Darya has fallen," Witt entreated him.

Aron called out, "Tevan, where are you?"

Witt nodded toward Tuller Kranf, who held a small whip. "Forgive me my friend," Tuller whispered then lashed out, striking Aron on the back. At the same time, Malik shouted Tevan's call for help: "Aron, help me!" Then cut it off with a painful scream.

At Witt's insistence, Tuller reluctantly struck Aron again. The whip had barely glanced off Aron's back, when he quickly whirled, snatching it from Tuller's hands, then charged his friend, intent upon killing him. The other men swarmed in response. It took all of them to pull Aron off poor Tuller, who had been so surprised at the sudden attack that he had no time to defend himself. Aron was now shouting incoherently and was twisting savagely trying to escape his captors.

The group finally managed to hold Aron still for Witt to approach. The Defender's eyes now burned bright with a fierce passion. He looked from face to face but did not recognize the other men. Witt acted quickly. Reaching out, he struck Aron across the face to get his attention.

"Defender, Temple Darya has fallen. Tevan has been slain. In the name of your ancestors, remember," he sharply ordered.

Aron screamed in pain and indignation, then stared at Witt briefly. His eyes softened in recognition. "Steward, is that you? The temple, the temple is destroyed." Aron's eyes blinked with tears. "Tevan! Oh, the ancestors, Tevan is dead. He and the other boys have been killed," he moaned and collapsed, sobbing.

Witt signaled for the circle to let him go. Aron bent over, sinking to his knees. He wept as the memories flooded back to him. Romal sunk to one knee. One hand covered his face in shocked grief as he witnessed what Aron had lived through that terrible night when Temple Darya fell to the Sankari.

Witt sat next to Aron, stroking his hair as a parent would soothe an upset child. He leaned toward the Defender and spoke in low, comforting tones. The other men brought food and drink, then left Witt and Aron in privacy. It would take many more hours for the steward to guide Aron back to full consciousness. But now Aron was peaceful and receptive. The Defender had awakened.

24

Dira essentially had been forgotten for a few days while Witt and nine other men attended to Aron. Adding to her distress was the change her body was undergoing. At first, she had denied the obvious answer. She thought her exhaustion was due to living through her harrowing experience and blamed her churning, sour stomach on the different Nuven food.

However, she could only fool herself for so long. The repetition of her symptoms soon made it clear — she was pregnant with Egan's baby. The day after Witt and the other men had helped Aron through his painful transition, Dira had confided her condition to the old man. Witt was sympathetic but his solution to her troubles was shocking.

"Not long after Temple Darya had fallen to the Sankari, another young Seer came needing help," he told Dira. "Only this young woman had recently given birth to twins, fathered by one of my young Defenders. She only had time to escape with her daughter." Witt took Dira's hand as he continued the tale. "This young Seer was frightened for herself and her children. She was terrified what the elder Seers would do if they discovered the truth."

The old man leaned forward. "There was ônly one place where she could safely raise her daughter — the Valley of Heroes. Friendly Nuvens escorted her deep into the valley to a village where the folk gladly took care of her and the child."

Dira sobbed: "Leave Verde Valley! But how would I live?"

Witt chuckled. "The other Seer not only survived but has risen to a position of honor. I am confident she will welcome you and help care for your baby."

The young woman thought for a long time before agreeing. "I know there is nowhere in Verde Valley I can go that would be safe from the Seers. Mother Verde help me, I will go to the Valley of the Hunters," she sighed.

Witt nodded. "The Nuvens call it the Valley of the Heroes and rightly so," he corrected her. "You will understand someday how they have sacrificed just to stay alive."

Dira bowed with embarrassment. "My apologies, I meant no disrespect. But I am worried. How will I make the trip?"

The old man smiled. "I am too old to make the trip, but I will make sure you are safely escorted through the mountains. Clan Pozos will be honored to care for you. I am confident they will treat you as one of their own."

Dira looked up surprised. "Egan's kin? That, that would be wonderful."

Witt rose, patting her on the cheek. "Don't worry young one. You and your baby will be safe soon enough."

Verinya woke with a gasp. Sitting straight up in her bed, she shivered in the chilly morning air, cold sweat soaking her night clothes and hair. How could it be possible? Her sight focused on her long-lost lover who appeared to be suffering from great pain. Or was it just a dream? The image had been so clear. Her lover lay doubled over in a faraway bed.

Hundreds of kilometers away, across the treacherous mountain, Aron suffered through another night of fitful sleep. The day before, Witt Peyser, along with his informal circle of family and friends had helped his Defender memories awaken. Now they haunted his mind.

Memories which had been buried for twenty harvests had resurfaced — his Defender training as a youth, bonding with his circle of brothers, falling in love with a beautiful young Seer and the most vivid of all — finding Tevan's body after the destruction of Temple Darya. Witt had helped guide him through most of his reawakened memories. The old man gently talked him through the events as they unfolded in his mind. One memory still lay buried in his subconscious, troubling Aron — the affair with the young woman.

A soft voice called to him in a dream. For many nights Aron had desperately tried to focus on his young lover's face, but each time the memory had disappeared just as smoke would dissipate from a fire. This time, however, Aron found himself facing a beautiful woman with long, dark red hair. The sight of her made his heart leap with joy. He tried to reach out to her. His arms would not respond. Aron was unable to move, but he could gaze upon her smiling face.

"My love, can you see me?" she asked in the dream.

"Yes, yes I can see you Verinya," Aron mumbled. He felt himself trying to wake up, but he did not want to leave this dream. "You have been a shadow in my thoughts for so long I almost forgot what you looked like." If he could just move, Aron was sure he could touch her.

Verinya sighed with delight as Aron responded. "What has changed?" she asked. "I can feel your thoughts again. It has been so very long. So much has happened."

Aron smiled. "I remember everything now, Verinya. My Defender memories have been awakened, except one, of you."

Her expression sobered. "Remember our moments together — those afternoons we spent hidden from the others. Something wonderful has come of our love." Aron could almost feel her breath in his ear.

"We have a beautiful daughter, a powerful Seer, and a handsome son, a famous Tarylan warrior — twins. I raised our daughter after I escaped from the Seers. Our son was raised in the fortress, but he is an honorable man. Do not fear for me for I am well. My life is full in the Valley of the Heroes. I have become their Protector."

Aron sat up, fully awake now. The dream had felt so real. He reached for a mug of water and almost dropped it when the voice continued, not beside him but in his mind. "We have a son and a daughter?" he asked out loud. "I did not know. So much has happened. I have bonded and fallen in love with another woman. We have made a life for ourselves and raised three beautiful children."

Verinya smiled. "I suspected that would happen if you remained alive. I am happy you have fared so well." Her image danced and faded a bit as Aron stretched. His body was sore from the stress of his awakening. Hunger gnawed at him.

"Be at peace Aron," Verinya said soothingly. "Treasure your memories. They will be with you to savor at will."

Aron frowned. "I may not have long to treasure them, Verinya. Sankari still live. I have my duty to carry out."

Verinya nodded. "May your ancestors protect you, my Defender." As her vision slowly faded, Aron was sure he saw her eyes well up with tears. He no longer felt troubled. No more hidden layers troubled his thoughts. It was time to prepare himself to face the Sankari. He stretched and jumped out of his bed. It had been two days since he had spoken with his circle. They had dutifully brought him food but did not otherwise disturb him.

Aron donned a long cloak and left his room. He strode down the hallway hungrily drinking in the aroma of freshly baked bread and cooked meat. When he reached the dining room, he saw his circle sitting at the large table enjoying first meal. The group of men looked up in surprise when one of them saw him.

Saying nothing, Aron walked over to the table and reached for a knife. He startled Romal by stabbing a piece of sausage off his plate. "Perhaps next time you will invite me to first meal so I don't have to steal food," he said, then winked at the others. Laughter erupted from the group. The others rose and heartily greeted him.

A young woman stood silently watching Verinya. Even though the Seer was in a deep trance, tears streamed down her face and her breath trembled with emotion. "What is it, Mother?" Arynna asked with concern after Verinya finally opened her eyes. The older Seer reached out to hug her daughter and gazed upon the lovely young face that reminded her so much of Aron.

"My Defender, your father, has awakened to his memories. But I fear for him now. He soon will challenge the Sankari. There are so many of them and only he is left."

Arynna kissed Verinya on her forehead. "Perhaps Father could use some help. Our Defenders have pledged to do your will after helping them ward off the Tanlians."

Verinya nodded. "Aron has kinsmen here. Ask Tarn to see me as soon as possible."

An hour had barely passed when a soft knock alerted Verinya. She called for the visitor to enter. A well-muscled man in his thirties bowed slightly but did not speak.

"Tarn, son of Raffin of Clan Nels, I have a dangerous task to ask of you and your circle." The Defender raised his eyebrows in a manner that eerily reminded the Seer of Aron.

"My circle will gladly do what the Protector asks," he said with pride. Verinya crossed the room and placed a hand on his shoulder. She could feel him tremble slightly. "This is no easy task, my loyal Defender. I want you and your circle to hurry to Verde Valley. One of your kinsmen, Aron of Clan Nels, is preparing to fight a great duel with many enemies. I fear for his safety as well as his family's."

Tarn's eyes widened momentarily, but he bowed at her request. "My circle will be honored to do your bidding," Tarn said without flinching. "Not only because you have asked it, but we have sworn to protect any kinsman at all costs."

Verinya smiled. "Forgive me, Defender, but I could think of no other I could trust with this duty. However, I fear for your safety as well."

Tarn bowed at the compliment. "This kinsman of mine must be a worthy warrior to challenge so many."

The Seer nodded. "He fights a blood oath. Many years ago the last temple of your people fell to his enemies. Many innocents were killed including his close kinsman, a quiet one.

All of his circle brothers have fallen in an attempt to fulfill their oaths. He is the last Defender in Verde Valley."

Tarn frowned at the news. "My circle and I will travel to Verde Valley with great haste. We will leave immediately," he said, bowing.

Verinya somberly bade him farewell. "You have my deepest thanks. This mission is very dear to me Tarn. Your kinsman is Arynna's father. May the ancestors protect you, my friend."

Tarn bowed deeply. "We will do all we can to protect our kinsmen. You have my oath."

25

The two men stood panting, sweat streaming off them. Large welts, inflicted by the flat wood paddles they both carried, covered their bodies. "Don't hold back," Witt Peyser called out angrily. "The Sankari will be fighting to the death. Now attack him!" Malik Klinfer took a deep breath and advanced on Aron. The grueling hand-to-hand combat training had gone on for two weeks.

Now in his 40s, Aron's reactions had slowed. His stamina and physical conditioning was nowhere near the deadly sharpness he possessed when he was 20 harvests old. He was slowly recalling some of the fighting maneuvers made famous by the Defenders. It had been a painful recollection. He suffered many cuts, bruises and those stinging welts his new circle brothers inflicted as they sparred viciously with him.

Witt had drilled Aron's new circle members time and time again they had to press the Defender to prepare him for what most likely would be bloody, savage duels. Once challenged, the Sankari would not stop fighting until either all of them or Aron was dead. A Nuven hunter, Malik was as close to a Defender training partner as could be found. His reactions were sharp and his fighting instincts were solid.

Malik advanced on his friend. He charged then quickly feinted to the left trying to find an opening to smack Aron with his paddle. Not fooled by the tactic, Aron smoothly deflected the attack, whirled and jabbed, lightly tapping his friend on the throat. Malik would have had his throat slit open if Aron's paddle had been a dueling knife.

Witt nodded with satisfaction. "Ah, that's better. You have to train at dueling speed. Otherwise the first Sankari to face

Aron will take his head home as a souvenir." The steward was noticing a pattern. The more exhausted and hurt Aron became, the more he fell back upon his instincts. When the Defender stopped being careful, his reactions were much quicker.

Malik rubbed his throat in surprise. He had never seen Aron move that fast. The two men had hunted together for many harvests. Malik had seen Aron dodge a wounded grazer as if he were dancing with the beast as it stomped by him, then drop it with a well-placed arrow seemingly without taking careful aim. But Aron's tap to his throat had been but a blur. Malik did not have time to raise his paddle in defense. "Well done, Defender, it seems you have killed me," Malik said smiling.

Aron nodded with satisfaction. "My blow must have been too light. You are still speaking." The two men laughed as they sunk to the floor, exhausted.

"You have two minutes to take water then do it again," Witt ordered. Aron and Malik groaned but complied. The two men had just started to face off again, when someone grabbed Aron from behind, pinning his arms behind him. He fought wildly but was forced to the floor by the stronger man. He was trapped, unable to move.

"Your opponent has just killed you, Defender," Witt snarled. "You have to feel another's presence, react as soon as you are touched or you will be killed." The "attacker" whispered an apology as he helped Aron up from the floor. "That is unnecessary," Witt barked. "The Defender should be apologizing to me. I trained you better than that."

Aron bent over from exhaustion but said nothing. He knew Witt spoke the truth. Staggering over to the water pitcher, Aron reached out for some refreshment when he was again grabbed from behind. This time, however, he instinctively let his body go limp. Slipping through the hold, he spun around quickly then kicked backwards, sending his opponent tumbling to the floor. With a triumphant yell, Aron rolled over and raised his fist, preparing to crush the other man's windpipe. He stopped himself before delivering the fatal blow, much to the relief of his surprised opponent.

"Thank you for not killing me," rasped a surprised Sef Jebo. Aron winced at the thought of what he almost did, then slumped on the floor, too exhausted to move.

"Much better. You are starting to remember how to react like a Defender," Witt called out. "That will be enough for today. Take refreshment and rest. We start at first light tomorrow."

For the next lunar, Aron was only allowed short rest breaks. The only exception was his nighttime repast. No longer haunted by nightmares of suppressed memories, he slept well, usually exhausted from the day's physically demanding regimen. While walking alone, Aron was subject to ambushes from around corners, out of the shadows in dark hallways or from the bushes in the lush gardens. Even during meals, an attack could be launched from behind him.

Day by day, Aron's dueling abilities grew sharper. His reactions became catlike when charged by an opponent. He usually turned a defensive move into a near-fatal blow to his opponents. By the end of the lunar, his training partners were the ones looking haggard and bruised from beatings they were taking after being repelled repeatedly by Aron. Even Malik was walking stiffly and with a limp after Aron flipped him through the air, causing him to hit his back on the stone floor after a creative but unsuccessful attack was easily rebuffed.

The Defender's personality also underwent a quiet transformation. Very seldom did Aron join in the jokes and storytelling with his circle. He now exuded a quiet confidence and a fierce determination to carry out his goal — to challenge the remaining Sankari to a death duel. Witt was pleased with Aron's growing Defender skills but was still worried how he would react to an actual duel when survival depended on killing his opponent. For too long now, when Aron fended off a practice attack, he always held up when it was time to strike that fatal blow or slash a jugular.

The old man was worrying about this as Aron and his circle were enjoying first meal when a messenger interrupted his thoughts. Witt tried to remain calm as he read the note. Excusing himself from the table, he sauntered away so as not to arouse suspicion. Finally out of sight, Witt hurried through the hallways, eager to meet the visitors who had requested an audience. The steward was surprised by the large group waiting to speak with him. About 20 people were gathered in a small courtyard.

Witt instinctively glanced around the room and was comforted by the presence of the Nuven warriors who were posted at regular intervals. These guards, who had vowed loyalty to Aron and his cause, were eyeing the group with suspicion. Witt was surprised to recognize a few members of the group. Standing in the forefront was Aron's mate, Stazia, and her daughters, Amaura and Lyllen. Next to her was Rissom, steward of Clan Nels with two of his lieutenants. A man of about Witt's age stood behind Stazia. It was the group of ten men who formed a protective semicircle around the others that drew Witt's attention. Their defensive postures and dress were eerily familiar. These strangers somberly eyed the old man as he approached.

"Steward, it's been too long. I pray all is well with you and those under your charge," Rissom said, stepping forward.

Witt bowed respectfully. "All goes well, Rissom. I am pleased how the Defender has awakened. He remembers everything and trains with vigorous passion," he said glancing towards Stazia. Aron's mate stood with her hands nervously clasped together. Amaura and Lyllen were on either side of their mother, their arms through hers.

Rissom nodded, smiling at the news. "Forgive the intrusion steward, but these people have asked for permission to see Aron. They all have compelling reasons."

Stazia approached Witt, concern burning in her eyes. "I beg of you, I must see Aron, it has been too long." Both daughters glared angrily at him.

Witt reached out, taking her hands gently. "Soon, very soon. I give you my word, Stazia. When you do meet, I must warn you, Aron is different from the man you know. His dreams no longer are troubled. They have been turned into memories."

Stazia shook her head emphatically. "He will remember me, he will remember his family."

Witt smiled. "Yes, he remembers, but he now has a new life purpose. The one he was born to carry out — to kill Sankari." Amaura approached the old man, demanding to know exactly when her mother could see Aron. The fire in her eyes reminded him so much of her father. Witt paused, taking a deep breath. He knew he could no longer delay this moment.

Eyeing the ten young strangers in the group, Witt agreed to a meeting but told them Aron also would have to consent to it. "I have one more test for him. It may be the most challenging yet."

After first meal was finished, the circle continued with their regular routine. Aron and several of the others left for the gardens to exercise in the warm morning sun. They stretched and moved through many elaborate kicks. Their arms waved steadily, blocking imaginary foes.

Halfway through a stretching maneuver, bushes behind Aron rustled slightly. Instinctively, he glanced towards the noise and barely had time to react to the body that hurtled toward him. Aron managed to partly deflect the kick, but the blow to his head still knocked him to the ground. Kicking defensively but striking nothing, the Defender back flipped into a defensive standing position.

A frowning young stranger faced him, standing in a similar position. His feet were spaced evenly apart, his hands held up in the classic fighting-ready position. Malik and the two other brothers, who also had been exercising, started to come to Aron's assistance when they were waved off by Witt, who stood watching from a far wall.

The stranger and Aron started to slowly circle each other. Both pairs of eyes studied the other cautiously. The younger opponent narrowed his eyes slightly and attacked. Seeing the movement, Aron blocked the kick, swiveled and kicked back, but the other man easily ducked out of the way.

Aron's foe kept up a savage attack, kicking, throwing sharp jabs. The Defender was able to defend himself but he could not manage to land any kind of a blow. His opponent moved with a frightening quickness, not seemingly bothered by Aron's counterattacks.

The two continued this deadly strategic match — kicking, punching, twisting and turning, trying to throw deadly punches at the other. During one of his attacks, the younger man grabbed Aron's arm, twisted it and threw him to the ground.

The Defender reacted as if he were a maddened snake, turning and twisting savagely until he and the other man rolled over and over in the grass. Neither could gain an advantage to strike a deciding blow. As they were grappling and growling with exertion, a huge wave of cold water slammed into them, knocking the breath out of both combatants.

Rolling over gasping and choking, both men staggered to their feet, rubbing their eyes looking for the other. "Enough, Defenders," Witt shouted as he struck a gong. Its chime reverberated through the garden. At Witt's signal, Aron's circle surrounded him, and nine other young men encircled his opponent to keep the combatants apart.

Aron watched curiously as Witt patted his opponent's shoulder in a "well-done" gesture. Then the Steward walked over to Aron with a proud smile.

"Defender, you have passed your last test," he said. Gesturing for Aron's opponent to approach, Witt said, "There will be no need for further animosity, especially between kinsmen."

Aron, who was still breathing hard from the fight, eyed the other man suspiciously. His opponent smiled. "You fight well kinsman. I am Tarn, son of Raffin of Clan Nels. We come from the Valley of Heroes to assist Aron, son of Ural."

Aron looked puzzled. "You are from the Valley of the Heroes? How do you know about me?"

Tarn bowed. "The Protector Verinya told us of your struggle with your enemies. We have come to help our kinsman."

26

High Seer Tanella was dumbfounded by the document. Manor Stillinger sat in front of her, shaking his head in amazement. Neither had expected this — a legal challenge from the Defender Aron Nels and his steward, Witt Peyser. The two men were formally accusing the Sankari of conspiring to commit war, destroying religious temples without due cause, treason and the murder of innocents. If they were found guilty, all the Sankari would face the ultimate punishment — execution.

Aron and Witt had filed their charges with Verdan authorities. Much to Tanella's and Manor's dismay, the authorities had found enough merit in the accusations to issue official charges. The only recourse for the Sankari was to stand trial in front of a panel of respected judges and truth seekers, whom were looked upon with great suspicion by the Seers.

The truth seekers were descended from a renegade Seer who was not born with the sight but possessed a different gift, the ability to detect if a person was lying or telling the truth. A granddaughter of the First Seer Taryl Bryann, the young woman frightened her kinswomen with her strange talents and her refusal to lie to favor the Seers. Unable to control or coerce her, the other Seers banished her from the fortress. To the Seers' dismay, her descendants thrived and soon gained widespread respect in the Verdan judicial system for their complete fairness in trials.

The writ left an out for the Sankari to avoid a trial. Aron noted he would consider death duels with the surviving Verdan warriors if challenged. The document named all nineteen Sankari. "We cannot stand trial," Manor growled. "Those damn truth seekers may side with the Nuvens. If the Defender and his steward witnessed what happened that night at Temple Darya, their testimony would refute anything my Sankari and I would say. I should have killed that fruit vendor when we had him in custody."

Tanella tossed the document down in disgust. "You have no recourse General. Challenge this Nuven vermin and kill him in a duel. He is only one man and you are nineteen. Losing a few more men would be a worthwhile price to finally be rid of the Defenders."

Manor stared out the window, nodding resignedly. "This Defender is a tricky bastard. If the Sankari issue a duel challenge, he gets to choose the time, place and weapons."

Tanella threw up her hands. "So what? He is one man. Issue the challenge and end this now."

———

A soft knock on the door interrupted Aron's meditation. Witt entered only when he heard the invitation called out. Looking pleased, he handed Aron a document and waited for his reaction. The Defender read the document carefully. Picking up an ink scratcher, Aron scribbled his answer on the piece of paper and returned it to Witt.

The steward read it solemnly: "I, Aron Nels, Defender of Temple Darya, have accepted your duel challenge. I will expect all living Sankari to be prepared to face me in the Arena of Champions three days hence. Dueling knives are my choice of weapons. We will meet one hour after first meal."

Witt sat next to Aron. The steward leaned back and stared into space. He was having trouble controlling his emotions. "This is the moment we both have been anticipating, but now I am at a loss for words. In three days, it will be your turn to stand against the Sankari. You have done all you can to prepare. May the ancestors and your fallen circle brothers be with you Defender."

Aron nodded. "I am ready to face the Sankari, but I have other business to attend to before the duel. I wish to see my family now."

———————

Stazia and her daughters rushed to Aron when he entered their rooms in the small stronghold. "Oh, Aron, I am so happy to see you well," Stazia said burrowing her face in his chest, hugging him tightly. Amaura and Lyllen wept for joy as they waited their turns for hugs from their father. Stazia noticed something different about Aron while he embraced his daughters. His expression was different. The good-natured twinkle in his eyes was gone, replaced by a cold seriousness.

"We were so worried after you were taken to the fortress," Stazia told him. "Then we were told a Defender sacrificed himself to save you. Now, I hear strange stories of you being a Defender. What is happening?"

With his daughters still clinging to him, Aron looked somberly at Stazia. "It makes my heart ache that you have suffered so much at my account. This past lunar has been the most difficult and challenging time in my life." Aron looked around the room searching for someone. "Flyn?" he asked.

Stazia shook her head. "He and his hunter circle are still hunting in some faraway canyon. No one knows where they are."

Aron sighed at the thought he may not see his son again. He then sat down and began to tell his mate and daughters the incredible tale of his life as a young Defender, the battle at Temple Darya, finding Tevan's body and being put into the waking sleep. Tears streamed down his face while he told them about the deaths of his nine circle brothers and then the painful experience of being made to remember all those tragic events again during his reawakening.

"I still cannot believe you are a Defender," Stazia said with disbelief. "I have been with you twenty harvests and never suspected."

Aron looked at her sadly. "I did not intentionally deceive you. I was made to forget all my Defender memories. I was happy with my life with you and our children." Looking away, he took a deep breath, dreading what he had to tell them now. "I have forced the Sankari into challenging me to a death duel, which I have accepted. In three days, I will face them."

The color left Stazia's face when she heard this terrible news. She had just been reunited with her beloved mate, and now he was about to face an enemy that greatly outnumbered him. The realization seized her that Aron, most probably, would be killed during the duels. Grabbing her mate, Stazia wept uncontrollably. She hugged him tightly, afraid to let him go. Amaura and Lyllen huddled close to their parents for comfort.

27

After third meal, Romal and Malik found Aron sitting on one the carved stone benches in the stronghold's garden. The Defender was staring at Luz Primo. The largest of Verde's two moons was almost full. It shone like a beacon in the sky. The smaller moon, Luz Nino, was a mere sliver, just showing itself above the opposite horizon.

"Good hunting moon. You could see the grazers from a hundred meters away," Malik said wistfully.

"There's nothing like a hunt to stir the blood up, riding into a herd of those beasts, dropping them with javelins and arrows," Romal sighed.

Aron smiled and returned to study the beautiful, glowing moon. "Flyn is out there somewhere with his hunting circle, probably tracking down some grazers even as we speak," he said, sadness tainting his voice. The Defender regretted he may not have the opportunity to see his son before the duel. Aron did not let himself dwell on the treacherous task he was about to face, an impossible challenge in which he could be killed.

Even the oddsmakers were against him. The best Verdan bet was he would kill nine Sankari. The Nuvens were a bit more optimistic. They had him dropping twelve opponents before finally succumbing. No one told Aron about this. They did not want to bring him bad luck. Knowing the close bond Aron shared with his son, Malik wanted to change his friend's mood. A natural storyteller, Malik could not resist the opportunity to retell one of his famous tales. He had a fresh audience in Romal.

Aron not only had heard these stories many times but had lived most of these adventures with Malik. With each telling the grazers got bigger and fiercer, and the hunters became more clever and skilled with their weapons. Much to Aron's chagrin, Malik had Romal guffawing about the time a large bull grazer had knocked him off his horse and then chased him into a grove of small saplings.

"There he was, running and dodging through those trees with that bull right on his heels. He looked a young rabbit trying to escape from one of our hunting dogs," Malik chortled while Romal bent over holding his ribs from laughing so hard. "I had to ride over and yell for him to run out of the grove so I could get a clean shot. Of course I dropped it with one arrow," he bragged.

Aron half smiled and cleared his throat. It was time to get even. "I remember a red-headed hunter falling off his horse when he was trying to retrieve one of his javelins in a fallen grazer. Much to his surprise, the grazer wasn't dead. It chased him almost 50 meters before he flung himself off a small ravine into a thorn bush."

Malik turned red at having the tables turned on him as Romal roared delightedly. Aron was not finished. "There was another time, I believe it was my first hunt. One of my brothers wanted to show how brave he was during a night very much like this. He charged his horse straight into a herd of grazers, yelling like a wounded hound. However, he didn't see this giant bull watching him from a small knoll overlooking the herd," Aron said, enjoying Romal's growing embarrassment.

"Well, this bull decided to fend off this threat and soon he was chasing down my brother and his horse. That bull chased him almost a full kilometer before he tired out. My brother's horse refused to turn after the bull, and the rest of the herd stampeded before we had a chance to get any shots off."

Now Malik let out a loud belly laugh as Aron smiled at the memory. Romal just shook his head. "You said the rest of the herd got away, but what about the bull?" Malik asked.

Aron grinned. "I got my first kill that night. It was a tired-out bull. He was breathing so hard, he didn't run from me, just let me drop him with an easy kill shot."

The laughter from the garden made it easy for the other members of Aron's volunteer circle of friends and family to find them. Tarn and his circle of Defenders had followed the others, hoping to find Aron.

"Can you still enjoy a sip?" Tuller Kranf said with a wry smile, holding up a large clay jug of his finest ale. Not to be outdone, Kaleff Remer proudly hoisted up two large jugs of homemade wine. Aron sauntered over to Tuller, accepted the jug and took a long drink. Putting it down, he let out a loud belch.

"Yes, I believe I can still enjoy a sip." More laughter echoed across the garden throughout the night as the Verdans and Nuvens shared stories and good drink.

28

The two men sat across from one another in a small dark room. Their faces were barely illuminated by a small flickering lamp. Witt Peyser looked solemnly at the meditating Aron Nels, who was sitting cross-legged on a thick rug. "Defender, on the morrow you will face the enemy Sankari in the arena. Are you prepared to accept the cleansing of pain from your body?" Witt softly intoned.

Aron breathed in and out steadily, opened his eyes and simply answered, "Yes steward."

Witt leaned close. "You will be in a shallow waking sleep, but the pain will feel very real to you. It will be very different than when you awakened to your Defender memories. Your body will be on fire. The injuries I will call out will feel very real, but you will not strike out. After the cleansing, you will feel no pain in the arena. You will leave it all here in this room."

Aron nodded slowly. "Prepare me for battle, steward. Without pain or fear, I will be able to face my enemies."

Witt looked sadly at this proud Defender who patiently waited to expunge any pain from his body. The old man wished he had the chance to prepare Aron's circle brothers thusly. Perhaps if they had been properly reawakened and trained, Aron would not be faced with such a monumental task in the arena. Much the same as he did with Aron's awakening, Witt started to sing and chant softly, repeating the same phrases over and over. This time the Defender easily succumbed to his steward. His eyes fluttered and half closed. His breathing grew slower.

Outside the door, Aron's volunteer circle of family and friends, as well as the Defenders from the Valley of Heroes, waited nervously. None of them knew what to expect from this

174

strange-sounding practice. Malik paced nervously, stopping every so often to speak to Tuller who stood with his large arms folded, staring intently at the door. "I thought that old man was through with this magic after his awakening," Malik whispered impatiently.

Tuller frowned and shrugged. "Witt said Aron would feel any pain possible one could experience in a duel. "This cleansing is supposed to . . ." Before Tuller could finish his thought, a high-pitched shriek jolted everyone to their feet. The cry was followed by loud, gasping sobs. "Mother Verde," Tuller gasped. "Is that Aron?" Malik was wide-eyed with concern. He had seen his friend wounded several times during their hunting forays, but Aron had never reacted in this manner.

A low groan came from the room. It grew steadily in pitch and crescendo, until the men covered their ears. Again and again, terrible sounds of someone being tortured rang out. A few of Aron's relatives grew ill from listening to the painful cries and reluctantly left.

Inside the room, Aron was bent over and gasping for breath. Witt had not laid one hand nor weapon upon him. The only instruments of pain were his words through the power of suggestion. The steward circled the half-awake man, describing a bloody duel. Aron felt as if he were a puppet. He responded to Witt's commands and reacted to the wounds that were inflicted in his mind.

"Your opponent has just lunged at you. His knife has cut a deep wound across your belly. Every time you move, your body is wracked with pain," Witt said, as Aron reacted with a deep-throated gasp. The Steward saw to it every one of Aron's body parts were broken, torn, cut off or slashed by Sankari weapons.

In his mind, Aron's fingers were broken or cut off, ears mangled, slashes covered every part of his body, deep gashes opened near vital organs, hamstrings were sliced, collar bones were broken, ribs cracked, even an eye was gouged out. Witt was relentless. He had to be. If this Defender was to keep fighting the Sankari to his death, his body would not go unscathed.

Aron's mind already had experienced every gut-wrenching pain imaginable. Once in the arena, his body would not react to any of these wounds. The cleansing continued for almost two hours until Aron was hoarse from screaming in agony. He now lay shivering in a fetal position on his blanket, gasping for air. His body was numb from the harrowing experience. In Aron's mind, he was at death's door, unable to move, think or react.

Witt knelt by his charge as he softly chanted. He could help the Defender fall into a peaceful, deep sleep, but it would take hours for the body to fully relax and recover. After several minutes, Aron's breathing again was slow and regular. His body stretched out a bit.

When the door opened, those waiting outside the room jumped almost as much as when Aron screamed for the first time. Romal was the first one to confront Witt as he left the room.

"It is done. He will recover but he needs to sleep now," Witt reassured Aron's family and friends. The steward looked haggard and exhausted. Tear stains dribbled down his creased and weathered face. "Take him a bed, water and warm blankets. It will be many hour before he awakens."

Witt looked gravely at his listeners. "Tomorrow the Sankari will feel the wrath of his knives. The Defender will only stop if he is killed. May the ancestors be with him. He is ready for the duel."

29

Aron's family sat in silence during an early first meal. All had risen several hours before so they could be together. Amaura looked at her father forlornly not touching her food. Lyllen stared at her plate, nervously playing with the fresh biscuits her mother had baked that morning. Stazia ate slowly. She paused occasionally to dab her eyes with her cloth napkin.

Her mate sadly watched his family while he forced himself to eat what normally would be his favorite morning feast of freshly baked pastries, fried strips of thinly sliced meat and of course a bowl of the finest honey fruit. None of the family members knew if this would be their last meal together. In a few hours, Aron would walk out into the Arena of Champions to face his hated enemy, the Sankari, in a duel to the death.

Aron plucked out the biggest honey fruit and took a long, lingering sniff of its intoxicating fragrance. Picking up a sharp table knife, he expertly sliced it into four pieces. Closing his eyes, he took a bite, savoring its sweet juices.

Seeing the contented look on his face, Amaura could not keep her emotions at bay any longer. "Oh, Father, none of this would be happening if you hadn't protected the secret of that damn fruit," she sobbed. Stazia moved over to comfort her crying daughter. Lyllen said nothing, but tears streamed down her cheeks, too.

"My precious ones, please understand this would be happening one day," Aron said softly. "This is my destiny. This is what I have been trained for since childhood. I suspect it is what I was born to do. If I hadn't been taken into custody over the honey fruit quarrel, I may not have been properly reawakened. At some time in my life I would have attacked a Sankari out of instinct and may have been killed."

Lyllen gazed at him questioningly. "How is that different from what you are going to do in a few hours?"

Aron gazed at his youngest daughter, wondering how he could make her understand. "Witt and all of your uncles and my friends have prepared me for this. I am ready to face as many of them as possible."

For the first time, he choked with emotion. "I was a young man, about Flyn's age, when the Sankari slaughtered all the Defenders and murdered innocents, including my kinsman." The women now were respectfully silent as they listened. "One dream still haunts me," Aron said in a slow trembling voice, fighting back tears. "Tevan calling out my name as the younglings were being killed."

Aron looked down at the table shaking his head. "Witt said I would not suffer the pains of battle, but I still feel pain here," he said, putting a hand over his heart. "I have to face the Sankari. The memory of Tevan and the others demands it."

The three women surrounded Aron, embracing him. Afterwards, he rose from his seat and asked them to consider a request. "When I enter the arena, I no longer will be your mate or your father. I will be a Defender prepared to kill my enemies. If I'm able, I will do terrible things to the Sankari, and they will try to do terrible things to me. I beg you not to watch the duel. I want you to remember me this way, not as a warrior killing others or being killed."

However, his mate and daughters were not to be dissuaded. "I know the odds are against you, Aron, but I will die slowly if I have to rely on others to tell me your fate," Stazia said. "Whatever happens in the arena will not change how I feel about you. I want to be there if you need me."

Amaura and Lyllen nodded in agreement. For the first time since his cleansing, Aron smiled. "It is obvious that courage and loyalty are not exclusive to the males of Clan Nels."

After the meal, Aron excused himself from his mate and daughters. He needed to prepare himself for the duel that was now only a few hours away. Amaura and Lyllen were too upset to stay and comfort their grieving kinsmen and friends. Needing to do something to keep from nervously fidgeting, they went for a walk and found the huge garden.

Walking on the winding path, seeing the beautiful colors and smelling the sweet aromas of the flowers reminded Aron's daughters of the times they had spent helping their father harvest fruit in the family orchard. Despite the dramatic events that were about to unfold, both smiled as they lightly touched the blossoms and watched the bees buzz through the plants.

Walking around a bend, the young women were surprised to see Witt Peyser sitting alone on a bench. The old man was bent over, holding his head in his hands. Lyllen glowered at the man, who had awakened her father to his Defender memories. Amaura fought to stifle the urge to slap the steward. They wanted to hate the strange man who had guided their father to this seemingly impossible fatal task.

However, Witt looked quite pitiful and lonely sitting there, quietly grieving. He sat with his head in his hands. His body slowly rocked back and forth. Witt reminded them very much of Ural, their deceased grandfather. Saying nothing, the women quietly sat next to him, one on either side.

The steward looked up, surprised to see who had joined him. "Forgive an old man for remembering too many brave Defenders dying for this cause," he apologized. "I was only able to help your father and Egan Pozos awaken. The Defenders before them fought bravely but were unprepared."

Witt gazed at the lovely young women. Amaura could almost be mistaken for a Seer, but her auburn hair was much darker not the fiery red of those secretive Verdan women. Lyllen's dark golden hair had reddish-brown streaks mixed in it. This was the first time the steward had closely studied Aron's daughters. He could see his beloved Gwena reflected in Amaura's face. Turning to Lyllen he stifled a gasp. She was the image of his beloved mother.

"Your father is a brave man," he said in a choking voice. "He fights for many today, but he should not have had to face such difficult odds." Amaura and Lyllen reached out and gently clasped the old man's hands. They looked and felt familiar, not unlike their father's.

Lyllen studied his face. There was something unsettling about him. "Romal says you brought my father when he was a baby to be raised by Ural and Norene. Did you do this with the other Defenders as well?"

The feelings welling up in Witt were new to him. He had been accustomed to training and mentoring young men, warriors who usually were driven to carry out their missions. Looking into the young women's eyes, he did not feel like the steward of a Defender circle. Loneliness burned in his heart. *What could it hurt to tell these young women the truth?* he thought. With Aron facing the Sankari shortly, the secret of Circle Sankarikiller no longer needed to be protected.

"Your father and his circle brothers were very special to the Defenders," he said proudly. "Yes, I am the one who took those precious babies to be raised by loyal and caring families."

Amaura wiped her eyes. "Then Ural and Norene are not our grandparents."

Witt shook his head. "No, but they are very close kinsman. Besides, they raised Aron as their own and were loving grandparents to you, correct?"

Both women nodded. "Yes, they will be so in my heart. But do you know who our blood kin are?" Lyllen asked, squeezing Witt's hand.

The steward paused a long while. His eyes focused on some far-off place as long-forgotten memories surfaced. He had never spoken of this to anyone, not even Aron and his circle brothers.

"Many harvests ago, the battles with the Sankari were going badly. It seemed no matter how many Defenders were posted at a temple or village to protect them, the Sankari always came in greater numbers. Somehow it seemed as if the Sankari knew the numbers of Defenders. Something had to be done to find out how the enemy could always breech our defenses."

As Witt spoke, he felt as if a heavy burden was finally being lifted from his aging shoulders. "One day the Nuven elders convinced a brave young woman, the daughter of a respected Defender, to follow the Sankari raiders after an attack. She discovered one of them was a Tarylan guard captain, a son of a Seer, who secretly joined Sankari raids. It took her many lunars but she finally seduced him and later bore a son."

Lyllen noticed Witt's voice grew soft and respectful when he mentioned the Nuven woman. "The Nuven elders studied the child as he grew but could not determine that he had any special talents," Witt said. "The young man was successfully trained as a Defender and was accepted into a circle. One day, while watching over a small Nuven mountain village, his circle came under attack by a large group of Sankari. The young Defenders fought bravely but all were killed except the son of the Tarylan."

Witt now stared off into space as he spoke. It seemed as if this was more than a story to him. "This young Defender attacked the intruders. Somehow, the enemy did not know he was there. He was able to approach them without being detected. The Defender killed the remaining Sankari. After that, he successfully attacked Sankari patrols, always catching them off guard. If others went with him, they would always be detected." Witt stopped for a moment, his voice choking with emotion. Amaura looked intently at the old man.

"The young Defender was you, wasn't it?" Witt half smiled and nodded at her deduction. "I am a grandson of a Seer, immune to their strange gift."

Lyllen interrupted him. "That is fascinating, but what does it have to do with my father?"

Witt looked at her patiently. "Over hundreds of harvests we Nuvens have learned how to cultivate a valuable trait amongst us." The old man now shifted on the bench and looked uncomfortable as he continued his tale. "Because I was just one warrior with a unique ability, the elders insisted I return to the

Valley of the Heroes. My orders were to produce sons with the daughters of Nuven Defenders."

Amaura gasped as she realized what Witt had just told her. Lyllen stared with wide eyes, not wanting to believe what she had just heard.

"Yes, when I returned to Verde Valley I brought eleven babies with me," he said blinking away tears. "Their mothers accompanied me on the trip. The infants were all given to their clan kinsmen to ensure they would be raised safely. The women returned to the Valley of the Heroes after the babies were safely adopted."

Amaura gasped. "You were not only the steward of my father's circle but are their father! You, you are our grandfather?"

Lyllen put a hand on Witt's shoulder. "You said you brought back 11 babies, but there were only ten Defenders. What happened to the eleventh child?"

Witt could not control himself any longer. He let out a soft sob as tears filled his fading blue-green eyes. "It was your father. He was born so small, the elders did not know if he would survive. Tevan was supposed to have been the final member of the circle."

Amaura covered her eyes with her hands. Sobs shook her body. Lyllen did not move, looking stunned. Tears ran down her chin and neck. The three sat on the bench together in silence for a long time. Amaura finally slid close to Witt, giving him a warm hug then looked at him sadly. Lyllen rested her head on his shoulder.

"You've have seen ten of your sons killed," Amaura said softly.

Witt nodded as he wiped away his tears. "Yes and now I most likely have sent another one to his death."

30

Aron Nels stood just inside the gate to the arena. At last, he was ready to face his enemies. He wore the simple fighting attire of a Defender — close-fitting clothes that would not impede his movement and the famous knife belts. Two belts crisscrossed his torso and fastened around his waist. The handles of numerous dueling knives protruded from pouches in the belts.

Slightly nervous but unafraid, a strange anticipation flowed through his body. A few minutes earlier, the Defender had said his tearful farewells to his mate and their daughters. Aron had handed a pouch intended for their son, Flyn, to Stazia for safekeeping. His only regret was he may not see his son again. Witt Peyser placed a hand on Aron's shoulder. "You are ready for this challenge Defender. Remember, you fight for all those who were killed by the Sankari, including the innocents."

A large bell sounded throughout the Arena of Champions, signaling it was time. The gate swung open to the arena. A great buzz greeted Aron and Witt as they walked out. The seats were filled with thousands of people waiting in great anticipation for this latest Defender/Sankari spectacle. The stadium was evenly split between followers of both sides.

On the other side of the arena, another gate swung open and two Sankari marched out with great bravado. Six officials stood in the center of the arena — three Verdans and three Nuvens. The men, who represented the hierarchy of the Nuven and Verdan societies, formally greeted Aron, Witt and the two Sankari as they approached.

The mayor of Verde City stepped forward to announce the combatants. "The Defender, known as Aron Nels, has accepted a death duel challenge issued by the Sankari, represented by Captain Manor Stillinger and his second in command. Warriors, I ask you, cannot a peaceful resolution be achieved here?"

Aron looked at Witt then addressed the group. "The Defenders who died before me all offered the Sankari the same option and now I repeat it. I offer you life if you admit to the slaughter of innocent Nuvens and the massacre of the Defenders. Do you yield?"

Manor stood with his arms clasped behind his back. He vigorously shook his head no. "I should have killed you when you were a prisoner in the fortress, fruit vender," the Sankari commander snarled.

Aron showed no emotion as he responded. "You will have an opportunity to carry out that threat. Will you be the first to die today?" Manor grimaced then spit on the ground to show his disgust.

The mayor called out. "This duel will be fought according to the established code of conduct, which has been agreed upon by both sides. Warriors, take your positions." Aron strode to the center of the arena to wait for his first opponent. The two Sankari retreated to the safety of their seats above the gate from which they had entered. Witt found his seat in the first row and murmured a quick prayer for Aron. The Defender was facing his first true test with an opponent who wanted his blood.

A tall, broad-shouldered Sankari appeared in the arena. He grinned widely as the Verdan crowd stood, shouting their approval. The Verdan, who was almost a head taller than Aron, started to walk toward the Defender. His pace quickened to a trot, then he broke into a full attack run. Aron pulled out two knives and stood his ground, waiting until his opponent was almost upon him. Just as the Sankari reached him, Aron sidestepped and kicked at his opponent's ankles, causing him to land with a clumsy crash.

Picking himself up quickly, the angry Sankari charged again. This time he leaped at Aron, who feinted, easily avoiding the attack, almost as if he were dancing with his foe. Growling with frustration, his opponent crept forward slowly this time.

The Sankari struck out with his huge knives again and again, only to find air where Aron had been. With each pass and missed thrust by his opponent, Aron lashed out finding flesh every time until his knives dripped with blood.

The larger man now stumbled through his clumsy attacks. He was in pain and growing weak from the loss of blood. In one last desperate move, the Sankari tried to grab Aron. The Defender blocked the attempt, but grabbed his attacker's arm, giving it a violent twist. The Sankari screamed in pain, holding his now limp right arm. He looked frantically for Aron but couldn't find him. He realized too late where the Defender had gone. Before the Verdan could react, Aron plunged his knife deep into his back. The Sankari staggered forward, a look of terror on his face, then fell to his knees. A quick slash across the throat ended the large man's life.

The Nuven crowd stood, cheering their approval. The Verdans were stunned. Many looked toward the Sankari gate, hoping their next champion would be more worthy. In a surprise move, Aron knelt by the body and said a prayer, asking for the Sankari's ancestors to accept him. He then stood and gestured for the man's body to be taken away.

Manor frowned at the outcome. His strongest man had failed to draw blood. He had even failed to touch the Defender. The general looked up and down the ranks of his men, many of whom looked to be in shock. Only one other returned his gaze, eagerness smoldered in his eyes. With a smile, Manor called on Taffa Ganu. The Sankari, known as "the crazy one," leaped forward and ran into the arena. Taffa quickly engaged Aron in fierce hand-to-hand combat. The Sankari was known for his unconventional skills. He would punch, kick, elbow, wrestle; whatever it took to win.

Aron traded blows, blocked kicks and skillfully warded off the Sankari's knives. Never losing his focus, the Defender returned the attack in Taffa's own style, which confused the Sankari. Again, Aron's knives slashed and stabbed into Taffa's body. The Sankari continued to fight in a frenzy. Some of his kicks struck Aron, but the force of most of them was blocked.

185

Each time Taffa rose, he moved more slowly, covered with blood from his many wounds. After Taffa's latest maneuver failed, Aron managed to bury a knife deep into his ribs. The Sankari groaned in pain and fell. Taffa tried to rise, but the effort proved too much. With a shudder, he collapsed to the ground, dead.

Aron also said a prayer for his second vanquished foe as the Nuvens shouted triumphantly. Three more Sankari ventured out to fight. Each was more cautious than his predecessor, but the outcome was the same. They all died under Aron's knives. After Aron had slain his fifth foe, a sixth Sankari came running out. The Defender steeled himself for the next attack. Even though unscathed except for a few deep bruises, he nevertheless was growing weary from the exertion.

Before the men reached each other, the crash of a large gong echoed throughout the arena. Both combatants stopped and glanced around to find the source of the sound. Witt stood on a platform at one end of the arena, holding a large mallet. Puzzled, Aron looked back to see the Sankari backing away. The sound of men approaching drew the Defender's attention. He whirled around and took a defensive stance but was greeted by the Defenders from the Valley of the Heroes.

Tarn smiled as he approached. "You have done well kinsman — five slain foes. You have earned a rest until tomorrow." Although tired, Aron was still full of adrenalin and did not fully understand what his kinsman was saying. Seeing this, Tarn gestured for Aron to follow them to safety for the evening. As he left the arena, the Nuven crowd rose up in admiration, shouting his name. The Verdans departed in silence, many shocked by what they had just witnessed.

Stazia and her daughters rushed from their seats to greet Aron after his bloody victory. However, Witt stopped them when they reached the room where Aron had been taken. "Give him some time. He is still in the battle trance and is cleaning up. He is very thirsty and hungry." Seeing the women's worried looks, Witt reassured them Aron had only sustained a few bruises. "Give him an hour, maybe two, then you can see him.

Aron has spilled human blood for the first time in 20 harvests. He is meditating after the difficult thing he has just done."

Two hours later, Aron solemnly greeted his family and friends. Even though he was showered with hugs and well wishes, the Defender did not share in their joy nor did he participate in more than perfunctory conversation. Stazia noticed her mate's aloofness. His eyes glowed with an intense seriousness she had not seen before. Witt, too, noticed the change.

"Aron is staying in battle trance because he has such a difficult task ahead of him," the steward told her. "What you are seeing now is a pure Nuven Defender."

After a few minutes had passed, Aron arose and addressed his well-wishers. "Forgive me, but I need to return to my room to rest for the next day's duels," he said slowly, almost as if he was speaking a foreign language. "It is difficult for me to see people before going into the arena. I beg all of your forgiveness, but I will not speak to anyone until the duels are over."

Without another word, he kissed a teary Stazia, Amaura and Lyllen on their foreheads and quietly bade everyone good night.

The next morning, Aron walked into the stadium to cheers from the Nuvens and jeers from the Verdans. Ignoring both sides, he walked across the arena to where the Sankari had gathered and once more issued the call for confession. "I offer you life if you admit to the slaughter of innocent Nuvens and the massacre of the Defenders. Do you yield?"

Manor Stillinger rose and angrily shouted "No!" Aron calmly walked back to the center of the arena to await his next opponent. The Sankari fighters changed their strategies on the second day. The combatants circled each other cautiously looking for an advantage. It soon became apparent the Sankari were trying to sap Aron's stamina, hoping to make him lose his concentration so he would succumb to a killing blow.

Much to the dismay of the Sankari, Aron's determination only grew more intense with each opponent. His fatal thrusts seemed to become faster. The Defender refused to get into a physically taxing fight with each Sankari. He killed at his first opportunity. The second day ended as did the first day — five more Sankari fell to Aron's knives. The Defender killed all his foes with a final slash across the throat, tearing open their jugular veins in bloody streams.

After every kill, Aron honored his opponent on bended knee in silent prayer. Out of respect for their hero, the Nuven crowd fell silent until he arose from the body. When the fifth Sankari fell, Witt hammered the gong again, signaling the end of another day's successful duels. Aron seemed to be even more detached after the second day. He said nothing to Tarn as the Defenders escorted him out of the arena nor did he acknowledge the adoring Nuvens in the seats.

Manor Stillinger was seething on the morning of the duel's third day. He again furiously rejected Aron's call for a confession of guilt. "Is there no Sankari who can bring down this Nuven pagan?" he shouted as he paced back and forth in front of the remaining nine Sankari.

Looking up and down the line for Aron's next opponent, Manor fixed on a somber-looking man. Mistaking his cohort's expression for eagerness to face the Defender, the general called out, "Tomar Yanti, make us proud." Tomar winced as if he had been struck. The Sankari had been haunted by nightmares for the past two nights. He remembered that terrible night at Temple Darya when too many young Verdans and Nuvens were killed during the bloody battle.

Tomar tried to control his shaking. The Verdan's heart was pounding so hard, his chest hurt. It was painful to breathe. Tomar slowly walked out to face Aron, who waited for him in the center of the arena. The Verdan's hands were clammy and cold. He did not want to fight the Defender who was out to avenge the deaths of his people.

Aron watched with a detached curiosity as the Sankari approached. His opponent walked slowly and stiff-legged. He brandished no weapons. If he had not sworn to kill this Sankari and all of his kind, the Defender would have felt pity for the man. Tomar stopped within about ten paces. A look of abject terror was etched upon his face. The crowd was strangely quiet as both men faced each other.

Aron wondered if this was another Sankari trick, refusing to attack, forcing him to go on the offensive. The Defender unsheathed his knives and took a step toward Tomar. The Sankari's lips trembled, his eyes blinked furiously as Aron cautiously approached, but he made no move to defend himself.

Manor screamed from the crowd. "Tomar, defend yourself, man! Don't shame us. Kill the Defender!"

Aron approached to within an arm's reach of the Sankari and stopped. "Verdan, defend yourself. I am not a murderer."

The Sankari took a deep breath. "Neither am I, Defender." Tomar took a step back, flung his weapon belt to the ground and knelt before Aron. "As Mother Verde is my witness, my father forced my brother and I to join the Sankari. I did not want kill to your people," he whispered in a trembling voice. "I was there, but I shed no innocent blood. I beg for clemency. Yes, the Sankari killed children and slaughtered everyone at the temple."

Aron stared in wonder at Tomar. He had never expected a Sankari to willingly admit to those tragic events when the temple fell. The Sankari did not move or look up, but Aron could see the tears streaming down his face. "Arise, Verdan, you are the first honest Sankari I have met. I give you back your life if you announce your confession to them," Aron said, nodding toward the Verdan crowd.

The Sankari nodded. "I agree. It is time the truth is known." Aron watched as Tomar walked slowly toward the Verdan side of the stadium. He wondered if this would end the duels, end the killing. Suddenly a woman's voice screeched, "Captain, do your duty. This man is a traitor." Tomar stopped in his tracks. He was visibly shaking again. But when nothing happened, he continued walking.The voice called out again. "In the name of Verdan honor, I command you!"

Gerro, captain of the Tarylan guard, frowned at the order, initially refusing to carry it out. Clearly this man had confronted the Defender and begged for mercy. Now he was returning to his people. When Tanella shouted her second command, Gerro reluctantly ordered his archers to fire. His guts roiled as a covey of arrows slammed into Tomar's body. The surprised Sankari raised his hands, took a step, then crumpled to the ground, dead.

Aron stared in disbelief at the scene. A slow anger swept through him as he watched Tomar's body be dragged disrespectfully out of the arena. This Sankari, who could have added validity to the Defenders' cause, had been executed before he was allowed to speak. The Defender took his wrath out on the next four Sankari. Aron changed his tactics. He viciously attacked each opponent. Not worrying about defending himself, Aron suffered his first wounds but kept fighting as if he felt nothing. He left each foe a bloody mess on the floor of the arena and did not offer a prayer for those he had slain.

When Witt sounded the gong signaling the day's duel was finished, Aron refused to leave the arena. Covered in his own blood and that of the men he had just slain, Aron marched to where the surviving Sankari were seated, threw back his head and screamed out a primeval triumphant call, which rang throughout the arena. All the spectators, Nuven and Verdan, looked on in shocked silence as the Defender finally allowed himself to be led out of the stadium by Tarn and his circle.

31

The thunderous applause startled Aron as he marched into the arena for the next day's duels. Half of the spectators exploded with happy anticipation when the Nuvens spotted their hero. They stood waving colorful clan flags, shouting encouragement to Aron and hurled long-secret insults at the Verdans seated in the other half of the arena. The Verdans were grimly silent. Most were stunned beyond belief by the past three days' events. Aron Nels, self-proclaimed avenger of the Nuven Defenders, had killed fourteen of their honored Sankari. Poor Taffa Ganu had been executed after begging for clemency. Only four Sankari remained.

Aron strode across the arena and stood before the surviving Sankari, who were sitting somberly in the front row above the gate their comrades had entered before. "Fifteen of your fellow Sankari have died," Aron called loudly, without malice. "There has been enough death. I offer you life if you admit to the slaughter of innocent Nuvens and the massacre of the Defenders. Do you yield?"

As they had done previously, the four Sankari rose and clamored for the duels to continue, although they sounded much less fierce now. Shaking his head, Aron brandished his two dueling knives which gleamed brightly in the morning sun. "Let it be finished on this day. May your ancestors welcome you," he said and turned to take his position in the arena.

Manor Stillinger could not contain his frustration. "Do not insult us with your pagan Nuven beliefs," the Sankari leader shouted. "You will be begging for mercy by the end of this day." Aron shook his head and held up four fingers, indicating the number of Sankari left alive. The Nuven spectators rose in unison and shouted their approval.

Aron turned and strode calmly back to the spot where the next duel would begin. He did not want the Sankari to see the wear and tear his body had suffered after three days of duels. The Defender had numerous slashes all over his body where Sankari knives had managed to slip past his defenses. His body was bruised from various punches, kicks and head butts. Turning, he gestured toward the Sankari, indicating he was ready.

The arena grew eerily quiet as Aron's sixteenth opponent cautiously approached. The Sankari was stocky with graying curly hair. He swished his dueling knives through the air in frantic, jerky motions. Manor stared quietly as his comrade approached the hated Defender. The Sankari general had intently watched Aron fight every duel, hoping to pick out a tendency or weakness that could be exploited. However, Aron had changed his tactics with every opponent. Not once did he repeat the same fighting stance or position his knives the same way. Every Sankari who faced him had no idea what to expect from this durable fighter.

As if in a trance, Aron watched the Sankari approach. His opponent's muscles tightened and his nostrils flared as he grew near. He cut through the air in fast, angry slashing motions. Instinctively, the Defender braced for the head-on attack he knew was coming. His opponent did not disappoint him.

The Sankari grimaced and charged in an attempt to bowl him over. Aron waited until his foe was a few paces away, took a step then snapped his arm forward. The knife left his hand in a blur. It rotated only twice before sinking deeply into the Sankari's throat. With a gasp, the man gagged with surprise and clutched wildly at his neck. Blood gushed from the wound as he stumbled a few steps before falling, mortally wounded.

The Nuven crowd again erupted in a loud tribute as Aron extracted his knife and wiped the blood off on the Sankari's body. The shouting quickly turned into a lusty repeated chorus of "three, three, three." Aron's followers had delivered this chant after the death of every Sankari. After each of his victories, the crescendo rose and lasted longer, taunting the surviving enemy duelists.

Aron waved off the customary rest time and challenged the next opponent to battle. The seventeenth Sankari circled cautiously. Aron stared into his foe's eyes and saw what he suspected — fear. This Sankari moved defensively, not willing to commit himself in any sudden moves. Aron moved from side to side, slashing with his knives, probing the man's guard.

The Defender pressed his attack, making the Sankari frantically protect himself. Aron did this again and again. In a surprise move, he suddenly attacked the Sankari head on and appeared to fall backwards when his foe kicked him in a defensive move. For the first time since the duel challenge had begun, the Verdans rose, shouting their approval at seeing one of their champions knock the Defender down. Likewise, the Nuvens gasped in fear. Surprised at having the advantage, the Sankari lost his composure and leaped toward Aron in a desperate move to end the fight. Aron deftly rolled away and kicked the other duelist in the sternum. Dropping his knives, the Sankari fell to his knees, choking and clutching his chest, barely able to draw a breath. The man never recovered to see a shadow loom over him.

Aron's knife cleanly sliced across the throat of his foe. The Sankari's life ended abruptly as his life's blood gushed out onto the arena's sandy ground. The Verdans sat down with a collective groan. Many covered their faces in disbelief and held their hands over their ears as a raucous chorus of "two, two, two," cascaded from the Nuven section. Aron turned and signaled he would take his allowed rest this time. He headed toward his tent to take refreshment and catch his breath.

———

"It is up to us now," Manor said glowering at his fellow Sankari. "We dare not let our people down. He is tired. I can tell by the way he is walking."

Porfio Kazmis stared in disbelief at Manor. "He will kill us both General. Not one of us has been able to even wound him severely, he moves so quickly." Porfio shuddered.

Manor gripped the other man's shoulder tightly. He smiled to the Verdan crowd, many of whom were now shouting encouragement to the two Sankari. "Now is not the time to be a coward," he hissed. "This Defender can be killed, but we have to work together."

Porfio gasped. "How can we do that? The Defender will only fight one of us at a time."

Manor loosed his grip on Porfio's shoulder, this time giving him a genuine, reassuring pat on the back. "Let me worry about that. We can accomplish anything. Remember, we have their favor," he said, nodding toward the rows of nearby Seers who were staring intently at the surviving Sankari.

Porfio glanced at the women and shuddered again. He was not sure who he feared most, the Seers who could penetrate his thoughts or the Defender who most likely would kill him. Following where Porfio was looking, Manor gave them a nod of respect. "I have their blessing to carry out my plan," the general said. "They have offered the protection of the Tarylan guards. We will leave here alive." Manor smiled. "One of the young Seers told me she will grant you special favors if you help kill this damned Defender."

Porfio blinked with surprise. He heard his leader's words, but they barely made sense to him. The Sankari's heart was pounding so fiercely his chest ached. *What was it Manor had said?* he thought, trying to clear his mind. *Seers, favors, a plan to kill the Defender?*

Porfio took a deep breath, trying to calm himself. He couldn't help but steal another glance toward the Seers. A young Seer with long, recognizable fire-red hair sat serenely, smiling warmly at him. Their eyes locked in a long gaze. Porfio felt his fears ebbing away, replaced by another strong emotion — desire. For the first time in four days, he smiled. He nodded toward the young woman. She nodded in return and sensuously licked her lips.

"General, let's kill this Defender," Porfio said with new-found bravado. "I will follow your orders. Tell me your plan."

Manor smiled. "I knew you would cooperate. If you follow my instructions, we will leave here alive as heroes. The rewards will be many." The Sankari leader leaned close so only Porfio could hear and explained his plot.

———

Gerro, the captain of the Tarylan guards, could not squelch his suspicions when he saw Manor Stillinger conferring privately with the High Seer. Her smile broadened as the Sankari spoke hurriedly in a hushed tone. When he finished she nodded approvingly and let him return to where Porfio was sitting.

Turning toward Gerro, she beckoned him. "May I be of service High Seer?" he said bowing in respect. Tanella waved for him to sit next to her. He could tell her mood had brightened since her discussion with the Sankari leader. During the past three days, the High Seer's disposition had transformed from surprise to frustration to anger to shocked disbelief to horrific desperation. She now looked almost relaxed and confident again. "I have good news, Captain," she said with a half smile. "Hopefully this tragedy will soon be over." She gestured disgustedly toward the arena, where seventeen of her prized Sankari had fallen.

Gerro cocked his head and raised his eyebrows. "How so, High Seer?"

She flicked an impatient wave. "You don't need to know the details, Captain, but General Stillinger has devised an ingenious way to dispose of this heretic Defender."

Gerro shrugged. "It is strange he has waited for seventeen of his men to be killed before devising such a plan. I am dubious. The Defender fights with great skill and purpose."

Tanella frowned at him. "I am not asking your opinion of the situation. However, I am ordering you to support Manor's actions."

Gerro's eyes narrowed. "It is a duel between the Sankari and this Defender. It has nothing to do with the Tarylan Guards or myself. The Sankari will have to kill him or be killed according to the dueling code."

The High Seer angrily held up a finger to stop the discussion. "It is of utmost importance that this Defender be killed," she snarled. "How it is to be carried out may be contrary to the dueling code. That is where you and your men may be needed. I am ordering you to protect Manor and Porfio, if they are still alive after the duel. There may be some, ah, objections after the Defender is killed. They will need to be escorted quickly from the arena."

Gerro sat up straight as a rod. He could not believe what Tanella had just told him. "All combatants have sworn an oath to uphold the dueling code — it is the law," he said and rose to leave.

Tanella stood up, facing him. "You have your orders, Captain. Carry them out. Get our Sankari out of the arena safely. How the Defender dies is of no concern to you," she snarled waving him away with disgust.

Gerro walked away. He felt angry and confused. Throughout the duels the Tarylan captain had watched Aron Nels in admiration and a bit of awe. He was fascinated how the Defender changed his tactics with every opponent he faced. Gerro found himself studying Aron's movements. He felt his body trying to react the same as Aron during the fighting. The Defender fought honorably, killing his opponents sometimes so swiftly Gerro doubted they even felt much pain.

As captain of the Tarylan guards, Gerro had been involved in many duels and skirmishes. He had killed when necessary but never relished it. Oftentimes Gerro fought so instinctively, he barely remembered how he had finished his foes. At first this concerned him but with each fight it became easier to trust this strange talent.

After the first five Sankari had been slain, Gerro watched with great interest as Aron offered each day to stop the killing if the Sankari would agree to his truce and admit to being responsible for the Nuven wars. The Defender seemed sincere and genuinely disappointed when they stubbornly refused to comply.

What could this plan be? Gerro thought, shaking his head. He felt disgust at the idea of protecting the Sankari if they managed to kill the Defender, especially if they broke the dueling code. The more he thought about the consequences, the tighter his stomach felt. Gerro did not feel this anxious and upset before he fought his own duels.

"Why should I worry about this Defender?" he muttered to no one in particular as he paced beside the stadium wall. He had sworn to do the bidding of the Seers, to protect them. Yet what Tanella had just ordered him to do felt so wrong.

———

The rest period over, Aron walked to the middle of the arena and waved for his next opponent. While waiting for the Sankari, he felt a strange urge to look into the Verdan crowd. Most of them sat sullenly, glaring at him. Some shouted encouragement to Porfio, who was preparing for the duel.

His eyes fixed on one figure, a young man who was gazing intently at him. Even from a distance, Aron could tell there was no animosity in the Verdan. Upon further inspection, Aron was surprised to discover the onlooker wore a Tarylan guard uniform. Something about him was oddly familiar. When their eyes locked for a few seconds, Aron nodded. It just felt natural. In an unusual gesture, the Tarylan respectfully saluted.

Aron tore his gaze away from the young man and watched as his next opponent approached, walking with a swagger. Porfio felt emboldened by Manor's plot. If everything went according to plan, he might escape this dangerous situation with a minor wound or two. The Sankari attacked then danced away from the Defender's knives. He repeated this tactic again and again — attacking just enough to draw Aron's defenses, then backed away.

His opponent's methods felt wrong, but Aron kept his defenses up. He easily withstood Porfio's thrusts and parries but could not manage to reach the man who kept retreating. The Sankari circled cautiously, keeping his knives in the traditional ready position. He would then charge in for a quick clash of steel, then back away. Porfio continued this tactic as Aron slowly pursued him across the arena.

When he was within twenty paces of the gate, where the Sankari entered the arena, Porfio circled halfway and uncharacteristically rushed Aron, who easily repelled the onslaught and managed to slash his knife across the Sankari's ribs, drawing first blood. Wincing in pain, Porfio dropped his knives and fell to his knees. "Have mercy, Defender, I was forced to do this, I yield."

Caught by surprise, Aron stared at the Sankari who was now prostrating himself. His back to the wall, Aron did not see Manor quickly rise, position himself atop the wall and raise a javelin. Shouts from the Nuven section caught his attention. He managed a half turn before he was knocked over from behind. His back exploded in pain, the breath knocked out of him.

Aron sank to his knees. Gasping, he clutched his stomach and felt the javelin point barely protruding. Another emotion swept over him in a heartbeat, blocking the pain, clearing his mind — the rage. A movement caught his attention as the surrendering Sankari scrambled to his feet. Porfio cautiously inspected the wounded Defender. Smiling wickedly, he picked up one of his knives and approached Aron.

Porfio stopped abruptly, looking past the Defender. "No! The kill is mine," he shouted to Manor who approached from behind Aron with knives drawn, a wicked smile on his face. "I risked my life getting him to you, he nearly killed me."

Aron waited until Porfio was within three paces, took a determined breath, then reached behind him. In one quick, excruciating motion he pulled out the javelin, launched himself at the approaching Sankari and jabbed the weapon into Porfio's chest. The Sankari was dead before he hit the ground. Everyone in the arena stood in shock, an eerie silence fell over the stadium. Already growing light-headed as the blood rushed out of his gaping wounds, Aron struggled to his feet and turned to face a shocked Manor. Taking a halting step, he pointed toward the surviving Sankari.

He screamed "COWARD!" His voice echoed throughout the stadium. Aron raised the javelin but the throw never came. The weapon wavered in his hand and dropped harmlessly to the ground. His legs trembled from the exertion of standing, then they gave out. Aron tumbled to the ground that was soaked with his blood.

Manor stared at the fallen Defender for a moment, visibly shaken. As he moved towards Aron, both sides of the arena — Nuven and Verdan — exploded in an angry unified chant of "COWARD, COWARD!" Stunned, Manor looked questioningly at Tanella.

The High Seer angrily waved for him to finish the Defender. Gesturing toward Gerro, she shouted. "Captain, do your duty." Gerro nodded, grabbed his bow and hip quiver of arrows and leaped into the arena.

Aron was still conscious as he watched Manor approach. He was filled with an odd feeling of detachment. He had no regrets. Seventeen of the enemy who had slaughtered the inhabitants of Temple Darya had died at his hands. That would have to be enough.

The Defender could barely focus on the Sankari who stood over him with a raised knife. He wondered if he would feel the killing stroke. It never came. Aron heard a familiar thud. Manor gasped in pain and stumbled backwards. An arrow protruded from his neck. The Sankari sank to his knees. Aron's and Manor's eyes locked for a moment, then Manor toppled over dead.

32

Almost in a dream, Aron felt himself being picked up and held in a stranger's arms. He strained to see the face, finally recognizing the Tarylan he had seen earlier. "You killed him?" he whispered hoarsely.

Gerro nodded. "It was not right for an honorable warrior to die that way. You were stopped by treachery."

Aron beckoned Gerro to come closer. The Defender's eye lids fluttered as he fought to stay conscious. "Tell Thella . . ." He paused, fighting to say the words. Gerro leaned close to hear what the last Defender of Verde said with his final breath.

Hearing screams of anguish, Gerro looked up as Aron's family members and friends rushed over. He delicately handed the body to them and stepped away, feeling confused and sorrowful. One of the mourners cautiously approached Gerro. The older man's reddened eyes were filled with tears. He tried to speak but could only managed soft sobs. Gerro stood respectfully still, his head bowed.

"I am Witt. I was his circle steward," the other man finally managed to say, nodding to where Aron lay. "He spoke to you, what did . . ." Both men paused realizing they had met before when a Sankari was killed in the marketplace.

Gerro eyed the old man for another moment then continued. "He had a message for someone named Thella. Is she here?"

Witt looked surprised. "She is his aunt," he said, pointing to a tiny white-haired woman who was making her way to where the mourners had gathered. She moved quickly for someone of her advanced years. Two middle-aged men, who looked to be her sons, walked alongside her.

"Oh my dear boy," Thella said, shaking her head and wiping away tears when she reached the body. With help from her sons, she knelt to kiss Aron's cheek.

Witt made his way to Thella to tell her of the message. After being helped to her feet, she gestured for Gerro to approach. "Aron said something to you? A Tarylan?" Thella asked bluntly.

In spite of himself, Gerro smiled at her candor, nodding. He bent down so the old woman could hear. "The Defender said to tell Thella that Tevan is avenged." She nodded as her crystal blue eyes watered. Her sons sobbed. Witt turned away, tears dripped down his cheeks.

Reaching up, Thella pulled Gerro close, kissing him on the forehead. "Now both my dear boys are at peace. Thank you," she said and walked back to comfort the other mourners.

"Traitor!" A high-pitched scream snapped Gerro around. The Tarylan captain looked up to see a furious High Seer gesturing for him to join her. Her face was red with fury and contorted in a grimace. All the Seers stood frowning at him. Gerro crossed his arms and glared back at Tanella. Shaking his head, he turned his back on the woman who had controlled his life. "Guards, seize that traitor and bring him to the fortress!" Tanella shouted.

Gerro readied himself for a fight as twenty Tarylans leaped over the arena's walls. They ran to within ten paces of their Captain, did an about face and faced the Verdan crowd with javelins lowered. Another Tarylan officer rose to order his men to capture Gerro but stopped in mid sentence when he saw the Guards' defensive stance. He had no stomach for taking on Gerro and his elite unit. In stunned silence, the Seers rose and made their way back to the safety of their fortress.

"It appears you may be in trouble," Witt said, nodding toward the furious woman.

"I no longer am concerned about the Seers," Gerro shrugged. "I have done their bidding all my life. The Sankari were cowards and apparently murderers."

Witt gripped the Tarylan's shoulder. "Is it you they told me about? The son born from a disgraced Seer and unknown father."

Gerro nodded slowly, not knowing what to say.

The Steward beckoned Gerro closer. "You can find your mother in the Valley of the Heroes. She waits for you."

Gerro's eyes widened with surprise. He stared at the old man, not daring to believe. "The Nuven valley? Why should she be there? What about my father?" he demanded of the old man.

Witt allowed himself a sad smile. "If you are brave enough to find your mother, she will have all the answers for you." The steward of Circle Sankarikiller gazed one last time upon Aron. His euphoria after watching Aron defeat the remaining Sankari one by one was washed away in a flood of grief when the last survivor of his elite Defenders was slain by treachery.

Aron's Clan Nels kinsmen gently draped him across a giant shield. They hoisted his body above their shoulders and carried him out of the arena. No cheers or insults were heard. All the spectators — Nuven and Verdan — stood in respectful silence. Witt allowed himself to smile at the scene befitting a hero. The steward was feeling his age of more than 70 harvests as he slowly shuffled out of the arena.

Witt thought of a lonely Dira Lineu waiting to bear her child in the Valley of the Heroes, not unlike another young Seer twenty-some harvests ago. *With any luck, I may have enough stamina to make the trip*, he thought to himself. If the ancestors smiled on him, Witt hoped to have the honor of witnessing the birth of a grandchild.

Verinya curled up in a fetal position on her bed in the Valley of the Heroes and sobbed for hours. The Seer had watched Aron's duel unfold from the start. She saw everything. The tragic events unfolded through his eyes — each duel with its bloody ending.

The Protector, as she was now known by the valley people, watched with horror when Aron was fatally wounded. Verinya felt his spirit slowly ebb away as his blood gushed from his body. She watched with shocked amazement as the oncoming Sankari was killed. The Seer almost broke the trance as her body shook with grief, but Aron refused to die.

The Defender was trying to fix his gaze on a face. The young man had short red hair and golden eyes. That face! There was no mistaking who it was. Verinya gasped as the two men shared a few words then her vision blurred and faded to nothingness. Death severed Verinya's connection to her long-lost lover.

Shortly afterwards, Arynna eased down next to Verinya and embraced her, stroking her hair.

"I'm so sorry. I saw everything, too." After a long pause, Arynna looked at her mother. "Do you think they knew each other?"

Verinya offered a weak smile. "I don't know. It appears Gerro felt a connection. He will be told the truth if he finds his way to us."

———————

Aron opened his eyes and was surprised to find himself at the base of a large tree. It looked like the giant tree he loved to climb in his family's orchard. The Defender looked around for a moment, confused. He thought he had been in an arena. Many people had been shouting. He strained to remember, but the memory slipped away. *Something bad happened but what was it?* he thought.

Shaking his head, Aron looked up after hearing a giggle in the branches above him. A small hand reached down. A blond-haired boy with blue-green eyes laughed as he looked down. "Come on, Aron, it's safe. I won't let you fall. I've been waiting for you."

A young Aron grinned, clasped the hand and scrambled up the tree after Tevan.

REUNION

1

His father was dead.

Flyn Nels was so grief-stricken his throat tightened with every breath. Aron Nels, the fruit seller and hunter had been killed in a duel with the Sankari. "A duel? Father was a Defender? Impossible!" Flyn shouted at his family.

He stopped his protests when his mother and sisters fought through tears as they told him of the dramatic events that had unfolded over the past lunar. Now, close family and friends, their eyes red and faces frozen with somber expressions, gently led him to where Aron lay in one of Verde's ice caves.

With trepidation gripping his heart, Flyn strode ahead of his family. When he drew near the entrance to a small cavern, ten men rose as one and drew dueling knives. One of the strangers stepped forward to intercept the determined young man. He looked serious but curious as Flyn came nose to nose with him.

"Do you dare keep me from my father?" Flyn demanded, his voice choking with emotion.

"Are you the one called Flyn, son of Aron of Clan Nels?" the other asked respectfully. The stranger had addressed him in the old Nuven way, as his grandfather would have. Flyn nodded, but his eyes wandered to his father. Aron was lying on a block of ice that had been carved to look like a throne. Huge flags hung directly behind the body — the black and gold of Clan Nels and the sky blue and white of Clan Vonn, the family of Aron's mother. Flowers were everywhere — some partially covered Aron and others lay in bunches around the ice throne.

"Ah, the blue-green eyes of a Nuven Defender. Not many are blessed with that color. We share your sorrow and offer our knives as protection to you and your family as long as we draw breath." The man then bowed and stepped aside. "Make way for the family of Aron, son of Ural of Clan Nels," he announced. The other nine men sheathed their weapons, bowed and stepped back to give the family privacy.

Flyn stared at the ten strangers in disbelief for a moment, then approached his father. Aron was dressed as a hero. He lay peacefully in a silken gold robe with black swirls on the sleeves. His arms were crossed over his chest. His hands clasped two of the most dangerous-looking dueling knives Flyn had ever seen.

Kicking some of the flowers aside so he could reach the body, Flyn knelt over his father and stroked his close-cropped beard. Aron had refused to conform to the Verdan custom of shaving. He preferred the traditional Nuven look. Tears slowly filled Flyn's eyes and spilled down his cheeks. He had never been overly emotional even as a child. His father had teased him that was his mother's blood in him.

The events of the past two weeks swirled in his mind. Flyn and his circle had been hunting in a newly discovered valley, about five days away by glider. Two of his cousins had frantically searched for Flyn to tell him about the duel all the folk in Verde Valley were talking about. The young man and his friends had dropped everything and rushed back. Flyn and a few of his circle managed to cover the distance in three days, stopping only for a few hours' sleep. He had not believed his cousins at first. A duel with the Sankari. Not just one, but all of them.

Aron had told his family he had been badly wounded while serving as an archer during the Battle of Temple Darya, but he never had as much as a quarrel with anyone after that. Flyn accused his cousins of taking part in one of Aron's jokes to get him to come home, maybe for a surprise celebration. Their serious insistence finally convinced him.

This scene was not right for the father he knew. It was common for the people of the Nels and Vonn clans to easily live past one-hundred harvests. Yet his father had not reached half that mark. The funeral ceremony should have been a simple affair in one of the Nuven temples, followed by a feast in honor of the deceased's life.

It was beginning to make sense why hundreds of Nuven families were camped outside the entrance to the ice cave. The strange experience of walking through adoring masses to reach his father now made sense. The young man had been so intent upon finding his father, he paid little attention to the people who stood and broke into song as he and his family passed.

Another thought snagged his attention. Those strangers seemed familiar. Turning towards the one who spoke to him, Flyn gestured to the man. "Who are you and what do you have to do with my family?" he demanded.

The spokesman stepped forward and beckoned one of the others to follow. "I am Tarn, son of Raffin of Clan Nels," the first man said.

His companion stepped forward, his blue-green eyes flashed with good humor. "And I am Ryyter, son of Martik of Clan Vonn. We come from the Valley of the Heroes."

Flyn stood wide-eyed at the revelation. "Are you Defenders?" he whispered not believing what he had just heard. "I am of Clan Nels and Clan Vonn blood. Are we kinsmen?"

Tarn smiled. "We all have been raised to be Defenders of the clans." He paused, taking a long look at Flyn. "Yes, we are blood through your father."

"Who has sent you?" Flyn asked.

"We are here to repay a debt owed to Aron of Clan Nels," Ryyter explained. "Our Protector came to us many years ago because of him, and now she asks us to defend you at all costs. We will do so proudly because you are of Nuven blood."

Flyn's head was swimming from all the events and stories he had heard in the past few hours. His father was dead after fighting a blood duel with the Sankari, the Verdans who had become famous by killing the Defenders, the hunter heroes. Now ten strangers who said they were kin from the Valley of the Heroes, were here to protect his family. Protect them from who?

"I have many questions for all of you," Flyn said, looking at his family and then at the Nuven guards. "But we have a life to celebrate first," he said gazing proudly at his father. "From everything that has happened, it seems it will be a large event. Something my father would not have wanted.

"If you please, I would like to be alone with him," Flyn gestured toward everyone in the cold cavern. I did not get a chance to say goodbye. He was in the fruit groves when I left, gathering honey fruit. We laughed and tossed fruit at each other . . ." Flyn choked, putting a hand over his eyes.

Stazia hugged her son. "It has been a long journey for you. There is nothing you could have done to stop it," she said looking into Flyn's reddening eyes. "Your father was very determined when his Defender memories returned." Flyn looked at her and shook his head.

"We will tell you everything once you have eaten and rested," she said.

Stazia gazed at her mate for a moment. She lovingly ran her hand down a sleeve of Aron's fine robe and turned to lead the procession from the room, leaving Flyn to grieve in peace. The ten Defenders followed but stopped just beyond the doorway, standing guard.

———————

The next morning after first meal, Flyn's sisters insisted he see them first. Amaura and Lyllen surprised him by their serious demeanor. Their story of their father dying in the arms of Gerro, the infamous Tarylan warrior, stunned Flyn. "Father whispered something to that awful Tarylan. We didn't even hear his last words," Amaura said sobbing. The two sisters then looked at each other. Neither wanted to relate the next part.

"What is it?" Flyn asked, seeing both frown. "How much more incredible can this story be?"

"This Gerro, he . . ." Amaura groped for the right words. Noticing her brother's exasperated expression, she blurted, "He looks like you, Flyn, but has the Tarylan red hair."

Flyn shrugged. "I've been told I resemble many people. There are many Nels and Vonn families."

"You don't understand Flyn," blurted Lyllen, usually the shy one. "His voice, his expression, even the way he talked to others. It could have been you."

Flyn sat deep in thought, his fingers drummed on their family's wooden table. "How old is this Tarylan?" Flyn asked, looking intently at his sisters.

"At least 20 harvests," Amaura said. Lyllen nodded her agreement. The three siblings sat in silence, occasionally tearing off pieces of the fresh loaf of bread Stazia had made that morning.

"Have you talked to mother about this?" Flyn asked, unconsciously raising one eyebrow the same way Aron would have done. "Did father tell her anything about this?"

"Mother only says she will tell us when she thinks we are ready," Amaura said.

Flyn looked at his sisters. "I think it's time we talk to her."

2

High Seer Tanella still fumed over events of the past few weeks. The crowds had jeered and yelled insults at them after the duel. The women practically had been chased back to their sanctuary.

"How dare they!" Tanella screamed, pounding her fist on the dark walnut banquet table lined with the Council of Twenty. "After all we've done for them. Our mothers and grandmothers and their grandmothers have spent their entire lives protecting these ungrateful scags. And that traitor, Gerro. He has escaped!"

The High Seer's cheeks were flushed with anger. Her long red braid flung around her head like a snake jumping at its prey. The Seers' guards had managed to disperse the people who had followed them to their fortress. It soon became clear the guards would do whatever it took to protect the Seers, whether it meant knocking people down or using clubs to keep them from advancing on the fortress founded by the sainted one, Taryl Bryann, Verde Grande's first Seer.

"Bring me the Verdan leaders," Tanella ordered the newly appointed officer of her personal guard. "Perhaps they will exhibit more gratitude after we show them how many attacks we have thwarted over the centuries."

Cara, an elder Seer, shook her head. "I fear the populace has grown sympathetic to the Nuvens. The outsiders have been among us too long. They have become intertwined in our society. Remember, we tried to eliminate their leaders, their temples and their Defenders, but the Nuvens have returned even stronger."

Tanella threw up her arms in frustration and paced around the room. Her actions unsettled the other women. The High

Seer was normally a serene and somber woman who demonstrated great patience in most situations, whether it was addressing the challenge of a new Tanlian attack or giving lessons to the young Seers-in-training.

The Seers were interrupted by a knock on the council room door. A lieutenant of the guard stepped quietly into the room and waited to be acknowledged. "What is it? I ordered no disturbances unless it was an emergency." Tanella glared at the young man.

"Pardon the intrusion, High Seer, but Seer Lenar demanded that I give you this message," he said.

Lenar? She is in charge of the watchers, Tanella thought. "Give me the message." The lieutenant handed her a small tube, bowed and quickly left the room. The High Seer read the note, frowning. Glancing up, she saw twenty pairs of eyes fastened upon her. "Lenar reports another Tanlian flyover, but there was no attack in the Valley of the Hunters. This is the third season the Tanlians have scouted but done nothing, very unlike them. Our watcher Seers have masked us. The Nuvens have not been attacked either, very strange."

Cara chuckled. "It almost looks as if the others are being protected, too." Tanella frowned at the older woman. She found nothing amusing about any mysterious protection of the hunters. "The Tanlians know there are people here. They will only grow more persistent and may find some of our settlements by pure luck." Tanella sat down forcefully in her seat at the head of the table and put her head in her hands. "Tanlians and ungrateful Verdans. Is something haunting us?"

Shrugging, Cara rose. "It is time for second meal. I, for one, always think better on a full stomach. Everything seems to be handled for the moment. The Tanlians have flown away, and our people have returned to their homes." Tanella looked up to see the other Seer smiling at her, waiting for the High Seer's permission to dine. After a wave of her hand, the women quickly left the table, discussing the recent events in hushed tones.

The High Seer hated to admit it, but Cara was right. She was comforted by the meal of roast lamb, sweet fruit, freshly baked bread and several kinds of the finest Verdan wines. The dark mood among the High Council members had been replaced by laughter and happy chatter. Tanella even looked at the bright side in what happened — the Tanlians, those persistent marauders from space, apparently had left, and the Verdan populace had quieted down and left the Seers in peace.

"That was a fine meal," she told the cook, who accepted the uncharacteristic compliment with an embarrassed smile. "Let's hear some good news. Cara, tell us how many fine young women have been accepted as Seers-in-training." A hush fell over the room as if all the Seers were holding their breath at once. Sensing something amiss, Tanella leaned forward with her chin on folded hands and stared at the older Seer.

"We do not have an accurate number, High Seer," Cara answered softly. "We are still evaluating some candidates. The ones we have chosen do look promising, though."

Tanella was no longer smiling. "How many have you found with the gift?" she asked, staring intently at Cara.

"So far, only ten," the older Seer answered. "We are looking at eight others, but they may be too young yet."

"Ten? From all the Verdan cities?" Tanella asked incredulously. "And when were you going to tell me this good news? Last harvest, there were only sixteen new disciples and the year before that nineteen."

Cara shrugged. "I did not want to bother you with another problem until we had determined an accurate number. I cannot answer why there are fewer young Seers each year. Many babies are born to families of Tarylan blood every harvest and at least half are girls, as expected."

Tanella glared at Cara, but knew the old woman was not frightened of her and refused to be bullied. The High Seer begrudgingly appreciated someone who would give her honest answers. "Do we need to encourage interfamily matings again?"

Cara shook her head. "Five generations ago, our Seers found their numbers dwindling much like what we are seeing now," Cara recalled. "The cousin to cousin matings produced more women with the gift, but they were sadly deficient in other areas. It took them almost two generations to correct those problems."

Tanella sighed. "We need more Seers for the growing population. More valleys are being settled every year. We are the only protection against the Tanlians."

"I heartily agree, High Seer," Cara said. "I have our historians reading many of the diaries of the first ones. Perhaps we will find an answer to our problem. We still have several hundred young women in watcher meditation."

Tanella nodded. "But who will replace them in another thirty harvests?" The High Seer rose and quickly left the table. Her stomach was churning, she needed a refreshing walk in the cool night air to calm herself.

3

The Council of Nobles on Betel 4 were stunned by what they had just heard from the defiant young woman standing before them. Contact an Earth colony for help? Break the Tanlian yoke over space travel? Her words were almost heresy, although many of the nobles had secretly wished for the very thing she proposed — just not publicly. If the Tanlians found out, the troublemakers would disappear and the planet's taxes could well be doubled.

"Do you know what you are proposing?" Erryl Masveld asked the speaker. "Have you considered the ramifications to our people?"

Willa Sydriker smiled and nodded. "Freedom from harm at the hands of those Tanlian animals? Freedom to travel freely and trade with whom we choose? Freedom to keep all our products for ourselves?"

Erryl shook his head. "I know it seems unfair to a youngster such as yourself, but this system has kept our people safe for centuries now," he said trying to soothe her. "No Betelan women have been kidnapped from their homes since we agreed to the treaty." Willa was not to be consoled. Even as a young girl, she had been furious as the arrogant Tanlians visited every year demanding more and more tribute from the planet — taking anything they could carry in their ships, except for the people.

Tanlian evaluators would travel through Betel's cities and countryside, dutifully noting any wealth or production they could siphon from the planet. Women were not kidnapped, but the intruders had no qualms about grabbing any female with whom they wished to take their pleasure. Betelan authorities were helpless to do anything for fear of Tanlian reprisal.

Willa's outrage had exploded and then taken focus after her younger sister, Branae, was taken screaming out of a bakery by Tanlians. She tried to fight them off. The poor girl was no match for her attackers. She was beaten and raped.

Willa blamed herself. She had left her 15-year-old sibling to buy pastries while she walked down to Middle River to watch a festival with musicians and craftsmen. When she returned to look for Branae, the sympathetic baker told her what had happened. She frantically tried to look for her sister, but the Tanlians had sped away with her in one of their fast ground vehicles. It had been six lunars and poor Branae still cried herself to sleep, refusing to leave the family home and barely talking to anyone.

"We are very sympathetic to what happened to your sister and have lodged a complaint with the Tanlian High Council," Erryl said. "But we have no other recourse. Remember my dear, others over the years have tried to do the very thing you propose and have been tortured and killed for their troubles."

Willa was not to be denied. "Others tried to fight the Tanlians on their own — attack small groups and their landers, holding them hostage. But, the Tanlians have no qualms about killing their own people along with ours. We need help from other colonies."

The tall woman shook her fist when she spoke. Her four blonde braids whipped around her face as she strode back and forth in the small, secluded amphitheater. "How many more daughters and sisters have to be taken for those beasts' sport?" she shouted. "Are we content to let the Tanlians take our best goods at their whims? Are we always going to be cows to these masters?"

Willa had pricked the nobles' pride and she knew it. "My father tells me we are descended from proud warriors who led the fight against Earth tyranny three hundred harvests ago. What would those warriors think of their grandsons?" The nobles were silent. A few glared at Willa, but many looked down in shame.

"What would you have us do? We have no ships to send for help," Erryl snapped.

"All I wish from you honorable nobles is your blessing," Willa said solemnly. "I have fifty young warriors ready to take action. If we fail, we die. If we succeed, you must be willing to support us."

An old man slowly rose from his seat. The others turned to look at this noble who seldom spoke. "I, too, have grown weary from these Tanlian intrusions upon our people. If this young woman is determined to give her life for Betel 4 then I support her."

One by one, all 35 of the nobles stood in support. "It seems we are in agreement," Erryl said surveying the room. "You have our blessing Willa Sydriker. How may we help?"

Bror Hepdogan could not believe his luck. A group of beautiful young Betelan women stood giggling before him. A tall blonde had just shyly asked him if her dance troupe could ride along in his cargo flier to visit the orbiting Tanlian transport ship. The dancers said they wanted to see what their world looked like from space.

Trying to act nonchalant, Bror asked the women to wait while he sought permission from the captain. Willa turned and smiled at her companions. The Tanlian pilot looked to be about their age. The women could sense his excitement. Bror returned shortly. "Permission has been granted for a visit," he announced officially. "How many of our Betelan, uh, guests will be joining us?"

Willa blinked her light blue eyes innocently. "It would be so kind of you to take our whole troupe, but I'm afraid there may be too many of us for your little ship."

Even more women than what he saw before him? Bror's eyes bulged with excitement. "You would be surprised how much my ship can accommodate. How many are in your fine troupe?"

Willa smiled. "Oh we have fifty or so, but that might be taking advantage of your generosity."

The young Tanlian gulped at the collection of beauties standing before him, all sweetly smiling. "Welcome aboard," Bror said, clearing his throat. "Find seating where you can, we will leave in less than an hour."

As the flier neared the Tanlian mother ship, Willa sidled up to Bror. "Will we have the honor of meeting all of the crew?"

Bror laughed. "Most of the crew is on the surface, enjoying your world's attractions. I'm afraid only 30 of my shipmates are on board."

"Thirty?" Willa said trying to stifle a smile. "I hope we won't be a distraction."

The pilot nodded. "It will be a most pleasant distraction I'm sure." Willa returned to her seat, her eyes gleaming like a predator about to pounce on wounded prey. While undergoing weapons and self-defense training in secret, she had read the diary of Ismala N'pofu. The woman single-handedly had taken over a Tanlian ship and coerced the crew to fly her home from an ill-fated mission on XR-309 several hundred harvests ago.

If one woman could accomplish this, just think what fifty inspired female warriors could do, she thought.

The flier docked smoothly. Bror walked into where the women were seated and offered to lead them to the mother ship. Willa smiled and took his arm as the hatch opened, revealing about twenty leering Tanlians.

"You have arranged escorts for us. How polite of you, Captain," she exaggerated and noticed his chest swelling with pride. Each of the Tanlians eagerly accepted the arms of two women and gave the curious visitors a tour of the ship. Upon reaching the bridge, Willa gasped with faked surprise. "Is this all that it takes to operate the ship?" she asked, looking at the six men at the control panels.

Bror nodded. "Only six at one shift on the bridge. We always keep about thirty to maintain the ship."

Willa smiled. In her tiny ear device, all her warriors had reported they had reached their destinations in the ship. She watched as six of her companions glided over to watch the men working at the controls. She coyly wrapped her arm around Bror's arm and touched off a signal. Almost as one, the Betelan women attacked their Tanlian escorts. Arms were broken, wrists cracked, eyes gouged, whatever it took to drop their victims to their knees. Sharp knives pressed against Tanlian throats.

Bror shuddered in pain, unable to speak. Willa had twisted his arm violently, forcing him to the floor. She waited and smiled as all the Betelan warriors reported success. Willa had memorized this section from Ismala's diary which described how the woman had taken over that Tanlian ship. And now the young warrior from Betel 4 was going to write her own chapter.

"Tanlian, you can choose life or a rather messy death. My companions and I have taken a blood oath to capture this ship or die trying," she told the gasping officer. "If you choose life, you will take us to Kenyatta. What they will do with you will be up to them, but you will continue breathing at least on the trip."

As Willa spoke, knives on all the Tanlian throats twitched slightly, drawing blood. "What is your answer?"

Bror was on his knees. He could not move from Willa's hold, his arm throbbed in excruciating pain and it felt like the knife was slowly cutting into his flesh. Looking at the terrified bridge crew, he had no choice. "We will take you," he choked. Turning to the communicist, who was trembling from a knife also at his throat, Willa ordered him to send the following message to Betel Central Command. "The performance is completed."

On Betel 4, Erryl Masveld heard Willa's signal and took a deep breath. Turning on his communicator, he gave the order. "Commence with Operation Cleansing." Then he whispered, "May the One have mercy upon us."

Dozens of Betelan warriors descended upon every Tanlian on the planet. When the general populace learned the foreigners were no longer protected, many joined the bloody fray. Most of the Tanlians were killed outright as they were eating, drinking or sleeping with women. The few who lived through the initial capture were tortured for the crimes they and generations of their people had committed. No trace of any of them would ever be found.

The Kenyattans were the only world in the Galaxy Exploration and Minerals Syndicate who were allowed to have their own space fleet. The Tanlians strictly forbáde any vehicle but their ships to carry weapons. The Kenyattan fliers were strictly transport ships that traveled occasionally to the other GEMS worlds.

As Willa's commandeered ship entered Kenyatta's orbit, it was hailed by a native vessel. Not wanting to reveal this was a captured ship, the Betel warrior ordered the communicist to politely invite the other captain and his entourage on board.

A graceful woman with a caramel complexion walked out of the hatch first. A few flecks of white were scattered through her dark brown hair. Both women blinked in surprise at seeing another female. "Kenyattan?" Willa asked suspiciously. A dozen of her Betelan warriors crouched on either side of the entryway, energy pulsers at the ready.

"A woman on a Tanlian ship? You don't appear to be a sex slave," the other said calmly while eyeing the armed Betelans. "Did you escape from your masters?"

Willa laughed and quickly told the Kenyattan about their armed takeover of the Tanlian ship and of her planet's revolt. She then invoked the secret name. "We pay homage to the sainted hero, Ismala N'pofu. We seek assistance from our GEMS allies."

The Kenyattan studied Willa and then bowed. "I am Sula Gallgos, captain of Kenyatta 27. If you are telling the truth young Betelan and dared to attack the Tanlians, you are an honored but dangerous guest."

Willa returned the bow. "I invite you to tour the ship and see for yourself. We could use your crew's expertise to travel to Sirius 7. I don't trust these Tanlians to get us there."

Sula stared at the other woman in disbelief. "You wish to contact a colony of the Colonization Alliance of Independent Nations? Why do you seek assistance from CAIN?"

Willa paused, not knowing how to phrase the answer without angering the proud Kenyattan captain. "Earth and its colony worlds have been fighting the Tanlians for centuries. They have warships. They may be eager to gain an advantage."

Sula nodded. "I cannot argue your point, Betelan. I believe the CAIN worlds will be impressed that we are finally fighting the Tanlians. In fact, you may discover this for yourself shortly. It is obvious you are brave. If you are patient, you soon may have answers to your questions."

Willa stared at the other woman. "Would you care to explain?"

"It must be fate or the stars have aligned in our favor," Sula laughed. "About a year and a half ago, one of our transport ships was 'accidentally' intercepted by a CAIN ship. They proved remarkably sympathetic to our plight with the Tanlians. It seems they have grown weary of defending their worlds against our common foe."

Now Willa was wide-eyed with excitement. "They are willing to help us? All the CAIN worlds? What did you mean when you said I will have my answers soon?

Sula grinned. "So many questions from such a young warrior." Then she laughed at the other woman's exasperated look. "We expect special visitors in about two lunars. That's why my ship was on patrol to intercept any Tanlians. We could not allow those parasites to interfere with our plans."

Willa looked puzzled. "Could not allow them to interfere?" she repeated. "How could you have stopped them?"

Sula gestured towards her ship. "A CAIN captain gave us some weapons as a token of goodwill. Any Tanlian ship would have gotten an unwelcome surprise. In fact, we almost were prepared to attack this ship before your signal aroused our curiosity."

Willa could not believe her good fortune. The people she was going to plead her case to — the consortium — were en route to this world. Would their distant cousins help Betel 4, too?

Sula studied the young woman's somber expression, "What troubles you, hero of Betel 4?""

Willa blushed.

"I imagine our new CAIN allies will be very impressed that you captured this Tanlian crew and flew here with the blessing of your planet's elders," Sula assured her. "This is the proof CAIN wants to ensure their assistance. They want to win back the GEMS worlds one planet at a time. I am positive they will not turn down help from an aggressive young warrior willing to fight for her planet."

Sula paused, smiling. "I for one would be proud to assist you. The more ships we can garner into a fleet the more effective we will be. I would be honored to serve with you. We Kenyattans have been waiting for another Ismala N'pofu to lead us against the Tanlians. I think I stand before her now."

4

Flyn tried to sweep the image of his father dying in the arms of Gerro from his thoughts but he could not. Even through the magnificent funeral celebration, he kept seeing Aron wasting his last words on that Tarylan Guard. *Why?* The question screamed in his brain even as Aron's body was carried carefully from the ice caves to the ridge where the pyre had been built.

All along the route, mourners — Nuvens and Verdans — tossed flowers along the path to show their respect. Many were Aron's favorite — the delicate azul trumpets. Aron's son was amazed at the numbers of people who came to watch the procession. At times, the crowd was four or five people deep, all were respectfully silent. The people followed the stretcher-bearers as they passed with the body. Clan Nels and Clan Vonn Defenders from the Valley of the Heroes walked beside the stretcher as an honor guard.

Flyn was in a state of shock during the many speeches extolling the bravery and kindness of his father. He scanned the crowd for Gerro, but the warrior was not among the mourners. The absence of the last man to speak to his father alive ignited a fire of anger in Flyn he had never felt before. How dare that Tarylan not pay his respects.

With the speeches finally completed, Flyn had the grim but traditional duty to light the pyre. He knelt before the huge pile of kindling upon which his father had been laid. He said a prayer, asking their ancestors to welcome Aron. Flyn took a trembling breath, looked at the tear-stained faces of his mother and sisters and touched the torch to the pyre. As the fire blazed and rushed up the wood, Flyn made a silent vow to find Gerro.

He had too many questions. The Tarylan was the only one who could answer them.

As the mourners passed by expressing their condolences, Flyn stopped Troz Dalkan, the governor of Verde Valley. "How may I assist you?" Troz said, surprised but honored to be singled out.

Flyn was abrupt, he had no time for niceties. "I wish to find Gerro, the Tarylan captain. I understand he spoke to my father before he died."

Troz nodded sympathetically. "Yes, I saw that; very unusual. I am told Gerro and his men have passed through the Verdan Gate and are traveling to the Valley of the Hunters."

Flyn scowled. "Do you mean the Valley of the Heroes, where my ancestors came from?"

The governor bowed. "I meant no insult, young Nels. Yes, that is where Gerro's party is headed."

Seeing Flyn's startled look, Troz shook his head as if to answer the unspoken question. "No, I do not know why they travel there. We are unaware of any connection Gerro and his warriors might have to your people."

Tarn of Clan Nels, one of the Defenders sent to protect Aron's family, stepped forward. He had heard their conversation. "If this warrior goes hunting our people, he and his men will be killed very quickly. Our fellow Nuvens have no patience for dangerous intruders," he said with a shrug as both men stared at him.

Ryyter of Clan Vonn apologized for intruding. "Flyn, our people are very familiar with the route to our valley. We could travel quickly and possibly overtake this Tarylan before harm comes to him before his time."

Flyn nodded and smiled at Ryyter's suggestion. "I always wanted to see where my ancestors came from. I need to find this Tarylan. My father felt it was important to speak to him. I want to know why."

Tarn and Ryyter exchanged quick glances. "We can leave at first light," Tarn offered. "The other Defenders will be proud to accompany you."

Malik Klinfer, who had been standing nearby, also offered his help. "I was watching when your father died. I too, want to know about the Tarylan."

Flyn reached out and slapped Malik's shoulder. "I would have it no other way. My father said you were the best he had ever hunted with."

Malik smiled at the compliment. "Do you think these Nuvens can keep up with us?" he asked with a half smirk.

Tarn glowered at Malik's audacity, but Ryyter just chuckled. "We shall see who can scramble over rocks the fastest. So, you are a hunter? You may be useful to us. There are many small rodents which can be caught for our stew pots." Malik stepped close to Ryyter, almost nose to nose. Both men stared at each other fiercely then, almost in unison, roared with good-natured laughter.

"We leave at first light then," Flyn announced. He turned and was surprised to see his mother, sisters and other relatives listening to the conversation. Stazia hugged Flyn and whispered: "We will pray to our ancestors and ask Mother Verde to protect you. Please come back to me my son."

———

Verinya looked proudly at her daughter. The younger Seer had easily manipulated the Tanlian navigator into seeing "nothing" on his scans of their valley. "They are gone for now mother," Arynna looked at her mother and smiled. "It was not difficult to convince him the search was fruitless. Is it always so?"

The older Seer shook her head. "Most Seers struggle at this task. It is difficult for them to change what the host is seeing and convince him otherwise. Your gift seems to be very powerful, my dear."

Arynna's eyes sparkled. "Even better than the other Seers across the mountain?"

Verinya smiled. "Perhaps better than many of them but not as powerful as the Elder Seers. The elders have been "watching" for many harvests. They can use the sight at will."

Verinya hid nothing from her daughter. She had told Arynna about Aron and also tearfully related how she escaped from the Seers but could only take one of the twins with her.

"You spoke of the other Seers," Verinya said. "I have been watching them for many harvests now, usually through their guards. Lately I have seen through the younger women, their sight is not very strong, they can't detect me."

Before Verinya could continue, tears filled her eyes as she gazed at her lovely daughter. Arynna bore one of the classic marks of the Verdan Seers — beautiful flame-red hair. However, her eyes were golden like her brother's, and her face was a haunting reminder of Aron, especially when she smiled or laughed.

"The other Seers have accomplished a terrible task," Verinya said slowly, trying to regain her composure. "They have overseen the extermination of all those brave Defenders. Your father gave such a heroic fight!"

A somber Arynna sat before her mother. She had never met Aron, but Verinya had told her so much about him. "Your brother was so gentle with Aron when he died," Verinya said in a quavering voice. She put her head in her hands at the sad memory. "Then Gerro refused to join the Seers after the duel. It's unusual."

Arynna sat very still and stared thoughtfully, but she was not focusing on anything in the room. For years she had watched her brother as he grew up. He had a difficult childhood. The other children teased him and called him names because of his questionable parentage. The taunts finally stopped when Gerro proved himself to be physically superior to his peers. His even temperament won him many allies. He was the youngest man ever to be named captain of the Tarylan Guards.

The younger Seer calmed herself and thought of her brother, hoping to connect with him. Verinya reached out to jostle

Arynna but stopped when she saw her daughter had gone into the sight meditation. At 20 harvests, Arynna was no longer a child and possessed a powerful gift of the sight which almost made Verinya jealous. The love for her daughter was much more powerful than any feeling of pettiness.

Verinya sat quietly while Arynna stayed focused. After almost a half hour, the younger Seer let out a deep breath and looked around the room. "Gerro and his men are coming," Arynna said matter-of-factly. "They have passed through the last Verdian gate and are making their way here."

This time it was Verinya's turn to gasp. "I never dreamed Gerro would travel here," she said stunned, almost missing her chair while sitting down. "Is he marching here to kill?" she looked fearfully at her daughter.

Arynna shook her head. "I cannot tell Mother. He does not seem angry, just determined. He and his men have weapons, but they are traveling light and moving swiftly."

Verinya clasped her hands over cheeks and rocked slowly back and forth in her chair. She, too, had followed Gerro as he grew up but never dreamed she would ever see her son again. Verinya gave her daughter a questioning look. "He is bringing men with him? The Seers cast him out. Who dares to follow him?"

Arynna smiled. "Twenty of his elite guard. They are the ones who protected him in the arena after he killed the last Sankari. They have pledged their loyalty to him." Arynna's expression changed to a frown. "Mother, another is preparing to come. My other brother, Flyn. He wants to follow Gerro. The Defenders you sent to help are with him."

Verinya stared in disbelief. Two of Aron's sons were on their way to the Valley of the Heroes. That other woman's son. That carefree hunter, who was liked by many, was pursuing Gerro. But why? As far as she knew, the half brothers had never met. Why would Flyn be pursuing Gerro?

Seeing her mother's concern, Arynna sat at her feet. "I do not know why they are traveling here, Mother. I suggest we prepare to welcome them and keep them apart if possible. Both are likely to be full of questions."

Verinya nodded. "Inform our Defenders that guests are on their way. Request that no harm come to either before we see them."

"What will happen if Flyn catches Gerro?" Arynna asked, hoping not to hear the answer she feared.

"May the ancestors protect them from each other," Verinya said holding up her hands in frustration. "Gerro is a trained warrior and Flyn is not. I fear the outcome would be bloody."

5

The CAIN space fleet approached Kenyatta with caution. The captains were wary of being ambushed by Tanlians. For almost three centuries, all of CAIN's colonies had been terrorized by Tanlian attacks. Each colony had a small defense force, but the Tanlians proved adept at slipping past to conduct their grisly business of kidnapping and pillaging.

After years of arguing over a solution, the colonies unanimously voted to develop a new generation of warships — smaller, faster vessels rather than the behemoths used in defensive orbits — to go on the offensive. It was agreed to send this fleet into GEMS-controlled space in hopes of destroying as many Tanlian vessels as possible. The colonies hoped to force their enemy to finally sue for peace.

Shim Murra stood on the bridge and double checked the scans of this GEMS world. The CAIN admiral wanted to be positive it was safe for his fleet. The captain of the vessel stood close by awaiting his orders. The young officer's intense dark eyes gazed at his superior officer, awaiting the order to push on to the planet.

Looking up at the taller man, Shim met the other officer's gaze for a moment and nodded. "We've been waiting for this moment for a long time haven't we, Captain Nandez? Order the first wave into orbit. Let's see if this GEMS world is serious about being free of the Tanlians."

"Yes, admiral," Jorn Nandez saluted. He relayed the order for the other five vessels of wave one to follow his ship into orbit. Jorn had been the first CAIN officer to volunteer for this duty. For years he had heard stories of how his ancestor, Hector

Nandez, had been ambushed and killed by Tanlians on a mission to colonize the far-off planet, XR-309.

Almost no one in CAIN officialdom remembered the planet's christened name — Verde Grande. At that time his family had been heavily involved in the discovery, bioforming and attempted settling of the planet, only to have it plucked away from them and turned over to the syndicate.

When a CAIN ship intercepted that Kenyattan vessel a year and a half ago, the GEMS scientists on board the vessel could find no record of Verde Grande. Jorn wanted to know what had happened to the planet. Was it unsettled? If so, why? He hoped to get his answers very soon.

First contact with the GEMS vessel had been a surprising success. The Kenyattans, whose ancestors had fought so bitterly to break away from Earth control, were ecstatic at re-establishing contact. They had answered every question the CAIN officers asked and offered even more information. The Kenyattan officers had a surprising knowledge of the Tanlian flight routes, schedules when the plunderers visited the other GEMS worlds and what they carried away as cargo. It seemed the Tanlians had turned into mercenary commercial shippers in their dealings with the syndicate planets.

In a show of etiquette, Shim hailed a lone Kenyattan vessel, asking for permission to orbit their world. A woman's voice quickly answered. "Greeting's Admiral Murra, I am Sula Gallgos, captain of Kenyatta 27. I have permission of the Elder Council to welcome you to Kenyatta as honored guests."

6

Shortly after landing on Kenyatta, Sula introduced Jorn Nandez and Shim Murra to Willa. The CAIN officers were impressed with Betelan woman's story. Willa seemed sincere. Sensing the officers' hesitance, Sula escorted them to a detention area, which housed the captured Tanlians. The admiral raised his eyebrows, not containing his surprise. Jorn studied both women intently, a smile slowly forming.

Tanlians? That almost made the long trip to Kenyatta worthwhile. To gaze upon their longtime enemy was too tempting of an opportunity. Maybe they could interrogate what was left of the crew and glean some information from them.

"We most certainly welcome the chance to meet these Tanlians," Shim said, glancing at his intense young captain, who nodded eagerly. "We are impressed with your courage, Willa. You have accomplished something CAIN captains have been unable to do for years — apprehend a Tanlian ship and capture its crew."

Willa smiled proudly. She appreciated his directness. "Thank you, Admiral. The Tanlians had grown complacent after having their way with our world and its citizens for centuries. They did not expect a threat from Betelans, especially females."

Shim smiled. "We Earthlings learned long, long ago not to underestimate a determined woman."

"A wise people," Sula said rising. "You seem very interested to talk with our 'guests.' The Tanlians we captured are not the fearsome warriors of folklore. None of them have been in battle. Come this way."

The Tanlians stared wide-eyed at the two men dressed in strange military attire who were looking them over. This crew

229

had never raided a CAIN colony. "These are the fearless raiders who have terrorized us for so long?" Jorn said, surprised at seeing the frightened young men. "This sorry-looking group looks like it would have trouble with children."

Shim agreed. "It appears these docile fellows are not the same ones we are seeking. I suspect the raiders we hunt would not be that different from our own soldiers."

Sula stepped forward. "We have questioned them at length, Admiral. I'm afraid these are not your raiders. They have never veered from their tribute routes. Our interrogation was thorough, Captain," she said after seeing Jorn's skeptical look. "We lost two uncooperative men during our questioning. The others were very helpful after seeing their comrades die unpleasantly."

Jorn nodded. "I can see why the survivors look frightened. Will they be of help to us?"

Sula grinned. "If you consider how many Tanlian ships are flying what routes, the times they are scheduled to visit GEMS planets and when they are expected to return to Tantalum 2 as valuable information, yes, I would say they have been most helpful."

Shim turned to the Kenyattan captain. "Most thorough indeed. I would be very interested in hearing these details if you would be so kind. This could be the opportunity both our peoples have hoped to find for so long."

At Shim's request, one of the Tanlian officers was brought forward to meet him. "This is Lieutenant Xang, the former communicist," Sula said. "He has served as the Tanlian spokesman. After a little convincing, he has been quite cooperative."

"Xang, eh?" Shim barked to get the officer's attention. Xang jumped at hearing his name in a foreign tongue and stared at the admiral. "Are you the only officer left among your shipmates?" he asked. Xang stared at the floor, not understanding what was being said to him.

Willa stepped forward. "He does not understand, Admiral. The Tanlians have developed their own language. They forced many on GEMS worlds to learn their speech so we could do business with them. With your permission, I will translate."

The admiral gestured his approval. Willa addressed Xang in what sounded like a series of growls and gibberish to Shim and Jorn. It sounded nothing like the universal Angle used by the CAIN colonies. After she finished speaking, Xang stared at Shim and Jorn not masking his fear. The officers looked at each other with a smile when he uttered one recognizable word — "CAIN?"

Jorn stepped closer to Xang. He towered over the much shorter Tanlian. "Yes, Tanlian, CAIN men!" he shouted "We are here to free all the colony worlds from you Tanlian parasites." Willa translated for Xang. The communicist who already was visibly shaken, turned pale and continued staring at the floor.

"Well, now that you have frightened him to the core, Captain, this Tanlian may faint before he can answer any of our questions," Shim said.

Sula chuckled. "Now may be the best time to talk to this Tanlian before he can gain his wits and discuss the situation with his shipmates. Come, let's take him to another room so he can speak freely."

Xang, not knowing if he was going to be executed or questioned, was relieved when he was allowed to sit at a small table across from the CAIN officers. Willa translated all their questions, which Xang answered quickly without question. Shim and Jorn learned the captured Tanlians — Talons in their tongue— knew they had no future on their home planet. If they returned to Tantalum 2, the kindest thing that would happen to them would be a life sentence in the mines. Most likely they would be executed.

Cooperating with their captors had kept them relatively safe so far. Xang had no qualms answering all the CAIN officers' questions if it would keep him and his shipmates alive and make them useful. As a young officer, he was not privy to high-level information. As a communicist, however, he had relayed many coded messages about the comings and goings of other Tanlians ships.

Xang spewed this information like an excited youngster sharing a juicy secret. With every detail he revealed, the CAIN officers seemed more and more pleased. Eventually their tone softened when they spoke to him, almost changing to friendly conversation. Shim and Jorn were surprised at first how cooperative this Tanlian seemed to be. After they understood his circumstances, they stopped pressuring him and just let him talk. When more than an hour had passed, the admiral stood up, smiled at Xang and patted him on the shoulder.

"Tell this young man if he and the other Tanlians continue to willingly cooperate and help us succeed with our mission I promise they will be given a new opportunity. Perhaps as colonists on a new world as free men."

The two women exchanged surprised looks. Xang looked shocked and nodded slowly after Willa finished translating. He said only one word. "No need to translate that," the admiral said, smiling with satisfaction. "I understand thank you in many languages."

7

High Seer Tanella read the report again very slowly to ensure she understood it. Seer Cara waited patiently, wondering what her superior's reaction would be to the document that apparently explained why the number of Seers had dwindled for the past two generations.

"Do you believe this?" Tanella asked, slowly putting down the almost translucent paper. "We possess an element in our blood that is responsible for the Seer sight?"

"Apparently so," Cara nodded. "This special element, or gene as the writer describes it, was added by Earth scientists to give our ancestors this special trait. It also is responsible for why all Seers have red hair and brown eyes."

Tanella shook her head. "That is not all. This ten-generation termination factor is particularly disturbing. It seems to explain why there have been fewer Seers every harvest. Is this writer to be trusted?"

Cara shrugged and looked at her copy of the report. "Hmm, this Rina Engstrom was a biologist. She kept a very thorough diary as well as an accurate journal of Verde Grande's plants and animals. She was among the first group that landed here from the Colonia Nueve along with the "Sainted One." At the mention of the first Seer, both women kissed the palms of their left hands and placed them over their hearts. It was the traditional sign of reverence for their ancestor, Taryl Bryann.

Cara returned to interpreting the report. "Her descriptions of our world are of someone seeing it for the first time."

Tanella gazed out her window which looked out over the courtyard of Fortress Bryann. The two Seers had disagreed over many issues over the years, but the High Seer trusted the other woman's judgment in the sciences. The report, gleaned from Rina's journals, explained their predicament in frightening straightforward logic.

"She writes sadly of the others who were stranded over Mount Barrasca. Obviously she means the Nuvens," Tanella said almost to herself while scanning the paper for the third time, looking for details that might help her Seers.

"Interesting that she thought the Nuvens had all been killed," Cara said softly, knowing this fact might be the most incendiary to the Seer society.

Tanella took a deep breath and stared at Cara. "I see this part is from her diary. I take it as supposition on her part. Even to suggest the Sainted One spoke an untruth will not be tolerated," she said with a sharp firmness, again kissing her palm and placing it over her heart.

"Of course, High Seer," Cara said, knowing this was one argument she would not win.

Tanella frowned. "We have to address one very important factor. Who is the Seer who found this information?" Despite herself, the High Seer's tone caused Cara to shiver. The chill coursed down her spine. Trista Hedlo, a young Seer who barely possessed the gift of sight but worked hard to please her superiors, had painstakingly read Rina Engstrom's diary and journals and had done an excellent job of summarizing the key points.

"Trista is waiting outside, High Seer," Cara said, warily eyeing her superior. "The young Seer should be commended for her hard work. Apparently she is the first one to have read Rina Engstrom's writing since the biologist died."

Tanella's smile was cold. "I want to make sure this young Seer is loyal. Has she spoken with anyone else?"

Cara steeled herself. "No, High Seer. Trista informed me of what she had found and worked in isolation under my guidance until the report was completed."

Tanella nodded. "We shall see that the young woman is *rewarded.*"

Cara quickly changed the subject to a topic dear to the High Seer's heart — producing more young women with the gift of the sight in hopes of diverting her attention from Trista, who may now be in danger.

"This report may also offer us our greatest hope in several generations, High Seer. The biologist writes that many of the lost ones — the hunters — also possessed this gene, which allowed their offspring to quickly adapt to different stresses."

Tanella's expression softened as she thought about the possibilities. "After all these years, imagine those damnable hunters being the key to our survival." She shook her head at the irony.

"Especially unfortunate since we have waged war on these people, perhaps wiping out the ones who carried the trait we need," Cara said, not masking her displeasure.

The High Seer glared at the other woman but did not contradict her. Cara always was abrupt and quick to speak her mind when she thought she was right. "How do we know the Defenders are the only hunters to carry the trait we seek?" Tanella sneered, hoping to catch Cara off guard.

The older Seer took a deep breath. "Remember the hunters we captured during the fighting? They all spoke with reverence about the Defenders – those warriors who possessed the skills of their fathers. They said the Defenders were born with special talents. It took highly trained instructors to find those with Defender blood."

Tanella sat very still, staring straight ahead. Her mind raced with different options. *Surely the hunter population still harbors those who carry this precious marker in their blood,* she thought. Perhaps among the children.

"The children!" she barked, startling even the usually unflappable Cara. "The Defender who was killed in the challenge — Aron Nels — he is being mourned by his family, is he not?"

Cara looked at the High Seer and slowly nodded, finally understanding what her superior was saying.

"His children — his blood relatives . . ." Tanella sat forward, her eyes gleaming at the thought. "How many offspring has this Defender spawned?" she asked eagerly.

"Three — two daughters and a son," Cara said. "Are you suggesting that Aron Nels's children may carry this trait?"

The High Seer looked like a predator sizing up its prey. "What did you say about the Defenders? They were warriors born with abilities from their fathers."

Cara shrugged. "How do we know if the Defender's son carries the trait we seek? To our knowledge, Flyn Nels, the son, has not been trained as a Defender." She stopped, considering a fact that just flashed into her mind.

"Yes, go on," Tanella said impatiently.

Cara stared straight ahead, her thoughts racing. "I am told Flyn Nels is an accomplished hunter and flier, even for one who is barely grown. He has concentrated on bagging game and has helped discover unknown valleys in our mountains. The hunter people say he has surpassed his father's considerable skill."

Both Seers looked at each other as the same thought occurred to both. "The son born with abilities from the father," Tanella chortled. "Even surpassing him, how wonderful! And born of a hunter mother, no doubt."

The frown on Cara's face dampened Tanella's glee. "Well, what is it?" the High Seer demanded as the other woman carefully scanned another document.

With a thoughtful look, Cara carefully put down her paper. "The situation is complicated," the older Seer said. "It seems the mother of Aron Nels's children is a Verdan, descended from a security forcer. There is no record of Tarylan blood in their family. It may be difficult to know if Flyn Nels carries this, ah, adaptor gene."

Tanella sat in silence, glowering at the news. "A Verdan and hunter mixed blood?" she mumbled, covering her eyes with her hands. "Is there any other *interesting* news concerning this family? Who do they worship, Mother Verde or the hunter ancestors?"

"The children grew up worshipping as Verdans. That is all we know about them so far," Cara said. "Does this change things since the son is half Verdan?"

The High Seer straightened up, scowling. "No, if this Flyn Nels is half Verdan, it may make it easier for us to convince him to assist us. Send our best spies among the hunters. I want to know everything about that young man. How many other characteristics does he have in common with his dead father? Let's consider the daughters, too. There may be some latent traits in them, too."

Cara met Tanella's gaze. "It may be worthwhile to read journals by Sankari who fought against the Defenders," the older Seer said thoughtfully. "Perhaps there is a common trait among them. It may help decide if Flyn Nels can be useful to us."

Tanella nodded in agreement. "Yes, excellent; do it."

Cara smiled. "I have the perfect person who can help us find this information."

The High Seer snorted impatiently. "Of course, put your best people on this immediately!" She then stopped, seeing the other's bright smile. "What is it?"

Cara stood up and bowed to her superior. "I shall inform Trista Hedlo of her new duties. She did an admirable job the last time, I am sure she is up to the task."

Tanella glared at Cara for a moment, contemplating the consequences of again using this young Seer who possessed dangerous knowledge about their past. "Can this Trista be trusted?" she snapped, not happy with being outmaneuvered.

"Trista desperately wants to please us," Cara said soothingly. "I doubt she even has considered what some of the implications in her report mean. I will speak to her about it and get her to concentrate on her new assignment."

Tanella dismissed Cara with an impatient wave. "Very well. Perhaps I will delay her reward."

8

Gerro walked carefully along the well-worn trail that apparently led to the Valley of the Hunters. His men followed behind single file. Some were hurling good-natured insults at their comrades and laughing as they trudged along. He walked quietly, concentrating on his surroundings, his senses on edge. Almost as soon as he and his men passed through the last Verdan gate and proceeded along the mountain paths, Gerro felt they were being watched.

The Tarylan Captain sensed there was something or someone lurking in the shadows. When he looked back at a place, the shadows often changed or had disappeared. Not to alarm his men, Gerro called for a break. He casually took a sip of water and stretched. Catching the eye of his second-in-command, he signaled him with a slight hand gesture, relaying his concern.

The officer confirmed and walked among the men, telling them in coded language to be on the alert. The mood of the men did not change. They had fought with Gerro many times and had come to trust his instincts. When Gerro gave the command to continue, his men got up slowly. Twenty pairs of eyes scanned the mountainside with professional precision, looking for anything suspicious or out of place. In code, each trooper gave the all-clear sign.

As one, the squad continued on their journey, but they walked closer to the rocks and carefully spaced themselves apart in a staggered pattern, making themselves a difficult target in case of an attack.

As they walked along, the second-in-command gradually caught up with Gerro. "Sir, you suspect that we are being watched?"

Gerro gave a slight nod. "I have seen nothing to confirm it, but I feel something, yes. If there are people here, I would be watching strangers, too, if I were one of them. Tell the men to keep alert and stay in groups. I want to be ready if we are attacked."

———————

Tren Warrod smiled as he watched Gerro and his men return to the trail after taking a short break. "Ha," he smirked looking at Erst, his son. "That leader is good. He knows someone is watching, but he doesn't know where we are or who we are."

Erst studied the Tarylan warriors. "I don't see any difference in their actions," he said. "How can you tell?

Tren, the leader of the Nuven Valley Defenders in this region, pointed to the Tarylans. "Did you see the leader talk to the other man?" Erst nodded. "They spoke briefly before calling for their rest," Tren explained. "All the men acted the same as they got ready to leave; they were looking about. See, their formation is much different."

Lev Klinfer also watched the Tarylans depart. "They are not laughing either. Just speaking softly."

Tren rose and signaled his circle to follow the Tarylans. "That leader is doing just as I would have. We need to be wary tonight. He may send out scouting parties to see if he can find us. They won't know where to look though. This is our land. We know its hiding places and hidden trails."

Erst started to rise to join Tren and the others when he stopped cold. He studied the Tarylans. "They did not wait until tonight to send someone after us," he whispered to his father. "Count them, they are one man short. They left one behind in the rocks, probably to try to trail us."

Tren uttered a low whistle which stopped his men. "Well done my son!" I will not underestimate this leader. His man will not find us. I will post a rear guard to make sure of that." He glanced at Lev who nodded. "Let us depart and leave no trace that we were here."

Erst followed as his father and the other Defenders climbed even higher and continued to follow the Tarylans. Lev watched as the group melted into the rocks. Snapping off a nearby pine branch, he brushed away their tracks. Finding a crevice in a nearby overhang, he pulled the branch upright and settled in to wait.

Not a half hour later, he heard someone scraping rather clumsily over the rocks. The Tarylan walked past cautiously. He stopped every few meters to investigate his surroundings. Looking around the area where the Defenders had stopped, the stranger scratched his head. He peeked over the edge of an outcropping. Finding nothing, he continued on.

Our children don't make that much noise when they're playing 'find me,' Lev thought shaking his head. *He's making enough noise, we won't have a problem being able to tell where he is.*

Lev waited until the Tarylan had walked a few meters away then tossed a small rock down the trail where the man had come from. The rock clattered and bounced off a few boulders and knocked some pebbles free, which made a respectable amount of noise as they clattered down the mountainside.

The Tarylan jumped behind a large boulder and waited a few seconds before he headed back down the trail to find what caused the noise. The Defender waited until the tracker was out of sight. Slipping out of his hiding place, he scrambled up the rocks to join his circle. So far, they were under no danger from this nervous Tarylan.

When Gerro and his men stopped for the evening, they lit a large fire well away from the group. Shortly after nightfall, a familiar whistle called from the darkness. After twenty seconds, the whistle sounded again but the call was slightly different. Assured it was his scout, Gerro answered in three short whistles, waited and gave a longer call. The other whistler answered immediately in reverse order. Not long after that, the Tarylan scout shuffled into camp and slumped to the ground, exhausted.

Handing the man a jug of water, Gerro waited for Domin Trullett to catch his breath. "Sir, I've been looking for signs of others since I broke from the troop, but I saw nothing, heard nothing, except for a minor rock slide," Domin said, relieved to be back among his comrades. "There appear to be trails, but they are broken up and lead to nowhere. They could be animal trails."

Gerro nodded. "A rock slide, eh? When was that?"

Domin shrugged. "It was close to where the troop rested before I left. I searched the area closely, did not find anything."

Gerro stared into the night and then turned his gaze to the scout. "What did you feel when you were up there? Was it too quiet?"

Domin shook his head. "It was rough going up there, sir. There were times I felt like I was being watched, but I didn't see a thing. No, there were no sounds, not like now when the night creatures are calling."

Gerro nodded. "I would have been surprised if you would have found anything. You may not have returned to us if you had found anyone. I suspect we are being watched," he said just loud enough so the troop, which had gathered nearby, could hear. "Let's just hope they are being cautious and not preparing to pay us a visit."

9

Admiral Shim Murra and Captain Jorn Nandez could not have been more pleased with first contact of the GEMS colonies. After being cut off for centuries, the populace of many of the renegade planets wished to be rid of the Tanlian parasites. Jorn had recorded everything the cooperative Tanlian communicist had told them — schedules and routes to the GEMS planets. The CAIN captain studied the seventeen worlds Xang and the two women had identified as being populated.

The captain had expected to learn about new GEMS worlds. When the syndicate broke from CAIN, there had been nine worlds. Eight more colonies had been added to the syndicate. Jorn pulled up a star chart on his wall vid monitor and added the coordinates of the new GEMS worlds. The worlds popped in one by one on his chart. Puzzled, the captain sat back and scanned his notes. The GEMS world he hoped to find — Verde Grande, his holy grail — had not been identified.

For generations his family had been connected to this promising world. Several generations of Nandezes had helped bioform the planet. Another ancestor, the brave Hector Nandez, apparently had been killed transporting colonists to the far-off world. Ever since he was a child, Jorn had dreamed of liberating Verde Grande from the GEMS and Tanlian usurpers. He wanted to reclaim this world for the alliance. The young captain yearned to stand on its tallest mountain and take in the view so many of his ancestors had a hand in shaping. Frustrated at not being able to find Verde Grande, Nandez sent a ship-to-ship message to Sula Gallagos.

The Kenyattan officer sleepily answered his page. "Yes, Captain Nandez?" Realizing it was the middle of their night,

Jorn quickly apologized for the interruption, saying his question could wait until morning. "Your question must be important to you, Captain, what is it?" she asked.

Jorn took a deep breath. "I'm looking for a GEMS world that has not been identified — it is charted as XR-309."

Sula repeated the name. "XR-309? That number sounds familiar, but it is not a GEMS world, Captain. We have identified all of the syndicate planets. Maybe it was a colony that failed through some natural disaster. Unfortunately, the syndicate suffered several such mishaps on planets it had attempted to colonize."

Unable to hide the disappointment from his voice, he thanked Sula and again apologized for the interruption.

"Try Willa. She is an avid reader of history. Perhaps she can find this XR-309 for you," Sula said. "Willa may still be awake yet, she keeps an unconventional schedule. Good night, Captain."

Jorn could scarcely hide his excitement. "Good night Sula and thank you." He swore he could almost hear the other woman laugh as she signed off. Holding his breath, Jorn sent a low-priority message to Willa. The captain did not want to disturb her if she was sleeping. He was relieved when she quickly answered. After offering a greeting, Jorn asked her about Verde Grande.

"It's one of our famous syndicate legends," Willa replied. "I'm not surprised Sula did not remember the chart number. It is known to most of us as the 'ghost world.' "

Jorn could not believe what he had just heard. "Ghost world? Why, what do you know about it?"

Willa was surprised at Nandez's reaction. "I have thoroughly read the diaries of Ismala N'pofu, the Kenyattan hero. It is a wonderful story. In fact, I have tried to model myself after her. She has been an inspiration to generations of women."

Jorn was speechless. He had not expected to hear anything like this. *Ghost world?* he repeated again and again to himself. *Kenyattan legend? Ismala N'pofu?*

"Captain are you there?" Willa asked after a long pause.

"Yes, sorry. This is just all so surprising," he answered.

Willa yawned. "Sorry about that, I was starting to retire for the night. Would you like to talk about this in the morning? I have many materials that may be of interest to you."

Jorn wanted to scream in protest, *Wait until morning?!* But he calmed himself, remembering the late hour. "Yes, Willa, I would enjoy that very much," he said trying to sound nonchalant. He thought he could hear her laugh, too, but he was not sure.

"Very good captain, let's meet during first meal. Until then, good night." Jorn bid her farewell and signed off. He sat staring at the wall at what he had just been told. He had no idea how he was going to get any sleep.

Willa smiled when she saw Jorn waiting for her even before first meal was ready to be served. She wondered why the CAIN captain was so interested in the ghost world. "Good morning, Captain Nandez," she greeted him warmly.

He jumped up not bothering to mask his excitement, gave her a polite greeting and stared at the books she was carrying. "Are those Ismala N'pofu's diaries?" he asked in a hushed, almost reverent tone.

"Yes, Captain, these are the words of the first woman from a GEMS world to commandeer a Tanlian ship," Willa said with a half smile.

As excited as Jorn was, he caught the reference. "She was the first? And, is it my honor to be standing before perhaps the second woman to hijack a Tanlian vessel?" For the first time this morning, Jorn smiled. She nodded. Even without knowing the story, Jorn sensed why this Ismala N'pofu was so important to Willa. This young Betelan woman had followed the example of this hero from so long ago.

"Before we begin, I must ask why you are so interested in the ghost world, I mean XR-309? Your alliance traded this planet to the syndicate centuries ago." Jorn winced when Willa described the loss of Verde Grande as a trade. Taking a deep breath, he told her his family's history with the planet. From its discovery to its bioforming and finally to the transporting of the colonists when Hector Nandez was mysteriously killed. He recounted the stories he heard from childhood.

This time it was Willa's turn to be shocked. It became clear to her why his interest was so profound. This young CAIN officer was connected to the planet through his ancestors. He had grown up dreaming of this planet, much as she fantasized about Ismala N'pofu's adventures. It was her turn to tell the story of the Kenyattan adventures. Willa told Jorn of Ismala's version of the second battle of XR-309 — the attack by the Tanlians and the courage and viciousness of the colony's Defenders. After it became clear the Tanlians had been defeated, Ismala boldly took control of the ship and returned to Kenyatta, where she was met as a hero.

Willa and Jorn were so engrossed in each other's tales, they did not notice when Shim and Sula sat nearby during first meal. The Admiral and Kenyatta captain grinned at the intensity of their younger counterparts. Jorn and Willa kept talking well after the last of the crew had finished dining. The young CAIN officer paused to reflect upon what Willa had told him. "You said Ismala N'pofu was the hero of the second battle. What do you know of the first battle?"

Willa shook her head. "That is the first mystery of ghost world. That was the mission of the Tanlian ship Ismala was flying with — to find another Tanlian vessel that disappeared when it apparently attacked the planet. She wrote that the colonists bragged of defeating the first group of Tanlians."

Jorn could not help but smile and shake his head. "What a fight they must have put up. My ancestor must have had a hand in the disappearance of the first Tanlian ship. The alliance lost all communication from the planet after that." The young captain paused, looking puzzled. "Why was Verde Grande never colonized by GEMS or the Tanlians? You still call it the ghost world."

Willa shrugged. "That is another mystery. Ever since the second battle, the Tanlians have been unable to successfully land on the world. We hear about secret missions to, ah, Verde Grande. Many Tanlians never return from those visits. Over the years, the legends have created ghosts that defend the planet, not allowing visitors to land."

Jorn stared at Willa, his mind racing. "Maybe they are not ghosts at all. Perhaps some colonists survived and they have been defending their world."

Willa shook her head. "Anything is possible but to go undetected for nearly three hundred years? The Tanlians are very persistent if they think there are prizes to be plucked. I have lived with those animals doing what they wish. They do not give up easily."

Jorn stared out a porthole. "I only hope I get the opportunity to solve the mystery for myself," he sighed. "There are many GEMS worlds to liberate and battles to fight before I dare think about visiting Verde Grande."

Willa respected the captain's resolve. She was reminded of her own drive to rid Betel 4 and the other syndicate worlds of the Tanlians. "I too have dreamed of looking upon the ghost world for myself. If fate allows, perhaps we can solve these mysteries after we free the GEMS worlds."

Rising from their table, Jorn cracked a shy smile. "I would be honored to have such a brave warrior assist us in our efforts."

10

Flyn Nels was startled to see the three red-headed women waiting for him in his family's cabin. He had started his trek to the Valley of the Heroes when a messenger intercepted them. His mother wrote to tell him he was needed urgently back home. After returning and greeting his mother and sisters, Flyn was shocked to see visitors — Seers.

After what his family and friends had told him about his father's deadly duel with the Sankari, the last thing he expected to see in his family's home were Seers. The three women rose as he walked in. He glanced out the window to see how many guards accompanied them but saw no one.

"Greetings Flyn Nels, I am Ines of the Tarylan Seers," the shortest and oldest woman in the group said as she stepped forward. "These are my escorts — Ewa and Mattia. On behalf of the Tarylans, we offer our deepest condolences on your father's death."

Flyn glanced at his family, the worry on their faces was evident. Pausing for a moment, Flyn's first instinct was to order the women out of the house, but all Verdans had been raised to respect the mysterious women. These were the first Seers he had met face to face. They were not at all as he imagined — wrinkled hags sitting in loose robes gazing into the sky with blank eyes. Rather, the three were striking with their long red hair and dark eyes. "Thank you, Honored One," he said cautiously. "Forgive me, but I am surprised to see Tarylans in the house of the man who killed so many Sankari."

Ines nodded and sighed. Ewa and Mattia bowed in respect. "There has been too much bloodshed," Ines said softly. "The High Seer wishes to offer her sympathies and requests your family's presence during a ceremony in twenty days honoring your father and the other brave Defenders who have been killed. The deaths of these brave men should usher in a time of peace for all the people of Verde Valley."

Flyn stared at his family and friends. No one spoke, all were thinking about the ramifications of the Seers' invitation. Many Nuvens believed these women were the guiding force behind the Sankari and their terrible attacks on the Nuven temples, which resulted in the extermination of the beloved Defenders. Now to have the Seers make a peace offering was startling. The Nuvens and Verdans had been living together in a strained peace. Many Nuvens left their small villages to band together in larger settlements that offered better protection against further attacks. This lifestyle was contrary to their culture, which revolved around smaller family groups. The Nuvens who refused to gather in the large settlements left to make their lives among the hundreds of small valleys, scattered throughout the mountains.

Flyn was suspicious of the Seers' offer. "My family and I offer our gratitude for your kind offer. We will let you know of our decision in three days."

The three Seers rose. "As you wish," Ines said. "We shall return in three days for your answer." She and the other two Seers departed after bowing to Flyn and his family. The room exploded in shouts of surprise and anger from Flyn's family after the women had left. Everyone had a different opinion of what to do about the Seers' invitation.

Amaura was the most emotional. "Don't trust those witches," she shouted. "Everyone suspects they were behind Father's death. You should have seen how they acted after the last Sankari was killed. They were angry." Their mother was more level headed but just as distrustful. Even though she was a Verdan, Stazia was suspicious of the Seers.

Lyllen sat quietly thinking. "I want to know why Father spoke to that Tarylan before he died. Maybe the Seers can tell us. They would not have invited us to this ceremony if they meant us harm."

Flyn nodded. "The only way to find out what the Seers want is to attend. We have three days to think about this. Let's talk to other Nuvens. If we go, we should have a large party with us. Perhaps the Seers want to use us to get back in the good graces of their people. So much has happened in the past two weeks, I want some time to think about this." The young man frowned as he thought about delaying his mission to find Gerro, but the Seers could not be ignored.

Flyn turned to hug Stazia. "I am going to the orchard groves, mother. Don't worry about me. I will return tomorrow for last meal." The young man had not been alone since he got back from his hunting trip to find his life had been dramatically changed by the death of his father. His Nuven blood cried out for solitude. He wanted to consider his choices without being interrupted or influenced by others. As his father had done as a youth, Flyn yearned for the peace of the fruit groves. One could think there. The only sounds heard there were made by birds singing in the branches and insects buzzing and flitting among the blossoms.

Stazia knew she could not change his mind, yet she still feared for her family's safety after all that had happened. Her mate was dead and now Seers had found their way to her home. "It will make me feel safer if you would allow the clan Defenders to accompany you," she said, patting his cheek.

Flyn started to object but stopped when he saw her tired eyes, reddened by days of grief. He could only imagine what sorrow she had experienced and did not want to add to her worries. Flyn agreed. "I don't think I could stop those kinsmen from following me. They have proven to be a most insistent group."

The Defenders were pleased to hear Flyn wanted to venture out. The ten men had grown restless while the young man visited with his family. They relished the opportunity to travel, stretch their legs and hopefully do some hunting. "My men and I will be happy to accompany you to this orchard," Tarn said.

Flyn smiled. "I am glad to have you as company. You and your circle have proven you respect my privacy. That is the only request I make of you."

———————

The trip to the orchard took almost half a day. Flyn and the Defender circle traveled by boat until they reached the entrance of a narrow canyon. Their boats barely squeezed through two giant boulders. They half pushed and half rowed their way through. The last stretch was spent climbing and following almost-hidden trails. The Defenders had no trouble following Flyn as he darted among the familiar paths to the Nels orchard, now attended only by Aron's oldest brother, who preferred to live as a hermit. The Nuvens felt quite at home in this rough terrain.

Rounding a bend and squeezing through a crevasse in two giant boulders, Flyn and the others found themselves standing in a sheltered canyon filled with the sweet smell of blossoms. Flyn turned to watch the Defenders but was surprised at their reaction.

"Ah, a sweet fruit tree is nearby," Ryyter said, inhaling the air with a deep snuffle. "Children in the Valley of the Heroes love to pick the fruit." The other Defenders smiled and casually walked among the trees.

Flyn turned to Tarn. "You know about the honey fruit? This is the only place in the Verdan Valley where they are grown. People would mob my father when he sold them at market."

Tarn laughed. "These trees are found everywhere in the Valley of the Heroes. You call them honey fruit? Yes, that is a good name for them I suppose."

Flyn shook his head at the revelation. "I am looking forward to visiting the Valley of the Heroes when this business with the Seers is finished."

Tarn smiled. "You would be most welcome, son of Aron. Your kinsmen would put on a magnificent feast."

Ryyter chimed in. "It would last for days. Just thinking about the food and drink are whetting my appetite." Tarn started to glare at the other man but stopped when Flyn chuckled. This was the first time the young man looked happy. Tarn was glad to see the young man's mood change.

"If we keep making this much noise, my uncle will greet us with an arrow," Flyn smiled as he pulled out a small sheep's horn. He blew three short, high-pitched blasts followed by a lower tone then waited, but there was no return call. Frowning, Flyn raised the horn and repeated the call — nothing. "Romal never leaves the grove unless he's hunting. His shelter is not far, perhaps we can find where he has gone."

Flyn and the others had not gone far when he signaled them to stop. Tarn and Ryyter no longer smiled. "Something is wrong here. There are no birds singing," Flyn said scanning the trees but seeing nothing. The Defenders said nothing. Tarn made two quick hand gestures to alert the other Defenders of possible danger. In unison they all loosened their knife straps and readied their bows.

"If there are no birds, perhaps something else is here. Something that may have frightened them away," Tarn said. "How far is it to Romal's shelter?"

Flyn nodded to his left, "Less than a kim away."

Ryyter looked at him, puzzled. "Ah, kilometer in Old Angle, I believe," Flyn explained.

Tarn signaled the group to proceed. "Let us walk with caution. I insist you allow me to walk beside you, son of Aron." Flyn started to argue but saw the intense look on the Defender's face. There would be no swaying him. Nodding, Flyn started walking through the trees, flanked by a circle of Defenders who made almost no sound as they made their way through the trees.

———

The path to Romal's shelter was much more open and well-worn than Flyn remembered. Seeing Flyn looking concerned as they walked, Tarn asked what was wrong.

"Strange, this path was not clear when I visited almost two lunars ago," Flyn whispered. "My uncle and father always took a different path. They said that was the only way to keep an eye on things and would throw off anyone tracking you."

Tarn nodded. "That is the Nuven way. I can see you have kept closely to our practices." At Flyn's signal, the band slowed as they neared Romal's shelter, a two-story structure hewn out of huge logs. It backed up to a large rock outcropping. Three generations ago, Flyn's forebears felled many of the huge oaks and maple trees in this small valley to build shelters and make room for crops and orchards.

Peering out from behind a large tree, Flyn saw Romal sitting quietly on the porch with his back to an open window. This was uncharacteristic of his uncle who was only happy when he was hunting or taking care of the grove. Tarn cast a questioning look at Flyn, who shook his head. "I don't like it, everything seems wrong. My uncle was never one to laze about during the middle of the day."

The Defender leader gestured for his men to take positions. "Let's not be in a hurry. We can keep watch from here until you decide whether it is safe or not."

Pulling out an old eye scope, Flyn could see his uncle clearly. Romal was staring straight at him. Flyn scanned the area carefully but could see nothing wrong. Looking back at his uncle, Flyn noticed Romal's little finger twitching ever so slightly. It moved back and forth, almost rhythmically. Focusing on Romal's hand, Flyn stared intently, finally recognizing the movement as a crude version of a hunter signal.

His uncle was signing the word "danger" over and over. Flyn studied Romal's face, the blue eyes stared vacantly ahead. There was no sign of recognition or his uncle's wry amused expression that he knew so well. "He is in trouble or hurt. He has not moved for minutes. Perhaps there was an accident," Flyn said rising. "I fear he needs help."

Tarn grabbed Flyn's arm. "We go as one, as a circle. Stay in the center. That way you are protected from any direction." The group moved cautiously down the path drawing near to the cabin. There was no shout of greeting from Romal who slowly turned his head to watch the approaching men. As they neared,

Flyn shouted a greeting, "Uncle, it's Flyn!" Romal did not reply. His eyes now focused sharply on Flyn and a frown creased his face. In a sudden move, Romal jumped up and yelled, "Run!" gesturing for them to leave.

He got no further. His body shuddered. He fell to his knees, a spear point sticking out of his chest. A shadowy figure looked out from the window Romal had been shielding with his body. In barely a heartbeat, Flyn let an arrow fly. The man in the window grunted in pain and collapsed.

The circle of Defenders formed a defensive circle as Verdans jumped out of hiding places. Dozens of arrows rained upon them from the brush and trees. Four Defenders fell. The other six, including Tarn and Ryyter, surrounded Flyn. Even though badly wounded, they limped for protection among the trees, returning fire with their arrows.

Attackers fell screaming from trees after being hit by the Defenders' and Flyn's arrows, but the deadly shower continued, dropping the stubborn Defenders one by one. Flyn lay wounded, one arrow in his shoulder, another gouged into his leg. Crawling to where Tarn lay, he gently lifted the Defender's head.

"I am sorry we failed you kinsman. May our ancestors protect . . ." Tarn managed one more trembling breath, gazed sorrowfully at Flyn and died in his arms. Flyn laid Tarn gently down and collapsed against a tree. His shoulder and leg were on fire from pain. Unable to move and starting to lose consciousness, he could barely focus on the figures who surrounded him.

"We were ordered not to harm this hunter," a gruff voice growled. Another voice whined, "It could not be helped. He killed at least four of our men. He had to be stopped."

The first voice grunted. "They won't like this, they wanted him brought to them right away. He can't travel like this; look at the blood he's losing. Bring a healer, hurry!" Flyn tried to open his eyes one more time but his vision swam. He slowly slumped to the ground — then blackness.

11

Gerro and his men stopped when the trail sprouted into three paths — one to the left, one to the right and another snaking up the mountain ahead of them. There were no signs or any other indication which direction would lead them to the Nuven valley. "We split into three groups," the Tarylan captain ordered. "Travel as far as you can go in an hour, then return to this place. Remember, we are being watched," he whispered.

The Tarylans had traveled hard for two days. During that time they had not seen anyone else, but Gerro was convinced they were not alone. After dividing his troop into three groups, Gerro led his small party on the path that led upwards. It was rough going but well worn and seemed to efficiently wind over the rocky terrain. After about an hour, he led his men back to where they were to meet the others.

The small party paced about nervously. Two hours had passed with no sign of the others. Gerro's mood grew darker with each minute, but he dared not let the others know he was worried. His men cast anxious glances at him, waiting for orders. He feared the worst. Had the watchers waited until he separated his group and then attacked? They had heard no danger signals from the others. "Let's find a place to defend ourselves," he ordered. "If the watchers have taken our men, they may be waiting for us also. We will not be taken easily."

As he turned to retrace their steps to find an appropriate shelter, a whistle trilled from nearby. Gerro spun around and listened. He answered and waited. The other caller responded appropriately, identifying himself as one of his men. Still suspicious, Gerro ordered his men to take defensive positions as he called the whistler in. Lieutenant Rooya walked slowly toward Gerro and his men. His face was frozen with a terrified look but he kept walking, then stopped a few meters away. "My apologies, sir," Rooya rasped. "They were on us before we knew it. I swear, they came out of the rocks."

Gerro motioned for him to continue. "What happened to the others, are they dead?"

Rooya shook his head, looking embarrassed. "No sir, my group is well. Just a few bruises and cuts." Gerro was shocked. His elite guards had been captured without anyone being killed or badly injured? He wondered if the same fate had befallen the second group.

"Why did they let you go?"

Rooya looked down, ashamed to look his captain in the eye. "The hunters sent me as a messenger sir. The leader told me they have the other group. He says they will not harm us if we put down our weapons. They even have offered to lead us wherever we want to go."

Gerro was stunned. He gaped at Rooya in disbelief. "Hunters captured you this easily? Put down our weapons? They will lead us? Lieutenant, do you believe what they say?"

The lieutenant swallowed hard and shrugged. "They call themselves Defenders, sir. They were upon us so quickly, commander, we hardly had time to lift a weapon. We may not have a choice whether to trust them. They watch us even now."

Gerro stared intently where Rooya was looking up the mountain. He swore he saw a shadow melt into the rocks. "Why have they not come forward to face us?" Gerro demanded.

"Their leader says he respects your command," Rooya said. "He claims he didn't want anyone hurt. Uh, one other thing, commander."

"Yes, what is it?" Gerro snapped, suspicious of the offer Rooya had presented.

The officer paused, looking frightened again. "They knew your name — Captain Gerro of the Tarylans. None of us told them when they captured us. The leader says their *Protector* is waiting for us."

Gerro did not know what to believe. He was not accustomed to being given ultimatums. As the most respected Tarylan guard on Verde Grande, Gerro was always the one to give the orders, the one who decided others' fates. Even more unsettling was the fact they knew him or knew about him. This gave him an unpleasant feeling of helplessness.

Feeling trapped, Gerro snarled, "And if we do not submit to their terms?"

Rooya gulped and glanced down at the ground. He knew his captain would not like the answer. "The leader said you have another sunrise to decide. He claims to want no bloodshed, just your cooperation. He gives his word."

Gerro frowned. Every instinct told him to protect himself and his men at all costs. But how could he protect them from an enemy that apparently could appear out of nowhere, almost at will?

"Who is this Defender who orders me in this way?" Gerro asked angrily.

"Tren Warrod is my name Verdan," came a shout from not far above the Verdans. Gerro and his men dove for cover, waiting for an attack. Seeing Rooya standing frozen, Gerro shouted for the lieutenant to find shelter. "No sir, they told me I would be killed if I moved from this spot." Gerro was startled when he looked at his men. What was left of his fierce troop huddled in fear, looking in terror around them. They had never been trapped before by an unseen enemy.

"Your man tells the truth Verdan," the same voice called. "We wish you no harm, but you must disarm. Our Protector has foreseen your coming. She has ordered us to give you safe passage."

"Who is this Protector?" Gerro muttered. "I do not know you, Defender," he called back. "You are courageous to send an unarmed captive to talk to me."

Laughter cascaded from all around the Verdans, causing them to back further in to their hiding places. "Very good," Tren shouted. "I expected no less from you. What will happen if I show myself?"

Gerro almost smiled when he replied, "Nothing will happen to you Defender — you have my word."

The silence that followed was almost worse for Gerro and his men. When the Defender was shouting, he was at least in one place. Now they did not know where the Defenders were. Rooya looked at Gerro and shrugged. Apparently, the lieutenant had not been told what would happen next.

Several minutes passed before Tren called again. He was much closer this time. "I am unarmed, Verdan." The Defender leaped out from behind some rocks directly behind Rooya. The lieutenant stood perfectly still as Tren walked up beside him. "You did very well," the Nuven told the grimacing officer.

"I will discuss that with him later if I get a chance," Gerro said, his eyes slitting threateningly.

Tren took a few steps toward Gerro and stopped. "He had no choice, Captain, we had knives at all your men's throats. If he signaled you in any way they would have been killed instantly."

Gerro stood and walked toward Tren. "You said you wanted to avoid bloodshed, Defender. That is not a polite welcome."

The Defender nodded. "Agreed, but you are in my protectorate. We do not allow strangers to have weapons. That is our first law. Our people are to be defended at all costs. Even the Protector honors our laws."

Gerro stepped closer, stopping only a meter from Tren. The Nuven looked very relaxed, almost amused. Rooya looked sick. His face was white. Sweat was pouring from him. Taking a deep breath, Gerro scanned the canyon's walls. "How many weapons are aimed at me?"

Tren shrugged. "Do you want to know the actual number?"

Gerro took a deep breath and shook his head. That answer told him all he needed to know. "Are you not afraid of dying, Defender?" The captain crossed his arms and stared at the smaller Nuven who sported a thick black beard.

Tren smiled. "I have been watching you. I trust your word. Besides, your men would be dead in a matter of seconds if you kill me." The easy, almost nonchalant way the Defender spoke unsettled Gerro. The Nuven did not wince. He stared straight into Gerro's eyes. The Tarylan captain had never been addressed in this way. Tren hurled no threats but had spoken with quiet confidence.

Gerro said nothing while he disarmed himself slowly, placing his weapons on the ground. The other Tarylans walked into the open and also laid down their weapons. Tren raised his hand in the air. At his signal, dozens of Defenders leaped from hiding places among the rocks and surrounded the Tarylans.

"I honor my word Tarylan," Tren said. "We will take you to the Protector. She has been waiting."

Gerro frowned. "Who is this Protector?"

The Defender leader smiled. "The Protector told me you would be familiar with another word — Seer."

12

"He has been wounded?!" High Seer Tanella shouted at Dallon Veser. "Flyn Nels was to have been protected at all costs. Those were my orders."

The leader of the Tarylan troop who captured Flyn shifted uneasily from foot to foot but kept eye contact with the angry woman. "We understood your orders, High Seer, but the Defenders proved difficult to kill. They fought viciously. We lost fourteen men. This Nels killed four before he was stopped by his wounds."

Tanella shook her head while massaging her temples. "They managed to kill so many even though they were ambushed? You had plenty of time to plan after following his kinsman back to the orchard."

Dallon stood patiently waiting for the woman to calm herself. After a few seconds, the High Seer looked up. "How badly is he injured? Is he being properly cared for?"

He tried to soothe her with good news. "We have Nels in a safe shelter. Two healers are caring for him. They removed the arrows with no problem, but he has lost a lot of blood. He is very weak."

Tanella paced about the room, muttering to herself. Dallon frowned while he watched the troubled Seer. The newly appointed captain was accustomed to following orders without question, but he was curious about this latest mission. He also was upset with having lost so many men to the Nuvens.

Dallon was the second highest-ranking Tarylan Guard. Only Gerro outranked him. The officer had jumped at the opportunity to prove himself during the dangerous mission. He had grown up in Gerro's shadow, never quite achieving the respect the other charismatic warrior had earned among the Seers for his daring and always successful missions. But now Gerro had disappeared, apparently pursuing some personal quest.

"Why is this Nels so important that makes it worth losing 14 loyal Tarylans?" Dallon asked. "He appears to be just another hunter."

Normally the High Seer would not tolerate such insubordination from anyone, especially a man, but Dallon was special. "You will not like my answer," she said, glowering at him. "This hunter may be worth one hundred Tarylans." Her answer stunned and angered the captain.

"No man is worth that much, Mother, especially not one of them — a hunter," he said not masking his defiance. Tanella looked up with surprise. It had been years since Dallon had addressed her as "Mother." Seers were not close to their sons. Many times they let other women raise the boys, preferring to shower their attention upon their daughters in hopes of fostering more Seers.

The males proved to be valuable as Tarylan Guards and as fathers of Seers. Over the generations, the sons of Seers had proven to be loyal warriors. Many of the vaunted Sankari were sons of Seers — proud, highly trained Tarylans who had finally defeated the Defenders.

Taking a deep breath, Tanella looked fondly at the son who always tried so hard to please her. Dallon should have been the champion of the Seers. Even though he was much taller than Gerro, the bastard son of Verinya always bested him. "It is very important to keep Flyn Nels alive, son. Yes, he is nothing but a hunter. But he also is the son of the Defender who killed our surviving Sankari."

Dallon's expression melted from from anger to shock. He could not remember Tanella ever calling him "son." The word was scarcely used by the Seers.

The High Seer sat down, folding her hands in her lap. "There are fewer and fewer Seers being born every year," she said softly. "We have discovered information from writings from a First One that hunters with Defender blood may have the ability to father more Seers."

Dallon slumped down in a chair in front of Tanella. "But Mother, Tarylan men have fathered Seers for years. What is different now?"

The High Seer shifted uncomfortably in her seat, searching for the right words. "It appears our blood needs to be refreshed by new family lines. They apparently carry a trait we require to produce more Seers."

Dallon sat shaking his head at this unpleasant revelation. The future of the Seers depended on hunters, particularly a special hunter. A knock on the door interrupted their discussion. Cara stood in the doorway waiting for permission to enter. "Is this important enough to warrant an interruption?" Tanella snapped at the other woman.

Cara nodded. "With your permission High Seer, we have uncovered more information regarding the Defenders." Tanella nodded her approval. She started to dismiss Dallon with a wave.

"If I may, I would like to speak with Dallon, too," the older Seer said. "Captain, I hear you captured Flyn Nels after a skirmish with the Defenders. This may seem a strange question, but did you notice anything unusual about these men?"

Dallon looked at Cara. "They were very quick and difficult to kill, even though we outnumbered them," he said. "There was one thing we thought strange, but it makes no difference. They are all dead."

Cara walked forward. "Tell me, was it their eyes? A blue-green tint?" she asked almost fearing the answer.

Tanella was startled by the odd question. "What does the color of their eyes have to do . . ." but was stopped by Dallon's look of surprise.

"Yes, how did you know?" he asked. "One of my men discovered it, and we checked all ten of the dead Defenders. They all had the same blue-green tint. Even Nels has the same color. Probably from too much inbreeding," Dallon sneered.

"The others were all killed?" Cara asked. "That is a shame, indeed."

The High Seer snorted. "What does all this mean?"

"After comparing the journals of Rina Engstrom with diaries of Sankari who fought with Defenders, we found one thing they always mentioned — the odd color of their eyes," Cara explained. "Eyes that seem to change in color depending on the light."

The older Seer continued. "Apparently the First Ones who carried the trait were produced artificially. They were all given the same eye color — a bluish-green tint — so they could be identified by the others. It is not clear why this was important to them, but now it is very important to us."

Tanella looked ill. "Do you mean all those Defenders carried that trait?"

Cara nodded. "Yes, apparently they all were potential carriers of this blood trait we seek. And now we are down to one wounded hunter in the Verdan Valley." .

Dallon rose shakily. "I will return to where we are holding Nels. I will take more healers and more men." Tanella waved him away. She was too upset to bid her son farewell.

13

To their surprise, the CAIN fleet found the GEMS worlds easy to liberate. The inhabitants jubilantly welcomed their former enemies and eagerly helped cleanse their worlds of any Tanlian influence. Admiral Shim Murra and Captain Jorn Nandez found the Tanlian tribute ships followed the same procedures for every GEMS world. This was very unlike the marauders who terrorized the CAIN worlds with stealth and vicious attacks.

When a Tanlian ship approached, the fleet would hide on the opposite side of the planet. Once in orbit, the tribute vessels did not have a chance. The Tanlians rarely put up much of a fight. CAIN surface fliers swooped down to intercept the landers, quickly destroying them. Their counterparts in space surrounded the orbiting transport ship, giving the captain only two options — surrender or die.

It only took three lunars to carry out eleven successful missions. In that time, only two transports tried to escape. The fleeing transports were no match for the faster warships and their laser-guided rockets. After every conquest, the fleet left behind an elite defense force on the surface. Surface-to-air missiles were strategically installed. Satellites armed with alarm systems and a potent array of missiles were launched. Any lightly armed Tanlian transport and its landers would offer little resistance.

After dispatching troops and weapons systems on the eleventh GEMS world, Shim requested a conference with Jorn, Willa and Sula. The women had proven valuable as the fleet leapfrogged the syndicate planets.

"The twelfth world will be much more difficult for us," Shim announced as the other three sat down across a table in the fleet flagship's war room. Not waiting for questions, he explained. "Our scout ship has just reported from Rossiya 7. It scanned at least ten Tanlian warships in orbit. It is unknown how many may be on the surface or hidden on its two moons."

Jorn studied the star chart. The planet Rossiya 7 was 20 days away. "Did the Tanlians discover our scout? Any pursuit?"

Shim shook his head. "They did not pursue. We do not know if they were aware of our scout. It appears they are ready to make a stand."

Willa looked at the two CAIN officers. "I am not surprised. The Tanlians have lost eleven ships and more than a thousand men. They have grown dependent on the GEMS worlds for many goods and supplies. We are their lifeline."

Sula agreed with her Betelan ally and now close friend. "The Tanlians are a greedy race and vicious as well. No GEMS colony has fought with them for two centuries. I would love to be on one of their flight decks. They probably think the Kenyattans are revolting."

Willa laughed. "They are, but they had some help."

Shim frowned as he studied the star chart. "The alliance has fought the Tanlians on their terms and in their space for years. I want to change that," the normally even-tempered man said thumping his fist on the table. "We need to make them come to us, fight us where we dictate."

Excitement coursed through Jorn as he studied the chart. The answer seemed too obvious. He looked at the chart again, like a chess player who can't believe he has a clear path to his opponent's queen. But there it was — Verde Grande. The world the alliance had given up as lost was about a hundred-day flight from their current location.

The planet his ancestors had invested so much in seemed to beckon to him. It was perfect. Verde Grande was undefended and, as far as anyone knew, was unpopulated. The other three at the table had stopped talking. The rhythmic drumming of Jorn's fingers and his look of utter concentration as he stared at the chart had caught their attention. It was unusual for the brash young captain to be so reflective.

After a few moments, Jorn broke his gaze from the chart and jumped when he saw the others smiling, waiting for him. The captain looked nervously at the others, afraid they would criticize his plan as being self-serving. They all knew his interest in that ghost world.

Shim leaned forward. "Well, Captain, are you going to honor us with your opinion or do we have to guess?" The elder officer saw tremendous potential in Jorn. The captain's ancestors were legendary in the early colonizing of CAIN worlds. Generations of his family had been leaders. Jorn eased himself out of his chair and walked to the star chart which filled the wall. He tried to organize his thoughts. The young officer didn't want to sound overly eager. Jorn desperately wanted to convince the others his plan was sound, not just a whim.

"Please let me explain what I believe will work," he said, trying to sound confident. "Verde Grande, the unclaimed world, lies here," he said using a laser pointer. We know the Tanlians are 20 days away at Rossiya 7, but they are at least 40 days away from Verde Grande."

Jorn stole a glance at the others and saw they were intently listening. "We don't know what the Tanlians are planning for us at Rossiya 7, but if we can get to Verde Grande first, then we can tempt them to attack our defensive positions. We would have the advantage." None of the others said a word. Each studied the chart as they considered his plan. Jorn could hardly stand the interminable silence. His heart thumped so hard he was sure the others could hear it.

"I see you are serious about this, Captain," the Admiral said. "How do you propose we induce Tanlian warships to attack Verde Grande?"

Jorn's stomach turned sour. That was the chink in his plan. He had not been able to work that out in so short a time. "I was hoping one of you had an idea," Jorn conceded. "Yes, Admiral, my plan is contingent upon drawing the Tanlians to Verde Grande."

Willa smiled as she looked at the two CAIN officers. "A decoy! We need to draw the Tanlians' attention and convince them to fly to the ghost world."

Shim cast a quizzical look at Willa. "That is our name for Jorn's planet." she explained.

Sula leaned forward. Her bright dark brown eyes shone with anticipation. "Can you spare some ships, Admiral? If the Tanlians are attacked, they would chase down any escaping vessels. When they 'discover' an enemy base on Verde Grande, I believe they will fly there quickly."

Shim's expression brightened as he considered the strategy. "A good plan. It's sound, except I'm concerned about losing any ships or crew in the decoy raid. We may need all our vessels and personnel for the full attack."

Jorn paced back and forth in front of the star chart and jerked to a stop as if he had walked into a wall. "Our autoscout ships, Admiral. We could use those," he almost shouted then looked embarrassed at his outburst. "We could program those ships to attack the Tanlian fleet and then have them attempt to flee to our 'base' on Verde Grande."

Shim stared at the chart for several moments. He ran all the scenarios through his mind again and again. "Even with the fully automated scout ships we will need a controller, a person to coordinate their flight paths and redirect their programs as the situation warrants. The Tanlians will be suspicious if they don't detect any ship-to-ship chatter."

Jorn smiled. "We can program the chatter, even make it appropriate to the situation. Our flight crews are very inventive. We can mimic ship-to-ship communications and even attack commands. As for the controller, we can ask for volunteers. That scout will have to be modified for life support and supplied with enough fuel to escape to Verde Grande."

Sula stood up. "I see I can finally be of assistance on this mission." The others were surprised the stoic woman had spoken. She had been cooperative in helping determine Tanlian flight schedules and patterns but was seen as shy, only offering her opinions when asked for them.

"It is time a Kenyattan did something in this campaign other than watch," she said, allowing frustration to edge into her voice for the first time. "All of you have already sacrificed much to free the GEMS worlds or to inspire us to be free," she said looking at Willa. "I am more than a capable pilot, Admiral. I volunteer to be the controller for the decoy mission. And I promise to get the Tanlians' attention," she said leaning over the table, her eyes glistening intently.

Shim rose and saluted Sula. "Good work. I am proud to serve with all of you. Let's get those scout ships retrofitted, programmed and ready to go. We need to fuel for the trip to Verde Grande. Captain, it looks like you will get your wish to see that world."

The ten tiny ships appeared out of nowhere, swarming around the moon of the Tanlian-guarded planet like bothersome insects drawn to a piece of rotten fruit. Darting in irregular orbits, the ships gathered into attack formation and swooped down on the transmission station hidden in a deep crater. Moments later, the ships streaked out of the crater, chased by an orange fireball from the destroyed station. Two large Tanlian fliers emerged from camouflaged spots on the moon in response to the station's distress signal which stopped abruptly after the explosion.

Instead of escaping, the attackers engaged the Tanlians. The little ships, barely bigger than satellites, easily avoided the larger fliers' defensive weapons and inflicted heavy damage with their short-range energy bursts. The vessels were quickly disabled. One of the Tanlian ships, its navigation system destroyed, careened toward the moon and crashed onto the surface sending debris flying. The second drifted helplessly into space, gaping holes in its side where it had been hit.

Four large Tanlian warships slowly rose from the moon's surface to engage. The autoships quickly reorganized and streaked toward the enemy. Picking the nearest vessel, the small CAIN fliers strafed it mercilessly, knocking out its weapons and heavily damaging its guidance system. The target of the attack barely stayed intact as it collided with the moon's surface.

Seeming to gain confidence after each attack, the scouts swarmed around the second warship, also inflicting heavy damage until it could no longer respond to their attack. It hung in a limp orbit around the moon, unable to stabilize itself. The two remaining warships joined ranks but did not advance or fire upon the autoships, which were now using the crippled Tanlian vessel as a shield. It was a stalemate.

"Those are the ships that have been attacking our transports?" screamed Tomar Jandon as he watched from his lead ship orbiting the GEMS world. The Tanlian fleet commander could not believe he had just witnessed four of his ships being crippled or destroyed by vessels so small that they had not registered on their scans.

"Tell Narfa and Inlof to hold their positions," the commander ordered the surviving warships orbiting the moon. Tomar had not predicted this maneuver. He had expected his fleet to fend off a few rebel vessels, possibly from one of the GEMS worlds.

Tomar grew angrier by the moment as he watched the scout ships hover around the crippled warship. The attackers were so close to the larger vessel, it appeared they were docked. After studying the scans, Tomar exploded in a fit of rage. "They are siphoning off Number Seven's energy supplies. They're refueling! Any contact from our ship?"

The communicist looked up from his console. "None, sir. It appears most of its systems have been knocked off line or destroyed."

Tamar glowered at the vid screen. "So, we do not know how many casualties they have sustained?"

"No sir," the communicist answered.

Glowering at the scene, Tomar opened a direct comm link to Narfa and Inlof, the captains of the remaining warships. "Fire full barrages at Number Seven. I want those attackers shot down."

Without argument, the two remaining warships fired on their wounded counterpart. The CAIN ships seemed to be caught by surprise as the laser-guided rockets streaked toward them but at the last moment all but one, which was still refueling, bolted away from the warship. The Tanlian vessel disintegrated from the full barrage, pieces flew everywhere. Some careened into space, the bigger chunks fluttered toward the moon. The nine surviving scout ships gathered back in formation and waited as if daring the Tanlians to attack.

"Any further orders, commander?" Narfa snarled. "We just killed 250 of our men and only got one of those damn bugs."

Tomar's bridge crew flinched when they heard the message. "Hold your positions, both of you," the commander ordered. "I will not tolerate another response like that, Narfa. I'm sure one of your bridge seconds would jump at the opportunity to take command of your ship."

Inlof interrupted the verbal jousting. "Shall we pursue, commander? Surely our two ships can ward off those vessels."

Tomar glared at the standoff between two of his large warships and their nine diminutive opponents. This was a new experience for the commander. No one had challenged Tanlian space superiority for centuries. "Yes, proceed," Tomar ordered. "Stay together. The attackers should not be able to withstand your combined firepower. Either drive them toward us or out into space and then we can pursue them."

The two Tanlian ships started to move toward the autoships, which held their positions. As Narfa and Inlof guided their vessels away from the moon, Tomar's communicist turned white when he saw six more of the diminutive attackers rise from the surface of the moon and speed toward the warships from the rear. The six new autoships swarmed over Narfa's vessel, splattering it with a series of precisely targeted rockets.

Most of his weapons were knocked out in the surprise attack. On cue, the autoships swept toward the lone unaffected warship. Inlof's vessel was caught in a crossfire of dive bombing attackers, who easily avoided his defensive fire. Inlof's ship fought back, firing rocket barrage after barrage, trying to protect itself and Narfa's vessel. Through the din of the battle, Narfa shouted, "Forget us! Escape to the planet while you can!"

Tomar cut in, shouting: "The fleet is on its way! Save yourself, Inlof! We will be there shortly." Inlof's ship refused to move. It hovered over Narfa's vessel like a mother bird stubbornly trying to protect an injured chick.

The nine CAIN ships concentrated their attack on Narfa's helpless ship, while the other six drew fire from Inlof. Their repeated energy bursts finally weakened the hull. Gaping holes ripped open, followed by explosions that spread throughout Narfa's ship. Inlof's vessel kept up its defensive firing but backed away from its dead fleet mate. The ship swung away from the moon and fired its thrusters to jettison itself toward the planet and away from its persistent attackers.

Instead of pursuing, the 15 scout ships sped toward the moon. They hit the defenseless Tanlian ship still in orbit with intense broadside energy bursts, then proceeded to the surface and destroyed the warship that had crash landed. Even the Tanlians were stunned by the viciousness of the attacks.

Tomar's communicist opened a comm channel for the fleet. To their amazement the Tanlians heard CAIN accents. The attackers were laughing and telling jokes as they went about their deadly business. The commander's face was red with rage. Veins in his neck popped out ominously, looking like they were going to burst at any moment. "Pursue those ships!" he screamed, his voice spiking two octaves higher, barely making it understandable.

A female voice calmly cut through the attackers' chatter as the Tanlians eavesdropped. "Mission accomplished, well done. Return to XR-309 where we will resupply. Those vermin will think twice about approaching a CAIN world." All of the attack ships formed in a pack and joined a larger vessel that lifted off from the moon. The Tanlians had concentrated all their attention on the battle and had not detected it. The CAIN fleet then turned and sped away.

Tomar fought to gain control of his emotions when he signaled the remaining fleet that was barely out of the planet's orbit. "Prepare a course for XR-309. We will wipe out those vermin there." Turning to his communicist, Tomar snarled, "Send a message to Tantalum 2. Tell them we have engaged the enemy, and they are retreating to XR-309. Request any available warships to join us. We will trap them there and kill them all."

On a scrambled channel in code, Sula warned the CAIN fleet of the approaching Tanlian warships. She had intercepted Tomar's message and passed it along. Even over the cold, vast distance of space, those listening to her messages could easily detect the satisfaction in her voice.

14

Gerro was shocked when he finally met the hunters' Protector — a Seer. Questions stormed through his brain but protocol must be followed. He bowed, showing the traditional Verdan sign of respect.

"Welcome Gerro, I am Verinya. We are pleased to finally meet you," the Seer said warmly, gesturing for him to be seated at a table filled with bread, fruit and a pitcher of water. "I have watched you mature into a formidable warrior. I am sure the Tarylan Seers value you greatly."

Gerro raised his eyebrows in surprise as he eased himself into a chair. "I am at your service Honorable One. Forgive me, but you called your sisters the 'Tarylan Seers.' Those are strange words." Verinya smiled as she gazed at her long-lost son. Sadness filled her as she realized how much he favored his father, Aron Nels. He was a handsome Tarylan with short-cropped red hair. Seeing him sparked a memory of the baby boy she had left behind. Tears slowly filled her brown eyes.

Gerro was trying to understand his predicament. Most of his troop had been captured by the hunters, and he had surrendered without a fight. Now this strange Seer, who had warmly welcomed him, was crying. He was speechless. He had rarely seen a Seer show any emotion other than anger. The affable Seer Cara was the only exception he could recall.

"Please forgive an old woman," Verinya said wiping her eyes. "You remind me of someone I knew long ago."

Gerro returned her smile. "You are not old Honorable One, and you are still . . ." he stopped, surprised by his boldness with the strange Seer.

Verinya's laughter unsettled him even more. "I see the Tarylan warrior before me is as charming as he is handsome." Her laughter grew louder as he blushed with embarrassment. Gerro had grown up hearing derisive comments about his parentage which only had fueled his desire to disprove those hurtful insults. Praise only came as he rose in stature as a formidable Tarylan captain. A movement to his left drew his attention. He instinctively reached for his favorite knife but clutched at an empty pouch.

Seeing his reaction, Verinya addressed the person lurking in the shadows. "You are making our guest nervous Arynna." Gerro watched as what appeared to be another Seer glided silently over to Verinya. This woman was much younger than Verinya, perhaps her daughter he guessed. He rose, bowed and sat back down. The young Seer wore her hair in an unusual style — a long braid wound four times around her head. Something else was different about the younger woman. Gerro tried to study her face without staring. With a start, he realized it was her eyes — not the typical Seer dark brown but lighter, almost golden. He couldn't tell from where she was standing. Her face was eerily familiar. It gave him an uneasy feeling because this was the first time he had met her.

"You surprised me, Mother," the younger Seer said giving Verinya a hug. "After all these years of waiting for him and then I hear laughter. Not at all what I expected."

Verinya reached up and took the other woman by the hand. "Let me introduce my daughter, Arynna. She has been worried about me and also is very curious about you." The young Seer blushed with embarrassment but smiled. Gerro could not mask his surprised expression as he stared at the two women.

The older Seer was somber. She frequently dabbed at her eyes. The younger woman acted curious about him. "You have traveled a long way, captain of the Tarylans. I am sure you have many questions for us," Verinya said, gesturing for Arynna to be seated.

Gerro took a deep breath. He had so many questions, they felt like they were tumbling over themselves in his brain. "If I may be so bold, Honored . . ."

Verinya stopped him with a raised finger. "I grew up and was trained as a Seer among the Tarylans, but I now call the Valley of the Heroes my home. Our ways are different, Gerro. Please address us by our given names."

He nodded. *These Seers are very different from the others*, he thought. "It would seem you have been watching me for many years. You even knew my men and I were traveling here. That is why the Defenders captured us so easily."

Verinya nodded. "Yes, we both have watched you with great interest for most of your life."

Gerro was stunned by her answer. "Why would two Seers among the Nuvens take such an interest in me?" he said, not hiding his frustration. Gerro's outburst even surprised himself. "I apologize for my words Honored, er, Verinya."

"We are not offended, Gerro," Verinya said. Her smile had faded. Sadness now shadowed her face. Arynna stared at him somberly. "Our answer will become obvious very soon. Please tell us, why did you put yourself and your men in danger to travel here?"

Gerro shifted uneasily in his seat. "An old man told me I would find my mother in the Valley of the Heroes. The other Seers told me she had died giving birth to me. This man had no reason to lie."

Verinya leaned forward. "Just a man, an ordinary man?" She was now staring intently at her visitor. "Were you well acquainted with him?"

Gerro shook his head. "No, not an ordinary man by any means," he said, remembering the conversation with Witt Peyser after Aron died in his arms. "He said he was the steward of Circle Sankarikiller. He was with the last Defender during a death duel. The old man told me I would find my mother here. I was curious."

Verinya had been preparing herself for this moment for many harvests. Her emotions now erupted after seeing her son for the first time since he had been a newborn. She could not speak. Tears trickled down her pale cheeks. Arynna moved to her mother, giving her a hug. "Shall I tell him?"

Verinya shook her head. The Seer looked as if she were in great pain. After several moments, she spoke haltingly in a strained voice. "Your journey has been successful, brave Gerro. I have been hoping all these years that someday I would meet my son. And now, here you are."

Gerro was stunned. His throat constricted. He had not prepared himself for this kind of revelation. His eyes darted back and forth studying both women carefully, looking for any nuance that would signal their deception. Both Seers, however, sat calmly. The young man eyed Arynna. "If she is my mother then that makes you my sister?"

The younger Seer leaned forward in her chair. Arynna's expression was intense. "More than that, brother. I am your twin."

Gerro was surprised to find himself standing, staring at the two women in amazement. "My mother and a twin sister," he mumbled. The words sounded foreign coming from his mouth. He slowly returned to his seat. Taking a moment to gather his thoughts, he grabbed a cup of water and drank deeply. "Why should I believe you?" he asked, almost fearing the answer.

Verinya held up her hands. "Why would we lie? Why else would we watch one Tarylan with so much interest? We only did so because we are connected."

Gerro shrugged. "To trick me perhaps. Many people try to curry my favor."

Arynna chuckled. "You have no status here, Gerro, no position. Our Defenders captured you easily. We could have had you killed."

He nodded and took another long gulp from his cup. "True, but perhaps you have plans I am not aware of. You may be trying to influence me."

Verinya had regained her composure. She felt a great weight had been lifted from her soul. The older Seer had anticipated these questions. "We do have plans for you, my son," she said softly. "But you will be fully aware of what they are. We have no secrets."

Gerro's mind was racing so fast now, he had trouble focusing on one thought. If what the women claimed was true, this could change his life. "I do not know what to believe," he said. "I never suspected to find such amazing discoveries."

As he sat contemplating these revelations, another thought came to him. "This all started with the dying Defender, Aron Nels," Gerro said, gazing at Verinya. "How did his steward know who you are?"

Verinya gazed lovingly at his familiar face. She wanted to reach out and caress his cheeks, wanted to hug him. The Seer let out a heavy sigh and steadied her breathing. "I saw Aron's death through your eyes, Gerro." The older Seer took a trembling breath. "The steward recognized you because Aron is your father."

Gerro dropped the cup he had been holding. It crashed and scattered into a dozen pieces when it hit the stone floor but no one reacted. The Tarylan champion had expected nothing like this. He had traveled to the Valley of the Heroes to find his mother and confront her, hoping she would tell him why he had been abandoned. Now Verinya's tears made sense. Gerro understood why Aron looked so familiar. It was as if he were looking at an older version of himself. The emotions that flooded him were unfamiliar, like being swallowed by a giant wave at sea.

Verinya arose, swaying uneasily. Arynna leaped beside her mother, steadying her. Gerro also stood, not knowing what to do or say. "This has been a trying day for both of us, my son," Verinya said. "It is night. Please allow an elder her needed sleep."

Gerro moved close to the two women. "I have many more questions," he pleaded.

"And we will answer them in the morning, after first meal," Verinya said. Reaching out, she touched his cheek lovingly. Gerro did not draw away. It felt warm, soothing. The two women slowly walked toward a doorway. Arynna's arm was around her mother's shoulders. Turning to gaze at Gerro, Verinya said, "Rest well, my son."

Gerro bowed but could not take his eyes off the women who had just turned his life upside down. "It may be a difficult night for me. Until morning then Verinya, er, Mother." That word felt strange but satisfying rolling off his tongue. "Good evening Arynna," he nodded to his new-found sibling.

Gerro hardly slept. He paced around the spacious room the hunters had provided for him. His heart raced, his head pounded. The Seers' news had been unbelievable, but everything they told him seemed to make sense. If it was a plot, it was an extraordinary one. The young man could not understand why these Seers would try to fool him. His thoughts always returned to the dying Aron Nels. Gerro sat numbly in a hardback wooden chair realizing he had held his father in his arms when the Defender died.

He finally succumbed to his exhaustion and managed a few hours of sleep before being summoned for first meal. Gerro politely turned down an invitation to dine with Verinya and Arynna, opting instead to eat with his troop. His men were in good spirits despite being weaponless and being watched constantly. They were allowed to roam where they wished. His troop peppered him with questions but Gerro begged off, telling them he needed more answers for himself.

After first meal, Gerro took his time making his way to Verinya's quarters, where she and Arynna awaited him. His stomach was in knots. For the first in many harvests, he fought to control his nerves. Politely greeting the two Seers, Gerro seated himself in the same chair as the day before and gazed at his mother and sister.

"Well, my son, what do you want to know?" Verinya asked gently.

Gerro leaned forward, his eyes intently meeting hers. "Everything, Mother," he said, noting the pleased look on Verinya's face. "I want to hear your story. If I have questions, I will ask them."

Verinya leaned back. "Very well, you certainly deserve to hear it after all these harvests." The older Seer left nothing out. She told Gerro about falling in love with the mysterious young Defender Aron Nels — their stolen moments together, which were all too few. Verinya's voice choked with emotion when she recalled being ordered back to Fortress Bryann before the battle at Temple Darya, when all the Nuven Defenders except for Circle Sankarikiller were killed. His mother told him she was horrified when the Sankari returned from the battle, claiming to have killed all the Defenders in Verde Valley.

After she gave birth to him and Arynna, the High Seer threatened to take the babies away if she did not reveal the name of the father. Her only way to escape was to take one of the babies — Arynna — with her. It broke her heart to leave him. Verinya wrote a note to one of the few Seers she trusted, begging her to care for her son.

Gerro listened to Verinya's story with fascination. He was not angry with this woman who claimed to be his mother. She spoke with utmost candidness, pausing occasionally to dry her eyes. "It is true then, the Seers guided the Sankari and were responsible for wiping out the Defenders?" Gerro asked. Verinya nodded. "You spoke of a Seer who you asked to look after me. Who was that?"

"Cara," Verinya answered quickly. "She and I were raised together, trained as sight watchers together."

Gerro smiled. "Cara. She was one of the few Seers to show me kindness. She encouraged me instead of insulting me as many of the others did. She was true to her word."

"I'm glad someone showed you kindness my son," Verinya said then broke down, sobbing.

Gerro knelt before his mother, taking her hand. When he moved, Arynna tucked her hand just inside the opposite sleeve of her robe. "Put your weapon away sister, I mean her no harm. If I wished, both of you would be dead already, but that is not my intent."

Arynna's laugh surprised Gerro. "Your bravado is impressive if not misguided. You would have been fallen before you could have done any harm."

Gerro smirked. "Do not misjudge me sister, but I mean neither of you any harm."

Arynna answered in a typical sibling taunt. "Do not misjudge us." Smiling, she called out. "Defenders, let me hear you." Gerro jumped up as voices answered from every nook and cranny in the darkness. He looked around intently but saw no one. Unsettled, he sat back down. The Tarylan captain had always prided himself on being able to detect danger but had sensed no threat.

"I should not be surprised that you have bodyguards," he said with resignation. "A wise move. I would have done the same."

Curious as to why their mother remained silent during this exchange, Arynna and Gerro turned to look at her, but she was strangely silent. The elder Seer stared somberly into space, her eyes darting back and forth as if watching some unseen drama play out. The brother and sister sat back and quietly watched their mother. They both were familiar with the sight trance. Verinya's face contorted as she watched the far-away action unfold.

Many minutes passed before she broke her trance. The elder Seer sighed heavily, shaking her head. "He is badly injured. The Tarylans have killed the Defenders we sent to protect him," Verinya said, looking sadly at Arynna. "They now are caring for him. I don't understand."

Gerro was startled. "Who is injured? Tarylans have killed Defenders? Where?"

Shaking her head, Verinya looked at Gerro. "I wanted to tell you in a different way. Aron's other son, from his Verdan mate, is in terrible danger. Tarylan Guards have captured him in a small canyon. The Seers want him alive for an unknown reason."

Gerro wondered how many more surprises these two women had in store for him. "Aron Nels has another son?!" Then, staring at Arynna, he remembered where he had seen that face before. One of the two young women who knelt at Aron's side after he was killed resembled Arynna. "He had daughters, at least two of them. I saw them with him in the arena. They were upset that Aron's last words were to me," he said.

"That is correct, Gerro," Verinya said. "You have two other sisters and a brother." A strange feeling swept over Gerro. In less than a day, he had gone from being an orphan to having a family — a mother and siblings.

"I always thought I was alone," he murmured, staring off into space. "The Seers told me I was an orphan." His thoughts were shattered by two loud gasps from Verinya and Arynna. Movement erupted from all around as Defenders swarmed out of their dark hiding places. Gerro started to rise but was ordered to stop by a scowling, large bearded man who knelt before the Seers.

"They are in trance. This one has not harmed them," the Defender said, looking at Gerro. My apologies Verdan, but it is unusual for them to make any noise when they are in trance."

"That is true. I have seen Seers in trance before," Gerro said amazed. All the men cast worried looks at both Seers, who stared into space. Verinya's face was frozen in a shocked expression, but Arynna seemed to be amazed. Their eyes darted back and forth as if they were trying to watch unseen insects flying around the room.

"So many ships, I have never seen that many, like a flock of birds," Verinya gasped as she broke out of her trance first.

The first Defender knelt before the elder Seer, fear etched in his face. "Protector, is it Tanlians? How many ships? Do we need to alert our people?"

Arynna broke out of her trance and waved the Defenders back. "These intruders are not like any Tanlian I have ever seen," she said as Verinya nodded. "They are not attacking but are scanning our world. There are men and women on board many ships, very unusual. I think they are trying to signal us."

Seeing the concerned look on the lead Defender's face, Verinya sought to calm him. "Alert our people to be ready for intruders if we give the signal. But they are not attacking yet."

Gerro was fascinated. The Tarylan Seers had always tricked the Tanlians into leaving. The intruders always arrived in one ship, never a flock as Verinya described them. Standing, he addressed Verinya and the head Defender. "If you need assistance, I give you my word that my men and I will fight beside you."

Arynna again stared off into space for a few moments, then turned to the others. "These people mean us no harm, Mother. I sense it."

Verinya sighed. "There are so many of them, it would be difficult to mask their eyes. Perhaps it is time to welcome visitors to our valley."

15

Ortelle Woodrud was gentle as she checked Flyn's wounds. He was barely awake long enough each day to take sustenance and then fell back into a deep but troubled slumber. The healing sedative was working. The Verdan healer dutifully changed the dressings. His leg was healing nicely. The arrow had not been deep, making it easy to extract. It took two healers, however, to operate on his shoulder.

The second arrow was imbedded so deeply, they had to cut through the back of the shoulder and pull it out. This left two holes, where it entered and where it exited. The healers were able to clean the shoulder and suture the wounds shut. Recovery depended on keeping the hunter still so the wounds would not tear open.

Ortelle watched over the handsome young man, holding his hand when he twitched and moaned from the nightmares that seemed to haunt him nightly. Elda Froller, the other healer, clucked with disdain at the younger woman's doting. The older woman reminded Ortelle they were helping the hunter to recuperate at the Seers' insistence. For all they knew, the Seers may want him just healthy enough to be executed. After all, he had been wounded in a battle with Tarylan Guards, obviously making him a renegade.

Ortelle doubted the Seers wanted any harm to come to the hunter. The Tarylans had treated him very gently when they brought the wounded man to the healers who were housed in Romal's cabin. *No, this hunter was important to the Seers to warrant so much attention*, Ortelle thought as she wiped sweat from his forehead. But what did the Seers want with him? The young healer absentmindedly stroked the hunter's thick dark brown curls as she sat near him humming to herself.

"Who are you?" a voice barely rasped, scaring Ortelle. The healer jerked her hand away and saw Flyn trying to focus. His eyes rolled, refusing to stay in one place.

"I am one of the healers looking after you," she said softly. "Do you need water?"

Flyn grimaced but managed to croak a "yes."

"Lie still," Ortelle gently ordered. She lifted his head so he could drink. Looking more alert, Flyn frowned as he glanced around the room, recognizing his uncle's shelter. "How long have I been here? Are any of the others alive?"

The healer leaned close to him. "We have been looking after you for eight days. Others? Oh my, you mean the men who were with you in the battle? You are the only survivor."

The hunter regarded her suspiciously. "Battle? We were attacked, not given a chance," he mumbled, trying to keep from passing out again. "All dead," Flyn sighed and looked away, his eyes misted over. "They were just trying to protect me."

Ortelle looked into those strange blue-green eyes. "Who are you?" she whispered.

Her patient's eyes fluttered as he fought to stay awake. "Flyn Nels," he slurred tapping his chest. "Son of Aron Nels, the Defen. . ." He sighed, slipping back into a deep sleep. The healer stared at her charge. Lying in front of her was the son of the infamous Defender who had killed all those Sankari in the bloodiest duel in Verde history. She still did not know why the Seers wanted him but sensed he was even more important than she first suspected.

Flyn stayed awake a little longer with each passing day. He chatted with Ortelle for hours, trying to learn what he could from the kind healer. He soon discovered she did not know why he was being held captive. Flyn did not reveal that he was familiar with the shelter. Romal, his uncle, had lived there for many harvests. Aron had taken Flyn and his sisters to the orchard often when they were children. He knew the shelter well, even its secret rooms, which emptied into caverns in the nearby mountain.

After several more days, Flyn started to move around. His wounds were healing well. The sore leg made him walk with a slight limp, but the shoulder was very tender. It throbbed with pain if he exerted himself too much. Flyn no longer required Ortelle's sedative to sleep. Much to her dismay, he also made it clear he wanted no one in the room at night. He sensed the healer had grown fond of him. Flyn appreciated her attention, but he needed his privacy to work his escape. For two nights, the hunter's injured shoulder kept him from prying open a hidden door along the side of the large fireplace.

On the third night, he was about to quit, when he gave the hidden latch one last desperate tug. The wall opened slightly, just enough for him to slip through. Grimacing from the pain in his shoulder, Flyn followed the escape tunnel.

It was just as he remembered it as a boy. The tunnel led into more caverns in the mountain behind the shelter. His father's family was not far removed from their Nuven roots. They still valued escape routes that emptied into confusing tunnels where only they knew how to navigate safely. Growing lightheaded from exhaustion and pain, Flyn stumbled back to the shelter. He required a few more days to gain strength and needed time to formulate a decoy maneuver.

Over the next few days, Flyn walked farther and farther into the orchard. The trees were scattered everywhere in the valley's rough terrain. Six Tarylans accompanied him everywhere when he ventured outside, but the guards kept their distance. At first they tried to engage him in good-natured conversation, but Flyn ignored them as if they were insignificant insects. The guards soon stopped talking and sullenly followed along.

Flyn took the same path every day, gazed at the same few trees, rested in the same sunny spots. He even settled down to nap against the same boulder in the bright midday sun, which soothed his throbbing shoulder. The routine soon bored his guards. At least half drifted off to sleep under nearby trees as he napped, and the others took advantage of their free time to play a gambling game. The Tarylans soon looked forward to this relaxation time. They were content to ignore him.

During one of these sojourns, Flyn noticed a small stone out of place. It was nestled slightly under the boulder where he usually rested. Familiar scratches were etched in its surface — Nuven code. Yawning loudly, Flyn sat down, keeping the rock between him and the boulder. It didn't take long for the Tarylans to fall into their routine as he appeared to doze off. With his good arm, Flyn slowly loosened the rock. It seemed to take forever.

Whoever put it there did a good job of securing it. He finally pried it loose and found a flat piece of wood and a sharp etching tool underneath it. Shifting his position as if trying to get comfortable, Flyn propped himself up so he could look at the message without being detected. Scratched in the wood were four words: "large oak look up." Flyn casually glanced around the clearing. The Tarylans were relaxing underneath a large oak. He slowly scanned the tree's massive branches. The leaves were thick, making it difficult to see anything but a dense wall of foliage. Flyn was patient, he studied every major limb until a slight movement caught his eye in one of the higher forks.

Marking the spot in his mind, Flyn glanced at the Tarylans. None of them were watching. Returning his gaze to the spot, he yawned and brushed his hand across his brow. Two large branches parted. A red-haired figure returned his signal. Flyn gave a slight nod. He recognized that smile even from a long distance — Malik Klinfer, his father's good friend.

Flyn expected someone would come looking for him. He just hoped whoever it was could avoid the Tarylans. Malik could walk unnoticed through a troop of Tarylans at night without them noticing. Now he was gesturing again. Flyn stared for a moment then recognized the age-old sign — a hand swiping across the neck. The older hunter was asking if this was a good time to attack the Tarylans. Flyn covered his eyes — the sign for "no."

He held up the etching tool and then shifted his body so he could scratch a message on the other side of the wood. Looking up into the tree again, his eyes met Malik's. The old hunter pointed at him and touched his heart — code for "I am with you." Flyn brushed tears from his eyes. Seeing Malik watching him and smiling filled him with hope. He could not see the tears of joy in his friend's eyes.

Flyn carefully returned the wood and the etcher to the depression and wedged the small stone back into its place. Rising slowly, he stretched stiffly and returned the way he had come, not saying a word to his guards, who also rose and followed him back to the shelter. Malik waited for Flyn and his captors to pass before lowering himself down on a rope.

The old hunter had grown worried along with the other members of Flyn's family when Flyn and the Defenders did not return. It took Malik almost a week to find the hidden orchard valley. Aron had taken him there only once, many harvests ago. It was an act of true friendship for Aron to allow Malik to accompany him to the valley. Romal had been distrustful of the outsider at first, but it didn't take long for the two men to start laughing and telling stories, sometimes at Aron's expense.

After finally finding the hidden valley, Malik immediately saw signs of the Tarylans. He was able to creep through the orchard unseen at night. That first morning in the orchard, Malik was grief stricken after discovering a huge pyre where many bodies had been charred beyond recognition.

Activity around Romal's cabin caught his attention. It was obvious the Tarylans were guarding someone in there. Malik could not get close enough to see who, but he suspected it had to be Flyn. His prayers were answered several days later when Aron's son finally emerged for a short walk. The young man obviously had been injured, perhaps badly by the way he moved.

Malik silently followed Flyn and his captors when the young hunter went for his daily walk. After seeing his friend's son was religiously keeping to the same routine, the old hunter left the message. He was ecstatic when the young man had found his note. Now Malik scrambled to the boulder and uncovered Flyn's message scratched on the other side of the piece of wood — "shoulder bad, need knife." The hunter smiled as he dug the hole a bit deeper to hide a knife and left another piece of wood. With Flyn armed, Malik had no doubt an escape was imminent.

―――――――

Flyn almost hummed as he walked along. He had grown up listening to Malik's and Aron's stories and later had joined them on the hunt. Gazing on that familiar face was almost as good as seeing his father. He knew the hunter would do everything in his power to help him. Flyn's mind exploded with possibilities while he made his way back to the shelter. He did not want to risk Malik's life, although he knew his friend would do anything he asked.

When Flyn reached the shelter, he saw Ortelle waiting for him as she always did after his walks. Much to her surprise, he returned her smile and greeted her warmly. Following him inside, she inspected his shoulder wound, added more of the healing salve and changed the dressing. For the first time, Flyn noticed how good she smelled as she leaned over him. Instead of staring glumly into space as he always did, Flyn looked into her bright blue eyes as she chattered happily away. She brushed her straight blonde hair out of her face as she worked. The young hunter felt her voluptuous body as she brushed closely against him while she attended to her duties. Flyn appreciated her attention.

When Ortelle finished, Flyn stood and gave her a hug. "Thank you for caring for me so faithfully," he said. "I think it is because of you that I am healing so quickly."

Ortelle returned the hug, practically burrowing into his body. After several delicious moments of enjoying his attention, the healer looked up at him. "You seem very different today — happy," she said, gazing into his eyes.

Flyn reached over and gave her hair a playful tug. "Yes, for the first time it feels good to be alive. My leg feels much better and my shoulder has stopped throbbing." Of course he could not tell her about Malik, but he was genuinely happy to be with her.

"I'm glad," she said. "You have been ill for so long, it's wonderful to see you happy." When she smiled, her whole face lit up. Her eyes twinkled and two dimples creased her ruddy cheeks. They were standing so close, Ortelle was rubbing her hand up and down his back. Flyn realized how much he liked her touch. "Would you dine with me tonight?" he asked softly. "I am weary of being alone."

Blushing slightly, Ortelle's smile revealed her answer. "I will return shortly with our meal," she said giving him a robust hug then scurried off.

———————

It did not take long for their meal to turn into romantic play. Ortelle tore off pieces of meat, dipped them in a hot wine sauce and hand fed them to Flyn. She also offered him fruit and bread, which he readily accepted. After every bite, he gently licked the tips of her fingers or kissed the palm of her hand. He offered her food in the same way. Holding his hand to her mouth, she playfully suckled and nibbled his fingers. Each bite took longer and longer as more attention was paid to lips, hands and fingers than it was to food. Eventually pieces of fruit were passed from mouth to mouth.

The meal was not half finished, when the couple turned their attention to the bed. Flyn's shoulder was still sore, making it difficult for him to disrobe. He did not object when Ortelle gently helped him. With his good arm, Flyn managed to unfasten her clothes a bit clumsily. This only added to the anticipation as they explored each other's bodies. Ortelle carefully guided Flyn to the bed. She proved to be very eager but gentle. It had been a long time since both had enjoyed the company of a lover. The tension of the past few weeks flowed out of Flyn as he and Ortelle made love again and again into the night. The couple eventually curled up together, exhausted and fell into a satiated, deep sleep.

It was well past first meal, when Flyn awoke. Ortelle was stroking his curly hair, her chin rested on his chest. She smiled when he finally opened his eyes. After a long kiss, the healer poured him a drink of cool water and then gave him some fresh fruit from the nearby orchard. The sweet juices triggered memories of his family, which only sharpened his resolve to escape. Gazing at the sweet Ortelle as she fed him, smiling lovingly as he accepted each bite, Flyn realized escape now would be much more difficult because of his new-found feelings for her.

16

Admiral Shim Murra paced back and forth on the bridge of his flagship as it orbited Verde Grande. All but one of the CAIN fleet ships had reported the same thing — heavy clouds covered most of the planet, except for one narrow valley. Their scans picked up no life signs. "What has Captain Nandez found?"

The communicist shook his head. "He has not reported in, sir, nor has he answered my hails."

Shim smiled. "Give him time. I'm sure the captain will search every square inch of the planet before he is satisfied. There is no hurry. This is where we will face the Tanlian fleet."

Jorn Nandez and Willa stared at the monitors at the control station on the captain's ship. Both were surprised at the results. "Those are the most unusual cloud formations I have ever seen," Jorn said as he rubbed his eyes. He had been intently studying the monitors for hours looking for a break in those impenetrable clouds.

Willa nodded her agreement while rechecking the scan information for perhaps the hundredth time. The captain looked at the view screen from the bridge on his ship. He had seen historical vids of the planet as it was being bioformed. It had been a bright, sparkling blue and green world, not unlike Earth, except there was only one huge land mass that rose from the oceans.

"What are the other ships reporting?" Jorn asked.

"They are confirming our scans," his communicist said. "Heavy cloud cover except for that narrow valley."

The captain shook his head. "I can't believe Earth colonists would travel to such a place. The early accounts of the bioformers said nothing about dense clouds."

Willa cast him a sympathetic look. "Perhaps there was a natural disaster. It may not have taken much if the ecosystem was still fragile." The young woman gasped as she looked down at her monitor again. "Thermal readings. I'm registering thermals in the smaller valley! Many of them, running in straight formations, starting about halfway up the mountain."

Jorn swung back to his monitor and smiled. "I see them too. Wait . . . And look, they are in a pattern." He stared at his screen for another moment then erupted in a happy shout. "Look at those thermals again. Do you see anything unusual about them?"

Willa studied them for a moment but shook her head. "Read from top to bottom in Old Earth Angle," he said excitedly like a small child who just found a hidden treat. Willa checked again and gasped. The word "WELCOME" was splashed in fire down the side of one of the mountains. She laughed. "Our ghosts are inviting us down."

From their well-hidden crags in the mountain, the band of Nuvens nervously watched the small ship land in the clearing. They had set a huge ring on fire in the clearing to guide the visitors safely down. After landing gingerly, the ship cut its engines. No movement came from it for several minutes.

"What are they doing?" the head Defender asked. Fear shone in his eyes. Every instinct told him his people needed to escape to the safety of their caves where they had successfully warded off Tanlians for three hundred harvests. "Why don't they show themselves?"

Gerro gaped in wonder at the sky ship. He had only read about such vessels in the early histories of Verde Grande. He found himself shaking with anticipation. "Perhaps they are doing what I should have done before walking into the Valley of the Heroes — taking their time to be sure they are not walking into a trap."

The Defender chuckled then continued to observe the ship. "The Tanlians seldom land in daylight, mostly in the dark like thieves looking to steal our women and children."

The hum of a door opening in the ship captured the Nuvens' attention. A tall dark-haired man slowly walked out, followed by a young blond woman. Their clothing was strange. One light blue piece of fabric covered their bodies. No weapons could be seen. After walking a few meters from the ship, the man knelt on one knee. Reaching out, he dug his fingers in the ground. Bringing his hands to his face, the man smelled the soil deeply, then let it trickle between his fingers.

The woman stood beside him with her hand on his shoulder, but her eyes never stopped scanning the rocks. She stopped to stare directly where the Nuvens were hidden then smiled. Gerro was fascinated by her. She seemingly had sensed or guessed where they were hiding. He couldn't help but smile at her. Arynna studied the kneeling man. He hadn't moved since first touching the ground. He appeared to be praying. His head was lowered and a hand covered his heart. "This is not the posture of an invader," she said, eyeing her brother.

Gerro smiled and stood up. He looked at the Nuvens who still suspiciously eyed the strangers. "It is time. Hide yourselves if you must," he said while walking out on an open ledge so the strangers could see him. Something brushed his shoulder. Arynna stood at his side.

Willa had sensed she and Jorn were being watched. The Betelan eyed the mountainside until spotting a cluster of boulders — perfect for hiding. She was startled when a man and woman seemed to appear out of nowhere. "Our ghosts have appeared," she whispered to Jorn, squeezing his shoulder hard. Rising slowly, the captain looked up to find two people looking intently at them from about 40 meters away. Holding his hands out from his body to indicate he had no weapons, Jorn walked forward a few paces.

The young captain had been practicing a speech for lunars in hopes he had the opportunity to find people on Verde Grande. Now, he could find no words after seeing these two people, obviously descendants of the Colonia Nueve colonists. The red-haired woman cocked her head as she studied him then smiled when their eyes met.

Finally finding his voice, he called: "Peace my brothers. We mean no harm."

"A strange accent," Gerro whispered. "Do you understand him?"

"I do," Verinya said, emerging from her shelter. "I believe he said peace. He seems sincere. I saw no danger from anyone in this ship or in the others orbiting." Holding her arms straight out, Verinya answered: "Welcome to our valley. I sincerely hope you come in peace."

Jorn and Willa walked toward Verinya. The captain turned in a circle, sweeping his arm. "Is this Verde Grande?"

The elder Seer nodded. "Yes, welcome. It has been our home since the First Ones arrived 300 harvests ago."

Willa leaned toward Jorn. "Her accent is similar to some remote areas of Betelan. She says they have been here for 300 years."

Nandez clasped his hands together. Despite his best efforts, tears filled his eyes. "The ship Colonia Nueva brought your ancestors here from Earth." Pointing to himself. "I am from Earth. I am Jorn Nandez."

Gerro and the two women were astonished to hear the visitor utter the sacred names of Nandez and Earth. To the Nuvens, Nandez was the name they called out when they needed courage in an impossible situation. Many Defenders used it as a war cry. The Verdans recognized the name as one of the martyred First Ones. It was only uttered with extreme reverence.

Earth, the legendary home of the First Ones, was a mystical place to the Nuvens. They believed their ancestors returned to Earth when they died. Verdans did not hold their ancestral planet in such high esteem. Most believed a great cataclysm must have destroyed it, otherwise why would the Earthers have abandoned them all these years?

Verinya called into the caves. "Nuvens, come out. Our brothers from Earth have returned." The small party, along with Gerro and his Tarylans slowly approached the strangers. Verinya walked up to Jorn, stopping only a few paces away.

He smiled and bowed slowly. "As the descendant of Hector Nandez, I am honored to meet the courageous people of Verde Grande," he said.

Verinya looked puzzled but smiled introducing herself and Arynna. "We are the Seer Protectors of the Nuven people. I am sorry Jorn Nandez, some of your words are strange to me."

Seeing his puzzled look, Willa stepped forward. "Captain, may I?"

"Of course. I would appreciate your help," he said. Stepping aside, Jorn introduced her. "It is my honor to present Willa Sydriker, warrior hero of Betel 4."

Willa glanced with surprise at Jorn then smiled and also bowed. Pointing to Jorn, she said, "The captain honors his grandfathers."

Verinya laughed as she first embraced Willa and then Jorn. "We have waited for many lifetimes for the brothers and sisters of the First Ones to return," she said tearfully. "So much has happened here." Willa translated for Jorn.

"The Tanlians kept us away for many years. We had to fight many to get here," he said. "We won't be driven away so easily this time. I swear on the name of Hector Nandez."

Gerro was fascinated by Willa. She spoke with an air of confidence he only had seen exhibited by the Seers, but, this tall blonde looked nothing like a Seer. "Warrior hero?" he asked. "I understand those words. I am Gerro."

She shrugged. "Some may call me that. My warriors and myself are trying to free our people from the Tanlians" Pausing, Willa shook her head. "Tarylan Seers? I do not understand."

Jorn interrupted. "Seers? The Colonia Nueve had a Seer on board." Without thinking, he reached into his pocket not realizing he was making a threatening gesture. The captain did not see the blow that knocked him to the ground. Seeing the stranger move his hand to his pocket, Gerro spun around to kick at Jorn. Willa reacted by kicking at the Tarylan's stationary leg, tripping him. Jorn looked over to see Gerro also lying on the ground with Willa straddling him, hand raised ready to strike a blow to his throat. Both prone men made eye contact.

The captain slowly pulled a small card from his pocket to indicate he carried no weapon. Despite the tense situation, Jorn let out a loud chortle then burst out laughing. Gerro glared at Jorn then heard a giggle as Willa stepped back. A moment later both parties howled with laughter, including Gerro who rose then helped Jorn to his feet.

"Forgive me, that was foolish," Jorn said, rubbing his chest where the Tarylan's foot had made contact. Gerro slapped the captain on the shoulder as an apology. The captain scanned the card in his hand. "Hmm, Seer. I believe the Colonia Nueve had a young Seer on board. Oh yes, here it is — Taryl Bryann was her name." Willa and Jorn were amazed at the reaction to the name.

"The Holy One," Verinya said softly. Then, the two Seers and the Tarylans gave the sign of reverence in unison — kissing the palm of their left hands and placing them on their chests.

Looking wide-eyed at Jorn, Willa said, "There is much we need to learn about these people."

The captain scowled in thought. "What did they say earlier that you did not understand? Tarylan Seers?" he asked.

Willa turned to Verinya. "Who are the Tarylan Seers, do they live among you?"

The older Seer smiled. "It may be more difficult to meet them. They guard the large valley on the other side of this mountain. The Seers are protective of their power and very suspicious of strangers."

Jorn shook his head. "Our instruments are scanning heavy cloud cover over most of the valley. We see no signs of life."

Verinya chuckled. "Ah, son of Earth, the clouds are only in your mind."

The Tarylan Seers were in an uproar. Never before had so many ships been detected orbiting Verde Grande. Watcher Seers from throughout Fortress Bryann rushed to the meditation rooms. Even Tanella and Cara put themselves in trances to help monitor the intruders. After a few hours, Tanella broke out of her trance. Aides helped her to a nearby chair and gave her water. It had been many harvests since the High Seer had been a watcher. The experience drained her.

A few minutes later Cara stretched and left her trance. "It appears the people in those ships have detected nothing in Verde Valley, High Seer. Our watchers are in control."

Tanella sat back in her chair. Her hair was disheveled and her eyes were bloodshot from the strain of maintaining a trance. "There are so many of them this time. Our watchers must keep vigilant! Keep me posted if there is any change in their actions." The High Seer started to rise but shakily sat back down with a grunt. She motioned for two aides to help return her to her room.

17

Malik was getting worried. Flyn had not returned to his usual spot the next day. The knife and message board he buried were undisturbed. The old hunter cooked over a small fire. Malik had found a small hollow in the rocks, where he could start a fire without drawing attention. He was getting tired of eating climbers, those bushy-tailed rodents, but at least they sustained him. The fruit was plentiful, and he never grew tired of snacking on the sweet juices.

"One more day, Flyn, and then I will go looking for you," Malik said to himself. This could prove to be dangerous, but he was determined to bring his friend's son back or die trying. The older hunter was rewarded the next day. About mid afternoon, he was surprised to hear voices. Flyn usually was quiet when he appeared with his Tarylan guards.

Today the laughter of a woman could be heard from a long distance. As the people grew closer to his hiding place in the giant oak, Malik heard a familiar voice — Flyn. Shaking his head, Malik watched as Flyn walked over to the giant boulder. A blond woman darted among the fruit trees picking up the delectable treats from the ground. "A woman! He brought a woman. The young fool," Malik snorted, but had to allow himself a chuckle. "He must be feeling better."

Peering out between the branches, Malik spotted Flyn's signal and waved back to acknowledge it. The young hunter was relieved to see his friend again. Flyn watched the chattering and laughing Ortelle for a time, then glanced up to see Malik wagging a finger at him. He suppressed a grin, remembering stories of Malik's conquests. Flyn had tried to convince Ortelle to stay behind while he went on his daily walk but she was insistent. After spending almost a day in bed together, eating, drinking and making love, she now refused to leave his side.

Pointing to a large tree sitting atop a large hill, Flyn convinced Ortelle that was where the best fruit would be. Feigning exhaustion, he slid down the rock to rest at his usual spot. Only more than willing to please him, Ortelle sauntered over to the tree. The Tarylan guards stretched out in their usual spots, ignoring him. Once in a while one of the guards would cast an admiring glance at Ortelle. Flyn worked the small stone loose, finding the knife and message board. He tucked the weapon into his boot and scratched a message while encouraging Ortelle to keep looking for the prized fruit.

Flyn was barely able to return the message piece back under the stone when Ortelle returned with a full basket. She nuzzled up to him as they sat in the sunshine. Glancing up the tree, Flyn could see Malik's smirk. Then, the branches slowly closed. Again, Malik waited for Flyn's party to be well down the path before retrieving the message board. The hunter smiled grimly as he examined Flyn's message. It was an ambitious plan, but the Tarylans should be caught by surprise. Malik retired even earlier than usual that night. He would need his energy tomorrow — it may prove to be a frantic day.

———————

Flyn veered from his usual path on the way back to the shelter. Unaware of the detour, Ortelle happily walked along beside him. The Tarylan guards were curious about the change in routine but followed at a respectable distance, confident the wounded man could not escape them.

This was the first time Flyn had visited the site where the Defenders were buried. After being killed in the ambush, the bodies of the Defenders had unceremoniously been burned in a large pyre then covered up in a common grave. The ground was still scarred from the massive blaze. A pile of charred logs lay nearby. The thought of this insult enraged Flyn, but he managed to mask his emotions. According to Nuven tradition, each one of those brave men should have been sent to his ancestors with a proper ceremonial pyre. Kneeling beside the grave, Flyn called out each Defender's name, blessed him and entreated his ancestors to welcome him among them.

Ortelle stood behind him with her head bowed respectfully. The guards watched from a distance, saying nothing. After finishing the ceremony, Flyn took Ortelle by the hand and walked back to the shelter. Once back in the room, he turned to her. "Please forgive me, sweet one, but I want to sleep alone tonight. I will be up half the night praying for those men."

Ortelle hugged him. "Let me stay. I want to be with you. I will not interfere."

Flyn pulled her gently away. "No, this is a private meditation. Those men were not properly honored. Their ghosts linger here. They are in turmoil."

She looked at him wide-eyed. "Ghosts?" Then backed away in fright. Flyn nodded somberly. Flyn hated to fool her into leaving him alone for the night, but it was the only way his plan would work. He cared for her but could not risk involving her with his escape. Her reluctance to leave made him heartsick, but he had to act out his plan.

"Will you be safe?" she asked trying to sound brave.

Flyn smiled and kissed her on the forehead. "Yes, I will be fine. I need to convince the ghosts to leave. Strange things may happen in this room tonight."

Ortelle needed no further convincing. She hugged him tightly. "When will it be safe to return?"

Flyn looked into her worried eyes, trying to soothe her without giving himself away. "Wake me for first meal, everything will be settled by then."

Ortelle reached up, putting both hands on his face and gave him a long, lingering kiss. "I will wake you in the morning my love," she said and reluctantly backed out the door.

Flyn smiled to reassure her, trying not to betray his heavy heart. His eyes drank in her image. After tomorrow, he feared he would never see her again.

———

Ortelle had been fitful most of the night worrying about Flyn. At first light she wanted to run to Flyn's room. She was anxious for his safety but honored her promise. He probably had experienced a harrowing night and may only recently have been able to finally enjoy sleep. An hour before first meal, Ortelle could wait no longer. She knew Flyn would forgive her. Something was out of place as she rounded the corner to walk down the hallway that led to his room. Curious, she hurried to his door but stopped with a horrified gasp.

A body lay crumpled in a pool of blood. Smudged bloody footprints led down the hallway. Shaking and sick to her stomach, Ortelle leaned over the body. It was a Tarylan who had been on night watch. His throat had been sliced open. Staring at the dead man, Ortelle stumbled into Flyn's room — it was empty and cold. The fire coals were long dead.

Not believing what she saw, Ortelle slowly made her way past the dead guard, following the bloody tracks to the outside door. She slowly opened it and discovered the next grisly scene. Both of the Tarylans who had been on guard duty lay dead on either side of the door. Pools of blood covered the porch floor. More bloody footprints led down the steps, disappearing down the trail.

Sinking to her knees, Ortelle couldn't help herself. Flyn apparently had managed to kill his guards and was trying to escape. Her sobs of grief turned into wails of brokenhearted anguish. Hearing her screams, other Tarylans came pouring out of the shelter's dining area. Their curses and shouts quickly mixed with Ortelle's cries. Seeing the bloody tracks inside and leading outside, a search party was quickly organized to comb the area.

"Remember to take the hunter alive!" a Tarylan officer yelled to his vengeful troops. "The Seers want him alive. If he is killed, you all will share the same fate as your dead comrades. If he puts up a fight, no one will blame you if you have to wound him again."

The troops acknowledged their leader and ran down the trail, fanning out looking for signs. Their shouts could be heard well away from the shelter as they followed broken branches and an occasional blood spot. To the Tarylans, it looked like the hunter was clumsily stumbling down the path trying desperately to escape. They were encouraged by this easy trail. It appeared the hunter was still suffering from his earlier wound. The troops soon were betting who would find the escapee and what they would do to him once they laid their hands on the murderer.

18

The autoship silently dropped out of the night sky into the Verdan Valley. It relayed no signals back to the fleet but recorded its every scan. No one in the CAIN fleet monitored its movements because Verinya explained to the officers that everything they would see would also be seen by a Tarylan Seer.

The ship detected thermals all over the valley. The vessel's presence went unnoticed. Not even the Seers detected it because there was no living being to sense in it. It sped across the valley, recording the location of the small villages scattered everywhere. The ship slowly swept over Verde City, measuring its size. Finally coming to Fortress Bryann, the mechanical spy carefully scanned the walls and hovered outside open windows, eavesdropping on conversations.

A young Seer was gazing out her bedroom window, admiring Luz Primo as it rose over the horizon, when a strange shape obscured her view. With a whoosh, the object was gone. Puzzled, the Seer looked all around, listening for the cry of what she thought was a night bird. Hearing and seeing nothing more, she shrugged and closed her window for the night.

The scout thoroughly scanned the valley until almost dawn and then climbed back into the sky, returning to its orbiting mother ship. No one in the ships watched or guided it back home. When the vessel had safely returned to its landing dock, maintenance crews nonchalantly attended to it, making sure their actions would not attract any attention from the Seers. After retrieving the scout's small memory cards, technicians inserted them into the ship's computer and went on about their business.

This was one of the longest hours Admiral Shim Murra had ever spent. He and thirty others in his ship had sat in pitch black waiting for the signal. The crew had to mimic sleep. Verinya told them the Tarylan Seers would stop watching as soon as their sight-hosts appeared to have fallen asleep. A gentle beep sounded three times. Shim quickly tapped his vid monitor and stared in wonder at the scene.

Cities and villages spread out over the Verdan Valley. He occasionally could pick out people walking in the streets. His monitor beeped again and blinked off. Verinya had recommended the Earthers stagger their viewings of what the scout found and keep each session short so as to not attract the Tarylan Seers' attention.

Shim's comm buzzed. "Sir, did you see that?" Jorn's voice cut through the darkness. "Cities and people everywhere — descendants of the colonists."

The senior officer smiled. "Yes, Captain, it appears the valley is full of people. Apparently those Seers don't want us to know about them." The monitor beeped again as even more scenes flashed across it. This pattern repeated itself again and again as the CAIN officers watched scenes flash intermittently on their monitors.

One of the last images was of Fortress Bryann. Shim and Jorn watched in wonder as a young woman peered curiously out of a window, her long red hair hanging loosely over her shoulders. Snippets of conversations poured out of other windows and more sights of red-haired women filled their screens.

"What do you make of all that?" the admiral asked Jorn as his vid blinked off again.

The captain was slow to answer but finally replied. "I've never seen anything like that, sir. Those Tarylan Seers all look alike with their red hair. They are the ones who have guarded these people all these years?"

Shim had noticed the same thing. "Those women have successfully held the Tanlians off for centuries. It would be wise for us not to underestimate them."

———————

What was keeping the Tarylans? Even those simpletons should be able to follow this trail, Malik thought as he hunkered behind a giant oak. Not long after daybreak, he was rewarded by their boisterous shouts. Most men feared being chased, but Malik looked forward to this hunter and prey game. The longer the Tarylans chased him, the better the chances Flyn's real escape route would go unnoticed.

Just before daybreak, Malik had worked his way to the shelter where Flyn was kept. He knew the guards were there but could only make out their silhouettes as they walked back and forth on the porch. The door to the shelter opened as a figure with a lighted torch stepped outside. It was Flyn. The guards rushed over to question him. The light illuminated all three men. The Tarylans were noisily interrogating Flyn who acted surprised at their reactions.

With their full attention on Flynn, Malik approached the shelter. Drawing his bow, he fired an arrow into the neck of one of the guards. The man barely made a sound as he staggered backwards. Forgetting about Flyn, the other guard turned to see what had happened. The young hunter seized the opportunity and thrust the torch into the second guard's face. As the Tarylan tried to protect himself, Malik saw Flyn's hand flash at the man's neck. The Verdan fell with a gurgling sound.

"Are you sure you can't go with me?" Malik whispered when he ran to Flyn's side.

Aron's son shook his head. "No, my shoulder would slow us down too much. I can follow the caverns that lead out into the mountain and disappear until you come back."

Malik smiled at the young man. Flyn reminded him so much of Aron, his good friend. "I will give the Tarylans a good hunt,'"Malik said, choking back tears. He wanted so desperately to take Flyn back to safety but knew the young man was not up to the journey.

"Stay safe young one. After I play with the Tarylans, I will return with help. We will bring you home," Malik said as he purposely stepped in the pooling blood, making sure he could leave a trail that a half-blind Nuven could follow.

Flyn gripped Malik's shoulder. "Father said you were a man of your word. Until next time, hunter." Both men turned away to make their escapes.

The pursuing Tarylans snapped Malik from his thoughts. The hunter was amazed at how noisy they were. Crouching high in a tree, he counted twenty searchers as they jogged underneath him. He was happy to hear how angry they were. *This will be even more fun that I had hoped*, he thought while effortlessly and silently slipping down the tree to begin following the Tarylans at a safe distance.

The search party paused for a short break after about an hour of crashing through the orchards looking for the escapee. This was the chance Malik was waiting for. One of the Tarylans found some bushes a short distance from the group to relieve himself. Malik fired an arrow at the easy target. The Tarylan shuddered and dropped to the ground without a sound.

The searchers gathered to continue their hunt. No one immediately noticed one of their party was missing. The Tarylans had not been on the trail long when Ravil looked for Utto to remind his friend he was in debt to him from the last game of chance. After checking the group twice, Ravil called a halt.

"Well go look for that slug and hurry," said an exasperated Lieutenant Lonan Rallik. "He will pull two night guard shifts for slowing us down."

Ravil hurried back to the spot where he had last seen Utto. The other Tarylans continued looking for Flyn but slowed to walk. A yell for help turned into a scream of pain that echoed through the trees. It was abruptly cut off. Rushing to the scene, the searchers found Ravil pinned to a tree by an arrow through his stomach. His throat had been cut. Blood was still dripping from the wound. Utto's body was found after a quick search of the area. An arrow had sliced through his neck.

"Find that damn hunter!" yelled an infuriated Lonan. "He's got to be in the immediate area. Stay in pairs. He wants to pick us off one by one." The attacks unnerved Lonan. He and his men were supposed to be hunting the wounded hunter. "Why is he attacking us when he should be saving his energy to escape?" he muttered to himself. Then a thought occurred to him. Of course! The hunter probably was unable to move any longer and was desperately lying in ambush.

The Tarylans fanned out over the area, checking every conceivable place a man could hide — nothing, not even a blood trail this time. It was dusk when Lonan called his men back. The setting sun cast long shadows throughout the orchard. He did not want them wandering about in the dark. They would make perfect targets for the hunter. The exhausted Tarylans made camp, posted guards and were settling down for third meal, when a high-pitched laugh cascaded through the trees from the next ravine. The Verdans jumped up, grabbing their weapons. A barely visible figure appeared between two large trees. It stood there looking at the Tarylans.

"What are you waiting for? Shoot him," Lonan yelled. The Tarylans let loose a barrage of arrows. Silence.

"Do you think we hit him, sir?" one of the Tarylans asked hopefully.

Lonan shrugged. "If we did, we will find him in the morning. It's getting too dark to take a chance if he's still out there."

As if answering the question, a second screeching laugh pierced the night, mocking the Tarylans. Cursing, several of the searchers loosed more arrows, which prompted even more laughter.

"Save your arrows. You will hit nothing in the dark," Lonan ordered. The nervous Tarylans gathered close. Camp fires were made to ward off the chill of the autumn night and to cook their rations. As they ate their meal, a hissing sound cut through the air, followed by a thud. A Tarylan who had been sitting on a stump clutched the arrow in his chest. He looked helplessly at his comrades and slumped over.

"Kill the fires!" Lonan screamed. "They're only giving him a target." A second arrow hissed into their midst but this time it embedded harmlessly into a tree. The troop posted guards to watch while their comrades lay shivering from the cold and from fright.

19

High Seer Tanella was enjoying a peaceful first meal. The first light of day was just starting to shine through her windows. She dipped pieces of freshly baked bread into the sour plum jam. Slices of apples and grapes filled a bowl beside her. A frantic knock on the door disturbed her reverie.

"Enter before you break the door," she snapped. Cara rushed in, forgoing the usual formal greetings. The normally good-natured woman's eyes were wide and her face was white.

Tanella frowned when she saw her friend. "What is it?"

The older Seer was having trouble speaking. Finally regaining her composure, she pointed out the window. "We don't know how long it's been there," Cara said hoarsely. "No one has come out."

Puzzled, the High Seer gasped as she peered over her balcony. A small black ship sat in the courtyard of the fortress. It looked like it belonged among the statues of past Tarylan leaders. The courtyard was eerily quiet.

"None of our watchers saw this ship approach? No one heard anything?" the High Seer asked in a barely audible whisper as if she was afraid the strange vessel would hear her.

Cara shook her head "no" as she joined Tanella in peering at the frightening sight. "We have posted guards around the perimeter, High Seer, but they are terrified. No one wants to approach it. Our weapons will be no match for whomever is inside."

Movement from the far side of the courtyard caught both Seers' attention. A hooded figure slowly approached the ship and walked around it. "Who is that?" the High Seer demanded.

Cara's curiosity overcame her fear. "Not a guard, it appears to be one of our Seers. What a brave woman!"

"Or a fool," Tanella growled.

Cara gazed at the figure. There was something familiar about her. At that moment, the Seer who had ventured forward removed her hood. "Trista Hedlo!" Cara gasped. Tanella said nothing but stared at the young woman who stood patiently before the ship. Trista had discovered and read the diary of Rina Engstrom, one of Verde's first colonists. A soft whir came from the ship as a long cylinder slowly rose out of the roof. Trista backed up a step but held her ground as two fan-shaped objects enfolded from the cylinder and spun to face her.

"Peace," a woman's voice crackled out of the cylinder. "We mean you no harm, Seers of Verde Grande. This ship comes from Earth. We have returned to rejoin our brothers and sisters." The same message repeated itself in eight of the major languages of Old Earth.

Tanella and Cara were stunned. The Tarylan Seers had long given up hope of seeing ships from Earth. For generations, all their energies had been spent protecting the Verdans from Tanlian attack. To their amazement, Trista stepped even closer to the ship, her arms spread out. Even from their lofty height, the two women could hear Trista. "We greet you in peace, welcome to Verde Grande."

A different woman's voice spoke from the cylinder. "We appreciate your gesture young one. We ask permission from the High Seer to disembark and seek assurance of no attacks by your Tarylan guards."

The High Seer felt her throat tightening with fear. "They know of us, of me. Who is that?" she rasped.

Cara gently placed her hand on Tanella's shoulder. "Whoever is in that ship is waiting for you. There is only one way to find out. It is beyond our control now. We are at their mercy. I doubt invaders would ask permission to leave their ship."

The High Seer just stared at the scene. The courtyard had slowly filled with Seers and Tarylan guards. No one spoke. All eyes were turned up at her balcony. Seeing Tanella's indecision, Cara gently pulled her away from the balcony and helped her out to the courtyard.

Tanella moved as if in a dream. No Seer leader had ever been faced with this situation. She had no history to guide her. She felt powerless. Fear washed over her like a shower of cold water, taking her breath away. For ten generations the Seers had protected Verde Grande from invasion and kept their ever-watchful eyes on the valley's population.

Fright gripped her as she approached the ship. Had she and her Seers failed their fellow Verdans? As Cara walked with Tanella, she felt the leader grow more tense with every step, her breath coming in short gasps. She expected to see more bravery from this woman who had ruled the Tarylans for more than thirty harvests.

The High Seer and Cara finally reached the ship, stopping next to Trista who had not moved. The young Seer greeted Tanella but received no response. Cara and Trista exchanged worried glances. Tanella's eyes appeared not to focus on anything. She slowly swayed back and forth. Trista glided to Tanella's other side to help support her.

Whoever was in the ship took the presence of the High Seer as permission to disembark. A buzz emanated from the vessel as a hatch opened in its side. Two pleasant-looking uniformed women slowly walked out. They were followed by three other women — a tall blonde and two others who resembled Seers. The last person to emerge brought startled gasps from the crowd. Tanella stared in shock as a young man approached her. Her focus sharpened as she found her voice. "Gerro!" she hissed.

The former Tarylan captain bowed to the High Seer, stepped aside and gestured to the two red-haired women. "I believe you remember my mother, Verinya. And this is my twin sister

Arynna." All eyes were on Gerro. No one had expected to see a familiar face step from the strange ship, much less the famous Tarylan hero.

Gerro's smile quickly faded as he watched the High Seer. All the color flowed from her face. Her eyes rolled up then her knees buckled. It was all Cara and Trista could do to keep her from collapsing. Her body was gently lowered to the ground as the crowd cried for a healer. Cara and Gerro knelt next to her. A healer rushed to the High Seer, checked her pulse and started chest compressions, pumping vigorously. Other healers rushed over to assist. Each took a turn pumping Tanella's chest.

The healers finally stopped after each had taken two turns trying to resuscitate Tanella. The first healer held the leader's wrist checking for a pulse. Another placed her ear over the High Seer's mouth. The two women held their positions over their fallen leader, not moving for several minutes. Finally both looked at each other, shaking their heads. "The High Seer is now among the stars. She has joined the Sainted One," the first healer said as she gently closed Tanella's eyes. All the Seers and Tarylan guards made the sign of reverence.

Cara sighed as she stroked Tanella's hair. "The High Seer was terrified of losing her power and the Seers' influence," she said gazing sadly at Gerro. "Many terrible things have happened because of this fear. People have died needlessly, lives changed forever."

The older Seer's eyes glistened as she held out her hand to Verinya. "Is that really you, my dear, after all these harvests?"

Verinya kissed Cara's hand. "Yes, I have returned," she said as tears streamed down her cheeks. "Fate has reunited me with my son. My daughter accompanied me here."

Cara gazed at Arynna, a puzzled look on her face. "Come close my dear," she implored the younger woman. Arynna knelt beside the older Seer. "Your eyes, the color . . . " Cara whispered. She beckoned Gerro. "The same eyes, they have the same beautiful golden eyes."

Verinya smiled. "A blend of Seer and Nuven eyes."

Cara looked intently at Verinya and grasped her hand. "A Nuven?" The older Seer paused, remembering the events of twenty harvests ago. "Was their father a Defender? It is very important."

Gerro looked at his mother. Verinya nodded. "Yes, he was the Defender who killed all those Sankari — Aron Nels."

Cara gasped. She felt lightheaded. The events of the day were overwhelming: A space flier landing in the courtyard, Tanella dying in her arms, the return of Verinya and Gerro. "Deep breaths, Cara, deep breaths," someone whispered in her ear. The Seer felt two arms around her shoulders. Verinya smiled and kissed her cheek.

Taking a moment to regain her composure, Cara was helped to her feet. Six Tarylan guards gently placed Tanella's body on a stretcher and carried it into the fortress. Cara held her arms out in greeting as she approached the strangers from the ship. Verinya took charge of the introductions. Willa and Sula knelt before Cara and offered their condolences on the death of the High Seer. She took the hand of each young woman and kissed it.

"I have much to discuss with all of you, but first we must attend to the High Seer," Cara said as she watched the stretcher-bearers disappear into the fortress. "All courtesies will be given to our guests. We will observe the traditional day of mourning and then she will be buried in the Meadow of Honor with the other High Seers."

A Tarylan officer came forward, stopping just in front of Gerro. Willa eyed him suspiciously, but the man gave no sign he was about to attack. "Is that really you, Gerro? How did you come to ride in a flying vessel? Did you capture it?"

Gerro guffawed at the idea he could manage such a feat. "No, lieutenant, I didn't capture it, but I can be very persuasive," he said, winking.

The officer stared at him for a moment then got the joke. Laughing, he turned to the crowd and announced, "Gerro has returned." The people in the courtyard roared their approval.

Guards and Seers crowded close to see Gerro and the others. Dozens of questions were shouted at once.

Holding his hands up to be heard, Gerro called out. "My friends, we have many stories to tell. The Earthers come in peace, but Tanlians are hurrying here, too. We have much to do."

20

Dallon Vesser glared at his junior officer. The Tarylan captain had just returned to the orchard when he was informed of the disturbing news of Flyn Nels's escape. "You outnumbered a wounded prisoner by twenty to one, and he chases you back here," he sneered.

Lonan Rallik did not back down. "He was picking us off one by one. The damn hunter knows the area too well. He killed three of my men last night. We chased him to the rocks at sunrise, but then he killed two more today. He appears out of nowhere, ambushes a man and then disappears again. We need many more men to flush him out."

Dallon shook his head. Five more Tarylans had died at the hands of this hunter. Normally he would hunt down the culprit and take delight in torturing him to death. However, the Seers wanted him unharmed. "Our orders are to bring him back alive. I brought a hundred more troops with me. Do you like those odds better, second captain?"

Lonan's face flushed with anger, but he held his tongue. "Let me have those men and I will bring him back. What is so important about this hunter? It would be easier to bring back a body than a wounded man."

Dallon grunted. He could sympathize with Lonan's anger. He would feel the same way if an escapee had put up that much of a fight. "Unfortunately, this hunter is valuable to the Seers. They want him for a trait he carries." Lonan stared at him, apparently not understanding.

"Genetics, captain," Dallon said curtly. "A family trait, the Seers need that trait. Now do you understand?"

Lonan was incredulous at what he was hearing. He had temporarily forgotten his anger. "A family trait? Do you mean they need him for . . ." the officer said flabbergasted, unable to finish the thought that made him sick. Dallon nodded grimly.

It was the ultimate honor for a Tarylan male to be chosen to mate with a Seer. Now these women wanted this enemy brought to them. "This hunter is going to pollute the Seer bloodlines," Lonan argued. "If he fathers women who will become Seers, that means his sons could become Tarylan Guards — unacceptable!"

Dallon held up his hand, ordering Lonan to stop his tirade. "You have your orders, now carry them out," he said brusquely. "Take all these troops and find that wounded hunter."

Lonan was about to continue the argument, but stopped when he saw the puzzled look on Dallon's face. "What is it, sir? Something wrong?"

Dallon nodded as he stared into the orchard. "Yes, maybe. If this hunter has such a bad shoulder wound, how can he run and shoot an arrow so effectively? How can he draw his bow?"

Lonan shrugged. That thought had nagged at him, but he had been too busy tracking the escapee and then being under attack to think it through. "You are correct. I have seen the wound. It is deep and is healing slowly. His movements have been limited."

The two Tarylan officers looked at each other. The same thought occurred to both. "We were chasing someone who ran like a deer and shot at us with great accuracy from far away," Lonan said, frowning. "Not like a wounded man at all."

Dallon pointed at the cabin. "You have been chasing the wrong man!" he shouted. "Search this shelter, tear it apart if you must. Nels must be hiding near here."

———

Ortelle Woodrud wept as Dallon questioned her. She told him over and over again how she had discovered the murdered guards. The healer slumped in her chair and sobbed every time she recalled the event. The Tarylan captain was unsympathetic. He found her relationship with Flyn distasteful. He could not control what the Seers might do with the hunter, but Ortelle had been under his orders to care for Flyn's wounds, not sleep with him.

Even the acerbic Lonan backed her story. He had been one of the first Tarylans to hear her screams when she had discovered the dead guards. He doubted she was acting after seeing Ortelle make herself sick with sorrow. These protestations only enraged Dallon. He was convinced Ortelle had helped Flyn escape. How else could a wounded man kill one or perhaps all three guards?

Ortelle's insistence reminded Dallon of the women he and Gerro had competed for attention. Much to his displeasure, the women usually chose Gerro. He now was determined to make this female tell the truth. Grabbing Ortelle by the arm, Dallon dragged the protesting woman outside and into the clearing outside the shelter.

With assistance of several troops, the Tarylan captain tied her spread-eagled to the giant oak that shaded the area. Pacing angrily around Ortelle, Dallon ordered her to tell him the truth. She continued to protest her innocence.

Making sure he could be heard from many meters away, Dallon shouted his threat: "Flyn Nels or whomever is helping him, come forward! I will spare this woman only if you return. You have one hour!"

———————

Malik's stomach soured as he saw the woman tied to the tree. He hoped Flyn had escaped to the safety of the mountain and remained unaware of her plight. The old hunter crept as close as he could and scaled a tall tree. He could go no further because the area was now swarming with Tarylans.

After an uneasy hour, Malik watched as Dallon approached the woman nonchalantly. The Tarylan chatted casually with his troops as they stood. Without warning, the captain nocked an arrow and fired at Ortelle. She shrieked as the arrow punctured her hand. Gasping and crying, Ortelle pleaded with Dallon to stop.

"Her pain is on your shoulders, Nels!" Dallon yelled. "I will use her as a target once every hour until you come forward. Don't be a coward and let this woman suffer."

Malik felt helpless and sick. It was midday, at least five hours until sunset. He could sneak no further because of all the guards.

Ortelle's wails could be heard clearly. Malik doubted the woman could last until nightfall if the Tarylan kept inflicting wounds. Another hour had passed when Dallon appeared out of the cabin again. Not heeding her pleas of mercy, he fired another arrow. This one shattered her knee. She screamed and passed out.

Dallon inspected Ortelle after yet another hour eclipsed. She had regained consciousness but was weak from loss of blood. He shot another arrow into her shoulder. The poor woman writhed and gasped.

"Enough, Dallon, Tarylans do not torture women," Lonan shouted as he walked toward Ortelle, intent on freeing her. Not uttering a word, Dallon raised his bow again and fired. Lonan staggered as the arrow pierced his back. He shuffled forward two steps, then fell.

With a collective yell, Lonan's remaining men rushed Dallon. Even though they were outnumbered almost two to one, it took almost all of the captain's men to beat them back.

Malik used the ensuing melee to drop out of his hiding place and rush to where Ortelle was tied. Flyn's lover had passed out again.

She was bleeding badly from her wounds, especially from the last arrow. Saying a silent prayer, Malik entreated Ortelle's ancestors to welcome her. The hunter drew his knife and ended her suffering. As he did so, he begged her ghost to forgive him and to find peace.

While the Tarylans continued to scuffle, Malik darted back through the orchard. As his men were dragging Lonan's

317

subdued men away, Dallon spotted Malik disappearing into the trees. A glance at Ortelle revealed the Nuven's act of mercy.

"A hunter!" he screamed. "Kill that hunter!" Eight of his troops set out in pursuit. They were all found dead the next morning with no sign of their attacker.

21

Sula Gallagos' air and food supplies were almost gone. She had put on her space suit three days ago to save energy. Most of the ship's power reserves had been transferred to the engines in an effort to stay ahead of the Tanlian fleet that was slowly gaining on her. The Kenyattan captain's ship was only two days away from Verde Grande and the CAIN fleet which protected it.

Sula grimly estimated the Tanlian vanguard could pull within weapons range of her ship in four hours, maybe six, if information from the Earthers was correct. Her autoship escorts were gone. They all had drained their power reserves into her ship along the way. One by one, out of power, they drifted off and self-destructed at her command.

CAIN engineers had quickly retrofitted this ship for Sula. They combined two of their small scouts into a small, deep-space flier. Three-fourths of the ship's space was devoted to an expanded engine and increased power supply. The remaining space was her living area and life-support systems.

Sula ran the calculations again, just to make sure. But the numbers told her the same thing. It was clear what her duty was now — warn the CAIN fleet of the oncoming danger. With a determined sigh, she powered up her ship's transmitter and programmed it to broadcast a warning every five minutes. Each 30-second transmission drained more of her ship's fuel, allowing the Tanlians to gain on her even more quickly.

Three hours after Sula started transmitting, her console flashed a warning: "Weapons range in ten minutes." Another glance at her console told her she had received no incoming messages. Sula was unafraid. She had volunteered for this mission fully understanding the Earthers could not guarantee her small ship could outrun the Tanlians.

Smiling, she was proud of her accomplishment to be the first Kenyattan woman since the famous Ismala N'pofu to rebel against the Tanlians. She not only had orchestrated the attack on the Tanlian fleet at the twelfth planet but also had created havoc. Another warning signal — "weapons range in eight minutes" — but it blinked off as a new alert flashed: "Incoming message." Sula took a quick breath as she listened.

Jorn Nandez's voice came over her comm: "Message received, Captain Gallgos. We are prepared. Our fleet and the people of Verde Grande are grateful to you. May your gods protect you."

Tears filled her eyes, but she brushed them away. "So your ghosts are real, eh, Nandez?" she said broadcasting her last message. "Good luck with your mission. These devils are persistent. Sula out."

Another alert warned: "Weapons range in six minutes." She brought her ship around, flicked on the vid cam, turned her engines to "full burn" and punched in her nav destination — the lead Tanlian vessel, a planet raider with light weapons, designed for speed not fighting. The raider barely had time to fire as Sula steered her ship straight into it.

A grief-stricken Jorn watched Sula's vid recording of the Tanlian fleet as she streaked toward one of the ships. Just before impact, she whispered a short prayer: "For Kenyatta and freedom." A bright flash lit his screen, then it went black. Bowing his head to pay his respects, he vowed her death would not be in vain. The captain retransmitted her vid message to the other ships in the fleet and to a receiver recently erected on Verde Grande. He wanted all to know of her ultimate sacrifice.

Jorn followed up with a call to duty: "In two days we will have an opportunity to free the GEMS worlds from centuries of tyranny, to make Earth colonies free from terror and to avenge this hero of Kenyatta. Prepare yourselves, my brothers and sisters, this is why we came here."

Verinya, Gerro, Cara and Willa were discussing with other Verdan leaders what actions should be taken if the Tanlians attacked, when Arynna interrupted the meeting. The young Seer had been raised to speak freely so she thought nothing of disturbing the others.

"What is it, my dear?" Verinya asked, seeing her daughter's troubled expression.

"Pardon my intrusion, Mother, but my other brother is in grave danger. He has escaped, but the Tarylan guards are close to finding his hiding place. He is still injured." Verinya nodded gravely. With the latest events, she had forgotten about Flyn's predicament.

Gerro hunched forward in his chair. His eyes glinted with concern. "Aron's other son? Why are Tarylans seeking him?"

Cara let out a gasp. "By the Sainted One, I had forgotten about Dallon's mission to capture Flyn Nels. Dallon's men wounded him during an attack." The older Seer told of Tanella's orders to find the son of Aron Nels at any cost.

Gerro's expression changed to astonishment after hearing why the Seers were interested in the Nels bloodline. "The Seers need a trait in his blood?" He paused, almost not daring to ask the next question. "In my blood, too?"

"Yes, we suspect so. You and Flyn Nels may share the same trait," Cara said.

Gerro combed his fingers through his thick red hair while absorbing this disturbing news. Arynna sat close to her brother, patiently waiting for his next reaction. "What kind of a man is he?" he whispered to his twin.

Arynna smiled. "Flyn is an expert hunter and flier. He is honest and true to his friends and family. He and Father were very close. I have watched him, too, for many years." Pausing, she clasped Gerro's hand. Tears filled her eyes. "You and he are very much alike. Please help him if you can. The Nuvens have suffered so much."

Gerrro squeezed Arynna's hand gently. "You have my word, I will go as soon as I can. Do we know where he is?"

Cara reached for a map. "Yes, but it will take you days to reach him. It is a difficult valley to find." She approached Gerro and placed a hand on his shoulder. "You have always served honorably, Gerro. As ranking senior Seer, I reinstate your rank of Captain. Does anyone here have an objection?" A loud chorus of cheers answered her.

After congratulating Gerro with a hug, Willa spoke up. "We can take the ship. It won't take long to fly there. I offer my services to help."

Gerro started to object when he remembered how easily Willa dispatched him when they first met. "I would be proud to have such a brave warrior by my side. Let us leave in an hour. Dallon is persistent. He won't stop until he finds Flyn."

Verinya surprised the group when she announced: "Good, I will meet you two and any others you choose by the ship." Gerro and Arynna implored her to stay because of the potentially dangerous mission. Their protests were cut short. "I understand your concerns, but it is my duty to go. I know the danger Flyn is facing. Only one lone hunter is trying to help him. Besides, Dallon and the Tarylan Guards may be willing to listen to an older Seer."

Seeing her determined look, Gerro knew he would lose this argument. "Not long ago I thought I was an orphan. Today I am going on a mission with a mother I recently met to find a brother I never knew existed."

As Arynna bade them farewell, she took Gerro aside. "Do not be overprotective of mother. Remember, she has lived all her life with the Nuvens. She knows how to protect herself."

Gerro shrugged. "Are there any other surprises I need to know about?"

Arynna gave him a farewell hug. "Yes, our other two sisters are safe. I am sure some day we will meet them, too." She laughed as he walked away, shaking his head.

————

Malik watched helplessly as the Tarylan guards tore apart the cabin during their search for Flyn. He had tried to draw their attention. After killing the eight guards who pursued him, no others followed. If they did find Flyn's hiding place, Malik vowed to follow them. He would kill them one by one if need be or die trying. He owed it to Aron. The two hunters had saved each other's lives numerous times during their many excursions together. He knew his friend would have done the same for him.

From his hiding place in one of the lush fruit trees, he barely heard the group approach nearby. The startled hunter could not see everyone clearly, but there was something different about these strangers — several appeared to be women. The old hunter became alarmed when the group of about twenty people stopped below him. He could see the men were heavily armed. Even the women bore weapons. Suspecting they were aware of his presence, Malik slowly strung an arrow and waited. If these strangers wanted a fight, he would give them one. It alarmed him that they did not move from under his tree.

A woman's voice broke the tension. "Do not fire on us, hunter, we have come to help you rescue Flyn Nels. Please let me talk with you." Malik was startled, but the woman's voice sounded sincere. The strangers knew his location. If they wanted to attack, he probably could only kill a few before the others reached him.

Malik eased the tension on his bowstring. "You look like Tarylans, why should I believe you?" he shouted. "Tarylans captured and wounded Flyn and now are trying to find him again."

A red-haired woman slowly walked out from under the tree. Malik could not see her clearly, but she looked like a Seer. "We are Tarylans, but we are not the ones who captured him. You have been an extremely brave and loyal friend. We only want to help." To Malik's surprise, the woman laughed, shaking her head. "We have a story fit for a hunter's night fire. Nuvens and Verdans both will be retelling this tale for many harvests if we are successful. We must hurry, though. I fear the other Tarylans are getting close to finding Flyn."

The woman paused and held up her arms, beseeching him. "I knew Aron when he was a young Defender. I give you my word in his name, we are here to help."

She gestured toward the group. A Tarylan warrior joined her, squinting up at the tree. "I am kin of Aron Nels. She speaks the truth." The young man carefully put down his weapons and exposed his chest, making himself an easy target.

Malik stared at the young man. It was almost like Flyn was looking at him, but the voice and hair were different. The other members of the group joined the two and also put down their weapons. In a few moments, a rope snaked down the tree and Malik lowered himself to the ground. He approached the group cautiously, his eyes darting everywhere looking for a trap or sign of danger.

The hunter gave the other members a careful look, then returned to gaze at Gerro. His expression softened as he recognized that similar bemused expression he had seen during all those hunts he and Aron had spent together. "Who are you? A son of one of Aron's brothers?" Malik whispered.

The Tarylan shook his head. "I am Gerro. You could call me the lost son of Aron Nels."

Malik's eyes widened with surprise. "Aron never said anything about another son," he said warily. His eyes darted to Verinya. "Woman, you look like a Seer." She nodded.

Cocking his head to one side, recognition flashed in Malik's eyes as he quickly took a step back. "That Gerro? Captain of the Tarylan guard?"

The younger man smiled. "I am as surprised as you are, hunter. I only recently discovered my parentage. Obviously Aron's blood has served me well. We are here to help the brother I have never met."

Verinya stepped close to Malik. "Yes, I am a Seer, but I have lived in the Valley of the Heroes for twenty harvests. It is a long story. Aron and I met when he was protecting Temple Darya as a young Defender."

Malik nodded. He realized there was so much more about Aron that he didn't know after he watched his friend's heroic but tragic duel with the Sankari. "You didn't bring many fighters with you. That Tarylan officer has more than a hundred under his command and about half again under guard."

Verinya explained their small flier had limited space. Malik gaped in astonishment. "A sky filer? On Verde Grande? Like the First Ones?"

Gerro held up his hand. "Our world has changed, hunter, but first tell me about the Tarylans. You said some were arrested?"

Malik nodded. "Yes, after the tall blond leader killed the short dark-haired one, the dead man's troops attacked the others, but they were all beaten and taken away.

"Dallon killed Lonan?" Gerro murmured as he glared toward the direction of the cabin. He had served with Lonan, whom he considered to be an honorable man. Malik gave the troop a quick account of the events that had transpired: Flyn's affair with the healer, his escape and Dallon's torturing of the woman in a crazed effort to find the wounded man.

Gerro's expression changed to grim determination. "Come, we have people to rescue and a friend to avenge. Lead the way hunter."

22

Dallon's men tore apart the cabin while looking for the missing Flyn. Walls were ripped down in the search for hidden passages. The Tarylans were inspired when their efforts yielded several secret rooms full of weapons. However, they found no sign of Flyn. This only infuriated Dallon even more.

Certain the hunter had to be hiding nearby, the Tarylan officer raised the reward for the group which captured him. Dallon was storming down a hallway after another false alarm, when one of his guards alerted him to a small party of unannounced visitors. He stomped out of the cabin, angry at the interruption. He stopped in his tracks when he saw the strange Seer with six Tarylan guards.

The Seer smiled warmly, introducing herself. "Greetings captain, I am Seer Verinya. We have come to tell you of sad news and a change in plans."

Dallon bowed. "I don't recognize you, Honored One." Almost all of the Tarylan Guard held Seers in high respect except Dallon. He was the son of the High Seer and only answered to her.

Verinya shrugged. "My mission has kept me far away from Fortress Bryann. It is my unfortunate duty to inform you of your mother's death. She collapsed in the courtyard recently. I am positive she felt no pain."

Dallon was emotionless as he listened to Verinya's news. He and his mother had not been close. Their relationship was formed by mutual need — power. As the second-most-powerful Tarylan officer, he had carried out many assassinations deemed "necessary" by the former High Seer. These murders were beneath Gerro, who was the public's hero. With Gerro gone, he commanded the largest Tarylan force.

"Sad news indeed," he said impassively. "I will pay my respects when I return to the fortress. What change of plans?" Verinya was surprised by the tepid response to his mother's death. She had hoped for a show of emotion that she could direct in her favor.

"Your mission to bring back the hunter Flyn Nels has been rescinded, Captain. You have served honorably. Here are your orders from Cara, the new High Seer." Verinya held out a parchment for him to read.

Scowling, Dallon snatched the paper from her and read it. Much to his displeasure, he recognized the official High Seer seal, but was unfamiliar with Cara's signature.

So that old fool is now High Seer, he thought. *She should be easy to manipulate.* However, more important matters needed to be dealt with. "What about the importance of the hunter to the Seers? I was told he carries an important trait. Everyone was in agreement on this, even Cara."

Verinya took a step forward. "We have discovered more information, Captain. There are more males who can be called upon to help us. This hunter is no longer important."

Dallon erupted when he heard this. "No longer important?! Do you know how many men I lost capturing this vermin pup? He escapes and another hunter picks off my men like they were wild game when we searched for him." He threw the parchment down in disgust. "All this time and trouble to bring back Nels alive and he is no longer valuable," Dallon snorted.

The captain stared at the parchment, which looked like the skin of a dead animal lying in the dirt. As he looked up, his mouth split into a wicked grin. "So, Nels is not needed alive. That makes our job much easier now and worthwhile!"

Dallon whirled around and started back toward the cabin. "Sergeant, tell the men I will double the reward to anyone who brings me the body of Nels!" he yelled.

Verinya's scream of indignation stopped him cold. "No, Captain! Call off your search. Let the hunter go," she demanded, stomping her foot.

Dallon smiled at her reaction. "I don't know you, Seer. You have no authority here. Your interest in this hunter means nothing to me. I suggest you and your pets leave immediately."

Verinya charged toward Dallon, her guards were right behind her. Seeing a threat to their captain, a dozen of his men surrounded the small group, weapons drawn. "I order you to stop this nonsense, leave the hunter in peace."

With a smirk, Dallon reached out to shove the petite woman out of his way. Before he could react, the captain was sprawled out on the ground looking up at the Seer. His men quickly grabbed Verinya and her guards. Dallon was helped up and dusted himself off. "Leave now, woman, before I get angry," he snapped.

"You will be punished when you return to the fortress," she snarled back.

Dallon mocked her. "By who? A group of old women like yourself?"

The normally calm Seer's face was flushed with anger. "You will have to answer to Gerro! He has returned. He will not take your disloyalty lightly." Verinya had no idea she had just ignited an old flame of hatred.

"Gerro?!" He spat out the name like an insult. "That bastard orphan had better stay in the mountains with those worthless hunters."

Straining against the Tarylans holding her only infuriated Verinya even more. "You will be the one who leaves when my son is through with you," she screamed.

"Son?" Dallon said, his expression turned cold. With a quick snap of his wrist, the captain plunged a knife deep into Verinya's chest and yanked it back out. The Seer uttered a soft gasp and sank to her knees.

"Looks like Gerro is an orphan again," Dallon said matter-of-factly wiping the blood off his knife. Verinya's guards struggled against their captors in vain. "Better kill them, too. No one will know that they found us." Turning back, he returned to the cabin with renewed energy to find the elusive Flyn.

Flyn's shoulder ached from the exertion of climbing over ledges and pushing through narrow cutouts that led to the escape route behind the cabin. He found the doorway to the outside but then had to hack his way to freedom through heavy underbrush. At last he was outside, standing in the midst of a small pine grove. Exhausted, he slumped against one of the trees. For the first time in weeks he was alone. No Tarylan guards hovered nearby watching his every move.

Each throb in his shoulder reminded him of Ortelle, the sweet young woman who had cared for him so tenderly. He missed her gentle touch and blue eyes that lit up when she smiled. He hated to leave her, but taking the healer with him would only have made escape much more difficult. The Tarylans would have concentrated their search on the immediate area. Using Malik as a decoy would not have worked.

Flyn had climbed to safety about a hundred meters above the cabin. He tried to ignore his aching shoulder he had re-injured during his escape. His shirt was wet from blood. Hearing shouting, he crawled to a ledge and peered down. Two groups of Tarylans were arguing. A large group had surrounded a much smaller group. Even from this height, Flyn recognized the tall captain. The Tarylan officer was arguing with a woman. She looked like a Seer, but he was not sure.

The shouting stopped when the captain lunged at the woman. He then turned and walked away. Flyn was surprised when he saw the woman lying on the ground. An even more grisly scene ensued when the larger number of Tarylans coldly murdered the others they had been holding captive.

Flyn was shocked that Tarylans had killed a Seer and her guard in cold blood. Seers were the highest social order among the Verdans. The women with their mysterious vision were revered. The events were puzzling. It appeared there was much more going on than an attempt to find him. He could not imagine what would cause Tarylans to turn on each other.

More movement caught Flyn's attention. Another small group of Tarylans had climbed up the large storage shed and were slowly shimmying down the roof. The shed was almost out of sight from the cabin. Looking closely, the young hunter saw the men on the roof were poised directly above the four guards on the ground. The guards near the shed were watching the commotion going on near the cabin.

"Why would there be guards there?" he said out loud knowing no one else could hear him. As far as he knew, there was nothing but baskets of fruit stored there. Before he could ponder the question further, the Tarylans on the roof jumped en masse, overpowering the guards in a blink and dragging them inside the shed. Hardly any time had elapsed when new guards appeared out of the shed.

Flyn was fascinated by the high drama unfolding before him. It was like watching a Verdan play but without the often-boring soliloquies. These actors were much more deadly with their intentions. An unusual sound drew Flyn's attention away from what was going on below. The soft rustling started and stopped regularly, similar to a large animal moving carefully through brush.

Instinctively, Flyn crept from his spot, taking cover among some young pines. The barely perceptible rustling got closer then stopped and started again. It was not unlike a predator stalking its prey. Between the pine needles, Flyn could barely make out a shape moving cautiously around the area. As the shape moved closer, he could tell what it was — a man deliberately moving from spot to spot, looking for something. Flyn had no doubt who the stranger was looking for — him.

A lone Tarylan was in no hurry to find Flyn Nels. The young hunter had to be nearby. He was probably resting after exerting so much energy to escape. His crew had been tearing apart Flyn's bedroom when one of their axes cracked through the hidden door in the fireplace. The searchers swarmed in but were soon overwhelmed by all the passageways that led nowhere.

The Tarylan was about to give up, when he decided to examine an almost hidden ledge. Holding his torch up, he spotted droplets of blood on the rocks where Flyn had pulled himself through an opening. He soon understood the route led upwards. Each time he was puzzled as to where to go, the Tarylan would look up and find another opening leading to another tunnel. An occasional blood spot gave him incentive to keep moving.

After endlessly stumbling in the dark with a dying torch, he saw light pouring through a half-opened door. Peering out cautiously, he saw the brush Flyn had cleared away. As one of the hunter's guards, the Tarylan had underestimated him. For weeks he and five others had trailed behind Flyn as the hunter walked the groves, always stopping at the same place. His troop had grown complacent. Half of them looked forward to those lazy afternoon naps while he and the others continued their ongoing game of chance.

The guard looked forward to exacting his revenge on this bothersome young man who caused the death of his friends. Perhaps he would bring back the hunter's head as proof and claim Dallon's generous reward. Dragging the body through those bothersome narrow tunnels would be too much work.

Flyn was impressed with how silently and cautiously the Tarylan moved, very similar to a Nuven hunter. The young hunter readied his knife. He could still lash out with his good arm. A distant commotion broke the silence. The searcher uttered a soft curse and crept to the spot where Flyn had been watching from earlier. The noise grew louder — shouts of a battle and clash of weapons could be heard.

The Tarylan grew restless and paced along the ridge, trying to get a better view. The guard was clearly upset by whatever was happening below. He swore loudly, slapping his thigh in disgust. Remembering his mission, the Tarylan spun back to resume his search but stopped abruptly. He didn't have time to react to the flash of steel flying towards him.

While the searcher was absorbed with the battle, Flyn had crept up from behind. Saying a silent prayer, the wounded youth readied himself. He threw the knife as soon as the Tarylan turned around.

The guard recognized Flyn just as the knife speared into his stomach. Drawing his knife, the Tarylan staggered forward and attacked Flyn. The two combatants fell to the ground in a deadly wrestling match. Flyn managed to locate his knife in his foe's belly and pushed it deeper.

The Tarylan shuddered but raised his knife and slammed it into the young hunter's side. Flyn gasped from the blow but found the strength to roll the Tarylan over and plunge his knife into the man's chest. Aron's son tried to crawl away but the pain was too much. He took a trembling breath and collapsed.

23

Jas Ronett and his comrades lay tied together by a thick rope in the fruit shed. He and the others had tried to help Lonan Rallik when Dallon attacked their leader, but the other Tarylans surrounded them and beat them into submission. The young officer was surprised he and the others were still alive. At least they had been fed and their wounds looked at by an old healer.

Dallon Veser had visited them once. The captain was threatening and brief — join him and his men or face execution. Lonan's men had been fiercely loyal to him. Their leader had treated them with respect as long as they carried out their duties. He had given up chasing the mysterious hunter through the orchards when it became apparent they were nothing but targets for the expert archer. They had watched with horror as the barbarous Dallon tortured the young healer. Their leader was killed in his attempt to help the woman.

The sullen group was not eager to join the power-hungry captain. Their self pity was forgotten by a series of unusual noises against the outside walls of the shed — scrapings and light bumps. The sounds slowly flowed up the walls and over the roof, like large animals moving overhead. Then they stopped abruptly.

A dark object briefly blocked Jas's view out a small window in the shed. The front wall shook from a scuffle outside, then the doors exploded open as bodies and bright light poured through. Jas and the other men squinted and then cowered, expecting an execution squad. The doors closed as quickly as they were opened. It was difficult to see in the half-light but about twenty men stood above them. Four bodies were dragged into a far corner.

"Go on, kill us, damn you and Dallon," Jas growled. "We refuse to join that butcher."

A familiar voice chuckled. "I was hoping you would say that, Jas Ronett. How would you like to join us?"

Jas stared in disbelief as a figure appeared out of the shadows and knelt beside him — Gerro! The young officer let out a heavy sigh of relief. "Is that really you, sir? You've come to rescue us?"

Gerro nodded, reaching out with a large knife and cut off Jas's bonds. His men followed suit and soon all the captives were free. "How many of you are able to fight?" Gerro asked, as he watched Jas and the others stretch and gingerly limber up. Most raised their hands. A few had suffered broken arms and ribs and were unable to be of any help.

Gerro was pleased as his troop armed the freed men with extra weapons. He had almost sixty men now. The odds were getting better. "Prepare yourselves. We attack at the next guard change," Gerro ordered. Looking at Jas, he asked how soon but was interrupted by three loud raps at the door — new guards were on their way. Another scuffle ensued outside but it ended as quickly as it began.

The door burst open again and four more bodies were dragged in and flung to their floor. Blood oozed from the chest of one of the new guards. The man lay in a crumpled heap, not moving. Gerro poked the body, giving Willa Sydriker a questioning look.

The Betelan woman shrugged as she wiped off her knife. "Apologies, Captain, but that one refused to surrender when he saw I was a woman. I had to defend myself."

Gerro examined the other three who were still alive but unconscious. "Rouse those men," he ordered. "We will need them to get close to Dallon's troops." The captured guards sputtered and gagged as cold water was dumped over their heads. The two older men glanced at their dead comrade, saying nothing. The youngest of the three, who barely looked twenty, was wide-eyed with fright.

Gerro paced somberly in front of the three men. "I will issue you a reprieve if you join us. If not, you will be taken back to Fortress Bryann for trial."

One of the older men glared at Gerro. "What do you think Dallon will do to us if you lose? I will take my chances with the Seers. I only was following orders." The other guard, who was close to his age, nodded in agreement. However, the youngest man rocked back and forth, grasping his legs in a sitting fetal position.

Gerro scowled. "We don't intend to be turned back. I don't think Dallon's men will have the stomach for what we intend to do."

Looking up at the captain, the young guard slowly stood up. "I will join you, Captain. I was conscripted to Dallon because my father owed him a debt. What he has done made me sick, especially killing those women the way he did."

Gerro grabbed the youngster by his shoulders. "What women?"

The guard winced from the hard grip. "Dallon tied up the healer who slept with that hunter and shot arrows into her until she was barely alive," he said, shivering at the memory. "Someone, a hunter we think, must have put her out of her misery."

Gerro stared hard at the guard, not daring to ask, but he had to. "What about the other woman?"

The young man shook his head in disgust. "She looked like a Seer, an older woman. She told him the search for Nels was called off. Dallon became angry and wanted to keep looking for the hunter — talked about killing him. He stabbed her dead when she screamed at him."

Gerro took a step backwards. His face creased in sorrow. He would never have allowed Verinya to confront Dallon if he suspected she would be harmed. The Captain sunk to his haunches, covering his eyes. He had barely known this woman but had felt an undeniable connection to her — the mother he had sought all his life.

Rising as if in pain, Gerro addressed the troops who stood quietly, waiting for their orders. "Kill all the others but save Dallon for me," he said with a cold stare. "I will settle with him personally."

The two older guards stood up sheepishly and asked to join Gerro and his men. Gerro glared at the men. "Why the change of heart?"

The man, who had spoken earlier, looked at his companion nervously. "We don't like what Dallon did to those women, either," he said spitting on the dirt floor. "The truth, Captain, we just want to go back to our families. We were going to leave the troop after this mission. You don't look like you intend to give up."

Gerro frowned but gestured for them to join his men. "Any sign you two plan to betray us and you will be dead before your bodies hit the ground."

As the men in the shed prepared to attack Dallon's troop, Malik approached Gerro. "I will be leaving you now, Captain. I want to look for Flyn. He may be in danger if those other Tarylans are looking for him that hard."

Gerro started to object. He suspected this hunter was worth four or five of Dallon's men. However, he stopped when he saw Malik's eyes shine with determination. "We will keep Dallon and his men busy, hunter. Good luck finding my brother."

Malik started for the door, then looked back. He paused and raised his right hand. "Good luck on your hunt, son of Aron. May you be stronger and faster than your prey." Gerro watched as Malik slipped out the door and disappeared into the forest behind the shed. The captain realized he had just received a hunter's blessing. Somehow it felt right.

———

"Captain, come here, you need to see this," one of Dallon's men laughed as he stood on the cabin's porch. "Looks like Lonan's men have changed their minds." Dallon walked over to where his trooper was pointing and grinned at the sight. Four of his guards were leading the men, all apparently still tied together. They shuffled towards the cabin, their heads lowered in shame.

It didn't take long for word to spread among Dallon's men. Most of them gathered nearby to watch, wondering aloud what their captain was going to do to the captives. The group approached to within twenty meters and stopped. Dallon loudly commanded the captured men to come closer, but they did not move. Three of the guards smiled and shrugged, a fourth hung his head slightly, a hood shading his face.

Dallon frowned at their insubordination. Taking a few steps toward the group, he called, "The first thing you worthless bastards need to learn is to follow orders! Now march over here." No one moved. Dallon stepped off the porch. "Damn it, you . . ."

A whistle rang out. The guards and the first row of prisoners dropped to their knees. Before Dallon and his men could react, a hail of arrows streaked into their midst, dropping many of them. At another call, the loosened ropes hit the ground and the former captives rushed the cabin. The two groups charged each other head on. Clubs and knives clashed, shouts of encouragement rang out, curses and screams of pain filled the air. Dallon swung his blade-edged club furiously again and again at his attackers.

In the heat of battle, a figure swept towards him with an angry shout. Dallon moved to counter the other's blow and was knocked to the ground. He rolled and leapt to his feet to face this opponent and got a good look at the frowning blood-streaked face.

"Gerro!" Dallon yelled. The two captains glared at each other for a moment then swung their weapons. Each man countered the other's blow. Spinning and changing the arcs of their attacks, they struggled to gain the advantage while their two forces fought on. Dallon grew angrier with each blow. He finally had his enemy where he wanted, in a fight to the death. Gerro sensed his foe's fury. He let Dallon swing first and easily blocked each blow, stepping aside and waiting for the next move.

Dallon kept pressing his attack, trying to beat Gerro back with sheer force. The two combatants parried back and forth. Dallon's frustration grew as the fight wore on. It only fueled his frenzy. He managed to force Gerro to back up to the tree where Ortelle had been tied. Seeing Gerro had no escape, Dallon put all his weight behind his next stroke. The blow knocked Gerro to the ground. Stepping quickly toward his downed foe, Dallon swung to deliver a fatal bash but it only struck the ground. Gerro rolled to one side, sprang to his feet and smashed his club into Dallon's back.

The other captain groaned and fell. He tried to rise but Gerro swiftly swung his club, striking Dallon's skull with a killing blow. Trembling from the deadly toil, Gerro sank to one knee, panting, his arms and sides aching from the force of Dallon's attack, sweat streaming out every pore. He stared at this dead enemy. No feeling of euphoria swept through him, only a grim satisfaction that the mother he had just discovered was avenged.

An eerie silence finally crept into his consciousness. Moments before, the crash of battle had echoed all around as he and Dallon fought. Now there was no sound, except for the occasional groan of a wounded man. Looking around the scene, Gerro saw all eyes were on him. He had not realized the battle ended as soon as Dallon fell. Many of his men were standing, covered with blood. A handful of Dallon's men were on their knees, their heads bowed in surrender. They fully expected to be executed.

Willa approached Gerro, kneeling beside him. "Dallon's men surrendered as soon as you ended him. Many of them are dead, a few wounded. The survivors are begging for clemency." She gripped his shoulder, trying to comfort him. Gerro eased himself to the ground to rest. Even though he was a tested fighter, the captain was alarmed when he looked up at Willa.

The young woman was streaked with blood and sweat. Her bright blue eyes peered out from what looked like a poorly applied mud mask. Dried blood crusted on her arms. Red splotches covered her clothes, all the way to her boots. Even her blonde hair, which had been pulled back in a tight bun, had turned an ugly copper color. Taking her hand, Gerro asked where she was wounded.

Willa looked at him, then grinned broadly. "I am well, Captain, although I can't say that for any of the men who crossed knives with me." Gerro looked approvingly at this fierce warrior. He now believed how she and her Betelan sisters could capture a Tanlian ship, using only their wiles and fighting skills. Willa squeezed his hand back. She had been impressed with his leadership and understood the emotions he had fought with.

"Treat the wounded — theirs and ours — equally. Bury the dead," Gerro ordered. He paused, eyeing the captured men. Some were weeping and shivering with fright. "Tell Dallon's men they are free if they vow never to take up arms again. Tell them to go home to their families. We are not murderers."

Rising, Gerro started to help Willa and the others with the wounded, when a scream echoed through the small valley. The cry came from somewhere up the mountain.

————

Malik's heart jumped into his throat when he finally found Flyn. The old hunter found the same passage the Tarylans had discovered in the cabin. However, he easily followed the coded etchings which led him directly to the escape route. He hastily scratched signs in the rocks so the others could follow later. He had hurried through the tunnels and scrambled up the ledges as fast as he could go. He was light headed when he burst onto the scene of the fight. His lungs felt like they were going to burst.

A horrific scene greeted him. Both men were covered with blood. An ashen-faced Flyn lay against a log. His head was rolled on one shoulder. A Tarylan lay at Flyn's feet. The knife Malik had snuck to his friend was gouged in the other man's chest. It appeared the two men had fought to the death. Overcome by grief and near the point of exhaustion, Malik stumbled over to where Flyn lay. The hunter couldn't control himself. Throwing his head back, all his emotions came rushing out in a frustrated, agonized scream. Putting his hands over his face, he doubled over in grief, sobbing.

"What's the matter, old man? I didn't lose your knife. It's in that Tarylan," a weak voice cracked. The old hunter's head snapped up. Flyn was still lying against the log but his eyes were open. A weak smile creased his lips.

Malik shouted for joy as he gently embraced the young man. Taking Flyn's head in his hands, the old hunter gingerly kissed the thick brown curls. Without another word, he attended to his wounds.

Not long after Malik had dragged the dead Tarylan a short distance away, Flyn's eyes widened with alarm. "What's wrong?" Malik asked, worried the young man had suffered an injury he had not found.

"Behind you. Tarylans!" Flyn whispered. Cursing his luck, Malik froze. He had assumed Gerro and his troops had taken care of the hostile Tarylans. The old hunter could not reach his bow, he only had a knife on his belt. He kept attending to Flyn. Leaning close, he mouthed, "How many?"

Flyn blinked twice. Malik nodded slightly. *Two was not impossible*, the old hunter thought to himself. Whatever move he attempted would put Flyn in great danger. The young man would be exposed to any kind of attack. Desperation filled Malik, he had to do something. Two enemies were behind him, and a wounded friend lay in front of him.

Acting as if he was fussing over Flyn, Malik shifted his body so his knife side was hidden from the Tarylans. He carefully moved his hand down the shaft and knelt in a crouch so he could spin around and throw.

If luck was with him, he would hit one of the Tarylans and force the other into making a mistake. He probably would get one opportunity to bring down the second enemy. Just as he got into a position to whirl around and throw the knife, a familiar voice stopped him.

"Don't throw that knife, hunter, you might hit a friend." Malik slowly turned his head and saw Gerro and Willa watching from a short distance. Shaking his head, he let out a huge sigh.

"The battle must have gone well, Captain," Malik said, standing looking at the two newcomers. They were an impressively gory sight — dirt and blood still clung to their skin and clothes.

Gerro nodded and stepped forward to get a closer look at Flyn. "Yes, Dallon is dead. His men have surrendered. You are free, young Nels," he said softly.

Flyn's eyes narrowed into slits as he studied the stranger, but he was buoyed by his words. He tapped Malik on the arm. "You know this Tarylan?"

Malik nodded. "I don't know where to start. So much has happened."

Flyn relaxed and let his head rest on the log. "Dallon is the one who attacked me and the Nuven Defenders in the orchard. Tarylans killing Tarylans, interesting. I hope someone will explain what is going on."

Malik smiled. "Plenty of time for that. Let's get you healed up and leave this place."

"No," Flyn said in a surprisingly strong voice. "Malik, this Tarylan called you a friend. Those are strange words."

Gerro and Willa walked closer to where Flyn lay. The Tarylan knelt by the young hunter. Willa gasped as she watched the two men measure each other up. "Gerro, he looks . . ." but the captain stopped her with a wave.

Flyn cocked his head to one side, staring intently at the other man. "Gerro? Are you the Tarylan my sisters told me about? You were with my father when he died."

Nodding, Gerro looked away for a moment. The events of the past few days had been overwhelming for the four people in this small mountain grove.

Gerro spoke hesitatingly, searching for the right words. "We have something very important in common," he said, choking back his emotions. "Our father was an incredible and honorable warrior. He avenged his people. He is a hero."

Flyn's eyes grew wide. He looked up at Malik who could only manage to nod while he brushed the tears out of his eyes. With a groan, Flyn raised his good arm. In the old Earth custom, the two brothers shook hands for the first time.

RECKONING

1

Tomar Jandon carefully studied the scan reports from the Tanlian scout ships which had recently returned from their mission. The reports confirmed only 14 Earth warships orbited the ghost world or XR-309 as it was listed on the star chart. No defensive forces were detected on either of the planet's two moons.

"So this is the mighty fleet the CAIN Earthers have sent to repel us," the Tanlian commander sneered as he tossed copies of the reports to his captains. "Even their warships are half the size of ours, barely bigger than our marauders."

Captain Inlof Spenlund did not join in his fellow officers' merriment. His ship had barely escaped from vessels much smaller than the warships they were studying. "We should have learned a lesson from the Earthers' previous attack — do not underestimate a small ship," he frowned while studying the reports. "Vessels barely big enough to carry one man destroyed four of our cruisers. Each of these Earther ships could carry dozens of those small ships."

Tomar normally would have punished an officer who dared to speak in such an accusatory tone, but Inlof was different. The captain had bravely tried to defend a sister Tanlian ship and managed to save his crew and ship. "The Earthers will not take us by surprise this time, Captain," Tomar bragged. "We have the advantage in ships and firepower. Small ships will do no good against our combined defenses."

The commander's mood was bolstered considerably when ships from a nearby planet rendezvoused with his Tanlian war fleet. He now commanded twenty-six ships — sixteen heavily armed warships and ten marauders, which were built for speed not intense fighting.

High Command had been unable to send more marauders. Most of those ships were busy conducting business important to Tantalum 2 — the mother world — whether it was transporting goods from GEMS worlds still under their control or attempting to plunder whatever they could from the CAIN worlds.

The Earther fleet, which protected the seemingly worthless XR-309, was the first serious challenge to Tanlian authority in recent memory. Earther ships for years had tried to protect their planets from the marauders. The fast Tanlian marauder vessels often escaped unscathed. Earther ships did get lucky occasionally, catching and destroying a marauder. However, those incidents were rare. Tanlian ships always had been faster, and their captains were savvy and daring.

The Earther attack at Rossiya 7 had shocked Tanlian command. Tomar had quickly been granted his request for as many battle ships as they could spare. High Command agreed with the admiral — the Earther threat needed to be quashed quickly before more uprisings occurred. Most of the warship fleet had been sent to aid Tomar, only a handful of ships were left behind as security for the home planet.

Tantalum 2 had been threatened only once before in its infancy after the prisoners had rebelled and taken over the mining world operated jointly by the Colonization Alliance of Independent Nations and the Galaxy Exploration and Minerals Syndicate. Brak Halpern led a vicious and successful defense of the planet when a small Earth fleet arrived to quell the uprising.

After that, no foreign ship had attempted to attack the renegade world. The Tanlians had concentrated their efforts on retrofitting dozens of captured Earther vessels into their planet-plundering marauders and transports. Only a token warship fleet had been built — mostly to serve as a reminder of Tanlian superiority.

GEMS worlds reluctant to increase their duties and tributes quickly succumbed when one of these huge vessels fired on defenseless cities, wiping out entire populations. The alliance refused to sign the tribute pact with the Tanlians. CAIN planets became the target of Tanlian forays.

Satisfied with his superior numbers, Tomar ordered the fleet to advance on XR-309 at a steady pace. The commander hoped to scare the Earthers away. If the intruders did not leave, he was confident his warships would destroy the outmanned and smaller vessels. Tomar was pleased at this turn of events. An impressive victory over this Earther fleet would ensure his seat on the High Council — a first for the Jandon family. Songs would be sung about this battle. For generations, Tanlian parents would name their first-born sons Tomar, in honor of their world's latest hero.

The commander broadcast his orders to the fleet. "Advance to just beyond weapons range, let's give the Earthers something to think about. Answer no hails from them."

Admiral Shim Murra watched as the Tanlian vessels slowly advanced toward his fleet orbiting Verde Grande. "Ah, they are trying to scare us off with their advantage in numbers."

Effana Zollorand stood nearby, intently watching the view screen. As Willa Sydriker's second in command, Effana took over as adviser for the Earth fleet. Willa was still helping with troubles on the planet.

"It's our turn to give them something to think about — order our ships into the net-defense pattern," Shim told his ship's communicist. As soon as the orders were relayed, the Earth fleet divided into three rows: five ships in the first line, four ships filled the gaps below them and five more vessels continuing the pattern below the second row.

Seeing the Earther defensive formation, Tomar nodded in appreciation of his opponents' strategy, then ordered his ships to mimic the pattern. The Tanlian fleet responded, moving to a nine-eight-nine net formation. The commander halted his Tanlian ships when they reached just outside weapons range. The two fleets faced each other, not unlike an old Earth giant game of three-dimensional chess.

Shim nodded to his communicist. The junior officer saluted and relayed the next order to the fleet. The Tanlians watched as two tiny ships — the same size as the ones that attacked them at Rossiya 7 — emerged from each vessel. The small vessels took positions above and below each mother warship. Tomar clapped his hands. "Look! The mother birds have hatched chicks."

Shim waited a few minutes then walked calmly over to his communicist, who opened a channel. "Tanlian vessels, this is Admiral Shim Murra of the Colonization Alliance of Independent Nations. This planet was illegally seized from the alliance. We now reclaim it, according to the CAIN-GEMS Colonization Treaty."

Waiting a moment, the admiral then delivered his ultimatum: "To the Tanlian commanders, as you can see, we now outnumber you. I advise you to retreat and return home before we are forced to take action." Barely a minute had passed when loud, hoarse laughter gushed through the comms of the Earth ships.

"Outnumbered? Retreat?" a gravelly voice asked incredulously. "This is Commander Tomar Landon, leader of these fine ships you are no doubt admiring. We have no intention of giving up our rights to XR-309. I advise you take your small fleet, including those gnats you just released, and return home." Tomar sat back in his chair, pleased with his bravado. The Tanlians waited for the Earthers to capitulate. The CAIN fleet responded by edging into weapons range.

The Commander grunted and shrugged. "Your attempt to challenge us is noble but unwelcome. If you leave within an hour we will not pursue or destroy you. This is my last communication before we take action. Jandon out." Tomar turned to his bridge crew. "The Earthers will be foolish to fight us. It's almost a pity we won't engage them. A Tanlian victory here would have been most impressive."

Shim sat back in his chair, a bemused look on his face. He was pleased on two accounts. Scans of the Tanlian ships and reports by Sula Gallgos from her successful attack at Rossiya 7 revealed the enemy's vessels were duplicates of old Earth ships from three centuries ago. Some modifications had been made and weapons had been added, but the design and size were basically the same as the Earth fleet that had attempted to thwart the prisoner rebellion on Tantalum 2 all those years ago.

The commander also was pleased with his opponent's braggadocio. "Are the Tanlians always this predictable?" he asked Effana.

"Yes, Admiral. He responded as we expected. The Tanlians have observed strict schedules for years. Their transports always arrive at the same time every year. They have become dependent on regular tributes from the GEMS worlds. No one has challenged them for centuries. I'm sure they feel invincible."

Effana was blonde and blue-eyed like Willa but was shorter and more muscular. Her cropped hair stuck out in all directions. A scar ran from her right eye down her face, finally trailing off in the middle of her throat. She shared Willa's keen hatred of the Tanlians. As a teenager she had been attacked by drunken Tanlians on leave.

The young woman had just returned from a successful fishing trip when the unwelcome strangers approached her. The Tanlians ordered her to surrender her catch and cook it for them. If she did so, they told her they would let her go unharmed. Furious, Effana flung the fish at the Tanlians' feet and tried to escape. But the men were too strong and fast. They caught her and dragged her away kicking and screaming into a grove. She tried to fight off her attackers but only stopped when a knife that was slowly cutting her face reached her throat.

Instead of crawling into a frightened shell as Willa's sister had done after her attack, Effana used her hatred to turn herself into a hand-to-hand combat expert. She was in charge of disabling the security forces when the Betelan women hijacked the transport on their world. The Tanlians who tried to stop Effana and her squad were quickly killed.

"Admiral, when we engage the Tanlians will there be a need for boarding parties? If so, I ask permission to be included." Shim looked at the young woman with surprise. She was staring coldly at the monitor, trying to envision the enemy.

"Why, yes. If we are successful, there will be need for boarding parties," he said. "We will have to search any disabled ships to look for survivors or hunt down any enemies who may refuse to surrender." Effana still stared at the monitor. Her crossed arms flexed with anticipation, revealing hardened muscles.

"Granted," Shim said. "You may lead a squad of your choosing if the time comes."

She saluted. "Thank you, sir. I will not disappoint you."

———————

Captain Inlof Spenlund did not like what he saw. The Earthers had unleashed those tiny ships that had wrought so much havoc in the Rossiya 7 battle. They obviously had enough confidence in these vessels to include them in their defensive fleet. Inlof and his crew had barely fought off those minute attackers when they rejoined the Tanlian fleet during the battle at Rossiya 7. He was unable to save a sister ship that was being bombarded, and to his horror, watched it and three other warships be destroyed.

During the journey to the ghost world, Inlof and his crew had never stopped working to repair and improve their weapons systems. After being so easily attacked, Inlof concentrated on defensive systems. The captain was sure long-range weapons would be useless against an enemy determined to fight ship to ship. He also had been concerned at the ease at which the

Earther attackers had avoided his ship's weapons, almost as if they were birds dodging sticks thrown by a child.

Inlof's crew disassembled six of eight long-range missile launchers and substituted them with short-burst energy cannons that could lay down an effective protective fire around the ship. They also improved the warship's maneuverability by adding more power to its thrusters.

The other captains showed no interest in modifying their vessels. They believed the sheer force of their fleet would be enough to repel and destroy any attacks. Inlof's fellow officers did not appreciate he was the only battle-tested veteran in their fleet. He had been the only Tanlian captain to survive a direct attack in centuries. Until now, just marauder ships had come under fire, but they were designed to escape, not stand and fight.

The captain also had expressed his displeasure at the deployment of the marauders among the warships. Admiral Tomar Jandon had ordered the smaller, lightly armed ships to be evenly dispersed among the battleships in the first three rows. Inlof saw this as a major weakness in the Tanlian alignment, but the admiral waved off his objections. Because of his insolence in challenging Tomar's battle plan, the admiral had punished the captain by sending his ship to the bottom row.

This incident had given Tomar the opportunity to remove Inlof, who was considered a hero for his actions during the battle at Rossiya 7. The admiral did not want to share the glory in what surely would be an impressive Tanlian victory. Tomar did not want a mere captain to overshadow his achievements.

Inlof officially registered an objection at Tomar's slight but he secretly did not mind the reassignment. From his experience in battle, Inlof felt the bottom row was just as important as the top line of ships. From his new position, Inlof's ship could help protect the fleet from a surprise attack at the rear.

Communicist Reth Marnad turned to Inlof and saluted. "Captain, I have registered something strange."

"What is it, Reth?" The brash young captain had changed after surviving the Earther attack. He now called the crewmen by their names instead of position as was the Tanlian tradition. His ship had escaped by the supreme cooperation of his crew. Inlof understood that well.

"Well, Captain, it might be nothing but several times over the past hour I have registered an irregular buzz. If it's a signal, I can't decode it. It only comes in short bursts."

Inlof was interested in anything unusual that might reveal the enemy's intentions. "Could it be coded signals from Earther ships?"

Reth shifted uneasily almost appearing embarrassed at what he was about to say. "No, sir, these bursts are not from the Earther ships nor the planet or even its moons. They, ah, seem to be coming from behind us. I can't pinpoint exactly where. They don't last long enough and seem to come from different locations."

The captain sat up as if he had been struck with a jolt. "From behind us, where? Have scans found anything?"

Reth shook his head. "No, sir. Our scans show nothing. These buzzes don't last long, perhaps they are just static echoes. I thought you should know."

Inlof slid off his chair and thanked Reth for his diligence. The captain walked over to the scanning monitors and spent several minutes studying the readouts. Finding nothing, he walked back to his post, deep in thought.

"Good work, Reth," he said, slapping the communicist on the shoulder. "Even if it turns out to be nothing, I want you all to follow Reth's example," Inlof told his bridge crew. "We don't know what tricks these Earthers might have planned, but anything you deem irregular may save our lives. Keep diligent, my brothers."

2

Sweat slowly trickled down Arynna's neck. The annoying sensation was almost enough to break her connection with the communicist on the large ship that anchored the bottom row of the threatening Tanlian fleet. The Seer struggled to keep her trance. She had to concentrate to use the gift, but she was more than capable.

The sister of Gerro and Flyn had never used her sight in such a way — to alter what another saw. Verinya had warned her of the seductive temptation to exert power over another, but now her talent was needed to help defeat the Tanlians. Now Arynna forced herself to relax and follow Reth Marnad's every move. She almost broke the trance from fright when he intercepted signals from the Earther warships that were now stationed behind the Tanlian fleet. The importance of her mission almost overwhelmed her.

Seeing Arynna's contorted face as she fought to hold her trance, Jorn Nandez spoke in soothing, reassuring tones. He did not know if she could understand him, but he felt she could sense his intentions. The captain's reassuring words helped Arynna keep her focus. Her breathing slowed to a controlled rate as she regained control.

Jorn was amazed his fleet of ten ships had been able to approach the Tanlians so closely without being detected. The Earther/Verdan plot was working so far. After hearing about the Seers' talents, the young captain and High Seer Cara had devised a bold plan to gain an advantage on the Tanlians. It had taken many hours for Cara and Jorn to convince Admiral Murra the strategy would work. Even if Jorn's fleet was discovered, the Tanlians would have to address the threat from two fronts.

Cara summoned most of the watcher Seers and any others who possessed the gift to Fortress Bryann. The newly elected High Seer told the women gathered before her about the threat they faced from the Tanlians gathered near their world. Cara called for volunteers to accompany a group of Earther ships that would attempt to secretly approach the Tanlians. To do this, Seers were needed to cloud their enemies' minds. Other Seers also were needed on ships orbiting Verde Grande. Their powers would be invaluable. Hopefully they could slow the Tanlians' reactions during a battle.

The vast group of young women gathered before Cara stood in shocked silence. For generations, they had been told the Nuvens were the enemy. Now they were being asked not only to abandon that thinking, but also to put themselves in harm's way in flying ships they had never seen or flown in before. Arynna was the first to volunteer. She walked out of the crowd of young women and stood beside Cara. Showing the same courage she exhibited when the Earthers landed in the courtyard, Trista Hedlo also stepped out. Seeing these brave young women come forward gave the other Seers courage to do likewise.

So far, Jorn's plan had worked perfectly. The captain had taken ten of the Earth warships to deep space and waited patiently. Each ship carried twenty Seers. It was the job of the women to use their sight to cloud the minds of the Tanlians as Jorn's fleet approached from the rear. The captain's fleet watched in silence as the Tanlian armada cruised by and took positions near Verde Grande. Like a giant unseen cloud, Jorn slowly maneuvered his ships behind the Tanlians. Only an occasional coded buzz was sent to alert the orbiting CAIN fleet of their progress.

3

The Tanlians did not disappoint Admiral Murra. The enemy fleet started moving slowly toward his orbiting ships as soon as the hour ran out. "Five, four, three, two, one," his communicist counted down. In the next breath, the lead scan officer called out: "The enemy ships have powered their engines and are moving to intercept us. They are traveling at cruising three, slow but steady."

Shim opened a clear channel to speak to all the ships in his fleet. "The enemy is on its way. This is the moment you all volunteered for — to meet the Tanlians head on. Remember the sisters and mothers on CAIN worlds who have been kidnapped and taken from their loved ones. Remember the brothers and fathers who died trying to save them. This battle will determine the safety of all the Earth colony worlds for centuries. I am proud of you all. Admiral Murra out."

As soon as he finished speaking, Shim pressed a red key at his control panel. At this signal the tiny vessels, which had been hovering close to their mother ships, gathered into three groups and sped toward toward the oncoming fleet. The Tanlian scanners barely registered them before the attackers were in their midst. Instead of engaging the easier marauders, the attack squad hit three of the warships in the front line. The Tanlian captains barely had time to lay down defensive fire. The tiny ships swarmed around them like angry bees.

The Tanlian marauder captains in the top row started to move to help their fleet mates when the next CAIN wave struck. The first row fired on the marauders before they could react. The lightly armed smaller Tanlian vessels were quickly destroyed in the first volley of energy rockets. The CAIN

353

warships maneuvered toward the middle row of the enemy, again obliterating the marauders.

Each Earth vessel then targeted the enemy warships in the top row, hitting them squarely with energy rockets as they swept by, easily avoiding the slow-release missiles of the enemy. With the enemy engaged in defending itself, the second row of Earth ships also aimed at the top row of warships. The reinforced attack quickly disabled the Tanlian vessels. The third Tanlian warship tried to retreat, but it came under fire by three CAIN attackers. The vessel exploded into a fireball after being hit with a barrage of energy rockets.

At this moment, the third row of Earth ships entered the fray and headed toward Tomar Jandon's vessel with deadly speed. The CAIN communicists had identified the location of the command ship. Shim made it a priority to knock the Tanlian commander out of the battle and hopefully mop up the remainder of the confused enemy. The Tanlians were caught off guard by the brazen attack. They had expected to instigate the battle and assumed their "superior" warships would easily penetrate the Earther defenses.

Tomar sat stunned at his monitor. The enemy vessels had easily cut through the top row. His Tanlian ships appeared to be firing at ghosts. One second an attacker wasn't there, but in a blink, a Tanlian ship would be hit by a broadside of energy rockets. Without waiting for orders, Inlof Spenlund left the back row to engage the oncoming Earther ships. He had no love for Tomar, but it was his duty to defend his superior officer as well as help any other Tanlian he could reach.

Seeing the hole left by Inlof, Jorn seized this moment to launch his attack from the rear. His ten ships struck the unsuspecting Tanlians at full force. The two enemy warships that were left behind were disabled by the first fusillade from the rear attack. Two of the weaker marauders crumpled into unrecognizable twisted hunks of metal and floated harmlessly away.

A third marauder abandoned the battle. Instead of escaping to deep space, the Tanlian vessel sped toward Verde Grande.

Seeing the fleeing enemy ship, CAIN Captain Fariq Talmari ordered his crew to break off from the attack and pursue the other ship.

————————

"Captain, they are attacking from the rear!" Communicist Reth Marnad screamed. Cursing, Inlof ordered his warship to come about and face the surprise attack. One of the CAIN ships attempted to strafe Inlof's vessel but was struck by the dense defensive energy bursts. It spun out of control after its thrusters were damaged. Manning one of the rocket launchers, Inlof locked onto the helpless ship and launched a missile. The CAIN ship exploded into a million pieces.

Seeing the other Tanlians under attack for their lives, Inlof started to maneuver his ship toward Tomar's command vessel, but it was too late. The admiral's ship was being swarmed by four CAIN attackers. Tomar frantically urged his crew to defend themselves and him. It seemed like only minutes ago his fleet was sailing confidently toward the smaller outnumbered Earthers, and now his ships were being destroyed.

Only one Tanlian captain answered his plea for help — Inlof Spenlund. Inlof tried to reach Tomar's ship, but the Earther attackers would not be denied. The captain watched helplessly as the command vessel's defenses were crippled. The CAIN ships docked and sent troops to board it.

After a quick assessment of the remaining Tanlian fleet, Inlof found only two warships that could still maneuver while attempting to fight off their attackers. The captain ordered the commanders of the other vessels to join him. They did so without argument. Fighting off the attackers with his defensive weapons, Inlof was able to regroup with the two ships. However, the surviving Tanlians found themselves overwhelmed by the Earth warships who now only had to concentrate their attack on this enemy trio.

In moments, the other two Tanlian vessels were rendered helpless. Inlof and his crew fought bravely, managing to damage two more of the enemy ships before their thrusters and gun ports were disabled. As their ship drifted helplessly, Earthers closed in on them. Inlof's crew turned toward their leader with frightened expressions. He sat quietly, his chin resting in a cupped hand.

Flipping a switch to open a ship-wide comm, Inlof addressed his crew. "We are about to be boarded by the people we have dominated for centuries. I fear it is their time for revenge." Inlof and his crew looked up as their ship rattled from a collision. Loud clanking told them Earther ships were attempting to dock.

Standing, the Captain saluted his crew. "You are the bravest crew a Tanlian commander has had the honor to serve with since Brak Halpern freed our world from the Earther oppressors. I now release every crew member to act in his best interest. I will not be taken alive." Picking up a short-burst energy pistol, Inlof headed down the corridor toward the nearest port the Earthers were attempting to enter. His crew grimly followed him without a word.

———————

Captain Fariq Talmari's ship quickly caught the fleeing Tanlian marauder and launched a rocket, hitting the vessel's engine compartment. A large flash erupted from the ship as it broke almost cleanly in half. The nose section spun crazily out of control, while the other half careened away, blackened from the rocket strike. The Earther crew cheered and watched as the spinning nose wreckage slowly drifted toward Verde Grande like a feather caught on a breeze. Fariq shook his head at how easily the Tanlian ship had broken apart.

Sujin Dhasgupta, the second in command, scanned the careening wreckage. "Captain, should we pursue it to check for survivors?"

"No need," Fariq said shaking his head. "No one could have survived that explosion. Besides, whatever is left of the ship will break up in the atmosphere or crash into the mountains. We've done our job. Return to the fleet, there are more captured Tanlian ships to investigate."

———————

Effana Zollorand begged Yulef Zaid to maneuver his warship close to the last Tanlian to be disabled. Before the battle began, she and some of her fellow Betelans asked to be transferred to a ship on the front lines. She had watched with great interest as the Tanlian ship had fought stubbornly to the end. It even appeared the vessel had tried to assist the command ship but was unable to do so.

"I have Admiral Murra's permission to lead a boarding party," she adamantly told the CAIN captain. A dozen Betelan women stood behind her, arms folded, waiting to be released into the enemy ship.

"Ordinarily I would allow it, but Captain Nandez has requested first boarding rights," Yulef said with a shrug. "There are other ships we could dock onto."

Effana snarled: "No, I want that ship, it put up the best fight. Please link me to Captain Nandez." The captain looked at her for a moment with a pained expression then punched in a code.

"Nandez here. Good to hear from you Yulef, how can I be of assistance?" Yulef gestured for Effana to speak. If the woman wanted to board that badly, she should argue her point. Jorn was silent for several seconds after hearing Effana's plea to board. "I will gladly yield in favor of our Betelan allies, but we will be right behind you. I trust you have even more to settle with the Tanlians than we do. Be careful, that captain appears to be the best fighter in their fleet. He is not answering hails to surrender."

Effana and her troop readied their weapons. "That is what I had hoped for, Captain, thank you." With a determined look, Effana and her fellow Betelans ran for the docking port. It took an explosive device to make a hole in the Tanlian port. The Betelans tossed an array of energy stunners up and down the halls. After the last thump, the women rushed in to find the enemy. They did not have long to wait. The Tanlian crew raced screaming toward the invaders. A few short-burst energy pistols were fired, but the battle turned to hand to hand. Tanlians and Betelans fought fiercely.

In the gloom of the poorly lit corridor, the fight turned into groans, gasps, and breaking bones. The heavy smell of sweat and blood hung in the air. The Tanlians fought desperately but found themselves trapped between the Betelans and a group of Earthers. Inlof battled like a madman, but the attackers kept pushing him and his men backwards. More and more of his men were slaughtered until he found himself alone, facing a short, bloodied woman. Both panted from the exertion of battle and the dwindling oxygen supplies. Looking at his opponent, recognition flickered in his eyes.

"Ah, Betelan, I see," he gasped trying to catch his breath. "Have all our protectorates rebelled?"

Effana raised her eyebrows. "Protectorates? That is the first time I have heard that word. Many of the GEMS worlds have been freed by the Earthers."

Inlof nodded slowly, realizing the days of Tanlian dominance was at an end. "Betelan, you have illegally boarded my ship. As captain, it is my duty to defend it." Without another word, Effana struck. Her leaping kick knocked Inlof to the deck, but he recovered to dodge a second blow. Her attack was relentless. She kicked and punched. He managed to block most of her jabs and tried to land his own blows with little success.

The two combatants finally wound up in a clinch. With the aid of his superior strength, Inlof spun Effana around and landed a sharp blow to her stomach, dropping her to her knees. In another motion, he grabbed her throat and pinned her to the wall. With a free hand, Effana managed to pull a small knife out of her belt — the small fish scaler she always carried with her for luck. In desperation, she thrust the knife into Inlof's side. The Tanlian released his hold and staggered backwards. In a rage, Effana rushed the wounded man, stabbing him repeatedly until he slumped to the floor.

Lying exhausted next to the body, Effana jumped when another shadow loomed over her. She flung herself backwards and held up the knife in an attempt to defend herself. No attack came this time. Instead, a voice softly urged her to drop the weapon. It said the Tanlians were all dead. She had killed the last of the enemy on the ship. Looking up, she tried to focus on the speaker, a tall, dark-haired man in uniform.

"You have no need to fear. I'm Captain Nandez. Your comrades tell me you are Effana Zollorand. We need to leave soon, the air supplies are almost gone." Effana stared at him for a moment. Her eyes were blurry and throat ached. She finally accepted his help to stand. This was the first time since her childhood on Betel 4 that she allowed a man to help her.

––––––––––

"Well done, Captain!" Admiral Shim Murra beamed as he slapped Jorn on the back. "We crushed their fleet."

Jorn smiled and saluted his superior officer. "Our plans worked perfectly, sir. We caught the Tanlians by surprise from the front and rear. What are their losses?"

Shim shook his head in amazement as he studied the reports from the fleet captains. "Only three Tanlian warships barely survived. Crews in two of the ships surrendered as soon as we boarded. You are well aware of the fate of the third crew after your men and the Betelans finished with them. The remainder of the enemy fleet was destroyed."

Jorn raised his eyebrows with surprise at the scope of destruction the CAIN fleet had inflicted on the Tanlians. "How many men and ships did we lose?"

The admiral cleared his throat as he steadied himself. "We lost two ships and their crews. It looks like several dozen men and women on a handful of the other ships were killed and several hundred wounded. Six other ships were damaged enough to require assistance but repairs are already being made to them."

Jorn was pleased with the victory but he grieved the loss of two of his fellow captains and their crews. He had witnessed the CAIN forces battle with the Tanlians, ship to ship and hand to hand. Each side had fought desperately for their lives. In the end, it was difficult to tell the difference between the bodies of ally and enemy.

Shim noted Jorn's pained expression. "We will retain our humanity as long as we remember the pain of battle and honor the brave people we have lost."

High Seer Cara choked back tears as she gazed out of the command ship's view screen. Forty young Seers also had perished on the two Earther ships that were lost in battle. Among them was the Seer who had won a special spot in Cara's heart — Trista Hedlo. The High Seer grieved as if she had lost a daughter.

"The Tarylan Seers for centuries have willingly sacrificed others so we could live safely. I have never fully understood the terrible feeling of loss until now," she said, looking forlornly at Shim and Jorn. "I pray the deaths of these young women will help Mother Verde forgive us for our transgressions against her other children — the Nuvens."

Shim walked over to Cara and put his arm around her shoulders. "Perhaps this is a day for many wrongs to be made right," he said. "The alliance should have sent rescue ships when the first colonists were stranded here. It is a testament to both groups' bravery that you have survived."

4

Effana Zollorand sat at a nearby computer console, busily inputting information. The stoic woman waited patiently for the computer to process. Her eyes lit up, and she had to stifle a laugh when the answer blinked on the screen. Curious, Captain Nandez strode to her station and looked at the screen. The captain let out an excited gasp as he read over her shoulder. "How did you get this information from the Tanlian commander?" Jorn whispered, amazed at the facts about Tantalum 2's defenses that covered the screen.

Effana chuckled. "The commander was very talkative after I explained what we needed. He just needed to be, ah, *convinced*. It didn't take long."

Jorn cast her a suspicious glance. "Did you harm him?"

The Betelan woman shook her head. "No, Captain, not one drop of blood was spilled nor bone broken. I sensed he was quite uncomfortable with me when I finished questioning him." Effana did not tell Jorn she interrogated the commander immediately after the deadly skirmish on Inlof Spenlund's ship. Her body and hair caked with rusty dried blood, she made an imposing questioner.

She flung Inlof's braid, which she had cut off, at the commander's feet. Tomar Jandon had never seen a woman in battle before, much less one who had just killed the bravest captain in the fleet. Grabbing Tomar by his beard, she held her fish scaler at his throat and threatened to take his braid as a souvenir too if she was not pleased with his answers.

Before questioning him, the Betelan woman had scanned information other Tanlian officers had volunteered to their CAIN captors. Effana offered no negotiation — either the

361

information matched what the other Tanlians had said or she would take his life. Tomar broke down and only stopped now and then to stifle a frightened sob.

"Well, Captain, are you going to keep us in suspense?" Admiral Murra asked. Effana and Jorn looked up and saw everyone on the bridge gazing at them in curious anticipation. Jorn looked at Effana, not wanting to take credit. The Betelan woman was embarrassed by the attention. She gestured for him to speak to the others.

"It appears Commander Jandon has been very talkative," Jorn said, giving Effana a wink. "He has given Effana very detailed information about the defenses on Tantalum 2. It seems only six warships and a handful of marauders are left to defend the planet."

Admiral Murra stared with disbelief. He hoped what Jorn was saying was true, but he was suspicious. "Can we be sure of this information? What if this is a trap?"

Jorn studied the screen again. "The Commander's numbers match perfectly with what the other Tanlians have told us. These officers seem to be more concerned about their personal safety than about their loyalty to their home world. It appears Tanlian high command fully expected an easy victory. We have captured or destroyed the majority of their defensive fleet."

Just as Jorn was finishing his review, Captain Yulef Zaid signaled the CAIN admiral's ship. "Go ahead, Captain," Shim said opening the comm so all could hear.

"Admiral, we have found important records from the surviving Tanlian warships. Most of their data is still intact. It is proving to be a wealth of information — battle plans, comm codes, planetary defensive weapons locations and marauder routes. I am transmitting what we have found so far. There appears to be much more information. We are deciphering it as fast as we can. Zaid out."

Jorn could hardly contain his excitement as Tanlians' secrets scrolled out before them. "Admiral, the planet is exposed. We may never have such an advantage again." Before the captain could continue his argument, the ship's communicist interrupted with a message for him from Verde Grande. Puzzled and a bit angry at being called away, Jorn excused himself. Adjusting his ear comm, his frown changed to a look of amazement.

"It appears we have reinforcements volunteering for duty," he said with a wide smile. The admiral, feeling the heavy burden of making a momentous decision, shot him an impatient look.

"Willa Sydriker and Gerro, captain of the Tarylan Guard, are requesting permission to be included if we attack Tantalum 2," Jorn said. "Gerro also is promising the services of hundreds of his best Tarylan guards and Defenders from the Nuven valley."

High Seer Cara stood. She dried her tears on her sleeve and addressed the bridge crew. "The Tarylan Seers also will travel with you to Tantalum 2. Our world and many others have been at the mercy of these monsters for too long."

Admiral Murra paced back and forth in front of the view screen, hands clenched behind his back as he considered the consequences. He was desperate to quell the Tanlian threat, but a small fear crept into his consciousness. Shim did not want to be the second Earth admiral to be defeated at the hands of the Tanlians.

Sensing his commander's misgivings, Jorn asked permission to speak. "Sir, we will not be surprised this time. In fact, we will have the element of surprise on our side as well as three Tanlian warships to lead us there. We know fully what to expect from them. I recommend we strike Tantalum 2 as soon as we can make repairs and travel to the planet."

Shim looked around the room. All eyes were on him, waiting for his decision. The admiral pushed his universal comm key and broadcast the situation to the other CAIN captains. He gave them an hour to consider the proposal to attack Tantalum 2. The other captains' responses flowed back in a matter of minutes. It was unanimous — all voted to attack the Tanlian one planet as soon as possible. No bravado was evident in any of the other captains. They all had seen their share of battle. All had lost friends. Many had lost crew members. They wanted to finish what they traveled all this distance for — to end the Tanlian reign of terror for the CAIN and GEMS worlds.

Shim gazed for a moment out the view screen. With a deep breath, he touched the comm key again. "The captains are all of the same mind. This fleet will make repairs. We depart for Tantalum 2 in eight days. I am proud to serve with you and pray for the success of our next mission."

5

Bralen Spenlund told his navigator to slow their erratic but controlled spin. He did not want a noticeable change to be discovered by any Earther ship that might be monitoring their descent to the planet. The captain had been the only other Tanlian officer to heed his cousin's advice.

Bralen had been impressed that Inlof had survived the battle with the Earther attack ships on Rossiya 7. Both cousins had been successful marauder captains. Their harrowing escapes with stolen treasure from CAIN worlds were almost legendary.

Inlof had accepted a promotion to be a warship captain. Bralen turned down a similar offer. He enjoyed the thrill of the hunt as well as accumulating a respectable fortune from his endeavors. On his last mission, Bralen's ship had narrowly escaped vengeful pursuers. His vessel had been hit by a rocket, but the damage was not serious.

Once back home on Tantalum 2, Bralen worked with engineers to redesign his marauder with an escape system. They came up with a breakaway pod. His ship was designed to cleanly separate into two pieces if it sustained weapons damage. Emergency shielding would slide into place to cover the hole. Hidden thrusters were added to the nose half to aid it during an emergency landing.

During their escape from the battle, only twenty of his crew were able to get safely to the nose section. The Earther warship caught them so quickly, the others didn't make it. The spin slowly stopped as the nose half entered the planet's atmosphere in a controlled descent. To the crew's surprise, no clouds or severe weather impeded their landing as was expected for the mysterious world.

"Captain, there's a large valley down there," reported the navigator. "I'm getting energy and thermal readings. There are people down there, lots of them!"

Bralen frowned. "It might be an Earther trick. Besides they may have comm and landing sites set up in many places down there. Pick a remote spot in the mountains and set down there so we can monitor the Earthers. Land slowly. I don't want to attract any attention."

After a moment, the navigator found a remote village that would be suitable. No comm signals were detected from the small cluster of log houses. The villagers watched in wonder as the small ship came to a skidding landing in a field. Smoke billowed out, and a dirt cloud followed it as the vessel finally came to a halt. Running to the ship, a small group of Verdans welcomed the twenty uniformed men as they stumbled out into the bright sunshine.

An old man approached the crew. He stretched his arms out in welcome. "Greetings Earther champions. I am Marn Stelforn, a village elder. Do you need assistance?"

Bralen brushed himself off and studied the curious villagers. The dialect was foreign but he understood a few words. He bowed to the Verdan. "Why yes, elder, that would be most appreciated. My men and I had a malfunction with our ship. We are a surveillance team and need to set up camp here for awhile."

Marn returned the bow. "You are the first Earthers we have met. Please share our food and our homes."

Bralen cocked his head. "Ah yes, *Earthers*? So who are you?"

Marn and the other villagers laughed.

"Why, we are Verdans of course, but I can't expect an Earther to tell the difference between a Nuven and us. Hmm, as a matter of fact, there is not much difference anymore. Come and rest after your ordeal. We are a simple village, but we have plenty of food."

Bralen frowned when he and his crew discovered the Verdans' primitive lifestyle. Turning to his crew, he shook his head. "They have no technology. How were they able to hide from us?"

6

Flyn Nels had grown restless waiting for the word about the Earther fleet's mission to Tantalum 2. He was upsetting his mother and sisters with his constant pacing and clumsy attempts to help them with their work. The last transmission from the fleet had been three weeks ago. The ships were preparing to engage the enemy and were ceasing all transmissions until after the mission.

Even though his mother had been overjoyed at seeing him after he returned home from his ordeal with his Tarylan captors, she now encouraged him to busy himself elsewhere — to go hunting, fishing or check how the fruit trees were faring. Flyn refused to return to the orchard valley that held so many painful memories.

During one of his frequent meandering walks through the village, a youthful shout snapped Flyn out of his troubled thoughts. Athal, his seven-year-old cousin, leaped out from behind a bush and charged at full speed. Flyn snatched his giggling attacker, spun the boy around by his arms and plopped him back on the ground.

Athal laughed as he lay in the grass, dizzy from the ride. "Where are you going Flyn? Can I come too? You don't play with me anymore," he blurted in rapid succession.

Flyn studied the brown eyes gazing expectantly up at him. "Have you been a good boy?" he asked, pretending to frown.

"Sometimes. I try to be good. I like climbing trees, just like you, Flyn," Athal said as he scooped up a bug from the grass and watched it crawl over his hand. Flyn flinched. Athal knew the Nels family climbed trees, especially to gather their famous fruit. The boy did not understand that climbing was second nature for Nuvens. Many of their kin were born with long, double-jointed toes, which helped them climb.

Athal was of Verdan heritage from Flyn's mother's family. His cousin had plenty of spunk and desire, but the boy kept losing his grip and falling out of trees. So far he had suffered no broken bones. "You have to listen to your mother," Flyn said squatting down so he could look the boy in the eye. "A fall could hurt you badly. You may not be able to walk or run again. You wouldn't like that now would you?"

Athal plucked out some long blades of grass and twisted them. "No, Flyn, I would not like that. I like to run, but I like to climb, too," he said, pouting.

Flyn mussed the boy's ginger-colored hair. "Tell you what, Athal, next time I decide to climb a tree I will take you with me. That way, you won't fall because I would help you."

The boy's face lit up. "I'd like that. Now? Can we do it now?!" he shouted, gleefully jumping to his feet, looking around for the perfect tree.

Flyn laughed as he watched the bundle of energy race around him. Many family members said Athal was just like him at that age. "No, not now but soon, I promise."

Athal paused, a mischievous grin on his face. "I know what tree I want to climb, but I don't know where it is."

Flyn looked puzzled. "What tree is that? How do you know you want to climb it if you don't know where it is?"

The boy looked up and squeaked excitedly. "The honey fruit tree. I want to climb that one. I love honey fruit. Uncle Aron gave us a bag of it last year. Mama only let me eat one slice at a time so it would last."

Flyn plopped down in the grass. Tears filled his eyes when Athal mentioned honey fruit — that delicious treat grown in the orchard the Nels clan had kept a secret for so long. Honey fruit reminded Flyn of his father. Ever since Flyn was a boy, probably starting the same age as Athal, Aron had taken him along when they visited the orchard in search of one special tree.

It had always been a great adventure. Aron and his brother, Romal, knew where the tree was located. To most, it looked like all the other trees in the orchard. What made it even more mysterious was the honey fruit came from a different tree every year. Only certain branches bore that mouthwatering treat. It looked the same as the other fruit on the tree and throughout the orchard. Only family members knew where the honey fruit could be found, and they were sworn to secrecy. .

A small hand patted Flyn on the head. "I am sorry, Flyn. I forgot Uncle Aron got hurt," Athal said solemnly. "He went to the stars, right? Mama says your Papa watches us at night. Mama says when a star twinkles, Uncle Aron is smiling at me."

Flyn nodded, too choked up to answer. Tears streamed down his face. Athal gave him a hug and sat beside him. Neither spoke for a long while. Finally regaining his composure, Flyn looked at Athal. "I'm not sure you will be able to climb the honey fruit tree, little cousin, but another tree maybe. It is time for me go back to the orchard valley. I have things to do there, perhaps I'll even find the honey fruit tree."

Athal grinned as Flyn took his hand and walked him home.

A week later, Flyn sat alone on the peaceful grassy knoll in the middle of his family's fruit orchard. He gazed forlornly at the row of boulders that marked the grave sites of all those who had died in the skirmish with his Tarylan captors. It had been several months since the bodies had been laid to rest in this private spot.

This was the first time he had come back to this valley, which had been such a happy place of his youth but had turned into a nightmare of torture and death. Three stones in particular held his attention. Two bore the names of those they honored — Romal Nels and Ortelle Woodrud. Etched in the third boulder were the names of the ten Nuven Defenders who had died trying to protect Flyn.

It was unusual for those of Nuven blood to be buried. For generations the hunters mourned the passing of a kinsman by gathering around a large pyre to watch the flames shoot into the sky. They believed the ghosts of their ancestors would be attracted by the blaze and come to guide the deceased's spirit back to their mystical world. However, the Tarylans had casually burned and thrown the remains of those they had killed into shallow graves. It would have been considered a sacrilege to disturb the remains.

The constant buzzing of bees interrupted Flyn's thoughts. The insects swooped by his head, narrowly missing him. Looking around, Flyn could seen the pollen gatherers were everywhere throughout the orchard. They swarmed to the fruit trees which were now in full bloom. Colors exploded everywhere in shades of white and pink. The air was full of delightful scents.

Despite himself, Flyn could not resist sitting back and drinking in those sweet aromas. The smell took him back to his childhood when he and his sisters, Amaura and Lyllen, ran through the orchard playing "catch me" and following Ural, their grandfather, as he inspected the trees.

A dim memory tried to surface. Flyn rose and sauntered through the trees, stopping often to look for something unusual. But what? The trees all looked similar except for the different shades of flowers and slight variations in the leaves.

As children, Flyn and his sisters were always in a hurry to climb a honey fruit tree when their grandfather relented and pointed it out. They would grab the biggest fruit they could reach and sit back and devour those precious treats like starving animals.

Ural always had to tell them how to look for the fruit and then he would recite a poem to help them find it. *Why was that?* Flyn wondered. Fruit bulged from every branch on every tree in the orchard. But the honey fruit was always in a special place in a specific tree. Flyn grew frustrated as he wandered through the orchard. He could not tell one tree from another. Finally deciding he was not accomplishing anything, Flyn started back toward the burial knoll. The sound of voices stopped him just as he was about to walk out of the trees.

Five people were standing among the stones. He recognized the two women putting flowers next to Romal's stone — his sisters, Amaura and Lyllen. A few meters away, a man and a woman with flaming red hair knelt by a stone that Flyn had purposely avoided. The name etched in that rock — Verinya — made him uncomfortable. A tall blonde woman stood a short distance behind them.

The red-headed woman was sobbing and rocking back and forth. Her companion stood silently, his hand on her shoulder. After a few moments, the man turned and stared in Flyn's direction, trying to see who lurked in the shadows. With a start, Flyn recognized Gerro. The honey fruit forgotten for the moment, Flyn strode toward his half-brother who grinned at his approach. The two young men gave each other a bear hug and slaps on the back.

The young woman with Gerro stood drying her tears. She, too, smiled at Flyn. She looked familiar. Confused, Flyn glanced at his sisters. Amaura, who was watching the scene, grinned broadly. Lyllen still knelt in prayer at Romal's stone. Stifling a gasp, Flyn realized he recognized the strange woman's smile — it was almost the same as Amaura's.

Gerro stepped toward the woman, putting his arm around her. "Flyn, this is Arynna, my twin, your half-sister." Even the somber Lyllen could not help but smile at the shocked look on her brother's face.

Back at Romal's cabin, which had been repaired after the Tarylans left the secluded Nels valley, Gerro and Willa Sydriker told the others about the conquest of Tantalum 2. "We are free from the Tanlians at last," Willa sighed happily. "The CAIN worlds no longer have to worry about guarding their populace against terror from space, and the GEMS worlds finally have self-determination."

Gerro leaned back in his chair as he sipped a mug of hot spiced cider. Looking at those familiar faces made him feel at home. It was a strange feeling. He had always felt out of place most of his life. Now his soul felt at peace. He didn't need to guard himself from these people.

The story of the Earther fleet's mission easily flowed out of him. "The Tanlians were completely fooled by our ruse. We used the three repaired Tanlian warships to fly point as the fleet approached the planet. The Seers again were magnificent at masking our intentions."

Arynna blushed a bit. "The Tanlians were expecting a triumphant return, we just helped manipulate the charade."

Gerro chuckled. "The fleet flew straight into their space without being challenged. Our ships surrounded the six Tanlian vessels and disarmed them before they could fire a shot in their defense. A handful or so of the marauders were destroyed when they tried to escape to the planet."

The former Tarylan captain shook his head in wonder. "The Earther ships were amazingly efficient when they carried out their missions. The shipyards on Tantalum 2's moon were captured first. They were poorly defended and were taken easily, within a matter of hours. Every defensive position on the planet the captured Tanlians told us about was accurate."

Looking at Flyn, Gerro shrugged. "They had no honor, no loyalty. We were able to attack troop barracks, communication sites, capture key personnel with very little struggle. The Tanlians had not been attacked in hundreds of harvests, they had grown completely complacent."

Flyn leaned forward. "Was there much fighting at all?"

Gerro nodded. "Oh, yes, the fortress their high council was holed up in was well defended. The Tanlians in the fortress fired on Admiral Murra's ship while he was giving them a chance to surrender. That was a serious mistake. The admiral ordered his ship to fire on the fortress. It was destroyed in minutes."

Gerro took a deep breath. His expression and tone grew grim as he recalled the next phase of the mission. "We landed troops — Earther, Verdan and Nuven — in their capital city after the fortress fell. The Tanlians there fought hard, but our weapons and troops were superior. The fighting turned into street-by-street, building-by-building battles. The Tanlians lost thousands of men before they finally surrendered. We suffered many casualties, too, probably several hundred dead and wounded. Most of our casualties came from hand-to-hand fighting."

Gerro's voice trailed off as he remembered his lost comrades. He choked up a bit as he remembered the bloody events. "All of our fleet allies fought bravely. Much blood was spilled on both sides. Willa lost a good friend — Effana Zollorand. We were pinned down by Tanlian snipers. They were hiding in a tower. Before we could stop her, Effana rushed the tower alone. She was hit but finally reached it. The firing stopped shortly after she entered."

Gerro stopped to take another long sip and regain his composure. "We got to the tower shortly after Effana, but it was too late. She must have taken on about a dozen Tanlians. They were all dead. Effana lay in the middle of the top room. Dead enemy troops were all around her."

Gerro stopped when Willa cupped her face in her hands and sobbed. He continued after a respectful moment. "Admiral Murra wasted no time defeating the remaining key cities after the capital was secured. Every captured city was given one ultimatum — surrender or face fire from his ships. Only two of the larger cities initially refused. Their leaders quickly changed their minds when building after building was destroyed. Most of the other cities surrendered without much incident."

Gerro finally stopped with a sigh. It was clear to the others that reliving the experience was difficult for him and Willa.

Flyn leaned forward. "What is to become of Tantalum 2? Can we be sure they have been subdued?"

Willa held up her hand as she recounted the key points of the new Tanlian treaty. "Admiral Murra and the GEMS allies have created a security plan for the planet. Its inhabitants are forbidden to leave their world for 10 years. Since many of their leaders died in the fortress battle, no further punishments will be inflicted on the citizenry."

She stopped for a moment and gazed out the window as she thought of her sister.

"All slaves who can be found and property taken from other worlds will be returned as soon as possible. Rewards are being offered for the Tanlians' cooperation. The shipyards will be under control of the Colonization Alliance of Independent Nations. Also, all marauders have two lunars to return home or risk being destroyed by Earth warships."

Willa drummed her fingers on the round oak table Romal had built many harvests ago. "Hmm, there was more. Oh yes, the planet will be subject to unscheduled visits by the alliance to ensure the inhabitants are honoring the treaty. For every broken violation, the inhabitants will be penalized an additional 10 years of restricted travel."

Amaura stood up to fetch another basket of fruit. She paused and looked at the others. "Will Tantalum 2 be forced to become a prison world again?"

Arynna shook her head. "No, the Earthers acknowledged it was a mistake to turn prisoners into slave miners. The Tanlians will be encouraged to develop their mining and agricultural resources to fuel their economy and feed themselves. The alliance also will monitor this progress and will help if necessary. We don't want them starving and creating martyrs."

Gerro looked approvingly at his twin. "You have an excellent memory, I am too tired to remember all those details." Arynna smiled at the compliment. The sibilings sat quietly on the porch, enjoying each other's company as a family for the first time. They watched the sun set over the mountains and listened as the night creatures chirped, sang and buzzed in the nearby trees.

"I am glad you both returned safely," Amaura said. Lyllen echoed her sentiment. Flyn nodded absent-mindedly as he stared at the orchard, his eyes darting from tree to tree in the fading light. The hunt for the honey fruit tree was starting to consume him.

Seeing his brother's perturbed expression, Gerro asked what was wrong. Embarrassed, Flyn apologized. "I am looking for something important to our family. It is nothing compared to what you have been through. We can discuss it tomorrow at first meal. I may need all of your help to find a family treasure."

7

Lyllen was the first to speak during first meal the next morning. She gazed at Flyn. "You are looking for the honey fruit tree, aren't you?"

Her brother sheepishly stirred his porridge. "Yes, I have been walking through the orchard looking for it, but all the trees look the same to me."

Lyllen gestured toward Amaura. "We have been talking about it, too. Father never got a chance to show us where it was this season. He and Romal died before they told anyone."

Amaura shook her head in frustration. "None of us were there to help them last fall. They always left a clue for the family. Uncle Romal would make a map or Father would give us hints where we could begin looking. Then they would watch us until we found it. But we only looked for it when the fruit was ready. I haven't been here during the blossoming since I was a little girl."

Flyn got a sick feeling in his stomach. If they didn't discover the location of the special tree in the next week, they probably would never find it. Once the fruit started to set, the trees looked more alike than ever.

"I loved coming here at blossoming," Lyllen said. "Remember when we would follow Grandfather through the orchard? He would help us gather the fallen flowers so we could put them in our hair."

Flyn laughed. "Oh yes, Amaura would look for those dark pink blossoms. And Lyllen insisted on wearing the white ones."

He stopped, trying to focus on a memory. "Grandfather would recite this funny poem when we asked about the honey fruit tree. He said his grandfather told it to him."

Amaura stared into the distance. Her mind raced backwards in time to when three little children tagged along with Ural as he slowly walked through the orchard. Their grandfather would chuckle as she and Lyllen gathered blossoms. He scolded Flyn for shinnying up every other tree, warning him not to knock down the blossoms.

Only when their pestering wore him out, would the old man find a stump and recite his favorite poem. Ural's words hung in the air before Amaura, waiting to be picked.

"She waves to passersby with her crown of red . . ." she spoke slowly, trying to remember then looked up in frustration.

Lyllen chimed in. "The bees attend her with a royal reverence."

Flyn nodded as he remembered. "The flowers of Nels worship at her feet. . ."

Amaura continued. "Her gifts grow golden in the sun."

The three siblings chimed in unison with the next verse. "When her leaves weep and mated branches grow heavy. Only then is her treasure ready."

Amaura rose and paced back and forth. "There's another verse. What is it?!" Flyn and Lyllen looked at each other and shook their heads.

Arynna smiled. "An interesting poem, but what does it mean?"

Amaura shrugged. "It never made sense to us. We were always so anxious to find the fruit."

Lyllen laughed as she remembered the last line. Her grandfather's words finally made sense. "Near the bridge of sorrows is her bed."

Flyn stood up and shouted: "It makes sense. Not far from here is what we call the Bridge of Sorrows. Our grandfather's grandfather slipped from the bridge and drowned during a flood. Years later, when his son was an old man, he also fell off the bridge and drowned. We now know where to start looking — near the bridge."

After about a half-hour walk through the orchard, the six honey fruit seekers stood before the bridge, which spanned a small river that coursed through the valley. They walked slowly through the orchard that lay on their side of the bridge, carefully studying the trees but found nothing.

Gerro stared across the bridge. "I see more fruit trees on the other side. Should we look over there?"

Flyn stopped at the foot of the bridge, examining its supports. "Yes, there a few over there, mainly new varieties Father and Romal were experimenting with or seedlings," he answered, squinting to see the blossoming trees across the river. By this time, their sisters and Willa had joined them. Amaura, who needed no further convincing, started to cross. The others followed with superstitious Lyllen reluctantly bringing up the rear.

Halfway across, Amaura stopped with a gasp and pointed. The others gathered around to see what she was looking at. A majestic fruit tree stood just a few meters on the other side of the bridge. At first glance, it looked very much like the other trees in the orchard. It was covered in white blossoms, except for the top third, which displayed contrasting light red flowers. The darker blossoms shimmered as the tree swayed gently in the breeze.

"She waves to passersby with her crown of red!" Amaura shouted and ran across the bridge and over to the tree. She and the others stood and gazed at the beautiful sight. Bees were swarming everywhere. The insects buzzed around the multi-flowered, double-scented tree.

Lyllen hugged Amaura and pointed to the base of tree. Wild daisies blanketed the ground around the tree. The flowers stood out with their black centers and golden petals — the family colors.

Flyn stood smiling. "It all makes sense now — the crown of red, the bees, the Nels flowers."

Gerro nodded. "Yes, that all makes sense, but what are *mated branches*?" Grabbing a thick lower branch, Flyn easily hoisted himself up. He climbed slowly so as not to alarm the bees. The others watched as he crept to the lowest layer of red blossoms. After about a minute, he laughed. "All these red branches have been grafted to the tree's original branches. They were taken from another tree and attached — *mated* you could say. We found it!"

Flyn eased himself back on a limb in relief. Tears filled his eyes. The treasure his family held so dear was not lost after all.

———————

Bralen Spenlund and his men had almost given up hope of escaping from the planet. The captain and 20 of his men barely survived after the battle in space when the Tanlian fleet had been destroyed. They landed their escape module in a remote, mountainous Verdan village. The Tanlians were shocked when the Earther fleet returned from its victorious assault on their home world. From their module, they learned the fate of Tantalum 2 as the warship crews chattered happily with surface troops.

The crew was distraught. Their module barely had enough fuel left to fly very far. Escape in their ship was out of the question. Surrender to the Earthers was discussed, but the Tanlians were frightened about the uncertainty of their fate. If they had been the victors, survivors would have been executed. The mood of Bralen's crew grew darker as they listened to the Earther comm chatter.

The Tanlians drank the sour wine produced by their village hosts growing angrier and more drunk as each hour passed throughout the night. The escapees had been on edge the past few weeks. The Tanlians and the villagers were beginning to grow weary of each other. At first, their hosts had been friendly and accommodating. Food and shelter were willingly shared. Now, Elder Marn Stelforn asked almost daily when they would be leaving. The villagers were aware the Earth fleet had returned to Verde. They wondered why their guests had not left to join the fleet.

The Tanlians stumbled from their module just as the early morning sun was breaking over the mountaintops. Bralen led the way back to the village as they trudged along in silence. A handful of elders stopped the Tanlians as they reached the village entrance. Marn greeted them. "You must be happy to hear the fleet has successfully defeated those savages. We have been most honored to host you, but we now ask that you leave us and return to the fleet."

Bralen sauntered toward Marn, shaking his head. He was tired of the facade. "My men and I have decided to stay longer. There is nothing left for us to do but eat and sleep with your women. Besides, the Earthers control the air space. How can we escape now?"

Marn's eyes grew large as he realized who the visitors really were. He started to take a step backwards when Bralen pulled his energy pistol and fired point blank. The elder collapsed to the ground. His body smoldered from the blast. The other elders turned to run but were cut down by a fusillade of blasts. Looking at his fellow crew members with a grim expression, Bralen walked into the village with his weapon drawn. The killing spree was on.

Many of the villagers were killed without warning as they prepared for the new day. The Tanlians methodically went from house to house, kicking in doors, firing on everyone they saw. Males were slaughtered without hesitation. Older women and children were slain, too. Only a few young women were spared to serve as sport for later.

The bloodbath was quickly over. With the village secured, the Tanlians finally rested, satisfied with their small victory. Later that day, Bralen was carefully nudged awake. He stared bleary eyed at the comm officer, who waited patiently.

"What is it," he growled, holding his throbbing head with both hands. He had drunk more than his share of the local wine and had grabbed one of the young women for the night. She lay sobbing quietly beside him. The captain reached under the bed for his knife, cut the ropes that bound her hands and feet and ordered her to bring him food.

The officer waited a moment then nervously reported his finding. "Sir, I've been monitoring the landing sites of the Earther vessels. Most are setting down in the large cities, except one. It just landed in a remote area less than a hundred kims from here."

The captain sat up with a start. "A vessel that close? Can we get to that ship?"

The comm officer nodded. "Yes, sir. The navigator assures me we can reach the site."

Bralen stood up a little shakily but dressed quickly. If he and his men could commandeer that vessel, they might have a chance to escape. "Gather the men quickly," he growled. "Capturing that ship might be our only hope."

Amaura and Lyllen startled Flyn as they poked their heads through the branches and joined him on a nearby limb. Laughing, Flyn's sisters studied their surroundings. The young women sat perfectly still as bees buzzed around their heads but lost interest in the newcomers and returned to their business.

Lyllen watched intently as some of the insects momentarily visited the white blossoms then stopped at the red ones. "Watch the bees," she whispered. "Every bee sniffs at a white blossom before it stops at a red one. They are bringing some of the white pollen to the red blossoms."

Flyn watched the bees do their work. He smiled at a memory. "Grandfather told me only the bees can cross pollinate. He said the best-tasting fruit came from this."

Amaura laughed. "It seems he and Father told each of us a part of the secret. We just didn't know they were pieces to the puzzle. I now see why Father taught me to graft twigs." She closely examined one of the branches which had been cut from its parent tree, inserted into then bound to a branch on this tree.

Her siblings looked at her with surprise. "When did father teach you to graft?" Lyllen demanded.

Amaura smiled. "After this past harvest, Father told me it was important to learn this. He said wonderful things can come from grafting, but I did not understand it at the time." She grabbed a twig with white blossoms and pulled it close to a red branch. Amaura frowned as she compared the flowers and leaves. "Father did not tell me which varieties he grafted, though."

Lyllen grabbed a pink branch and studied it carefully. "Father told me you can always find related trees by comparing the leaves — the color, texture, shape, even the number of veins." Reaching out, she carefully broke off a twig with a red blossom and three leaves, then scrambled down the tree.

Walking in a slow circle around the honey fruit tree, Lyllen paused at every red-blossomed tree to compare the leaves and flowers. She stopped in front of a small sapling which grew only a short distance from the honey fruit tree. "It's this one!" she shouted, waving the twig at the others. "Come see! Half of its branches have been carefully cut. Its flowers and leaves match perfectly."

Amaura climbed down and examined the sapling. "Now it makes sense. Father said some of his favorite flavors come from a sapling joined with an older tree. We have found the secret of the honey fruit!"

Gerro was about to join in the celebration when Arynna moaned softly and clumsily sat down. Her head was cocked to one side. Her eyes looked vacant, as if she were focusing on nothing nearby.

"What is wrong? Is she sick?" Willa asked as she knelt by her.

Gerro had seen this expression many times with the Seers. "No, she is in the sight trance," he explained as his three siblings joined them. Concern shadowed their faces. "Arynna, what do you see?" Gerro asked in a low, calm voice. He waited for a moment then repeated the question.

The Seer slowly rocked back and forth then turned her head looking vacantly into the trees. "They are looking for us," she said dreamily. "They haven't found us yet, but they are close."

Gerro leaned close to his sister. "Who is looking for us?" he asked.

Arynna paused, her pupils danced wildly as she surveyed the scene playing out in front of her. "Tanlians," she said matter-of-factly. "Maybe twenty of them. They are running through the orchard."

Before Gerro could say anything, the others instinctively crouched in the tall grass. He pushed his sister into a hiding place. Moments later, figures appeared across the river. They skittered from tree to tree in an apparent search for something or someone.

8

Bralen and his men tracked the Earth lander to a remote tree-filled valley. They found the ship in a clearing near a large cabin, but there was no sign of anyone. The Tanlians began a systematic and careful search through the orchard. They needed one of the Earthers to help them gain access to the vessel. The searchers heard echoes of voices from far away but could not tell where they were coming from. The sounds of people nearby were enough to spur them on.

The Tanlians hunted with desperate seriousness. Their only hope was to capture this small ship, fly it into space and dock it to one of the orbiting Earth warships. Bralen gambled the Earthers would not expect danger to come from the planet.

After a long space mission, it was likely most of the warship crews were recreating on the planet, leaving only a few members behind to maintain the vessels. Activity from the fleet confirmed this, as lander after lander headed toward Verde Grande.

Once on board, Bralen and his men planned to kidnap the remaining crewmen and force them to fly the stolen ship to freedom. The Tanlians swore a blood oath not to be taken alive. If escape proved impossible, they were prepared to fly the warship into the heart of the remaining Earth fleet and destroy as many of the enemy as possible.

Finding the crew of the lander was proving to be an aggravating first step to their plan. Even though the temperatures were mild, Bralen and his men were huffing and puffing with exertion as they ran through the orchard. The Tanlians were unaccustomed to long, surface foot searches.

They preferred to land, attack their targets, grab what they could and quickly leave.

Bralen now leaned against a tree to catch his breath. He looked out over a river that cut the valley in half. A nearby bridge looked in good shape, but it was wide open. His men would be exposed to attack if they crossed it.

"Where could they be?" one of his men wheezed as he doubled over with exhaustion. "Do you think they know we are here?"

The captain glared at his man. "If you keep up that noise, they will think a sick animal is after them. We are bound to flush them soon so be prepared."

Looking around, Bralen was disgusted at the sight. All his men were sitting or lying against trees. Most were red in the face and sweating profusely. "You have all grown soft in that village," he hissed. "Too much food and drink have made you lazy. Get up and continue the search."

Peering through the tall grass, Gerro intently watched the men across the river stumble to their feet. Flyn, Willa and Arynna crouched nearby. Amaura and Lyllen lay behind them. "Do you notice anything interesting about those men?" Gerro whispered.

Flyn nodded. "They are exhausted. I can hear them from here."

Gerro looked at him with surprise. "You can hear them? I can see why you are an expert hunter."

Willa and Arynna crawled closer to the brothers. "Tired men make mistakes," Willa said. "We should take advantage of that before they have time to rest."

Flyn stared at the searchers. "What kind of weapons do they have?"

Pulling out her bi-scope, Willa scanned the group. "Looks like the old-style energy pistols the Tanlians used when we attacked their planet. Effective at close range, but they can't compare to this," she said, pulling a new energy pulser out from her shirt.

Flyn grunted his approval and watched with envy as Gerro displayed a similar weapon.

"I only have these," Flyn said, tapping the bow slung around his shoulder and pointing to his knife belt.

Gerro shook his head. "Don't worry, I know what those can do. You have greater range with your bow than the Tanlians have with those old weapons."

9

The sound of laughter froze the Tanlians in their tracks. They watched in wonder as three beautiful young women sauntered out of the orchard and walked toward the river. The women threw petals into the river and watched them in apparent merriment as the flowers swirled and danced on the current. After a few moments, Lyllen, Arynna and Amaura stretched and preened at the edge of the water then started to walk lazily back into the orchard, moving away from the bridge. Bralen chuckled as he signaled his men to pursue the women. It was apparent they were unaware of the Tanlians' presence.

One of the women was dressed in a quasi-military uniform. *She must be the pilot of the ship they hoped to steal,* Bralen thought. At his signal, the Tanlians snuck toward the bridge and started crossing it in single file.

The lead Tanlian had almost reached the opposite side of the river bank when he stumbled backwards with a gasp. A trailing comrade caught him as he fell. An arrow protruded from his chest. Before the stunned Tanlians could react, another arrow hissed into the group, slicing into a Tanlian neck. The second target slumped over dead without making a sound.

The troopers instinctively drew their weapons and started to rush toward the bank when they were cut down by the rapid "whump, whump" of energy pulsers firing from both sides of the bridge. Another arrow sliced into a Tanlian body.

Caught in a crossfire of energy bursts and arrows, the Tanlians turned and fled back across the river. Bralen screamed at them to turn around and rush their attackers, but his panicked troops were intent on escaping to the safety of the trees. Furious at being ambushed, the Tanlian captain fired intermittently across the river, but his weapon was ineffective at that range. The grass on the opposite shore barely twitched from the subsiding energy burst.

As he turned back into the orchard to rally his men, an arrow whizzed by his ear, just missing him, popping into a tree to his left. As Bralen broke into a frantic run for safety, a tree to his right exploded after a muffled crack echoed from across the river. A series of energy bursts followed him into the trees. Limbs shattered from above, showering the hiding Tanlians with debris. Clouds of dirt erupted all around them. After what seemed to be an eternity, the firing stopped.

Bralen was shocked as he counted his surviving troops — only half remained. Grabbing his bi-scope, the captain confirmed his fear. Ten Tanlian bodies lay strewn across the bridge. Bralen turned around to see three of his surviving men being treated for shoulder, back and leg wounds. Slumping against a tree, he stared across the bridge.

Doubts and fear clouded his mind. How many of the enemy were they facing? Did he have enough crew left to effectively man a ship if they made it that far? Bralen was startled out of his troubled meditation by a voice from across the river.

"Tanlians, surrender now and we will show you mercy. Your fleet has been destroyed and your home world has surrendered to Earth forces. There is nothing left for you to fight for."

The captain's men looked at him with fear. He could see defeat in their eyes. Tanlians had never faced such a situation. They were shocked and frightened. "Earther, how do we know we won't be killed as soon as we give up our weapons?" Bralen called back. Willa and Flyn looked at Gerro and shrugged.

Gerro called back. "We are not Earthers. Most of us are native born. I am Gerro of the Tarylan Guards, I give you my word you will not be harmed."

One of Bralen's men gasped. "Not Earthers?" he asked incredulously. "We've been attacked by natives. Captain, even if we do make it to the ship, we would need Earther codes to take a warship."

Bralen leaned back in exhaustion. He played out all the options in his mind. None of them had favorable outcomes. "Can you guarantee us safe passage back to Tantalum 2?" he shouted. "We only will surrender if you can convince us."

Gerro called back. "You will have safe passage as long as you have not killed anyone on Verde Grande."

Bralen's men stared at him with fright. The slaughter at the village may have cost them the opportunity to return home. "We accept your offer," he bellowed. "I will meet your leader on the bridge to discuss terms."

Turning to his men, their captain answered their unspoken questions. "As far as these Verdans know, those villagers all died in the fire we set. We were very thorough — no need to worry about these ignorant natives." A plan formulated in his mind. "Be ready to act. I intend to capture the leader. We still will have a chance to escape."

Bralen waved off their protests as he rose and headed toward the bridge.

The two men studied each other intently from either side of the bridge. Gerro held up his arms and turned around slowly to show he carried no weapons. Bralen was overly demonstrative. He twirled and pulled at his clothes. No weapons were visible, but Gerro's suspicions were aroused. The Tanlian was shorter than Gerro, but he was broad-shouldered and stocky.

Tanlian and Verdan slowly advanced towards each other, carefully stepping over the bodies. Bralen could not help glancing at his fallen men. Despite himself, the Tanlian grew angrier with each step. Six of the men were slain as they ran for cover. The ambush had been perfectly executed. As they drew closer, Gerro noticed the Tanlian's mouth twitch slightly as he examined each man. His gait quickened a bit becoming more unsteady the closer he got. The two stopped in the middle of the bridge, only a few meters separated them.

Gerro stood in a relaxed position with his legs apart and hands at his sides. Bralen stood at attention and crossed his arms, hoping this would reflect his superiority.

"You Gerro, the leader of these Verdans?" the Tanlian snarled. He looked across the river but saw no one. "I am Bralen Spenlund, captain of the most feared marauder in the Tanlian fleet."

Gerro locked eyes with the Tanlian. "I am the leader of this troop. You hunt us, Tanlian, why? Your people have surrendered. The fighting is over."

Bralen was surprised at the Verdan's abruptness but admired him for it. He would have addressed an opponent in the same manner. Trying to smile, the Tanlian looked more deadly than cordial. "My men and I crash landed in a remote area during the battle in orbit. I cannot believe Tantalum 2 has surrendered. We saw your ship land and were investigating."

Gerro noticed Bralen's arms flinched as he spoke. His fingers edged a bit deeper into his sleeves. "Are you and your men prepared to surrender to Earth forces" He did not want to anger Bralen whose breathing was growing quicker by the second.

Not masking his emotions, Bralen snapped. "Can you guarantee our safety? We have done nothing other than try to survive here."

Gerro pointed toward Bralen's troopers who were peering out from behind trees. "My *men* will do no harm, but Earth forces will insist upon questioning you. They will determine if you will be returned to your home world. Tell your men to show themselves and drop their weapons."

Bralen shrugged a bit too broadly. His lips cracked into an insincere grin. He turned to gesture to his men to come forward, but the scene that greeted him drained his ruddy face of all color. His surviving men were on their knees at the foot of the bridge with their hands over their heads. The helpless looks on their faces told him everything. He could not believe his eyes.

Only two Verdans — a man and a woman — stood behind them brandishing energy pulsers.

Flyn and Willa had snuck through the grass when Gerro and Bralen faced off at the bridge. They found Romal's old boat that had been moored just around a short bend and crossed the water. The two easily snuck up behind Bralen's men as they intently watched the action on the bridge. It did not take much of a threat to scare them into submission.

The Tanlians had no idea they had been captured by only two people. They dropped their weapons as they were ordered and marched out of the orchard. Bralen could not believe his eyes. His men were captured by two people and one was a woman.

"Cowards!" he screamed. "You let two natives capture you!" Bralen's men were shocked at their leader's revelation. Several of the Tanlians stole quick glances back at their captors. Willa sternly warned them not to move. The men cowered when she fired a short burst that kicked up a puff of dirt behind them.

Bralen was about to turn around when he felt a sharp point at the back of his neck. "Your fight is over, Tanlian. Put your arms down slowly and drop the weapon you have hidden in your sleeve," Gerro commanded. "The Earthers will be very interested in talking to you."

Rage filled Bralen as he saw all his plans dissipate. He and his men were captured. Their chances of escaping were all but impossible now. The captain was certain the Earthers would execute them if they discovered the truth about the village.

Staring at his men, Bralen's expression told them of his intentions. With one last look of admonishment, he dropped his hidden energy pistol on the bridge. Using that gesture as a signal, the captured Tanlians sprang to their feet with a collective shout and rushed Flyn and Willa. Startled, Gerro was momentarily distracted by the commotion.

In a surprisingly quick move, Bralen sprang at Gerro, knocking the knife from his hand. The two grappled in a bear hug, thrashing back and forth across the bridge as screams of pain and the sounds of energy pulsers filled the air. Spinning around like a pair of crazed dancers, the combatants crashed violently into the bridge railing, which collapsed from the collision. The two men plummeted into the river, creating a resounding splash.

As soon as they hit the water, Gerro instinctively kicked away from the struggling Tanlian, who tried to reach out for him in desperation. Bralen frantically gulped for air and reached for something to grab onto but there was nothing. Gerro could hear no sounds of the fight on shore. He swam as fast as he could. Pulling himself up the grass with a gasp, he looked back at the river to see the Tanlian's hand disappear underwater.

It took him another minute to crawl up the shore. Slowly rising, he saw bodies strewn in a circle. Some were still smoldering, blood seeped from others. Flyn and Willa sat quietly amongst the bodies, surveying the scene. Gerro stumbled over to them. They looked up at him with dazed expressions.

"Are either of you hurt?" Gerro asked, carefully examining them.

Willa shook her head. "It all happened so fast after they attacked. I only had time to fire my weapons twice. Then we had to fight by hand."

Flyn breathed heavily as he blankly stared into space. He was still tightly clutching two bloody knives — the weapons his father had used in the last fatal duel with the Sankari.

Willa looked at him with wonder. "One of the Tanlians attacked me. We fought for a few seconds before I gained an advantage and killed him. When I looked up, Flyn had already killed the others."

Gerro grimaced. "Flyn experienced the rage. I have had it overcome me in battle. You focus entirely on the combat, everything moves slowly as if in a dream. You can almost sense your opponents' moves."

Gerro whirled around at a sound from behind him. He relaxed as Amaura, Lyllen and Arynna crossed the bridge and gingerly stepped over bodies. The young women had watched the battle from the edge of the orchard in the safety of a tree.

"Yes, it's the rage," Arynna said softly as she and her sisters knelt close to Flyn. "The rage comes from his Defender blood. It's a mechanism to help one fight with every sense." In soothing tones, Arynna chanted to Flyn. "It's over, the fighting is over, come back to us." After a few moments, Flyn shuddered and blinked as if he were waking up.

Looking up at Gerro, he reached out to touch his brother, who was drenched from his tumble in the river. "It was very strange. Even through the fight, I saw you fall in the river with their leader. All I could think of was the bridge had claimed another Nels then something happened to me."

He rubbed his head as if trying to remember a bad dream. "I could count my heartbeats. I saw Willa fighting with one of the men, but I could not help her, a group attacked me. How is she?" Flyn said as he scanned the group, looking around for the Betelan.

Willa touched Flyn's shoulder. "I am well, I killed two Tanlians. You killed the others who attacked you with uncanny quickness. I have only seen that one other time." She gazed at Gerro. "He fought exactly as you did when we faced the Tarylans near the cabin. Especially when you killed their leader."

Flyn looked around at the scene — bloody bodies lay nearby. He opened his hands and watched the knives drop to the ground. "It's over?" he asked in a hoarse whisper. His siblings hugged him as they helped him to his feet.

Epilogue

It was a crisp early morning autumn day on Verde Grande. Trees of all hues splashed the mountain range in vibrant colors. The young couple had just opened their kiosk in the already busy market when a herd of children saw them and ran screaming toward them.

"Honey fruit! The honey fruit sellers are open!" the youngsters yelled with delight as they raced toward the stand. The man looked at bit startled, but the woman laughed at the sight. "Easy now children," she said patiently. "You all know the rule, buy a bag of fruit and there will be one special treat inside."

A dozen little hands thrust Verdan coins at the sellers. One by one, all the children received bags and raced off to find their parents. A large group of adults smiled at the children as they waited patiently in line for their turn to buy fruit and take home the treasure inside to their families.

A short time later, the couple had sold all their bags for the day. "We will have more next week," the man announced to the disappointed people still in line. With a heavy sigh, he slumped back on a stool.

The woman chuckled as she leaned over and put her arm around him. "You see, our brother was right. Selling is a lot harder work than harvesting. I see we have more visitors." The woman nodded towards the front of the kiosk. Three young children shyly approached. They stood hand in hand, looking up at the man and woman. The smallest of the customers, a petite girl with curly golden brown hair, peered over the wooden counter. "May I help you?" the fruit seller asked patiently.

She stared at him somberly and nodded. "Do you have honey fruit left?" With the question out of the way, the taller of the two girls also approached the counter, her bright blue eyes shining with anticipation. The seller started to explain they were all out when the woman stopped him with a gentle touch.

The first girl's head suddenly shot up over the counter — an older ginger-haired boy had lifted her so she could get a better view. Now clinging to the counter with both hands, she looked around with disappointment. "Uncle Aron always had honey fruit for us," she said sadly.

The seller leaned over the counter, smiling. "Well, let's see. Flyn told me to save honey fruit for some special children. I believe their names are Athal, Maelys and Varie," he said rubbing his chin.

"That's us!" the taller blond girl shouted. Three pairs of eyes shone with eager anticipation. Smiling broadly, Willa brought out three large golden honey fruits and handed them to the children.

"Thank you," Varie said holding hers like a precious gift. "Mm, hmm," the other two mumbled as they hungrily tore into the treats.

"Flyn picked those especially for you," the man told the younglings. "He said they were growing at the top of the honey fruit tree." Athal stopped eating for a moment, examined his fruit then continued his joyous chomping. Juice ran down his chin as he smacked away.

The children's parents approached the kiosk. "Thank you, Gerro and Willa, that was kind of you," Athal's father, one of Stazia's brothers, said. "It is good to see the Nels family selling this delicious fruit. People so look forward to it."

Gerro smiled. "I never thought harvesting and selling fruit could be so satisfying, even though it is a lot of work. I will be happy to trade places with Flyn in the orchard tomorrow. It will be his turn to face the hungry crowds when he delivers the next load of fruit."

Willa laughed as she wrapped her arms around Gerro's waist. "Ah, Gerro of the Tarylans, the feared warrior."

Tugging at her father's tunic, Maelys begged to be lifted to the counter. The little girl had stopped eating for a moment and studied Gerro. "You look like Flyn," she said matter-of-factly.

Gerro shrugged good-naturedly. "Brothers sometimes do look alike."

Maelys cocked her head to one side, "Does that make us, uh, make us . . ." she stumbled searching for the right word. "Cousins," Athal finished for her. "Does that make us cousins?"

Gerro shook his head. "No, we have different mothers, it's a long story. But we could be good friends."

"We would like that," Maelys said, grinning. Athal and Varie nodded vigorously in agreement, their mouths full of honey fruit.

"So would I," said Gerro Nels, the orchard keeper.

END

A NOTE FROM THE AUTHOR

Dear reader:

Thank you so much for taking the time to read my book. I hope it was a worthwhile experience. If so, I would greatly appreciate it if you would write an honest review and indicate a rating on amazon.com or goodreads.com. It can be as simple as one sentence. Reviews help authors know how they are doing and also can influence potential readers.

I also would enjoy hearing from you — pros and cons. Feedback from readers is another way for authors to learn if they are doing a good job. Following are the various sites you can contact me.

Happy reading!

M.L. Williams

mlwilliamsbooks.com
mlwilliamsbooks@gmail.com
www.facebook.com/mlwilliamsbooks
www.pinterest.com/mlwilliamsbooks/
www.instagram.com/mlwilliamsbooks/
Twitter: @MLWilliamsinCR